Heroes and Traitors

Heroes and Traitors

B B Elsin

The manufacturer's authorised representative in the EU
for product safety is Authorised Rep Compliance Ltd,
71 Lower Baggot Street, Dublin D02 P593 Ireland (www.arccompliance.com)

Troubador Publishing Ltd
Unit E2 Airfield Business Park,
Harrison Road, Market Harborough,
Leicestershire. LE16 7UL
Tel: 0116 2792299
Email: books@troubador.co.uk
Web: www.troubador.co.uk

ISBN 978-1-83628-503-8

British Library Cataloguing in Publication Data.
A catalogue record for this book is available from the British Library.

Printed and bound in Great Britain by CMP UK
Typeset in 11pt Minion Pro by Troubador Publishing Ltd, Leicester, UK

This book is dedicated to those who work to help people with hearing impairment, and to those who work to help people with autism spectrum condition, to achieve their full potential.

Warning to readers:

This book contains scenes of violence, scenes of a sexual nature and offensive language.

It is set in an imaginary early modern world, similar to our own in that period, when life was "nasty, brutish and short". Despite this, people managed to love and laugh, and some worked hard for progress and enlightenment.

1

The Great Moor above Tamsit in the Edgelands, west
coast of Kimalloa. Early morning. The third day of the
Fourth Moon, Year Fifty.

YONNIS'S SKIN PRICKLED. He peered into the grime, not
knowing which way to turn his horse. His eyes and nostrils
were stinging. He tried to salivate to reduce the pungent taste
of gunpowder smoke. Rhythmic musket fire and the cries of
men were fading, and, most chilling of all, he could not hear the
drums. This did not make sense. His tactics always worked. His
men always followed his lead. Was he deep behind the enemy
lines? He must be. He had felt fear in battles before, but this was
something worse. It was dread.

Yonnis started to pray. "Eternal Spirit, my light and
inspiration, please forgive me my many wrongdoings, help me
to endure my passage to the afterlife, and grant me everlasting
rest." He felt a flicker of warmth in his heart. He had given his
all for the Doctrine of Truth. The Spirit would not forsake him.

Thunder cracked ominously. Rain followed—a pitter-patter
at first, and then, suddenly, a downpour. This might disperse
the smoke. He urged his horse to step round again. There was
something not far off. The smoke swirled, and he caught a clear
glimpse of a conical helmet.

Instinctively, Yonnis urged his horse into a canter towards the helmet, his sword raised. If these were his last moments, so be it. He would go down fighting. As he closed in on the helmet, he could see a huge man underneath it, encased in heavy armor and sat astride a well-padded saddle on a finely caparisoned horse.

Yonnis's stomach lurched with hatred. It had to be him. He tried to suppress it. He shouted, "Sir, surrender yourself to the Army of Truth! Your cause today is hopeless! You are greatly out-numbered." Yonnis hoped that this was still true. He had no idea where his men were.

The metal head turned slightly towards him. Was this the chance that his gut urged him to take? Yonnis's head shuddered with memories of the screams of the Day of Lamentation. So many innocents wounded and dying, and somewhere in that cacophony had been his beloved wife, gasping her last breath.

Slowly, as if he might be conceding, the figure raised his gauntlet. He opened the visor of the helmet. Then he bellowed, "Never! You diabolical god-killer widower of a whore!"

It *was* him! Yonnis charged, feinting to provoke a mighty blow. His target swung at him. Yonnis parried. The swords parted and clashed again, and again. The armored man was big, but how much of it was brawn? Yonnis backed away a few paces and then charged. His opponent's horse stamped and tossed its head, as if starting to panic. Yonnis saw his chance and used his broadsword to push the bigger man with all his strength and fury. As he connected, the horse bucked and bolted. The mighty column of metal was dumped into the black mud of the moor. The stricken man flailed like an overturned insect. Yonnis jumped from his horse and used his sword to flick up the visor of the helmet. He hesitated. This was King Navvan, for sure. Was he gasping or laughing? Yonnis plunged his sword into his enemy's face. He opened his mouth and lungs, expecting a roar of triumph to come out. Instead, it was a howling sob of despair.

Time passed. How many moments? Yonnis had shut his eyes and tried to blank his memory. Then he found himself blinking, as the sun in the east pierced the last few raindrops of the storm. The mist had cleared as suddenly as it had formed. In the distance, purple mountains wrapped with conifer forests were emerging from the cloud. In front of him, dead and wounded men were scattered across the grass and scrub. Crows and gulls were diving from the sky to eat the faces of the fallen. Some of Yonnis's own Yerallan Adventurers were rushing towards him. The Sudarite soldiers were on their knees wailing, and they appeared to be looking at him in amazement. Their red-tattooed priests, the Raas, were staring too. Yonnis turned his head. There was a glorious rainbow reaching out from the indigo waves of the Arna Gulf and arching over the moor, its colors clearly defined. That would explain their awe, and it was useful. He turned back, took off his green-plumed, lobster-necked helmet, and yelled at the groveling wretches of the enemy army.

"King Navvan Glantar is dead! Submit to the Army of Truth! Long live the Republic of Kimalloa!"

The Army of Truth, exhausted after a long campaign, found the energy to cheer in relief. Some fell to their knees, praising and thanking the Eternal Spirit, some blessed each other, hugging and backslapping, some were exuberant and roared their triumph. Some chanted for their general, but Yonnis did not raise his hand to draw attention to himself. This was a time for their comradeship. Since the previous battle, they had endured days of mud relentlessly sucking at their boots and wagon wheels, encountering the cinders of villages that the enemy's devastators had torched, trying to help frightened women and children while building barricades and traps to cover the army's rear, skirmishes, sleeping on straw under wet canvas, eating pottage, and longing for home.

Yonnis felt a warm joy wash over him as he saw his men smiling and cheering. May the Spirit bless them—his brave, uncomplaining heroes who had followed him through a plague of hardships. The previous afternoon, they had caught up with the King's men, who had halted on this moor, trapped by the flooded pass into the town of Tamsit. The Army of Truth arrived in driving rain and camped beneath the brow of the moor on its east side. Yonnis had not felt overly confident then, despite having superior numbers. Tamsit Moor was a large plain, big enough for thousands of men to engage in warfare, but laden with risks. Uneven clumps of twisted, wiry blue-gray moor grass sprouted from the thin, rocky soil. To the west of the moor, a steep drop into the town on one side and the sea on the other could be navigated by goats, but was dangerous for men and impossible for horses. The pass to the south of the moor, a wide, straight road in summer, had been overcome by the spring rains, transformed into a fast-flowing river. To the north, a rocky outcrop scattered with prickly briar loomed. It was a forbidding place, and this was the Sudarites' last stand. They would be resolute.

Yonnis had ordered an attack as soon as the black of night turned a navigable gray. It began with a bombardment of light cannon and muskets. The enemy responded with heavy cannon which they had secured in a niche in the rock. One blast caught the right flank of the Army of Truth, including Yonnis's second-in-command, Lord Grakko of the South Mountains. Yonnis ordered ranks of pikemen to push the King's infantry up against the rock, intending to compromise their angle of fire. The Army of Truth gunners watched how the enemy moved as they absorbed the assault, and picked their target. At last, there was a great boom and crumbling rock—the King's main cannon had been hit. It was time for a cavalry charge. Or was it? The smoke from the cannon and musket fire was dense and acrid. Yonnis charged on, but as he disappeared into the miasma, the Army of Truth had retreated. In hindsight, Yonnis was impressed with their discipline. They had been trained to hold back when they couldn't see their own noses. It was he who had made a mistake.

Yonnis could hear Commander Magg shouting orders now.

"Stretcher-bearers, wrap up the wounded as best you can! Get them on to carts. Head back to the field hospital! Scavenger duty men, strip those carcasses! Get what can be salvaged on the baggage train! Engineers, we need rafts to get into the town. Anyone who can row or steer, get on those rafts. Secure the town. Dump the bodies at sea. We'll never get them to burn up here. Chain those priests! Have we got any fencing posts left to pen the prisoners? Clerk Konnu, get messages tied to the word-birds and release them—quick as you can!"

Yonnis walked up to Magg, and grabbed and shook his shoulders in comradely admiration. "Well done, Commander!"

Magg saluted him.

"This victory is yours, Magg. You did absolutely the right thing to order the retreat, or we would all have been lost and confused. That smoke was the worst I have ever seen and smelled." He paused, and let go of Magg. "May the Eternal Spirit rest the souls of dear Grakko and his men."

"Aye, General. A great loss to Kimalloa. Let's try to get his body—well, the bits we can find—to a Temple of Truth."

"Yes. Let's find a boat to get it back to his home temple. You stay in command here and I'll go down to the town with my personal regiment. You know how we Yerallans can manage watercraft! We will dispose of the Glantar body first. I will come back for Grakko."

Magg looked slightly quizzical. He opened his mouth and a faint noise came out, which he suppressed. He started again. "Aye, General."

Yonnis signaled to his men, who had already tied the body of the King to a solid piece of wood. Then he was distracted. He saw some braziers with slivers of smoke rising out of them. He investigated, and the smell hit him like a punch. Ugh! Those wretched red priests with their hocus-pocus! Had he inhaled that?! He raked through the ashes and gathered whatever sizable cinders he could find. Beckoning to a sergeant, he took a cloth from his pocket to wrap and tie them securely. "Find a fast horseman and get these to a Healing Elder for investigation. Tell him to report directly to Squire Tallier."

The sergeant saluted, took the package, and ran as best he could over the debris of the battle. Yonnis returned to the edge of the flood. The soldiers working at the waterside were happy to see him as he approached, and rushed forward to shake his hand. He shook a few and then made his excuses as the Yerallan Adventurers guided their precious, grisly cargo into the flood. Yonnis followed them. The urge of the icy cold water to reach the sea was strong, and it was hard to guide the rafts through the chest-deep water. There was a solid, stony road underneath, but the uncomfortable journey into the town needed a great deal of concentration. It had its consolations. Each man ducked under the water from time to time, hoping to drown the lice that had been driving them mad. As they got nearer the sea, the floodwater rushed away to their left and they had to drag their burden to the right, onto the harbor front of Tamsit.

Tamsit in the Edgelands, west coast of Kimalloa. Midmorning. The third day of the Fourth Moon, Year Fifty.

TAMSIT SMELLED OF fish and salt. The atmosphere was eerie. All the windows were shuttered and the doors barred; dozens of fearful eyes peered through the gaps. Although armed and wary, the Yerallans did not expect much resistance. They issued a few shouts of "Lend us your boats! We have coin!" A few doors creaked open.

Yonnis could not suppress a grin as the faces behind the doors gasped. "Don't be afraid. We are not ghosts. We are from Yeralla, and from the Army of Truth. You are now free, brothers and sisters. Your tyrant king is dead."

He waited for a reaction, but didn't get one. They must have heard the guns, the drums, the cries. But why should they know what to believe? In civil war, if you want to just go about your business, it helps if you believe nothing.

He got down to the practicalities. "We have bodies to take out to sea. Who will take our coin for the use of their boat? *Coin*, brothers. Not promises you can't read on paper you can't eat. Coin! Or do you want us to dam the pass with dead men?"

Several men with braided hair and beards, in faded blue woolen thrum hats, jerkins, and breeches covered by resin-coated aprons, emerged and crept forward. The smell of fish got stronger to the point of overwhelming. Deals were done.

Yonnis got into a long rowing boat with five Yerallan Adventurers and Navvan's body. The storm had passed, the sea was calm, and they rowed swiftly out into the Bay of Dilmas.

On their return, all that was left of King Navvan Glantar was his helmet, which Yonnis carried in a plain sack. More men, from a variety of regiments, were arriving in the harbor with rafts piled with bodies. They were loading boats while also haggling with the fishermen's wives to cook them fresh fish for their return. The town was opening up for one of the most interesting days in its history.

An old man with a bushy white beard in a threadbare orange gown approached Yonnis and his rowers. "Yerallans, are ye? I can tell so. You don't see them gray faces on the living in this land. This is your lucky day, my lads!"

"How so, brother?" Yonnis was suspicious about the old fellow's accent, although he had learned that each village in Kimalloa had their own special way of mangling their language.

"I'm taking wool to your fair country on my ship, and if you've the right coin, I can take you home, sir."

He got no immediate answer. Yonnis just looked at him with a furrowed brow.

The old sailor started to explain, demonstrating real pride in

7

his product. "Our sheep may look like nuffin' up on the moors, but their *hard-wearin'* wool—spun 'n' dyed 'n' woven in our *intricate* local patterns—it's quite a curiosity for the discernin' ladies of your capital. Rightly so, sir."

One of the men, Ennis, moved close to Yonnis and hissed at him in Yerallan as fast as he could, in case the old man understood a few words. "Perhaps we should go, sir. Some Kimalloan men have already been whispering. Some suspect that what happened… was our revenge."

Yonnis hesitated. This was indeed a lucky offer. To quietly slip away home, leaving the Kimalloans to sort out their own peace—why not?

"Sir?" Ennis insisted.

"Make sure that this is not a trap, and then you five go. I… I can't—well, I promised to sort out the return of Grakko's remains, and—"

Ennis stiffened. "It is my duty to tell you, sir, that I fear for you—"

"Thank you for your concern, Ennis. You have done your duty. Now I have to do mine."

Ennis saluted, and then went with the other men to check the captain's ship.

Yonnis was left on his own on the harbor wall. He felt a deep urge to run after them, but the more he called silently to the Eternal Spirit for guidance, the more he felt drawn to stay. There was the dead king to account for; that was a matter of honor—honor lost which had to be regained. But the images that the Spirit sent to him, they were of Kimalloans who needed peace. Those Kimalloan soldiers just now who had wanted to shake his hand—they were going back to villages that had been burnt, or devastated by famine or disease. And the men who died—what was his duty as their leader to their widows and orphans? Yonnis Krusa's job was not done, because no victory is whole until peace is secure.

Rather than struggling back to the moor upstream through the flood, he contemplated the rocky climb. He noticed that a cluster of Tamsit's urchins had gathered to stare at him.

"Hey, children!" he called to them. "Show me the quickest way up that cliff and I'll give you a quarter-penny each."

They rushed over, giggling, and pulled at his hands to lead him. How wonderful it was to hear the voices of happy children. He would have liked a big family. It had been several years before a seed of his had grown in Farida. And then that seedling of hope had died with her. Because Navvan needed to show the high priests who were funding and fueling his war against his people just how devout he was. At least Yonnis's boy—or girl— was at rest. Navvan would now be learning just how long and dreadful eternity can be when you have violated the Eternal Spirit of the Doctrine of Truth.

The children peppered him with questions, demonstrating what they had been taught about Yeralla.

"D'ye worship bears?"

"Is yer dad a pirate?"

"What's it like without sunshine all the year?"

"Will you show us yer eelskin back?"

Yonnis laughed. "None of this is true! Just show me the path and I'll tell you all about Yeralla..."

While the innocent interrogation was going on, a huddle of young girls ran up and then scattered, leaving one standing naked in front of Yonnis. The children backed off. Nearby soldiers jostled to see.

The girl curtsied deeply and awkwardly, wobbling on the cobbles. "You must be fulla seed after battle, Divine Lord Marko. I offer myself to you. Plant it in me."

Yonnis put a hand over his eyes, appalled. These Sudarites, he thought, are so depraved! He was angry and wanted to throw her to one side, but he checked himself. He must be gracious in victory. She was just a young girl who did not know what she was asking for. He greeted her politely. "May the Eternal Spirit bless you, miss." Yonnis focused his gaze on her eyes, and tried to ignore the curves of her body. He could not control his physical reaction, but his buff coat covered the swell of his member. "I am not who you think I am. Today there is a new Kimalloa, where we value chastity and modesty. Please cover yourself up and go home."

"Would you prefer my brother, sir?" she asked.

"No!" Yonnis felt angry again. "Stand aside, miss, or I shall have to throw you aside."

The girl lowered her head and burst into tears. "My friends'll taunt me that I'm not fair enough for ya!"

He looked down with pity at her. She had a pretty pink face, circled by flowing golden hair catching in the sea breeze. She would be fair enough for any man. But what of her character? "I'm sorry that your friends are mean. But we can all learn something from humiliation. Reflect on what I have told you. Follow the Doctrine of Truth and you will never be judged again on what you look like."

The soldiers started to titter.

Yonnis bellowed at them. "You, men! You are witnesses that I did not violate this girl, despite her provocation. I expect the same restraint from you."

"Aye, sir!"

"Aye, sir!"

One shouted to the girl. "Best hurry off, sweetheart, or he'll give you a lecture on cockpox!"

The girl bobbed up abruptly, still shaking with sobs. As she did so, an arrow thudded into her back and through her chest, stopping a few inches from Yonnis. She dropped like a stone.

Yonnis threw himself on the cobbles, peering up carefully to assess the threat. "Watch the yellow door on the left!" he yelled, as fishermen and soldiers scattered for cover.

Before Yonnis crawled forward to search for the archer, he stroked the cheek of the poor girl and said a quick prayer for her.

Another life wasted that might have been fulfilled and fruitful, and yet again, he had been spared. Was it a pointless coincidence? Or should he reflect more deeply on his debt to her?

Whiteleaf Castle, Region of the South Mountains, Kimalloa. Early morning. The seventh day of the Fourth Moon, Year Fifty.

M *Y DEAR RESPECTED Squire Clayhills, Leader of the Assembly of Commoners,*

What a joy it was to hear about the convincing victory for the Army of Truth at Tamsit. I was so relieved to know that my uncle was defeated. The messenger said that there were clear signs from the beliefs of both religions that the victory was blessed. This can only augur well for a new, prolonged, and prosperous peace for our dear country. I have prayed long and hard for an end to the fighting, as it grieved me to know that my people of Kimalloa were suffering and dying.

Of course, my pleasure in the victory is clouded by my grief at the loss of my Lord Grakko, who has been such a kind and generous foster father to me in the past few years. The whole of Whiteleaf Castle is heavy with sorrow, especially dear Lady Deneesa.

I am so grateful that your agents saved me from the evil intent of my uncle and ensured that I have been cared for in this safe haven where I have been able to study and understand the Doctrine of Truth, and prepare myself for the new way. You and Squire Tallier have been such true friends, and I have such a deep obligation to you both.

I am writing to assure you that I am deeply committed to the future of our beloved Kimalloa, and I am ready to serve as consul queen with the guidance of the Assembly,

of course. I hope that we will meet soon, so that I can
assure you in person of my gratitude and my longing to
serve my country.
    Your humble servant,
    Esta Glantar

Esta looked hopefully at her "foster mother". "Guardian" would be a much better word. Or, perhaps, just "guard". Lady Deneesa's face was red and puffy, her eyes were still full of tears, and of course she just wanted to spend time with her children in the temple, mourning her husband. But she was an important noble. Surely, she knew that affairs of state don't wait for hearts to heal? They certainly had not when Esta's father died. How glad she was that Navvan knew defeat before his death. What an uncle. He had promised to protect her. With his brother still warm in the grave, he had undermined her, tried to deflower her, and then tried to kill her.

"Please, Your Grace. May it be sent?"

"I don't know that it is wise, Esta." Lady Deneesa looked at her eldest son, the new Lord Grakko.

Esta looked at him too, harboring the flame that had been flickering for the past few years. What a handsome young man. But he had chained himself to some copper-haired cousin. Just as well. It was not fitting for a queen to marry a subject.

"I'm not going to censor your letter, Lady Esta," Young Grakko told her. She marveled at how the peddlers of Truth could sound respectful and condescending in the same breath. "It will go to Nasrin by the fastest boat we have. Just remember that Squire Clayhills is a very busy man."

Esta looked out of the small window of her room, down to the long black lake, dotted with all manner of watercraft, over which all things came and went to this dreary settlement. Then she turned back to the black figures at the door. "Thank you, Your Grace!" She curtsied deeply.

"Now," said Lady Deneesa, "please come and join us in the temple, to reflect on my husband's sacrifice for Kimalloa."

The grieving widow held out her hand to Esta, and Esta took it. What else could she do? She was still trapped in this tyranny of humble kindness. For now.

The Seat of Learning of Divine Crafts, religious house of Her Grace, Grand Duchess Kirina, Southwest Osiran. Late afternoon. The seventh day of the Fourth Moon, Year Fifty.

WHOOSH! A NOVICE screamed as her glass vial spat fire. She dropped it and the glass tinkled as it broke. Another novice threw sand over the fiery mess on the floor.

"Be careful, girl!" Her Grace had little sympathy. "Think what the word 'experiment' means! You are trying something. You don't know what will happen. Now make a note of what *did* happen. See if you can make it happen again—that would be magical, don't you think?"

Her Grace the Grand Duchess Kirina of Osiran, once (a long time ago) Queen of Yeralla, continued to walk up and down the benches where she taught novice priestesses their craft. Her silver hair was woven into a headdress shaped like a crescent moon that sat across the top of her head. Her dark eyes, deep-set in her well-lined, buttermilk face, watched the girls like a hawk. Her robe was bright blue, and decked with rows and rows of silver necklaces, each laden with a different charm.

She observed the novices mixing colored liquids in glass vials, applying heat to some and cold to others. She knew that she made them feel nervous, and so it should be, because they needed to concentrate. The older ones tried to supervise the younger ones and keep them sensible, but nobles thought that they could send just any unwanted daughter to her institute these days.

After a while, her gaze was drawn to a jar of kakko ash on the shelves, and it prompted her to call to the mother of the house to take charge. Kirina walked from the laboratory, across a covered causeway that looked out across red rocks to the foaming gray sea. She came to an atrium lit by dozens of high windows which linked the causeway with the building that she shared with her sick brother. It was hewn out of the white-and-yellow mottled sandstone cliff. Apart from only having windows on one side, it was, to all intents and purposes, a small palace. Courtiers loitered in the atrium, desperate to be seen, and to see her. As she approached the tall portico of the Imperial Winter House, handsomely uniformed armed men bowed deeply to her, one after the other. They should never be looking at the floor at the same time, in case it gave a moment of opportunity to an assassin.

She acknowledged a woman waiting by the door and asked, "How is His Majesty?"

"Your Grace, His Majesty sleeps," the woman replied.

Kirina nodded. The guards opened the heavy bronze door for her. Kirina, flanked now by a posse of maids, strode purposefully through corridors lined with fine wood and hung with glittering tapestries, to her personal apartments. In the center of the main room, there was a wheel set over a large bowl of milky blue liquid, illuminated by lamps underneath it. She sat down and started to adjust the wheel. There were many cogs within the wheel, including moon phases for time, a compass for place, a gauge for the closeness of a relationship, a marker for the features of a subject, and a dial for the information sought. Setting them prepared her mind for her meditation. She added a large pinch of ash to the watery mixture and started to stir it with a lever on the side of the bowl.

An old man, wrapped in lush blankets in a well-padded wheeled chair in front of the fireplace, snuffled and woke up. "Where am I? Where am I?!" He wept.

She rose and went to comfort him. "Shush, Zanda, my darling. You are with me, Kirina, your big sister. You are safe."

"Who are you?"

"Kirina."

"My wife?"

"Your sister."

"Sister?"

"Do you remember us playing in the gardens of Larriklias? We used to have some little furry animals in golden cages. We let them out and played hide-and-seek with them."

Zanda smiled. "Oh yes. That was fun. Can we go back there, then?"

"Zanda. Alas. You are ill, my dear one. We can't go back there. We're preparing everything for young Ikra, remember?"

"Ikra?"

"Please, Zanda. Please try to sleep again, while I do some work."

She stroked his face, whispering calming incantations, until he fell asleep. Oh, how she loved him, even though there was so little of the real Zanda left. She gazed at his face and remembered their extraordinary lives. She had been blessed with a sweet younger brother. So many royal siblings became estranged, but the Princess Royal and Crown Prince of Osiran had been fiercely loyal to each other. They had eventually been forced apart. She had been given a duty as a brood mare to Yeralla while he, so young, struggled with the burden of empire. When she came back as his regent, with a useful dose of new knowledge from Yeralla's rebel Raas, she set out to be a priestess as well. She had needed that mystic power to reinforce her political power, to keep the perfidious Grand Dukes in check.

Kirina watched over Zanda for a while, and then returned to her divining wheel. As she adjusted it, the lights under the bowl flickered and the blue of the water changed into many shades, dancing, reflecting on her face. Kirina had to look, but she was dismayed by what she saw. "Oh, foolish boy! It makes you adorable that you are honorable… but when will you learn that it makes you vulnerable to those who are not?!"

A maid tapped gently on the door.

"Enter!"

"Your Grace, news from Kimalloa."

"I know," Kirina replied.

The maid offered her a beautiful white bird with a scroll on its back. Kirina cradled the bird, blessed it, stroked its breast, and kissed its head. She untied the scroll and returned the bird to the maid.

"Make sure that she eats the best corn in the granary!"

She unrolled the paper, translating its code as fast as she could. Briefly, she thought of strategy. Thanks to the victory of the Truth cult in Kimalloa, North Boriela was now cut off from other Sudarite states and would be more dependent on Osiran. It was always gratifying to extend buffer zones on borders and set country against country. So much for strategy, but Kirina's work was never done. The strong bond with her youngest grandson was twisting and tugging. She stroked a hammer hanging from one of her necklaces and spoke to the goddess of her bloodline.

"Oh, Divine One, help me find the words to let them know— those perfidious Kimalloans—that if they touch a hair on his head, I am the one who can, and will, unleash the sleeping wrath of Osiran on their miserable, misty mudscape."

2

The approach to the New West Gate of Nasrin, capital city of Kimalloa. Early morning. The eleventh day of the Fourth Moon, Year Fifty.

NEWLY HATCHED FLIES buzzed with glee around the long procession of soldiers. The smell of hundreds of unwashed humans, carts full of bloodstained armaments, and scores of tired horses was drifting in the spring sunshine. The Army of Truth had covered over a hundred leagues in eight days from the far west coast of Kimalloa. The sun had been shining ever since their victory at Tamsit. They were hot under their uniforms, exhausted, and their feet were raw in their worn boots, but they kept marching, driven by the banging of the drums. They daydreamed—welcoming crowds... a weighty pay packet... the warmth of family love and the hearth at home.

Through his small telescope, Yonnis could see the ten-stride-high earthworks that the women, children, and old folk of Nasrin had built to defend their city. Last time he had seen them, they were a mighty mass of red mud splattered with gray gravel. Now, they were coated in luscious green grass and flowers. The dots of blue, yellow, white, and pink were cheerful, and he paused his telescope on them for a while. He thought about how wonderful it was when nature softened a human structure. It was a momentary distraction. His men were anxious to get back to a garrison with some home comforts. And he knew how well they had earned it.

"Nearly there, my heroes!" he called back to them.

They cheered and started to sing.

Army of Truth, we are the ones.
Army of Truth, with better guns.
Were you at Grettin, boy?
Boy, were you there?
Kasbrit and Tinmas too?
Estlorn and Santair?
We won, we won, we won again,
And never shall be slaves again.
Whoa!
Were you at Grettin?

Yonnis sensed their urgency, and ordered the drummers to a faster pace.

After a short time, Yonnis focused his telescope again, this time on the massive New West Gate. The neatly hewn white stone was glistening, and the hubbub around it reassured him. On the approach to the gate the militia were sorting people into lines. To the right, Yonnis could see the ragtag remains of the King's Pozarian mercenaries arriving under guard for deportation. His own auxiliary services such as engineers and nurses had arrived ahead of the main army with some carts carrying wounded men, and they were on the left. He was relieved to note that well-dressed men with barrows of goods were in the left middle line; at least the capital was still trading. A miscellaneous collection of desperates, probably non-residents seeking work, was in the right middle line.

He raised the telescope to the battlements over the gate. The sun glanced off the helmets of the militiamen. And then he spotted a tall black hat. It was easy to guess the sinister presence under it, waiting like a bird of prey. The motivation Yonnis had felt on seeing the end of the journey melted away. The end of the journey also meant a reckoning, and the man under that hat would influence what it was. Nevertheless, Yonnis waved the men forward. Dust, smell, and the clip-clop of many trotting horses were announcing their arrival.

Initially, the people waiting were solid in their lines as they strained to see what was coming along the cobbled road. Soon, the left line surged with energy and some men chanted, "Whoa! General Yonnis!" They abandoned their places and rushed towards the riders at the front of the procession.

Yonnis stopped his horse and was soon surrounded. He leaned down from his saddle and shook hands. Some folk were just happy to touch his boot, or his horse.

He heard a woman shouting, "Thank you for what you did for my hospital! May the Spirit bless you, M'Lord General!"

Yonnis looked up and spotted her, noticing a mark on her face—a scar, perhaps. She seemed familiar. He waved to her over the heads of the raucous men thronging round him, and then gave a two-handed general wave to the lines.

The cheering seemed to get louder and louder. The crowds greeted all the men with enthusiasm, but their desire to get near to Yonnis was overwhelming. He could not help pride surging. He felt so energized by it, as if he were floating above them, bathing them in the light of his success. These people loved him—he had reached into them and inspired them. Why was the joy of having done something so monumental starting to curdle in his stomach? He wanted someone or something to blame for that awful feeling. But the Doctrine of Truth urged him to look within.

Two militiamen marched up to Yonnis, apparently intent on doing their duty without fear or favor. Of course they would. Spymaster Tallier, who relished his nickname "All-Ears", was listening.

"'Oo are ya?" they barked.

"General Yonnis Krusa," Yonnis replied, modestly presenting a wooden token to prove it, to the amusement of the crowd around him.

An army sergeant shouted at the militia. "Open the gate for your victorious general, brethren! The King is dead. Long live the Republic of Kimalloa!"

The crowd started to roar its approval and Yonnis was seized by a desire to keep them roaring, loud enough to make a lasting impression on All-Ears, who was still gazing down from the battlements. Yonnis reached behind him to the panniers on his horse's back and snatched out a large steel helmet circled with a gold coronet which looked like it had been kicked around a slaughterhouse. He held it high. The crowd gasped in awe. One woman fainted. After a few moments, the eerie quiet was smashed by a throaty cheer from one soldier, and others soon chimed in. The despised tyrant was dead, and they were privileged to see the evidence.

Yonnis looked up to the black-hatted man, who offered him a mechanical, official wave.

Bankside Place, Nasrin. Midmorning.
The eleventh day of the Fourth Moon, Year Fifty.

A s YONNIS AND his entourage, swelled by curious and excited citizens, approached the Bankside Place gatehouse, Elders rang the bells to call Followers of the Doctrine of Truth to observe their routine of reflection.

Yonnis dismounted and placed his right hand on his heart. "Eternal Spirit, bless us with enlightenment and inspiration. Protect us from evil and temptation. Please comfort the living and give rest to the dead." He then bowed his head and shut his eyes for a few moments of private and silent entreaties.

'Eternal Spirit, help me to reassure Squire Clayhills. May Arlo be restored to health. Please rest the souls of my dear Farida and all the loved ones that I have lost. Please guide me and protect me in my time of reckoning…' When the bells rang again to close the reflection, he turned to the guards and ordered them to open the gate to him.

It was over two years since Yonnis had seen this fine castle on the north bank of the River Binar. The battlements, which towered over the city, were clad in masses of newly opened, heart-shaped green leaves. Within the walls, Bankside was like a bustling small town. The accommodation encompassed everything from the former king's apartments in the inner courtyard, to the rooms of clerks, soldiers, and servants in the outer courtyards. Dovecotes, hog pens, and beehives, a bakehouse, a brewhouse, and a slaughterhouse kept the occupants well fed. Storage rooms, dining halls, a laundry, offices and meeting rooms, the Archive and the Treasury kept the processes of government running. Stables, a forge, an arsenal, and a gunpowder store served the garrison. There was even a bowling green, now being churned up by off-duty soldiers playing groundball.

This was the headquarters of the War Cabinet and the beloved Father of the People, Squire Yoshi of the Clayhills. Yonnis deeply admired the brave squire, who had been a thorn in the side of the kings, risking an awful death, long before launching the Great Rebellion. He longed to see him and deliver confirmation that the war was won, but he knew the news was tainted. Yonnis had promised to bring the King back alive for trial. He had not, and he had to admit why not. The courtyard seemed wider and wider as he strode across it to an uncertain reaction. Perhaps guards were waiting to arrest him. He would soon know.

The door opened and Squire Clayhills stepped out. Servants, clerks, and soldiers, flocking to see this historic moment, stretched their lungs with loud cheers. Yonnis felt a sense of wonder as the Father extended his right hand to him. He felt the warmth of the old hero's blood pulsing in his lean palm as they shook hands firmly. The Father looked much as Yonnis remembered him—tall, lean, handsome, hampered by a limp and sporting an eyepatch from the battle injuries that had nearly killed him three years ago. He was wrapped in a black gown and had put a black cap on his gray curls to answer the door. Yonnis sank to his knees and offered him the King's bloody helmet. The old man winced with disgust, but he took it and held it up, which pleased the crowd.

Squire Clayhills leaned down to Yonnis and hissed in his ear. "Welcome back, Lord General. Thank you for your endeavors that have delivered victory. But I hope that there is a good explanation for this—this thing."

Yonnis whispered back. "I am so glad to see you again, Father of the People. May the Eternal Spirit bless you. Sir, there *is* an explanation. It is not one that either of us may like." He stood up.

Squire Clayhills turned to a guard and issued a curt order that chilled Yonnis. "Infantryman Eevo, take the general to his quarters."

Yonnis interrupted. "Sir, may I see Arlo? I was so happy to hear from the field hospital that he was sent home. He is still recovering well, I hope?"

The Father looked straight at him. Yonnis was dismayed to see a tear trickling down his cheek. Squire Clayhills spoke softly. "Get cleaned up and come to the Great Hall after the midafternoon bells." He swung round and went back into his residence, closing the door quietly behind him.

The General's Quarters, Bankside Place, Nasrin. Early afternoon. The eleventh day of the Fourth Moon, Year Fifty.

IT WOULD TAKE several baths to get the stink of the last few months out of him—the smoke, sweat, mud, blood, horse. Yonnis soaped and scrubbed vigorously at his grimy skin, and then just soaked. He could not imagine any luxury worth more to him than a hot bath. For the sixth time, a boy opened the door and asked if he wanted more hot water. He had to say no. He wanted to spend time in the temple before his meeting with Squire Clayhills. He gazed longingly from his bath in the dressing room to the bedroom. A bed with a well-stuffed mattress was luring him. Clean linen. Soft pillows. Warm blankets. What a world away from his sagging camp bed in a moldy tent. Sleep beckoned. Then it pulled and yanked at him. He had to resist. Momentarily, his eyes flickered. Then he was trying to scream and couldn't. The next thing he knew, he had received a blow to the face, was snorting soapy water, and was staring into the sparkling hazel eyes of a woman with a red mark on her face.

"M'Lord General!" she shouted in frustration. "'Eck! Y'nearly drowned! Fat use it is to survive battles if you fall asleep in the bath!"

"Did you have to slap me so hard?" Yonnis croaked as he rubbed his cheek.

"Aye, I did, sir! It were such a fright to hear the noises you were making—then to find you slipping under the water."

"Ugh!" Yonnis spluttered and wiped his face. "Thank you. Who are you, and what are you doing in a man's dressing room?" He checked that the bathwater was murky enough to offer him some privacy.

"I'm Suki. Army nurse—I mean, I *was* an army nurse—and I don't hesitate to enter a man's dressing room when his life depends on it… sir."

"Thank you, Mistress Suki, thank you again. May the Eternal Spirit bless you for your quick wits and strong hand." Yonnis felt that he knew her, and he struggled for the right memory in his tired head.

It was after Grettin, a big and bloody battle. He had given thanks to the Eternal Spirit for victory, and then went straight to the field hospital. The cacophony of groans and screams from the wounded burdened his heart, but he could not show it. They needed him to put a hand on their shoulder, praise them, thank them. Some were delirious, some were crying for their mothers. Some just saw an officer's sash and swore, some forgot the Doctrine of Truth and thought that he was a sky god and begged him to take them to the Dome of the Divine. Yonnis went from bed to bed for half a day, offering sympathy and encouragement.

Nurses in their distinctive uniforms, conveniently dyed a brown like dried blood, were hurrying around, their linen coifs wet with sweat. The Healing Elders barked orders at them. The nurses helped the worst wounded to drink sleeping-herb drafts so they could pass peacefully— not so easy if a man has lost half his face, or his guts are falling out of his belly. They scrubbed down the amputation blocks after each operation. They washed and bandaged the wounds that might heal. They carried hot water and surgical instruments to where they were needed, and they waved brooms to chase away the rats.

When Yonnis could do no more, he asked the Elder in charge if he could gather some nurses so that he could speak to them. A cluster of them came to the flap of the tent. Yonnis thanked them for their devotion to the wounded, to the Doctrine of Truth, and to Kimalloa, and then, as he was about to turn to leave, he thought to ask how they were managing, and if, assuming supply were possible, there was anything that they needed to help the wounded.

This woman, with the lovely eyes and the red mark on her face, had spoken up first. "M'Lord General, the Truth tells us that cleanliness is one of the Nine Great Virtues. We need more pine spirit to keep men's wounds clean. We don't like losing men to reeky."

"Don't I remember you from the field hospital at Grettin? You were talking about pine spirit…"

"Aye, that were me, sir." Suki beamed. "I… I feel so honored that you've remembered! You asked us about our work, and we told you what we needed, and—may the Spirit bless you—within a few weeks, things came."

"I'm very glad to hear that they did. Of course, it was the supplies people here who made it happen. You must bless them. I just sent the requisition. And were there fewer cases of reeky?"

"Maybe so, but really, I didn't have time to count. Not long after, we'd to pack up and move on to Estlorn, and then Tinmas—"

"Of course." Yonnis felt a wave of anguish about the casualty rate, and his stomach turned. He hadn't been counting either. And perhaps he should have been. "You and your sisters did a wonderful job for the cause, Mistress Suki. Really. Our hospitals were a beacon of the mercy of the Doctrine of Truth."

"Thank you, sir."

"And what will you do now?"

"I'm your housekeeper, sir."

"Oh, so I am in very capable hands. That is good to know. Well, I must get out of this bath and get dressed. So, you can go now." Yonnis was conscious of the housekeeper looking at him. Was she looking at him with desire? "Go *now*, Mistress Suki."

"Shall I bring some salve—for your skin, sir?"

Yonnis was embarrassed. He had flattered himself, and disrespected her. She had noticed the clusters of tiny scabs on his arms and chest from the ravages of lice. Of course, as an army nurse, she would have seen them before, and other things, far worse. "Yes. Please."

"Sir." Suki bobbed a slight curtsy as she swept out of the room.

Yonnis hauled himself out of the bath and rubbed himself dry with a cloth. There was a looking glass on the dresser, and he dared himself to use it. The white-blond stubble on his head and chin had grown spiky. His pale face was unscathed by disease or battle scars, but it was deeply lined. He had spent many years on campaign in all weathers, and it was as leathery as the face of the poorest peasant. He was in his thirty-fourth year, but looked older. Perhaps he would be lucky enough to see forty-five summers.

After a few moments wondering what Farida had ever seen in him, and what she would make of him now, he wondered about shaving, but didn't. He donned the fresh linen undergarments and the newly tailored dark gray breeches, doublet, and hat that were laid out for him. He left the officers' quarters in the outer courtyard and headed for the storeroom that had been converted into a Temple of Truth.

The Cause of Truth Printing Company yard, Words Street, Nasrin. Early afternoon. The eleventh day of the Fourth Moon, Year Fifty.

"OH, ILLIO! WHAT joy! Praise be to the Eternal Spirit! The priests of Sudar are defeated! And Navvan the Nasty is dead! If I could get on my knees, I would!" Seemo, clutching his crutches in one hand and holding a newssheet in the other, beamed at the busy printer. He came here every day at dawn, his old green army coat already brushed, his face washed, and he hoped for work. There was none that morning, but Illio had been up, waiting for some words from All-Ears' office, and he had told him to come back after his midday meal. Meal. Ha! He'd been lucky enough to get some thin gruel at the Goodwives' soup kitchen.

"There's no time for prayin'—I pay you to get to yer stump and read news." Illio was always focused on business. He washed and dried his hands, which were stained completely black with stinking ink, then he counted out some newssheets for Seemo.

In the background, the printer's apprentices were busy rocking ink balls across type, placing damp paper onto the packing, and lowering it onto the printing frame for the pressman to apply his brawn. The smell of the fresh oil-based ink was oppressive in the small workshop. It mixed with the equally offensive smell of the grease used on the presses and the urine used to tan the leather of the ink balls. The men and boys worked skillfully and speedily, placing and pressing paper. The machinery creaked and they grunted. The boys pegged up wet sheets to dry on strings.

Seemo read the newssheet again. "There's some odd stuff 'bout lightning 'n' rainbows—"

"And a dead king, when we were promised a monumental trial that would sell lots of newssheets. Very annoyin', that."

"You should try being in a battle someday, Illio. You can plan all you like, but then it's all different—'specially if the weather kicks in!"

"No thanks, Seemo. Ev'ry day I see what battle did to you, you poor cotter!"

"Some of us had to make sacrifices for the cause, Brother Illio, so we could all be better off—now those thieving Raas and lords can't own us!" Seemo could barely think of a name for what he felt today. Could it be "rapture"? Was that what the Elders said about the Spirit's perfect state for the world? It must be nearer today than yesterday.

"Think so, old soldier?" Illio laughed heartily. "Bless you for believin' fine words, but they butter no parsnips! The squires'll feather their nests and we'll still be scrapin' along. I reckon it's all been about diggin' into Mother Earth to make more bricks. Those clay hills will be gettin' shorter soon—but you and me, we'll still be livin' behind walls made from shit 'n' straw."

"Illio! Shame on you for slandering the Father! Think on! You can say that now. Five years ago, the likes of you or me criticizing the high-ups—they'd 've had our tongues pulled out."

"Point taken!" Illio held up his hands to acknowledge his agreement. Then he grinned at Seemo and offered his stained hand for him to shake. "It's a momentous day. And I'm not complainin'. Ol' All-Ears keeps my presses runnin' and he's a good payer—not like the King's men. Assholes, they were. But really, Seemo, are you expectin' jam for breakfast tomorrow?"

Seemo shrugged, and ran his hand over his bare brown head. "Mebbe not. But I'm expecting veterans to be looked after some'ow."

"Really?!" Illio's small black eyes suddenly glowed like coals under his mop of gray hair. "Don't hold yer breath for that, friend!"

"Oh, I'll be reminding squires of their promises, Illio! I'm with the Distributors!"

"Idiot! Why tell me that?!" Illio spluttered. "Just don't start one of their fanciful rants when you've got my newssheets in yer hand!"

Images of his landlady chasing him out of his hut with a broom because he couldn't pay the rent flashed through Seemo's mind. "Sorry! Sorry, Illio, friend! We go back a long way and you've been good to me. I won't cause any trouble for you. You know I need the work!"

"Yeah, yeah!" Illio grumbled. "May the Spirit bless you, Seemo, but you think too much for yer own good! Now fuck off and get yer stump to yer first readin' stump!"

The Temple of Truth, Bankside Place, Nasrin. Early afternoon. The eleventh day of the Fourth Moon, Year Fifty.

As YONNIS CROSSED the courtyard, clerks and maids scampered up to him to bow or curtsy. He nodded back—

what else could he do? Their behavior was curious to him. If they dared to look at him, they were wide-eyed. It made him uncomfortable. Did they know what he had done? Was that worth staring at?

In the temple, a whitewashed former storehouse, two bright-faced little children were collecting a jug and plate from the Elder, who hugged and kissed them before sending them back to their mother. The younger boy guided the older girl. Yonnis felt his heart warming. This was the sort of love that he believed in, that he believed he had been fighting for. Fighting for love—a contradiction he had wrestled with every day since childhood; its roots ran deep into his earliest memories. His best friend Merutis had limped because of a clubfoot, and woe betide any boy who decided to push him around for it. Yonnis would make sure that the aggressor would limp for a while himself.

Yonnis clasped his good friend, the Army Elder Yeribbi, in a hug of desperation. His emotions since Tamsit had been building up like a menacing boil. Yeribbi was one of the new Elders, chosen by Followers for his inspirational reflections. A roistering laborer with no time for any sort of piety, Yeribbi had been overwhelmed with love when he became a father. His baby daughter's eyes could not see, so under the old religion she would have been condemned to misery as one of the "flawed folk". His little family had escaped to the capital just as the war started, and Yeribbi signed up as a pikeman in the Army of Truth, vowing to fight for his daughter's right to a better life. This was a man with his own contradictions, and one who had seen Yonnis both at his most invincible—planning battles with his commanders, barking orders, and charging into enemy cavalry, and at his weakest—nurturing misgivings, faults, and guilt.

After a few moments summoning some words, Yonnis blurted them out. "I killed Navvan Glantar. And I did it for vengeance! I disobeyed the orders of the War Cabinet to arrest him, and I have blighted the Doctrine of Truth! Oh, Yeribbi!

29

What am I? How did I start to become a monster? The penalty that good men pay for not defending ourselves and our dearest ones is to be at the mercy of badness, but then we—*I*—do bad things to defeat the badness. What can I do to put things right?"

Yonnis felt Yeribbi shaking him gently, urging him to look at him, eye to eye.

"Why d'ya think that you should be perfect? Not many men could pass up an opportunity to avenge personal grief. We all knew what we were signing up for. The followers of the unjust king may not have deserved what we did to them, but it was kill or be killed. Now that the fight against the unjust is won, there's a chance to establish a just peace. That's because of *your* victory."

"But what about my soul? Please, Yeribbi, let me tell you what is happening to it. I am haunted by a nightmare, every few days." Yonnis closed his eyes, to recollect the dream in detail.

"I am on my favorite horse, with my wife sitting in front of me. We are in the mineral mountains of my home, North Yeralla, gazing in wonder at the colorful rocks, and the purple heather, and the green moss where the glacial rivers run. The sun is shining. All is bliss. I am kissing Farida's neck, and then my horse whinnies in fear and I look round.

"There is a large red catlike creature in scaled armor, with the horns of a ram and a leering human face, right behind me. Its breath is like soot. It roars at me. 'How many have died at your hand, boy? Corpses follow wherever you are!'

"There are hundreds of bodies, marching… some in simple winding sheets, others just naked and sliced like meat. Then there are glimpses—memories of my sword slicing through limbs and guts. And the demon shouts, 'How many widows and orphans did you make at Tinmas, at Daktor, at Kasbrit, at Redmor, at Grettin…?' The list

goes on and on. 'And you think that you do the work of your Eternal Spirit?' The creature laughs… and leans into my face and whispers, 'You are no man of Truth! I am Marko, god of war, and I am come to claim you as my disciple.'"

Yonnis opened his eyes again and looked at Yeribbi. "Marko claims me as his disciple! He says that I cannot be a man of Truth. Could he be right, Yeribbi?"

"Yonnis, this war had meaning and purpose. That's why men followed you. And you weren't reckless with our lives. You never risked us fighting on bogs or hills. You made sure that the cannons did most of the work. And the enemy? You were more merciful to them than they expected! Let me warn you against wallowing in self-doubt!" Yeribbi stood up and paced the waxed earth floor, frowning, searching for words that would help. "When crushed with guilt—that's when the Eternal Spirit is closest to us and we to It. You may feel like you're trembling at the edge of the abyss… but you *are not* chained there—you can move towards the light. *You* have to make that move. He who wants peace in the afterlife must make a contribution to it in this one."

Yonnis shut his eyes. First of all, he noticed sounds from outside filtering through the open eaves. He could hear the rhythmic whine of swans' wings overhead, and their splashdown into the Binar. He could hear the shouts of wherrymen and the grind of oars in rowlocks. Then he heard Yeribbi's breathing. Then he could hear his own heartbeat. Here, in stillness, Yonnis felt sure that he would gain awareness of the Eternal Spirit's guidance. He concentrated so hard that he shook. He saw colors swirling on the insides of his eyelids. He waited. First of all, he tasted salt from the sweat popping from the pores around his mouth. He felt hands in his hands, pats on the back. He smelled tired men and horses. He heard the monotonous chant "Whoa!

General Yonnis!" from Kimalloan troopers, relieved to have been on the winning side again. Finally, he saw faces—hopeful faces, faces that had been condemned as "flawed", faces that had seen hunger and toil, and then children's faces. A strange voice, a Kimalloan woman's voice, speaking in Yerallan, whispered, "Come with us, Yonnis. Show us how the Truth delivers prosperity and peace!" After some time in profound reflection, he was comforted and calm.

"I can do it, Yeribbi. How could I ever have doubted that the Spirit is powerful enough to turn a warhound into a peace-builder?! I must make Farida proud of me." He paused. "But what might come to me—for what I did to Navvan—before I can redeem myself?"

Yeribbi replied sternly. "Go to the Father! Explain yourself, and offer yourself."

As Yonnis left the temple, a group of five green-jacketed drummer boys barreled into him.

"Hey, boys!" he complained. "If you want to play tag, do it on the green where there are no people carrying pots and pails!"

They stared at him. They had heard that voice before somewhere.

"Are you…?"

"Yes—where's your salute?"

They saluted and then mobbed round him, cheering and laughing, hands extended to shake. Yonnis obliged.

"Thank you, boys, for your bravery in the war. Stay strong to build the peace."

"Aye, General!" said some.

One declared proudly, "I'm signin' up to have a go back at the Pozzies, sir!"

Yonnis had made his commitment to the peace of Kimalloa, and immediately he was confronted with the enormity of his quest. The war had unleashed the instinct of humans to hate. What would it take to change that?

The apartments of the Leader of the Assembly of Commoners, Inner Courtyard, Bankside Place, Nasrin. Midafternoon. The eleventh day of the Fourth Moon, Year Fifty.

I T WAS BARELY credible.

"So, the mighty general is in one piece—of course! While poor Grakko, who stepped into my shoes, was blown to bits. And a girl—a Sudarite girl—takes an arrow for him! Why am I not surprised?"

Commander Arlo Clayhills sat propped up on a cushioned settle, nursing a heavily bandaged left arm. He had bags of weariness under his big gray eyes. At the Battle of Kallo Mill on the border between the Western Region and the Edgelands, a musket ball had burst through his buff coat and settled in his muscle. It had been skillfully extracted and the wound had been thoroughly cleaned and sewn, but no Healing Elder had been willing to advise him whether or not he would regain the use of his arm. Arlo hoped for the best outcome, but expected the worst.

He was in the Bankside quarters of his father, Squire Yoshi of the Clayhills, now the Head of State of Kimalloa, who was sharing some intelligence reports with him. The "Information Officer" of the Cause of Truth, Squire Ellis Tallier, had some expert agents, including some deep in the enemy's camp, and they all seemed to have observed different battles at Tamsit. Just exactly how victory had been achieved seemed just as unclear with more information as it had been with less.

"Arlo! What is this?" Squire Yoshi Clayhills chided like the gentle parent he had always been. "I know that you feel bitter about your injury, but you are still in the army and should respect a senior officer."

Arlo held up his good hand to accept the point. His father's advice was always wise, which was why Arlo had to share him with the whole nation. It had been his first experience of jealousy, as a child, when his mother said that his father had to be away from home "for the people of Kimalloa". Who were they, to take *his* wonderful father and call him their own? "Sorry, Pa. But it irks me that our soldiers are—dare I use a reference to magic? —entranced by Yonnis's reckless bravado." He screwed up his face in distaste. "I mean—they *sing* for him. It's awful. They should sing about *your* courage, *your* leadership. All those years that you have been devoted to this country, how you have suffered for it—riddling with old King Rikko in the Parleys, attacked by Navvan's heavies, making something of the rebel army when it was just a bunch of hopeful escaped serfs..." Arlo knew it well. As he transitioned from boy to man, he had lived in fear, knowing that the loss of his father and his home might only be one speech away. Kimalloa did not appreciate how much it owed Squire Yoshi Clayhills, or what it owed the rest of his family for their sacrifices. Yet his father was so *reasonable*, so much a Follower of the Truth, that he sought no entitlement; he played a team game. It was admirable, but sometimes Arlo just wished that his father would seize his due and put others in their place.

Arlo's father sighed and rubbed under the rim of his eyepatch. He spoke calmly, as he always did. "Yonnis was capable, willing, and available when I was badly injured. And it has worked. His tactics are demanding, but they are masterful. He has not lost a battle. Here we are—we have won the war in less time than we might have expected, and we are planning the peace." He sighed again. "I wonder why we aren't drunk with the joy of victory?"

Arlo's good hand groomed his neat brown beard. He was breathing deeply, trying to calm down, but he was angry and he felt driven to share it. "Perhaps, Pa, because there's something missing! We wanted to put the King on trial for all the Kimalloan blood shed in this war. Now we can't!" Suddenly, Arlo's big voice reverberated, shaking all the air in the room. "He—Yonnis Krusa—appointed himself judge, jury, and executioner! What flagrant disregard for his orders! How can you be so calm?"

His father replied quietly. "Remember our Doctrine and suspend your judgment. There is probably an explanation. Even if there isn't, we have to tread carefully."

As soon as he had felt the searing sting of the musket ball in his arm, Arlo had felt cheated. He might not have been cheated of his life, but he had certainly been cheated of triumph. What if he had swerved and the bullet had landed in Yonnis? Then he, Arlo, a true son of Kimalloa and the son-in-blood of the brilliant man who had imagined the new Kimalloa, would have had the glory at Tamsit. How much more fitting would that have been? What would history make of some minor royal from some remote country doing the job?

Arlo winced. His healing wound stabbed and itched. He reached for a small vial of liquid. He noticed that his father was watching him, very deliberately.

"Take care with the poppy juice, Arlo."

Arlo grumbled, then unfurled his tall frame from the settle and went to open a window. "I'm still in pain, Pa. I need it."

3

Office of the Information Officer, the Archive, Bankside, Nasrin. Midafternoon. The eleventh day of the Fourth Moon, Year Fifty.

THE DOOR OF All-Ears's office creaked ominously. He liked it that way. He rose from his chair in front of the fireplace to thrust a piece of paper at the visitor, before there was even a breath of a chance for greetings.

"Read this, Yoshi! Just read it!"

Yoshi Clayhills stood and read quickly, then again, slowly. He looked up from the letter and shook his head. "The trouble with change is that very strange things can happen." He drew up a chair opposite All-Ears and sat down heavily. "I hadn't been expecting Navvan's niece to claim the throne. This is, at best, a naive but well-meant offer of help. At worst…"

All-Ears noticed a faint tremor in Yoshi's hand clutching the letter. Why was victory so difficult? Why did he feel so angry? "Agh." His dry cough hacked when he drew breath to speak. "She didn't waste any time! How many Glantars have offered to be humble in the face of revolts, and then turned and slaughtered their new friends? She would have learned at her father's knee that she should smile while taking the hand of friendship and then chop it off. She is not to be trusted. Saving her from her uncle was a righteous thing to do at the time, but now she's showing her true Glantar instincts." He had risked his own life to save her. Had it been gallantry? Or just strategy?

All-Ears pulled his mind back to the present and grunted. "We didn't come all this way through the darkness to have her step onto a throne and push us back into the shires." He felt a seething resentment racing into his head. What inspired her to think that, just because she was the daughter of a powerful man, she had the right to any power herself? Obviously, she had not learned much in the past few years. "Just imagine the Pozarians queuing up to marry her and claiming to be the Sudarite King of Kimalloa... Kimalloa could not take that. There isn't another Kimalloa to waste."

"Ellis, we can't ignore this letter. When the War Cabinet calls the Assembly of Commoners to establish a new constitution, they must have choices..."

All-Ears nodded. "Absolutely, and I have complete faith in your ability to persuade them to make the choice that is right for *our* Kimalloa... or all our efforts will have been for nothing." He deeply admired the way that his cousin could maneuver debates to the right ends without losing his integrity. Yoshi could always make colleagues see things his way. He would steer the Assembly.

A log spat and flared in the grate. The squires watched the flames for a while, sipping their beer. All-Ears had aching joints and he made sure that his office was always stiflingly warm. It was for his comfort, but his favorite excuse was that warmth made ink flow better, so he could write faster. This room was his sanctuary. He loved his banks of locked cabinets, which were made of tin in order to keep the nation's secrets safe from damp, fire, and mice. He loved his plain, sturdy desk, his inkstand, his baskets of messages in and messages out, but above all, he loved the chair by the fire where he did his plotting. This was his life's work, and he cherished it so much that it hurt. He stamped out some sparks that the burning wood in the grate had spat onto the tiled floor.

"Agh. I can't wait for us to have plentiful coal. I wonder how many bell pits we can sink in the first year of peace. Now, Yoshi, let's put the Glantar woman to one side and discuss the more urgent issue, which I'm sure was your reason for coming here. One of my agents in the King's camp at Tamsit has confirmed that Yonnis disobeyed the order to arrest Navvan and smashed his sword into the head of the late king. There were mitigating circumstances, including the knavish Raas burning kakko..."

"He handed me the bloody helmet in public so that I couldn't refuse to take it."

"So I have heard! Very brazen!"

"Yes. But the onlookers loved it. Well, I was surprised, and I was very sad. Of course, things do happen in the heat of battle. I had to make quick decisions that I regretted when I was general."

All-Ears huffed with indignation. "Sometimes, Yoshi, you are just too reasonable! What are we to do with him now the war is over? The soldiers revere him—too much. The army has the power to support the Assembly of Commoners in creating the Republic, or to crush it."

The spymaster waited for a reaction. All he got was a raised eyebrow. He carried on.

"After all, history tells us that successful generals can't stop themselves from filling the gap in power that their victories create. Do you know what I heard this morning?" He had a short fit of coughing, and drank deeply from his beer mug. "Militiamen asking each other if Yonnis was king now that he had killed Navvan. I have to tell you, Yoshi, those comments have rattled me into a state of unreason and strange imaginings. On his mother's side, Yonnis has a claim to be an heir of Rikko IX..."

It was All-Ears' vocation to be a very suspicious man, but he would be relieved to be wrong. Now, he looked at Yoshi, who seemed to be amused. If Yoshi found his accusation fanciful, that was reassuring.

"My dear Ellis! So we have a new queen *and* a new king days after declaring a republic! I share your frustration with Yonnis—but we've known him for years, and you've admired his piety as well as his prowess. I can't imagine him turning on us—no, not at all." Yoshi paused. "And we have to consider... it wouldn't be righteous for us to be blatantly ungrateful for his commitment to winning the war for us."

"Agh! Or was it his commitment to personal vengeance?! But, of course... we would not want to seem ungrateful—that might provoke the army, as well as our allies." All-Ears paused. "But we need to do something with Yonnis... as we need to do something with the Glantar woman." With a force that surprised himself, he slammed down his beer mug. "I do have an idea, cousin."

Yoshi looked at him expectantly. All-Ears felt a glow of satisfaction. Of course, his cousin knew above all others that no discussion with him could be concluded without a plot of some kind.

"Please share it."

All-Ears feigned reluctance. "It's an unlikely scenario..."

"Is it a *possible* scenario?"

All-Ears paused again. "I suppose that it depends on how repentant he is."

"Please, Ellis, spit it out!"

The Great Hall, Bankside Place, Nasrin. Late afternoon.
The eleventh day of the Fourth Moon, Year Fifty.

YONNIS WAS TOLD that he could not miss the Great Hall, because it was aptly named. But he was not to be allowed to find it for himself. On this journey across the courtyard, he was beset with soldiers finding some excuse to approach, salute him, and offer an escort. Six of them guided him to the Great Hall and they pushed the tall, heavy oak doors open.

Yonnis felt insignificant in this room, as people were supposed to do. Five tumblers could stand on each other's shoulders before one would touch the ceiling. It was so wide and long that you could have stabled twenty horses in it. Yonnis looked up to the ceiling and his eyes were assaulted by colorful, finely painted pomp. In the central panel, an unrealistically handsome king in magnificently shiny robes, dripping with ermine and jewels, looked down proudly. In the panels surrounding him were fat, naked children with wings, looking adoringly towards him. Yonnis flinched and quickly turned his head away, screwing up his face in disgust.

The spring sun pierced through neatly arched high windows, stained to depict scenes from the Sudarite myths, creating delicate patterns on the floor. Tapestries of silver and gold thread covered the walls. Everywhere Yonnis turned, the Great Hall shouted wealth and power, just as the Glantar kings had intended. A huge fireplace was surrounded by black marble, with coats of arms either side and above it—red and blue with glittering gold lion heads. He smelled a hint of roses in the air, perhaps from the beeswax tapers squatting in heavy silver candlesticks on carved blackwood cabinets.

He suppressed his awe and asked out loud, growling with frustration, "Why haven't we sold these furnishings to feed the poor and whitewashed that *obscene* ceiling?"

"Ah, Yonnis." He heard Squire Clayhills' stick on the tiles behind him. "I know what you mean—but we haven't really thought about this place until now, we just locked it up during the war. Now we are in charge of the country, we need some continuity for the affairs of state, somewhere to meet ambassadors—"

"Continuity? Do we need continuity?" Yonnis thought about the hungry, ragged wretches he had seen up and down the country. "Let us make the grand ambassadors notice that things have changed. We fought for *change*." He realized immediately that he had started this conversation badly. A blunt challenge to an unimportant comment and a stark opinion spoken like a general giving orders. And his Yerallan accent made it worse. Clipped. Staccato. Formal. Humorless.

"An interesting point of principle—that is not for you or me to decide. These items are owned by the state. The Assembly of Commoners must discuss what happens to them, and in the meantime, continuity is indeed the prudent course."

Yonnis remembered that his uncle had grumbled that the heavy pull of continuity corrupts all progress. But he must show humility to the Father of the People. He nodded. "Of course, sir."

"Now, General." Squire Clayhills looked squarely at Yonnis, and got straight to the point. "You have put me and the whole of the War Cabinet in a very uncomfortable place. I've seen the reports from our agents. I know that you found yourself in a position where you had to engage the King in one-to-one combat, but also that you killed him when he was on the ground and could have been taken prisoner. What on earth were you thinking?"

Yonnis knelt at Squire Clayhills' feet, with his right arm clasped across his chest.

Squire Clayhills snapped, "I'm not a king that expects a man to grovel! Get up and look me in my one good eye and tell me the truth!"

Oh! The Father of the People, the man of reason who so rarely raised his voice, had shouted at him. This must be righteous anger indeed! Yonnis was stung, and jumped up quickly. "Sir, I confess that I was not thinking. I was full of rage and vengeance. But the circumstances? The smoke, the rain, the confusion? Really, I could not have anticipated them. For all I knew, I was about to meet my own end at the hands of the King's guard, and I made the judgment that I could not wait for our men to find me—I had to finish Navvan there and then. I did try to get him to yield. He would not yield…"

"And?"

"He bellowed at me, 'Never! You diabolical god-killer widower of a whore!'" Yonnis looked sorrowfully at the Father. Surely, as a man who loved his wife and family, he would understand?

"Go on."

"He was reveling in what he did, and insulting the memory of my wife!"

Squire Clayhills blustered back, "Are you claiming that some goddess of fury blinded your reason? What superstitious nonsense! What kind of hypocrite are you? You broke your uncle's rules of war!"

Maybe there was no defense for Yonnis the warmonger. He had betrayed the trust of a great man, which made him a worm of the vilest nature.

"What happened to the body?"

"Buried at sea by some specially chosen Yerallan Adventurers, who have, at my order, returned to Yeralla."

"How convenient. No Kimalloan witnesses."

"Sir, I could not ask any Kims to be a focus for retribution."

Squire Clayhills nodded.

"I am sorry, sir. I am very sorry. These were not the actions that our Doctrine requires. I was not a man of reason, or a Follower of the Truth, in that moment at Tamsit. I have reflected, and I know that I committed a great wrong, especially to you. You have always supported me and trusted me. I will accept whatever punishment you see fit."

Squire Clayhills barked back at him. "Ha! You've spared me the responsibility of trying a king—do you think I want the responsibility of trying a popular general instead?"

Yonnis tried to persist in showing his repentance. "Dear Father of the People, let me serve Kimalloa—" He was cut short.

"You've done what Kimalloa needed from you, General Yonnis. Your military strategy played a great part in freeing the people from the yoke of serfdom and the superstitions of Sudarism. For that, I'm grateful."

Yonnis tried again. "Please, Squire Clayhills, sir—let me contribute to the peace-building. I have a debt to the men who followed me into battle and did not come home. Whatever I can do to help their widows and orphans, tell me and I will do it. I can work in a soup kitchen or a hospital, or run a craft shed for the wounded—"

"We're not short of people to ladle soup and wrap bandages. If you are offering a sacrifice, it'll have to be something more than that!"

"Sir? It is so important to me—may I ask for *your* forgiveness?"

Squire Clayhills hesitated, and as he did so, there was the thud of a baton on the door.

"Enter."

Yonnis's heart sank. Squire Clayhills looked so glad and grateful to have the interruption. Yonnis deduced that he had not been forgiven—yet. He would have to try harder.

A sergeant appeared. "Squire Clayhills, sir, I am sorry, but the Pozarian Ambassador wishes to 'drop by' immediately, as he puts it."

Squire Clayhills smiled. "Well, let's be sociable to our neighbor. He may drop by."

"Yes, sir," said the sergeant, saluting and clicking his heels together.

He returned swiftly with Excellency Onfri, loudly dressed in red and silver. Onfri looked askance at Yonnis, and openly took a deep inhalation of his pomander.

"Thank you for seeing me, Your Grace, Father of the People of Kimalloa." He bowed deeply to Squire Clayhills and turned to Yonnis. "My Lord General?" Onfri bowed less deeply to him. "I've heard much about you."

"I am sure that you have, Ambassador." Yonnis extended a hand for Onfri to shake.

Onfri looked full of disdain, as if he had been offered a grizzly paw, but he shook it. Then he looked about the Great Hall. "What a surprise. Just as I remember it—"

Squire Clayhills interrupted. "To what do I owe this pleasure, Excellency Onfri?"

Onfri bowed again, with exaggerated deference. "My lord—"

"I'm not a lord. Surely you have done your research? I refused to take a title when Rikko Glantar was offering me one, twelve years ago. He wanted to buy me, and I was not for sale. But you can call me what you find comfortable. Now, pray, Excellency, what is so urgent? The Assembly is very busy building the new republic."

Onfri looked around for somewhere to sit.

"Let's not sit, Excellency," said Clayhills. "I find that meetings go so much quicker when the people in them have to stand."

Yonnis wondered whether he should leave, but Squire Clayhills did not dismiss him. Perhaps he was grateful for a witness.

"Very well, I will get to the point." Onfri's tone was acidic. "My king commands me to ask after the health of his cousin."

"Which one?" Clayhills taunted him.

"Her Majesty Queen Esta, of course."

"'Her Majesty'? I recall that your king decided four years ago that she was not the rightful heir?"

Onfri gave no indication of humility. He looked defiant and amused. "Sir, the other Truth states have symbolic figures as Head of State. Who will be yours, if it is not her, the princess that you took great risks to rescue? Do you have another, more distant cousin of my king in mind?"

He stared at Yonnis, making Squire Clayhills notice his inference. The squire's face remained resolutely blank.

"The Assembly will debate the new constitution in due course, Ambassador," Squire Clayhills asserted. "Tell your king that the Lady Esta is well. I have had a letter from her, full of delight that the Army of Truth had won the war."

"That is very reassuring. Thank you. I'll let His Majesty know that she is well." The ambassador paused and then smirked. "You had better not take too long with your constitution, *Mr.* Clayhills. The people are always impatient. And the army…" He stared at Yonnis again, with as much curiosity as contempt. "The army will turn on you if your fine promises to them are not delivered. The new land of truth and freedom, of peace and plenty! Pah! I wish you luck, gentlemen." Onfri bowed, yet again, and strode out.

4

A quayside inn, Nasrin. Early evening. The eleventh day
of the Fourth Moon, Year Fifty.

"... OUR TROOPS, NOW famed for their speed and deadliness,
began the onslaught. The bodies of the enemy were all
around! A storm broke and there was much smoke and noise.
As the smoke cleared, in their thousands the soldiers witnessed
a mighty lightning strike which lit up the sky and struck the
so-called King Navvan Glantar from his horse to the harsh
ground—dead. Our men sank to their knees in prayers of thanks
to the Eternal Spirit that It has saved Kimalloa from the Sudarite
Glantars that have enslaved us for centuries. Citizens, it is your
time now to pray for our wise Assembly and its victorious army
who have delivered truth and freedom to our glorious land!"

The listeners did not react. What was wrong with them?
Seemo's voice hacked into the quiet, like an axe.

"This is great news, brothers and sisters! You should be
cheering!"

One toothless old man managed a throaty cheer. "God save
the Army of Truth!"

"Good riddance to that Glantar scum!" cried a younger man
with a disease-scarred face.

"So *that* was all the fuss uptown this morning," someone
grumbled.

Another man sneered, "What good does it do us? Fuck me if I don't feel as hungry today as I did last week." His blood-spattered sputum whistled from his mouth and splatted on the earth floor. He added as an afterthought, "No offense to you personally, Seemo."

There was a smattering of applause and mumblings of approval, but that was all. The landlady dropped a copper coin in Seemo's pocket, commenting, "Thanks for the news, soldier. Even if it was all shit."

Seemo spotted a well-dressed man with a military bearing and a groomed beard—an unusual sight in this particular hostelry, with its earth floor, walls made from shit 'n' straw, and roof of rotting thatch. He started to stride towards the newsman. Seemo soon noticed that his left arm was in a sling.

"Is that a recent war wound, sir?" he asked.

"Yes. At Kallo Mill. Musket shot. I am lucky that I did not succumb to reeky. I'll take two newssheets please, brother. Where did you lose your leg?"

"At Sentur, in the rye fields of the northwest, two years ago."

The man nodded in sympathy.

Seemo continued. "I've been reading out the news ever since. It's all I can do for the cause."

"May the Spirit bless you for your devotion, brother. What did you do before the war?"

"I was a shepherd—on the moors."

"You're a countryman. Don't you want to go back?"

"I heard most of the sheep had been eaten. And for any sheep left, a one-legged shepherd ain't any good to 'em."

"There're plans to set up craft sheds for veterans—maybe you could operate a rope lathe or a potter's wheel with one leg?"

Seemo shrugged. "How long does a plan take, sir? If they're ever real, I'll try."

"I wish you success." The man grasped the newsman's hand firmly and pressed several copper coins into it.

A quayside inn, Nasrin. Early evening, some moments later. The eleventh day of the Fourth Moon, Year Fifty.

THERE WAS A short interlude of awkward looks in the half-light of the inn as Yonnis and Arlo glanced at the newssheets and quaffed the bad beer. Arlo had spent most of the walk along the quayside berating Yonnis for his reckless conduct at Tamsit. But, thought Yonnis, he had a right to his opinion, and friends should be able to clear the air from time to time. Last time he had seen Arlo was in the field hospital. The musket ball had been extracted from his wound and he was still dizzy from the dreaming herbs he had been given to dull the pain. Yonnis was just so glad to see that his friend was now fit enough to spoil for an argument.

Suddenly, Arlo reached across the sticky table and grasped Yonnis's arm. "Would you have done differently… if—"

"I missed you, Arlo, of course I did. I was very aware that I did not have you organizing the ranks behind me, and that made me so anxious just to finish the job. We had to press on and stop that man of blood from regrouping ever again." Yonnis paused and looked with concern as Arlo winced when moving his injured arm. "How long will it take to heal completely?"

"It might not." Arlo sighed.

Yonnis struggled to find some sympathetic words. "You will heal. You're of strong stock and had good treatment. And think how the ladies love a wounded war hero. They'll fuss over you like a lamb. And men will respect you. The army will need your leadership when I've been disgraced. You *will* succeed, Arlo."

Arlo gazed at the beer in his mug.

Yonnis continued. "You will be a great general."

"So, you will support me—to the Army Council?" Arlo looked up. He seemed surprised. Why should he be surprised? Hadn't they supported each other time and time again?

"Of course!" Yonnis exclaimed.

"Thank you. Well, I hope tomorrow's outcome is nothing more serious than exile—"

"Oh, I have reflected with Yeribbi and I know that I must do my penance here. I am committed to building the peace of Kimalloa."

Arlo took a big mouthful of beer. He swallowed hard and screwed up his face.

The conversation paused. Yonnis's head filled with memories of saddle-sore and foot-weary days in the cold, the wind, the rain. The mud, blood, smoke, lice, rats, screams, oaths, the hunger and hardship, the sweating disease, the shitting disease, the reeky disease. What had it all been for, if not to build a better peace?

Sometimes, he wished that he hadn't made the boastful boyish remark that seemed to have determined his destiny. Yonnis's uncle, the deputy consul of Yeralla, had taken him to the harbor to look at ships. He asked the five-year-old which one he liked best. Yonnis pointed at one and said, "That ship. It has the most guns." His uncle roared with approving laughter, then started training his precocious nephew for war. Having adopted the new creed proselytized by Yerobis the Liberator, Yonnis's grandfather had enabled technical and economic progress for Yeralla, but conflict with the forces of the old ways was bound to come.

Learning the art and science of war was an outlet for Yonnis's energy and intelligence which pleased him at the time. It took just one battle for him to realize that real war was messy, ugly, and cruel. He vomited and he wept and he had nightmares. He still did. But after all his practicing and studying, he was good at combat, and he was his uncle's talisman. He could not let his uncle down, even when duty dragged him from the arms of his sweet wife to fight for kinsmen trying to establish the Truth in Boriela. When that quest seemed secure, Yonnis was ready for peace. For a short while, he seemed to have it.

Then came that day...

Yonnis and his uncle Artoris had been riding at the head of the Yerallan Adventurers to the celebration of comradeship with South Boriela, taking place in the central park in the Yerallan capital. Other members of the family, together with Yerobis the Liberator, their spiritual leader, had gone ahead in carriages, greeting the crowds of people who were so happy to have a day of sport and entertainment. The sun was shining and the atmosphere was light and cheerful, until they heard furious yelling off to their left. Militiamen spilled in front of them, asking for help. Artoris ordered a left turn, as dozens of brawling fishermen piled into the troops. It did not take long for the trained soldiers to sort them out, just a few moments. They were turning back towards the park when the mighty explosion rocked the ground and blew them sideways. There was a painful ringing in Yonnis's ears. Then he could smell the smoke, the black, sulfurous smoke. Then he heard the cries, the screams... A ghastly realization dawned on Yonnis. As he howled in anger and grief, he felt like his body and soul were turning inside out.

For Yonnis, the desolation of losing his wife and unborn child was like having his heart ripped out. The desolation of surviving the explosion himself was another intolerable burden. His hatred of the Sudarite zealots funded by Navvan who had murdered and maimed in Yeralla that day knew no limits. So many people that he loved were reduced to fragments of scorched flesh. His wife, his child, his best friend Merutis, his cousin Anya, his Aunt Gulda. And all those he did not know who were just out for a day of fun—soldiers, servants, clerks, merchants, and more and more, all with their wives and children. Yonnis threw every energy into the search for the perpetrators. He wanted to execute the plotters personally, but his uncle made sure that the rule of law applied to the few who were caught. When the call came to help Followers of the Truth in Kimalloa, a chance to defeat Navvan, Yonnis had nothing to hold him back. He sailed with his uncle's men and guns, and an inner rage that would not succumb to reason.

It had always troubled his prayers and reflections that vengeance was a driving force that offended several core virtues of the Doctrine of Truth, but Navvan had planted the monster in his soul. When he slew Navvan, he slew the monster. Now, and only now, he could concentrate on his penance.

A skinny dog crept towards Yonnis and Arlo. These were days when folk would sooner eat a dog than feed it. It sat, and looked hopeful. Gazing at its doleful eyes, Yonnis contemplated the suffering of so many innocents caught up in the consequences of "the cause", however just it was. He remembered a favorite horse that had been shot from underneath him. He felt again the shuddering impact, saw the fountain of blood, and heard her pitiful scream as she collapsed and died. He stroked the dog's coarse gray fur. When they left the inn, Yonnis beckoned to the dog to follow them. He couldn't save all the dogs of Kimalloa's capital, but this one had asked nicely and asked first.

Yonnis put his arm round Arlo. "Oh, my dear friend. I'm so pleased to see you recovering so well! Let's get back to quarters for some more wholesome sustenance."

They set out alongside the wide, slow, powerful River Binar that made the capital, Nasrin, such an ideal inland port. Yonnis noticed with satisfaction that it was somewhat cleaner since the local administrators of "Free Nasrin" had organized street cleaners and soil collectors to take the city's filth to the south bank where it could warm and fertilize the vast expanse of fruit trees, hopbines, and vegetable fields that should soon be feeding the capital.

On the quays of the north bank where they were walking, there were ships waiting to take Pozarian soldiers and Kimalloan Sudarites choosing exile away to the east. There were food aid ships from Boriela. Both had long lines in front of them, being policed by the local militia. The militia were also holding back young lads who were throwing stones and jeering at the "Pozzies".

Yonnis and Arlo switched to a parallel street. There they ran into a crowd watching a quivering, shirtless old man being tied to a whipping post. Arlo asked a militiaman what crime he had committed.

"He's a cutpurse. Ten lashes."

The whip whistling through the air, its slap onto the old man's back, his howls of pain, and the audience's gasps disturbed Yonnis, and he moved on. Arlo and the dog followed.

As they strode up Embassy Street, they were passed by ragged citizens running in the other direction, calling out to others, "There's meat at the soup kitchens! Hurry!" Some soldiers in the brick-red uniforms of the Yerallan regiment marched past, smelling of deer.

Arlo looked down at Yonnis with absolute exasperation. "Ah. Your personal regiment. Raiding the city's parks to feed the hungry, eh? Really, Yonnis! With all that you have to face tomorrow, was acting like a bountiful king today your best move?"

Bankside Place, Nasrin. Sunset. The eleventh day of the Fourth Moon, Year Fifty.

"MY LORD GENERAL." Sergeant Loomis scolded Yonnis in their own tongue. "You should take a guard when you go wandering the streets." He looked at the dog. "And you shouldn't pick up souvenirs. Look at the state of it."

"We've looked like that after some battles, Loomis, and we brush up afterwards."

"It won't stand the journey back to Yeralla—assuming we are

going?" All the Yerallans were anxious to get back, hoping that their families had not forgotten them.

Yonnis had nothing waiting for him at home. Home was a hearth flanked by gravestones. "Well, some of us will be going home soon, Loomis." The vagueness of his answer did not impress.

"Don't stay here, sir," Loomis pleaded. "No offense to your mother's kin, but these Kimalloans don't have very deep veins when it comes to loyalty. They love you one day, but they will drop you for the slightest error, real or imagined, the next. I've heard some gossip—"

Yonnis smiled. "Take care, Loomis, we are still their guests for now. Please call someone to bring some scraps for the dog, and bring a big basin with clean, warm water—I want to wash her."

Loomis shook his head and muttered at the idea of warm water for a dog. "The poor beast will think that you are going to cook her!"

A basin and a jug of warm water, and scraps, were soon brought. Yonnis knelt down, poured some water into the basin, and lifted the nervous dog into it. As the warmth spread through her, the flea eggs in her fur started to hatch. Yonnis quickly started to squash the insects between his fingernails.

"I thought you might have a few of these," he said to the dog. "I've had a few myself over the years and I hate them. Oh, how they make you itch. It's torture. When you are clean, you'll feel better, and I'll let you share my quarters. I think I'll call you Nessi. You know, you are the first Kimalloan life I have saved since my pledge to the Eternal Spirit."

Nessi licked his face.

He squirmed away. "Ugh! I must teach you manners, Nessi!"

Nessi was a medium-sized dog, of the sort that Yonnis usually saw with shepherds, although there was a hint of a cross with a leaner hunting dog, and a longer, wolfish snout. She was very patient and calm, looking at him with curiosity, but complete acceptance. Yonnis could not work out why a street dog would be so trusting. He felt immediate affection for her. He fed the scraps to her carefully and slowly, so that she did not gorge.

He had no recollection of his own ablutions or how he fell into a deep sleep on the bed. He didn't notice Nessi climbing up from the rug where he had told her to stay. After sleeping peacefully all evening, and through the night, as the light of dawn started to creep through the window, Yonnis had the dream—Marko was leering at him again. Yonnis tried to scream, and couldn't.

Something warm and wet slapped his face. He woke and whimpered. Nessi slobbered another smelly lick over his face. He met her eyes, which expressed astonishment that he was back with her.

"Thank you, Nessi," he muttered. "I was in a bad place."

He then realized where he had woken up, and how heavy his bladder was. As he reached for the pot, he wondered what the War Cabinet would do with him today. Had he befriended poor Nessi only to leave her homeless and nameless again within a day?

5

The approach to Maylan Castle, Eastern Region, Kimalloa. The end of the eleventh day of the Fourth Moon, Year Fifty.

WHEN THE ARMY of Truth made a castle unusable as a fortress, they called it a "slighting". There was nothing slight about the holes that the Army of Truth had blown through the walls of Castle Maylan. The ravaged battlements loomed like a giant's black and broken teeth. Sitra remembered the castle from before the war. It had been a magnificent and intimidating sight. It surveyed vast areas of cropland and the long, flat Eastern coast. That had been when Pozaria, just a few breaths from the god of wind across the sea, had been a friendly trading partner, before the plains had been ripped up to build extra defenses for the town, and before the confiscations of the Army of Truth.

As Sitra approached the castle, dusk was slipping into night. It was a night bereft of the comfort of moon or stars. A cold mizzle was clinging to her. She could hear the sea rumbling from the other side of the castle. She wrapped her cloak closely around her and squelched step by step at the foot of the flood defense dike which surrounded the headland. She was avoiding using the path at the top of the dike, which would expose her to the cold sea breeze and, perhaps, prying eyes. Sitra was disguised as a clerk, in the brown jerkin, breeches, cowled cap, and soft boots that a Follower of the Doctrine of Truth would wear. She was confident of her disguise and her paperwork, but the less contact she had with the local militia, the better. The bells for the final reflection of the day were clanging when she left the port of Maylan, and curfew was not long behind it. The winds had been favorable and the sea had been gentle, but the journey had still been uncomfortable. She stopped to stretch and rub, and stared longingly at the castle. Welcoming flickers of light were evident at every casement window. She trudged on.

As most of the household servants were finishing their duties and shuffling away to bed, she approached the guards at the portcullis across the main gate.

"His Lordship is expecting me," she announced.

The guards knelt to kiss her hand. "Yes, Mother Raia."

Sitra was escorted to the oak doors of the keep, which were swung open, letting loose a huge and very welcome blast of warm air. Although she was tired and aching, she moved as fast as the guards as they marched her to Lord Rubin Aldor's office.

Light blazed from the sconces on the walls and a large fire was crackling in the grate. She was so glad of the heat. Her feet were wet and chilled to the point of cramp. Her cloak hung heavy with mud.

Lord Rubin Aldor sat in a very tall chair, well-padded and upholstered in red leather, drawn up at a very large desk made from beautifully marked walnut wood which was carved with the emblems of lavender and iris, sacred to the goddess of wisdom, Feena. Walls draped with crimson-and-silver checkered tapestries complemented the finely tiled floors which were scattered with sheepskins. Sitra drew in the fragrance of gently scented spring flowers which were in a green vase on a side table, countering the odors of an office—paper, ink, and woodsmoke.

Aldor wore a vivid blue silk doublet, trimmed with lace, and open at the neck, hinting at a smooth chest. He had a shock of thick, glossy dark hair which was swept up into a knot behind his head. His face was like burnished bronze, decorated with a trimmed mustache and beard. Sitra's eyes rested on him longer than they should. He was handsome and he knew it. He grinned broadly at the Raia, his brown eyes warm with welcome. She swept into a deep curtsy and indicated her deference loudly.

"Your Grace!"

Aldor curtly dismissed his clerk, who seemed not at all surprised to see a stranger arriving at a very late time, looking like a man and curtsying like a woman. "Well done for making the journey."

Aldor looked impressed, and Sitra felt relieved. She curtsied again.

"It was quite grueling, Your Grace. May I sit?"

"Sit. It is a joy to see you. I have so longed for a proper ceremony of grief for our losses."

"Your Grace. I am ready. May Sudar bless you for trying to save our relics." Sitra wondered how Aldor managed to keep finding money for them.

"Oh, the War Cabinet," spat Aldor, in a heavily sarcastic tone, "have been very reasonable. They take my money for our treasures to finance their ugly infrastructure projects. In return I may live in a ruin. I do not have freedom of movement or freedom of communication. I can practice my faith in private, but they know that is not our way. The fuckers are going to build one of their gloomy temples in our august and beautiful sacred grove in Maylan. Ugh! The delights of living in turbulent times! Chancellor of State to a glorious king one moment, and under house arrest, begging concessions from grim-faced clerks the next." He banged his fist on his desk.

Sitra listened sympathetically. The infighting among the Glantar Dynasty had turned the fortunes of their aristocracy time and time again. The Aldors had almost always been on the right side, or hedged their bets by prudent political marriages so that their lands were kept or extended whichever claimant to the throne came out on top. Their strategies had worked for centuries, but Aldor seemed to be struggling to work out how to protect his interests from a bunch of commoners with a new religion which challenged all that he had ever known.

"So. Raia Sitra. How did you get away from Tamsit? I thought that you might have been rounded up and deported… or worse."

Sitra was ready for this. How on earth could she have escaped the clutches of the all-conquering rebels? Surely, they would pay handsomely for her head. What did Aldor want to believe? She made eye contact with him and held it. "I spend many long years learning the skills of a Raia. There are good reasons for them to be held sacrosanct. I will not explain myself. I'm here. It's a result. It has causes. Some magical, some mundane."

"I appreciate that you take great risks for our faith… On your journey, you must have been able to listen to the gods. Can you explain? What have we—we true and devout Sudarites of Kimalloa—what have we done to so offend the Dome of the Divine?"

"Your Grace, our people have been comforted by our gods for so many centuries! The upstart Truth can't stamp that out. Wherever there is an evergreen branch in a house at midwinter, wherever there are girls reciting love charms with rosemary flowers in the spring, even whenever a workman invokes Sudar when he bangs a hammer on his thumb, we will prevail. It is natural for people to believe that their fortunes and misfortunes are decreed by our gods. They will return. We have to be patient." Sitra checked that Aldor had heard her last word, knowing that patience was not one of his virtues, and then she offered a glimmer of hope. "Excellency Onfri told me to tell you that King Rolan had proclaimed Esta Glantar as queen, even though the rebels claim that she is now following their god-killer creed."

Aldor's eyes glazed over. "Ah. The lovely Esta. Do you remember her fifteenth birthday party?"

"Yes indeed. She was dressed in a shimmering pink silk dress that matched her dark honey skin and black curls so well. She laughed a lot, and was utterly charming. It was such a relief to me that she could be cheerful again, after the tragic loss of her brother and mother."

Aldor nodded, and then huffed. "And then her dear father so overindulged that he didn't wake up in the morning. I couldn't think of anything to do but scream at his body, 'You stupid fucker!' I could see that was the beginning of the end."

"The squires may yet make Esta a puppet—a consul queen."

Aldor raised his eyebrows and laughed. "They must have saved her in order to control her, but she was brought up a Glantar, and they only pretend to consult! Perhaps she is pretending for now, but harbors the iron will to restore our faith? Or we must find a gods-fearing foreigner with the guts for a holy war, and marry him to her by proxy—even the second son of a North Borielan duke would do. Worth a try, Raia Sitra?" He gave her no time to reply, but blustered on to answer his own question. "Well, it would be better than the fucking Assembly of fucking Commoners! The ingrates! They're descended from our bastard sons and the artisans we chose to marry our plain daughters. We rewarded them with land and businesses, and this is how they repay us! Well, Raia, let me tell you what I predict. Those self-important scriveners will talk themselves up their own assholes and the country will collapse. Then we—that is, we, the bounteous lords of the land—we can ask the rabble, 'Why not have a proper king who encourages jollity and beauty, rather than a gaggle of dour managers and merchants who give you bread but no roses?'"

"It may be years—"

"Pah! What if Old Clayhills gets the sweating disease tomorrow? I need to plan. It will give me hope."

The Great Hall, Bankside Place, Nasrin. Early morning.
The twelfth day of the Fourth Moon, Year Fifty.

YONNIS STRODE INTO the Great Hall to some applause, and some cursory nods. He heard his boots creak at every step. He was reminded of all the backroom work that had made the Army of Truth successful. Where would he have been as general without Squire Beechwoods sending pay and arranging shipments of equipment from allies? Or Squire Coppermills who organized the logistics of the war, making sure that food and weapons were in the right place? Elder Yersil, of the North Middlelands, wrapped up in the unbleached robes of his calling, was the healer with special responsibility for the field hospitals, an awesome hero. Elder Yerbun was also there—the engineer who could design and organize pontoon bridges, trenches, cannon positions, catapults, and temporary forts.

What did they think of Yonnis now? Did they think that he had honored or dishonored their hard work? Besides the experts were a few men that he did not know so well. He noted the eagle-like stare of Lord Ulfan, an imposing figure in fine black silk and lace with a neat copper beard. He was the ruler of the remote Northern Mountains Region, the guardian of the border with Osiran.

A fire flickered below the black marble. The tapestries were still in place, but Yonnis was pleased to note that bleached linen had been hung in tasteful swirls across the ceiling to cover the images of rich kings and naked children. A solid table sat in the middle of the Great Hall, and around it sat the War Cabinet. At the head of the table was Squire Clayhills.

As Clayhills called the meeting to order, a clamor began for a report from the Battle of Tamsit.

"Patience, brothers!" Squire Clayhills demanded. "Let us pray first. Let us give thanks for deliverance and seek guidance for our deliberations. Elder Yersil?"

Elder Yersil prayed for the Eternal Spirit to inspire those present in their responsibility for healing the nation and building the peace. The members of the War Cabinet respectfully reflected for a short while after he finished speaking.

Eventually Squire Tallier spoke up. "Let us celebrate our momentous victory, brothers. Here are the hard facts from the final battle. In total, our casualties were 254 men. The enemy lost 742 men, mostly from our small cannon fire. We marched 436 prisoners back to Nasrin, mostly Pozarians. The rest dispersed from the battlefield, and are still being rounded up by the local militia supported by the Seventh Battalion, whose colonel knows the terrain."

Squire Coppermills, a very squat fellow from the North Middlelands, cut in. "We are all, of course, mightily relieved that the military campaign is over. However, our victory did not go according to plan. We should explore that. I'm anxious to hear from the general."

"Hear, hear," said some.

Squire Clayhills nodded and looked at Yonnis, who rose to his feet. It was a long time since Yonnis had addressed the War Cabinet. He was not comfortable with close eye contact, but he knew that he had to look from person to person around the table, long enough for them to feel that he had been talking to them, and talking sincerely. He stood up straight with his hands by his sides.

"Gentlemen, you will have received my dispatches from Inker and Kallo Mill. Let me take you on from there using the notes of the army clerk. My positioning at the Battle on Tamsit Moor meant that I did not get a full picture of what happened—"

"Spare us the protocol, General," Squire Coppermills demanded. "We've read agents' and prisoners' reports. We know about the weather and the smoke. Somehow, you ended up in the fog on your own with a dead Navvan Glantar. I don't know about anybody else, but I'm very curious about *that* episode in particular."

61

Yonnis felt his pulse quickening. He had done what he had done, and it was his duty to give an honest answer. "I became separated from my men in the smoke, which was dense and acrid. Through the grime, I saw an enemy helmet. I rode towards it, and when I realized that it was him, Navvan Glantar, I told him that he was outnumbered and urged him to surrender. He refused, yelled foul things about my wife, and engaged me in one-to-one combat. Despite his greater weight, I unhorsed him, and, being weighed down by heavy armor, he was not able to quickly recover from his fall. I got down from my horse and I killed him."

There was a huge collective gasp which seemed to sway the drapes on the high ceiling, followed by a noise that sounded to Yonnis like growling. The men around the table stared at Yonnis. Some stares were just astonishment; others were clearly hostile.

Yonnis ploughed on. "Our Doctrine urges us to recognize that when the truth is suppressed, the lying will create more evil than the original mistake. I have told you this because it is the truth that I killed Navvan Glantar when he was prostrate on the ground, and I did so because he insulted the memory of my late wife. I could tell you that things happen in the heat of battle, and they do. I could not tell, in the smoke, whether my own men would soon find me or whether his men would find me and kill me. But I do not seek to excuse myself. I am very sorry for this act of vengeance, which, I acknowledge, was contrary to my orders, contrary to the Army Code, and—"

Lord Ulfan leapt to his feet and Yonnis heard the familiar sound of a sword being wrenched out of its sheath. The sword shone in the sunlight cascading through the high windows. Its sharp point hovered close to Yonnis's neck. "D'ye fancy a taste of your own justice, General?" Lord Ulfan stared at Yonnis with eyes like flaming coals. "Because you have disgraced us!"

Yonnis showed no reaction. He had deliberately not worn his sword.

Others around the table jumped up, shouting, some roaring disgust at Yonnis and others telling Lord Ulfan to calm down. The next surprise was the frail Squire Beechwoods drawing his sword to tap Lord Ulfan's blade away from Yonnis, and shouting in his wheezy voice.

"P-put it away, Milord Ulfan! I'm g-glad for what he did." Beechwoods smiled at Yonnis. "May the Spirit bless you, General, for your honesty. Who among us has not been blinded by fury?" He re-sheathed his sword, and sat down.

"Poppycock! I'm with Ulfan!" Squire Coppermills struggled to his feet and put his hand on the hilt of his sword.

"For pity's sake! Brothers, do you want to do the enemy's work for them?! We are on the same side!" Squire Clayhills shouted from the top of the table, and the room was instantly silent. "Put your weapons away if you love our cause, and I assume that you are here because you do. My Lord Ulfan, do you have a question?"

Lord Ulfan switched from hotheaded aggression to respecting protocol in an instant. "Father Clayhills, I would like to ask the general what he did when a man under his command disobeyed a critical order?"

Yonnis started to feel nauseous. He knew that it was something that had to be done in any army, but that did not make it less loathsome. "I would hang him, in front of the men, and kick away the stool myself, so his comrades did not have to."

"And yet you expect us to forgive you?" Ulfan glared at Yonnis, then turned away from him. "Father Clayhills, I can't believe that you condone this vanity—for it was vain of this servant of the Assembly to put his personal vengeance before his orders!" Lord Ulfan looked around the room, fixing each colleague in turn with an angry stare. "Who are we, brothers? We are Followers of the Truth and we are liberators. But we need discipline, too." He stared coldly at Yonnis. "I'll say what a pikeman would say to you if he were here—you're a *fucking* hypocrite." He sat down. "I apologize for my obscene language, brothers."

A murmuration of excitement soared around the table, and all eyes turned to Squire Clayhills.

"I'm sad, brothers, that within a few days of our victory against the forces of darkness, we're arguing among ourselves." He gazed pointedly at Lord Ulfan. "Reflect on that. And reflect on the world watching us. What do the veterans expect of us? What do our allies expect of us? That we punish a good servant of our cause? No. We're at a critical point in the aftermath of war, and we shouldn't do something which would cause uncertainty when we need stability. But we could ask General Yonnis to show his repentance—if you'll allow the details to be left to Squire Tallier and myself."

Quickly, Squire Tallier clipped in, happy to relieve the tension in the room. He coughed, and waited for everyone's complete attention. "We can't—and we won't—get away from the gravity of Duke Yonnis's action, but it should be considered in the light of his overall contribution to the war effort. Also, I must say, gentlemen, I haven't heard any complaints about the general's conduct in any previous battle, and he has always, as he puts it, 'led from the front.'"

Murmurs, grunts, and nods rippled round the table.

"And will he be suspended and… monitored… while these investigations are going on?" Squire Coppermills inquired.

Squire Tallier coughed. "He'll be… rested. Arlo Clayhills is recovering well from his wound and will take charge of the army."

Yonnis bristled. *Rested*. It felt insulting.

Squire Clayhills spoke again, and the word of the Father of the People was usually the last word spoken on any matter. "Brothers, if I were defending Duke Yonnis in a court of law, I would say to the judge, 'What did the War Cabinet expect when they knew his history?' Does the country care about a trial as much as we did? No. They just want the war to be over and to have food in their bellies again. Let's concentrate on giving them that."

Yonnis heard the formal minuting of the War Cabinet's grave concerns about his conduct and his "resting", pending investigations. The meeting moved on, but he had not been dismissed. He sat and listened. At any other time, he would have shown great enthusiasm for the proposals for reconstruction—the repair and extension of dovecotes and fishponds in villages to ensure a ready supply of meat for the winter; building roads and canals to encourage trade; mining stone, metal, and coal. The old religious houses of the Raas were to be converted into schools and hospitals. Some small pensions would be paid to veterans and widows of the Army of Truth. The War Cabinet also decreed the building of craft sheds in every town according to the natural resources of the local area, which would enable maimed veterans to take up suitable occupations. It was everything Yonnis wanted and expected for a country embracing the Truth, but his mind was troubled. He wanted to be leading the reconstruction, not "resting".

As the War Cabinet dispersed, Yonnis suggested to Arlo that they take Nessi walking on the south bank and share a meal afterwards.

"Sorry, Yonnis." Arlo shook his head. "I'm going to be very busy consulting with the commanders on demobilization. But if you go walking that hound, why not take some of your regiment with you? You can talk to them about packing their bags to go home."

Yonnis sensed indecent haste in the dismissal of his countrymen. They had been the shock troops, the ones who went behind enemy lines, the ones who knew the arts of sabotage and ambush, the ones who trained the Kims. Shouldn't they be honored before they were sent home? They were also his personal guard. It occurred to him that he was being isolated. Then Yonnis remembered Yeribbi's words. He must not give in to self-pity.

Ah well, at least a dog is loyal. Nessi was waiting outside the Great Hall. Her unconditional delight to see him, wagging her tail, whining a greeting, and licking his hands, helped to melt his anxiety. He took her with him to find Loomis, to let him know that he could soon go home to his loving family, and the beautiful lakes and forests of his homeland.

The Pozarian Embassy, 3 Embassy Street, Nasrin. Late afternoon. The twentieth day of the Fourth Moon, Year Fifty.

YOSHI CLAYHILLS WAS not a king, and he was keen to demonstrate that a certain amount of informality was quite tolerable in the new Kimalloa. If the Pozarian Ambassador could "drop by" him, he could "drop by" Onfri. It was another fine spring day. There had been several since Tamsit, which, for Sudarites, would be another indication that their gods had abandoned them and were blessing the god-killers. Yoshi hoped that the sunny weather would last a long time.

He arrived at the door to the Pozarian Embassy with a small guard in their ivy green. He nodded to one of the men to use the knocker, which was a carved image of the green-haired god Sudar. He did not want to touch it. The metal-barred door was opened cautiously, and he stepped in. The ambassador's steward ushered him, as an honored visitor, through the embassy and out to the courtyard garden. White and pink blossom was luxuriating on the espalier fruit trees and jaunty red tulips were nodding in the breeze. Yoshi and Onfri sat close to one another on woven-willow chairs, as if they were old friends enjoying the spring sunshine. The conversation began with the weather, as polite conversation should. The bonhomie was even more pronounced when the wine arrived and was tasted.

"You like this robust, earthy wine, from ancient Pozarian vineyards?" Onfri asked. "So sad that it's no longer being traded for succulent Kimalloan beef. They should be experienced together. But I think you miss the money more than the cuisine.

Our trade embargo can do a lot more damage than armed men."

Clayhills felt a little pang of regret that he did indeed enjoy the wine. "Your Excellency, it's a shame if we deny each other excellent products. We should talk about trade, but not today."

Clayhills produced from his pocket a newssheet, which he read aloud to the ambassador.

Brave Kimalloan soldiers of Sudar fleeing from the foul cruelty of the god-killer hordes of the upstart devil Yonnis the Yerallan have told of his cowardly crimes committed in a field in the Edgelands. He summoned demons to create smoke, darkness, and lightning while his men slaughtered the true Kimalloan defenders of their land and the Faith. The rightful King Navvan Glantar was dragged from his horse and martyred by the savages calling themselves soldiers of Truth. Kimalloa is now in the hands of vandals from countries to our west, who have been paid by the traitorous Assembly to force their pitiless, miserable creed on the population. Thousands of good Sudarites have set sail for Pozaria, seeking refuge from their hellish homeland. There, His Noble Majesty Rolan IV is wearing black to mourn his cousin, and is praying for Her Majesty Queen Esta, who has been held hostage these past four years in a grim castle in the South Mountains, seized by the Assembly's troops while still in her mourning dress after the tragic death of her father, King Rikko X. Civilization is aghast at the hellish madness in Kimalloa. Rituals will be held across Pozaria for Navvan the Martyr, son of Her Highness the late Princess Royal, Louisa. Good citizens of Kimalloa, stay strong in your beliefs! Rescue is coming. Endure like martyrs the punishments of the god-killers, and your reward will be in the Dome of the Divine where you will sup with the god of gods, Lord Sudar.

Yoshi smiled at Onfri. "Colorful, isn't it? Your Excellency, I know that all newsmen have to sell their product by exaggeration and invention. They are free to do so in the new Kimalloa—up to a point. What troubles me is the implication, in the phrase 'Rescue is coming', that King Rolan is planning an invasion. Would you like to comment?"

Onfri hesitated. "No, Mr. Clayhills. You cannot trap me into saying something on this matter." He raised his glass to Yoshi.

Yoshi raised his glass in return. "Well, let me help you, Your Excellency, because if there is one thing that you can be sure of about the new Kimalloa, it is that we have informers everywhere. King Rolan's had his fill of wasting money in Kimalloa. And he knows that it's not good for his popularity at home to send more Pozarians to feed Kimalloan fields with their lifeblood. It's cruel to raise the hopes of your friends here, knowing that they are false hopes."

Onfri laughed, but not very convincingly. "Of course, I admire Mr. Tallier. He's the best spymaster that there has ever been—in the world, in history! However, he knows as well as we do that information can sometimes be—accidentally or deliberately—*false*. You should be careful, Mr. Clayhills."

Onfri grinned, and Yoshi felt chilled by the way that his lips were drawn back, revealing a full set of yellow and black teeth. It was time to leave.

"Your Excellency, I thank you for your hospitality. Now let me extend some to you. The War Cabinet has decided to hold a Victory Festival across the country in a few weeks' time. Would you like to come?"

"Thank you, I would *not*." Onfri looked like he had been invited to his own funeral.

"That worries me—you don't know any lunatics who might plan nasty surprises, do you?"

"We both know that wherever there are passionate beliefs, there are plots." Onfri shrugged.

Yoshi felt infuriated by the gesture, but his face remained blank. "I wish you a good day, Your Excellency. I hope that you change your mind about attending. I would be gratified to see you there." Yoshi struggled to his feet and put on his hat. He felt a certain surge of energy from doing diplomacy with the condescending Onfri. And when it came to playing games with Pozaria's intentions towards Kimalloa, there was more excitement on the horizon.

6

Parley Square, Nasrin. Midmorning. The twentieth day
of the Fifth Moon, Year Fifty.

YOSHI HAD INSISTED on accepting the enemy's letter of
surrender in Parley Square, rather than at Bankside. It was a
fine square in the center of Nasrin, built in the classic pale pink
stone of West Kimalloa. In the Glantar era, lords had access to
kings at court, but only here in Parley Square would the King
"consult" his selected commoners. The square had six deep steps
on each side, where the selected sat. In the middle of the square
there was a podium for whoever was speaking. The King would
sit on a throne on a platform on the north side of the square.
It was on the Parley Square podium that the struggle of Yoshi,
selected squire from the Clayhills, had begun—riddling with
Rikko X for small freedoms and sensible taxes. Rikko huffed
and puffed, but always made some small concessions. He had
probably realized that, bit by bit, he was being surrounded
by reformers. Navvan did not. He saw kingship in his father's
terms—absolute.

Now, there was no king. It was Lord Lazzar, the surviving
commander of King Navvan's army, who would deliver the
formal letter of surrender and submission to Squire Clayhills,
Leader of the Assembly of Commoners of the Republic of

Kimalloa, on the twentieth day of the Fifth Moon. He would also formally accept the terms of peace, carefully crafted with concessions that looked generous, but were prudent. Yonnis had been the main architect of the document, although that would never be publicly acknowledged. He had been willing to rest his sword in return for picking up his pen, which he wielded with enthusiasm. He stood on a step behind Yoshi. He was there to indulge the public's curiosity, and as a display of military and political unity. And he had begged, oh, how he had begged to be there, to be close to the act.

Yoshi had wanted this exchange of documents to be very public. Lazzar, resplendent in purple and wearing a large, feathered hat, was watched by hordes of dockers, tailors, peddlers, and washerwomen as well as squires, as he bowed stiffly to his social inferior. As Lazzar proffered the letter, the Father of the People looked into his face. He saw defeat, but he also saw disdain, resentment, and defiance. The stare-out was uncomfortable. The joy that had been bubbling within Yoshi in anticipation of this event momentarily faded.

Yoshi took the scroll, briefly inspected it, then turned to raise the roll of paper to the spectators. Peace was officially declared. The crowds clapped and cheered, then clapped and cheered again. As Lazzar ungraciously grasped the terms of peace and was marched away, and the crowds dispersed to the inns, Yoshi had to return to work. He was helped into his carriage, which headed west.

A hut in the backstreets of East Nasrin. Midmorning. The twentieth day of the Fifth Moon, Year Fifty.

"MISTRESS OONA! MAY the Spirit bless—"

A scrubbing brush whistled past Seemo's ear, thudded into the shit 'n' straw wall of the hut, and landed in the pile of dirty rushes below.

"Bless me with the half-moon's rent you owe me, Seemo Shepherd! How could a man of Truth rob a poor widow so, when y'know I've to pay the tallyman pronto?"

"I have it, my dear Mistress Oona, I have it! And this too!" From the battered leather satchel in which he carried his newssheets, Seemo produced a very large white egg.

"A swan's egg! Ain't that bad luck?"

"Bad luck for the poor mama swan—but she can lay more, and we have to eat. An innkeeper gave it to me after I read in his place. Too tightfisted to give me coin, the ol' ballbag. And, Spirit be praised," he rustled in a pocket in his threadbare breeches, "here's your rent." He slapped some copper coins into her outstretched hand, which was red and blotchy from the hard soaps of the laundry.

"Thank you." Mistress Oona graced him with a smile, which made her face light up under her floppy white coif. "And thanks for takin' Little Pollo to the peace ceremony. Where's he now?"

"In a long line at the baker's. I thought that mebbe we could have a proper midday meal today? Have you finished your shift?"

Mistress Oona went to retrieve the brush that she had thrown at Seemo and put it back in the large basket that she carried on her hip. "I've got some more collections to do, and if we eat now, what'll we eat tonight? I don't like the boy goin' to sleep hungry."

Seemo rustled in his pocket again and proudly produced some wooden discs.

"Soup tokens!" Mistress Oona's eyes widened. "We ain't s'posed to have 'em when we got work!"

Seemo shrugged. "Folk give an old soldier all sorts."

Mistress Oona started to cry. "Men dead and maimed, world turned upside down, and we're still beggars!"

Seemo wanted to hug her, but worried that it was improper. "Chin up, my dear lady! There's better times coming."

Mistress Oona's tears turned quickly to laughter. "You silly fool!"

Seemo joined in with her laughter.

"Now there's peace, Seemo, are you goin' back up north to convert the Sudos?"

Seemo's mood plummeted. Did she want rid of him? The Elders were so keen for widows to remarry and have more children, and a one-legged pauper like him was no use to her, so perhaps he should get out of her way. When he did not answer, she answered for herself.

"Thought not. I like the tune of them Distributors as well. Stickin' up for veterans and widows—you're good at that. I like to see ya speak up at meetings."

It was the nicest thing that she had ever said to him. And now he knew how to make her like him, what was there to lose?

The Seat of Government, Victory Park, Nasrin. Midafternoon. The twentieth day of the Fifth Moon, Year Fifty.

YOSHI'S CARRIAGE GLIDED through the gates of the Mighty Grove of Sudar, now renamed Victory Park, on the western outskirts of Nasrin, on the north bank of the mighty Binar. An enormous tent had been erected here, thanks to the ingenuity of Elder Yerbun, and this was now the Seat of Government of the Republic of Kimalloa.

The ancient evergreen willow trees sacred to Sudarism, that gave the park its mystical peacefulness, surrounded the tent. Yoshi took a few moments to watch their long, twisting leaves glistening in the sun and swaying in the breeze. Perhaps there was still a bit of Sudarite in him. He did not like to see the groves desecrated, as they had been in so many towns. At least he had managed to save these majestic specimens, on the grounds that they might deter Sudarites from attacking the Assembly at work.

Yoshi was about to face hundreds of land managers,

merchants, and professionals who were obsessed with the new order and what they might gain from it. Much as they espoused the Doctrine of Truth, modesty and humility had been hard to find in the last few weeks. Everybody claimed their own victory, except the penitent Yonnis. He had been working very hard to support Yoshi. When he wasn't working, he was in the temple in deep reflection. Arlo, Ulfan and Coppermills grumbled that he had not been punished, but they did not know Ellis Tallier's plan.

Yoshi watched in grateful awe as landowners and lords lined up to take their oath of allegiance to the Republic of Kimalloa and the Doctrine of Truth. It was something he had not dared to dream of as he had faced up to Rikko in Parley Square.

It was the imposing Arch-Elder Yeramo, in his deep black robes, square cap, and cowl, with his long dark wood staff of authority, who started the proceedings. He had been Navvan's Chief Raa and his conversion to the Truth was a bitter blow to the king. Yeramo raised his hands in blessing and began with a prayer that settled the excited crowd of over two hundred men and about thirty widows. He had a gruff tone combined with a Greenlands accent, which made entreaties sound like menacing orders.

"We have a great weight of responsibility on us today, brothers and sisters, and you must search your soul to do right by your country and by the Doctrine of Truth! Our Eternal Spirit is knowledge and fair judgment. Many people have died and suffered so that we can sit here today, speak our minds without fear of retribution, and work together to build a country that will be the envy of the world—where citizens are prosperous, healthy, and happy. That can only happen where reason prevails and people aspire to the Truth. Drive out your instincts for retribution, drive out any temptation for corruption! Approach this meeting with an open mind and a clean conscience. Whatever you decide today will have consequences! Think them through! Through to the very end! Will you be able to defend what you did today in two years' time, ten years' time? We are all held to account, either in this world or in the next. I call on the Eternal Spirit to be with each one of us and guide us to the Truth." He held his hands up high, shut his eyes for several moments and then sat down.

Yoshi looked around for reactions. Some of the audience might have preferred to hear more about smiting their enemies and glorying in victory. Many attendees immediately jumped to their feet to acclaim the War Cabinet for the successful conduct of the war and the convincing victory. After a few votes of thanks and congratulations were accepted, Yoshi raised his hands until the Assembly was quiet again.

"Brothers, thank you for the recognition that you pour upon us. However, we have important things to do today and we need to move on—"

Yoshi had worried about this debate for weeks. Each person in the tent had a different view about what the new government should look like. In a civil war, when people have to take sides, they make compromises. Sitting out there were men who had just wanted a monarch that wasn't Navvan, alongside men who wanted self-governing communes in every village. The postwar constitution would not please them all.

"We will start with a debate and a vote on the broad structure of our new constitution. The War Cabinet have accepted four proposals, brothers and sisters." Yoshi began. "The first, which is similar to the model of Yeralla, is to have an elected Assembly of Commoners, an advisory body of major landowners, and a consul—"

A crescendo of shouting and a chant of "No more kings! No more kings!" drowned out a few individual shouts of "Gods save Her Majesty!"

Yoshi allowed the protests. Esta Glantar, sitting in a curtained and guarded enclosure nearby, needed to hear them, even though it must hurt her. After a few moments, he called for order. "Brothers and sisters! Let me remind you that the Lady Esta has converted to the Truth. She has indicated her willingness to be subservient to the people's government—"

This attracted hoots of derision.

"You will have your vote in due course, but I urge you to consider all options with objectivity. This country has had kings for centuries. It's what the people know, and we may wish to comfort them with some familiar symbols."

Chants of "No, no, no!" met this suggestion.

By putting that option first and stirring up the outrage, Yoshi could be confident that it would lose heavily. Then he continued with proposals that were jeered for giving too much power to the army, or to Elders, until putting forward the one that he wanted to win.

Most members seemed satisfied at that point, but Squire Glass, a self-proclaimed radical, was not. "Honorable Father Clayhills!" He had sneering lips that looked like slugs dancing under his thin mustache. "I'd like to know who's going to *vote* for the members of the Assembly. We're all landowners, and sent here by fellow landowners. But this war was won by the sacrifices of people *without* land. What say the soldiers? Indeed, what say the widows? We promised them that we fought the war to make them free. So why can't *they* vote for who governs them?"

The radicals cheered loudly.

The monarchists jeered. "Anarchy is what you want, Glass!"

Yoshi was resolute. "Your question, Brother Glass, with its implication of extending voting rights, comes from a togetherness with the people which is admirable. There will come a time when we can consider a broader base for our Assembly. For now, we must work with what we know. People who own land have a stake in how it is governed. We can prove who they are and where they are—"

"Let's give veterans land, then!" Squire Glass shouted. "What says the general?" He looked very deliberately at Arlo. "Oh, goodness me!" Glass feigned surprise. "The general who led us to victory seems to have been set aside for a new model—a *clay model...*"

A few radicals made a sound as if they were children spotting adults doing something they knew to be naughty. "Ooooooh!"

Squire Petron, who had fought for Navvan Glantar until the Battle of Inker, rose and yelled, "Look how loud and rude and raucous we are! Trying to govern by consent will weaken Kimalloa! Shut him up, Honorable Leader, or I will!"

Yoshi was riled by Glass. He seemed not a bit grateful or graceful, and he was too fond of the sound of his own mean rhetoric. Had he, Yoshi Clayhills, seemed like that to Rikko? The world had indeed turned. Now the Father of the People was the authority to challenge, and Glass must see himself as the rebel leader. Yoshi struggled to maintain his composure, remembering that he owed his popularity to his reputation as the calm and wise one. "We can discuss the welfare and rights of veterans in our first legislative session. But before we have any sessions, we must decide how we'll make laws and run the government. And I ask you to withdraw your offensive implication about favoritism in the appointment of General Clayhills. You surely know that when a general has to take leave of his command for whatever reason, his second-in-command is duty bound to take over."

There was quiet. Squire Glass stood and said simply, "I withdraw, and I apologize, Father."

Yoshi had expected some posturing. Men will be men. But Squire Glass had been looking for personal combat. He only had a small clique of supporters in the Assembly, but it was his influence outside, with the veterans that he claimed to represent, that was worrying. Why did he call on Yonnis? Well, Yonnis the soldiers' icon was just about to disappoint the likes of Glass, more than they could guess.

The Seat of Government, Victory Park, Nasrin.
Midafternoon. The fifth day of the Sixth Moon, Year Fifty.

YONNIS WAS SITTING dutifully, but he was daydreaming.

He was watching himself, dressed in a linen smock with his hands bound behind him. He was walking behind a large man covered in red tattoos with a long black braid swinging on his back. There was a crowd shuffling behind Yonnis, singing joyfully in praise of Sudar and Pollo, and beseeching them for a good harvest. They were taking a path across a marsh towards a black lake. It seemed such a long way. His feet were so cold that he could not feel them. The rest of him wanted to shiver, but he must show no fear. Step by step, the lake got bigger. At the edge of the lake, he knelt. The tattooed priest yelled incantations that Yonnis did not understand. A thin band of animal gut was put around his neck. Someone pulled it, choking him. Then he saw Marko, laughing.

He knew what it was—the Sudarite sacrifice of a prince to appease the gods. And it was also the self-pity of Duke Yonnis Krusa of Yeralla, vain enough to believe that he was sacrificing himself to Kimalloa. He had done so willingly. Did he expect it to be easy? His grandmother's latest letter had unsettled him. She had written:

Remember the playmates and soulmates of your childhood—Farida, Merutis, Anya. Navvan's gunpowder blasted them to dust. You should take pleasure in having avenged them. Remember your unborn child, my great-grandchild. It was your duty as a father to avenge him. And it was your duty as a duke of Yeralla to avenge your country. I curse the soul of Navvan! My dear Yonnis, you

owe Kimalloa nothing. That country will be as dangerous
a place in peace as it was in war.

The constitutional debate of the Assembly had not seemed dangerous, just very slow. It had taken half a moon. The Assembly had voted for a constitutional model which included the role of a negotiator, called the Arbiter, between two houses of government—the Assembly of Commoners and the much smaller Senate of the regional lords and Elders. The Arbiter was nominated by the Army Council. The role would be like that of the arbiter in a groundball match—calling out breaches of the rules and stopping members of the two houses of debate from crippling each other. It was an unattractive role for squires or lords who wanted to showcase themselves in speeches, so who had they chosen to pilot it? The penitent Yonnis. When he was not waving a red cloth at political foul play, he could represent the Seat of Government, visiting and encouraging reconstruction projects. However, this role was just part of his repentance. The other part of it was a bizarre emotional challenge.

But that would be at a later date. Today, Yonnis had listened to Magg announce him as Arbiter, and watched the reaction of the two houses, assembled together to hear it. He stepped forward to accept, shaking Magg's hand. The monarchists were tight-lipped, clapping politely. The moderates clapped a little more enthusiastically. The Elders were pleased enough. What was curious was that some radicals were cheering. What did they hope for? Or was it just a case of "rather him than anyone else"? Out of the corner of his eye he saw a huddle by one of the entrances to the tent. They were looking on blankly. Lord Ulfan, Grakko's widow, Squire Coppermills, Elder Yerbun, Squire Coppermills, Squire Tallier, and General Arlo Clayhills. Their lack of expression felt churlish and menacing.

Why, Arlo? Why are you not pleased for me? I have only ever wanted the best for you, my friend.

7

The quarters of the Leader of the Assembly of Commoners, Bankside Place, Nasrin. Midday. The twelfth day of the Sixth Moon, Year Fifty.

YONNIS WALKED UP and down the short gallery over the reception rooms in Squire Clayhills' accommodation in Bankside ten times, and then again—briskly, slowly, slower again, normal pace, very fast, then slow. He gazed out of the windows across the courtyard of Bankside, where a few servants and clerks scurried to and fro, trying to avoid the rain. When Squire Clayhills first told him what he wanted him to do alongside "arbitrating", Yonnis had been so surprised, he had almost fainted. He had heard of the local code of honor: after a war, the victors should marry the orphaned daughters of their enemies or the widows of their fallen comrades. There was good logic to it. Perhaps Squire Clayhills was right that he should set an example. But what could he hope for from a marriage to a stranger? A partnership of some sort, but there could never be the deep friendship and romance that he had experienced with Farida. Could there be children? He wanted children. If she could not bear them, he would foster orphans. What about her? He could not possibly be the man of her dreams. What could he do to make her happy? Followers of the Truth were not supposed to disturb the peace of the dead by calling on them, but he could not help trying to ask Farida's advice. What would she say, that sweet, fair-minded, dutiful woman? She would say, "Fulfill your vow to the good squire, enjoy your marriage, have children, and cherish them."

The bells rang for the midday reflection. Yonnis put his right hand on his heart and prayed. "Eternal Spirit, fill me with divine inspiration today, to do the right things, to say the right things, to honor the lady I am to meet..."

A maid appeared after the second bell indicated the close of prayer. "Squire Clayhills'd like you to come down now, sir."

Yonnis followed her, and entered a large room where Squire Clayhills, his wife Mistress Inga Clayhills, and the gracious but stern Lady Deneesa of the South Mountains, widow of Grakko, were gathered. Mistress Clayhills ran across to hug Yonnis, while the squire and Lady Deneesa nodded their acknowledgment.

Yonnis bowed to Lady Deneesa. "My lady, you gave an excellent speech at the opening of the Seat of Government. It was so clear and informative."

She curtsied and said, "Thank you, Duke Yonnis. It's a pleasure to meet you properly, cousin. Your maternal grandmother from the Kimalloan Greenlands was my father's older sister."

"Indeed, we are both fortunate to come from remarkable families."

"Ye've many reasons to hate the Glantars, and yet ye're willing to marry one. That is remarkable. Perhaps it's the blessing of having been immersed in the Doctrine of Truth since birth."

"Two generations of Yerallans have been so blessed. And look how our country prospers from it. I wish the same for Kimalloa."

Yonnis wondered whether he was now supposed to start some small talk about the weather. Squire Clayhills came to his rescue, asking him about his first official engagement—a visit to the craft sheds on the south coast that were building new nimble fighting ships for the navy. Yonnis was happily recounting his observations when he heard even footsteps approaching the reception room. He stared at the door, wishing that he could stare through it.

A firm knock was heard, and Squire Clayhills called, "Please come in."

There was a hush. Yonnis listened to the handling of the door latch. It sounded confident; slow, but not reluctant. A sweet aroma of spring flowers wafted into the room first—from a swaying pomander, which was followed by a tall, upright figure. Yonnis was intrigued. How did a person born to rule behave in a social setting? So, this was what it looked like. She held her head high, and looked at him as if he owed her his life. She was dressed head to toe in a deep black silk robe and a pure white veil. The robe was cut thinly enough for her figure beneath it to be imagined, as she walked with a certain sway of the hips that swished it around her body. She stood in front of him and smiled slightly. All that could be seen of her was her oval face with glowing cheeks, big, long-lashed, deep brown eyes, and soft, full lips.

It was enough to stir Yonnis. He swept into a deep bow and was glad to be carrying his cap so that he could hold it over the embarrassment in his breeches. He was very uncomfortable, and a pinkness shone through his pale skin as his blood pressure rose. He tried to be dignified, but spoke in a slightly higher tone than normal. "My lady. It is such an honor and pleasure to meet you."

The Lady Esta looked up and down at Yonnis. He deduced that the tidal wave of physical attraction that he felt for her was not mutual.

"I suppose that I should thank you, Duke Yonnis, for killing my uncle," she said. Her voice was not as imperious as her stance. It rose and fell like music. "Whatever your reason for it, I certainly had good reason to want that result."

Yonnis bowed again. "I am a professional soldier, my lady. I did what was required to win."

"Of course." Esta paused, holding his eye contact and making him feel even more aroused. Then her face clouded with a frown of curiosity. "I hear that we're some kind of cousins?"

"We share one grandparent, my lady—King Rikko IX, your father's father, and my mother's father."

She seemed to bristle. He supposed that she was thinking that his mother was born to a concubine, which was not how things were seen by his family. Rikko IX had married Yonnis's Kimalloan grandmother in secret and without the consent of his father Rikko VIII. So Rikko VIII forced the first wife into exile in Yeralla with her daughter, and married his disobedient son to a Pozarian princess. Yonnis decided to say nothing more on that subject.

"Hmm. And yet you look so completely Yerallan. Your father was the second son of a Yerallan consul and an *Osiranian* duchess?"

"That's correct, my lady... But I am not here because I think that my parentage entitles me to your hand. I am here because I have given four years of my life and risked my life to secure a happy and hopeful future for Kimalloa. I have proved myself a successful leader, I have commanded the army, and the army has now chosen me to arbitrate in affairs of state. I would be honored to have you at my side—Lady Esta." He spoke her name with a soft and respectful tone of admiration. "We both know that the job of rebuilding the country after a devastating war will not be easy. The people will do the hard work, guided by the Assembly, but we—*we*—can encourage them."

Esta gave him a gracious smile and, at last, a deeper curtsy. "I'm giving it serious consideration, my dear Duke Yonnis."

She had said, "my dear", and that gave Yonnis hope. Of course, in the bizarre courtly love that was espoused in the Glantar culture, a lady should not seem too keen. In reality, so he had been told, the aristocrats of the court had all been fucking like rabbits. But perhaps she was feigning reluctance when she was at least resigned to the convenience of the match.

"Dear lady," Yonnis looked at her adoringly, "I will leave you to talk to your advisers. I will be back shortly in case you have any other questions."

Yonnis excused himself and moved hurriedly out of the Clayhills quarters to the privies.

"Caught short, sir?" a sergeant joked as he sped past. The sergeant would have been even more amused if he knew that it was Yonnis's balls that needed emptying rather than his bladder.

He wrenched the door open and was relieved to see a high pile of dried moss beside the hole in a wooden platform, over a chute that spewed its contents directly onto the outer wall over the river. The unpleasant smell of the privy did not deter him from doing what he had to do into the moss. The relief nearly caused him to pass out. He dropped the sticky moss into the hole. What had just happened to him? He needed physical relief from time to time, of course he did. Like other men, the sight or thought of a woman could stir his member, sometimes in most inconvenient circumstances. So, he found the Lady Esta attractive. Very attractive. Well, if he must do his duty, why should he not get pleasure from it?

As Yonnis re-entered the reception room, he was surprised to see that Arlo had joined the gathering. Esta and Arlo were chatting amiably. Arlo, with his soft brown beard and big gray eyes, and his arm in a sling, the wounded hero. Esta was looking at him with wide eyes, as women do when they find a man attractive. Yonnis immediately thought, It should be Arlo. Surely that would be a better way? Absorb royalty into the squirearchy and show that class was meaningless. But Yonnis had been told that it had to be him—his faint streak of royal blood would avoid causing too much offense to the monarchists. That might be so, or was it that the squires did not want to risk their own sons with a Glantar? Whatever the politics, his penitence suddenly seemed like a blessing. He was a man with the opportunity to make love to a stunningly beautiful woman. He had never been so driven by lust before. It was a difficult force to resist. The wedding could not happen quickly enough. He now had a deep yearning to make Esta Glantar pregnant. Their children would personify the peace of Kimalloa!

The quarters of the Leader of the Assembly of Commoners, Bankside Place, Nasrin. Late evening. The twelfth day of the Sixth Moon, Year Fifty.

ARLO HAD BEEN thinking about Esta for half a day. She was gorgeous. And she was attracted to him. Her eyes had told him so, as soon as they met. She was sympathetic about his arm, and even stroked it gently, which was quite improper. They would be a wonderful couple, and have strong children. Once Yonnis was out of the way, of course. How could it be that his "punishment" for willfully killing Navvan was to marry the most eligible young woman in Kimalloa? Why did that self-righteous, reckless hypocrite have such a charmed life? What's more, why was Arlo's beloved father proposing that he should marry Deneesa, who was plain, sharp-tongued, and old? Had he no consideration for his feelings and hopes? Here they were, father and son, alone together at the end of an extraordinary day, and the tension between them was breaking Arlo's heart.

"Why, Pa, why do you ask me to do this?" Arlo raged. "Why can't I marry the Lady Esta? Why do I have to marry that sour widow?!"

At a simple supper of broth, bread, and beer, the conversation had been polite and intelligent, largely thanks to the skills of Lady Deneesa in managing its flow. The ladies had retired to a particularly well-guarded guest suite in Bankside, and Yonnis had taken his dog for a walk. Arlo and his father sat opposite each other at the table in the Clayhills' Bankside dining room, where the fire was still warm and the candles cast ghostly light on the anger twisted into Arlo's face. He waited impatiently for his father's excuses.

"You find the Lady Esta attractive, of course you do. But she's a poisoned chalice. There are still evil forces plotting around her, and she's too vain to stop them. Yonnis—"

Arlo squirmed. He felt hot. He could not stop himself angrily interrupting. "Yes, Pa, *him*! The 'never retreat' reckless warhound who squandered Kimalloan lives, the vengeful murderer, the upstart who rides the wild horse of history and never gets thrown, the person we are supposed to be punishing—he gets the beautiful princess. Where's the Doctrine of Truth in that?!"

His father waited several moments before replying. It was a tactic he used when infants in the family were having a tantrum, and Arlo was annoyed by it.

Eventually, his father carried on. "Yonnis knows the risks, and he has less to lose. As an outsider, he's less likely to suffer from whatever she does, whenever she does it. And she *will* do something stupid or vicious, eventually. Glantars always do. Surely you remember your history? The closer you are to them, the more likely they are to hate you and harm you. It would worry me—worry me to distraction—if you wanted to make an offer to her... but... you are free to do so. Bear in mind, son, the likelihood that she might refuse, and then how would you feel? And if you did make her an offer, Deneesa would be humiliated. You wouldn't get a second chance. I'll not force you to marry the Lady of the South Mountains, but if you think about it clearly and calmly, as our faith requires, I think that you'll come to see why I suggest it. First and foremost, I'm confident that Deneesa will cherish you. As your father, I want you to have that in your home life. You deserve to be cherished, Arlo."

Arlo was comforted by these words, but he glared resolutely at the fire.

His father continued. "Now consider the practicalities. She's a wealthy widow, and although Grakko's lands and castle have passed to his eldest son, she has reserves of money that most squires can only dream of. She manages her money well, so your future will be secure. Also, and perhaps more importantly for your ambitions, dear son, she has tremendous influence the length and breadth of Kimalloa, and she'll make sure that you have power. How rare is it for a man to have true power everywhere in this fractured country?"

Arlo was still simmering. "What about my needs as a man, Pa? *As a man?!* Am I not to have any, since my arm is crippled?"

His father sighed. "I was young once, you know. Physical urges were a daily occurrence. She's a pious woman and she'll do her duty as a wife in all ways, I think we can be sure."

Arlo was not convinced that Lady Deneesa's wifely duty would be enough for him. "Even if she does take my seed, will she give me children? She has thirty-six years, Father! Thirty-six!"

"Of course it's possible! She has delivered children to Grakko. At least you know that she's not barren."

Arlo ignored his father's answer. "Don't you want a grandson from me? Is my sister producing so many grandchildren that you don't have room to want just one from me?"

"How can you think that I prefer your sister? Can you imagine how hurt I was by her romantic adventure? Had I been such a monster as a father that she needed to do that? Her headstrong insistence on what she thought was love has paid her few dividends other than her children. If you feed your heart on fantasies, reality will violate them soon enough... I don't want you to be unhappy, Arlo. The Spirit knows as I do what a true son you have been to me. You're a treasure beyond words, and I'm sorry that my suggestion has upset you so much. After all your years of deprivation out on campaign, are you not ready to settle?"

Arlo's rage was starting to boil itself dry. He had said some things that he should not have said. He had a deep love and respect for his father. He would show his love in a way that his sister had not. Esta's face was in his head, but it was probably the case that no man would ever have her heart. Deneesa would be an ideal partner for his career, as she had been to Grakko's. Finally, he looked at his father, grabbed his hand, and smiled at him. "I'm ready to settle my personal life, and I'd like to be a father, but my greatest ambition is to follow in your footsteps as a statesman. You're the Father of the People, and I'd like to be a Father of the People. I've loved my country and our faith beyond all bounds of personal love."

They sat and looked at each other. Arlo remembered playing with his pa in the orchards of their family home in the northwest outskirts of the capital, and fighting by his side at the beginning of the war. They had a close bond. Ultimately, Arlo trusted his father's instincts more than his own.

"I do understand. Lady Deneesa will help me. But… why the haste?"

Arlo saw a tear form in his father's eye as he gasped out his reason for haste.

"Because you nearly died, and who knows what perils you'll face as general? There'll be rebellions and plots. If you delay much longer, the risk of not having children is greater."

Arlo nodded. He felt warm filial love slowly washing away his resentment and anger.

His father smiled. "Dear Arlo. I knew you would be sensible. How fortunate Deneesa will be to have a husband who is both sensible and handsome. You'll be a fine trophy that will soften her heart and rouse her spirits."

Castle Kallo in the Edgelands. Early morning. The
fourteenth day of the Sixth Moon, Year Fifty.

AGENT KANDID, KNOWN for the time being as Sergeant Mollin, descended the narrow winding staircase to the dungeon again, and lit all the wall sconces. What had he missed? Everything that the staff had been storing down here had been moved out. He had checked the walls and floors for stains and graffiti so many times. They were suspiciously clean. There were no signs of chains on the walls, no smell of piss near the drains, the room was not even damp. It was as if it truly was just used for storage. It had occurred to him that the floor might be false, and the original dungeon was underneath it—probably filled up with rubble. That looked possible from the outside, but it would be a huge job to try and prove that theory.

Those who were not locals had been allowed to march out with musket balls in their teeth to grimace their pride, provided they agreed to go home. Prudently, they all took the road east. The locals were another matter. Soldiers and household staff were questioned again and again—

"Who stayed here? What happened to them?"

Squire Tallier was keen to have tales of Glantar cruelties to feed to his newsmen. But the serfs of Kallo just claimed to be simple, local folk who kept the castle clean and safe. Kandid had obtained only one hint of past improprieties. A visiting Pozarian duke had raped the steward's wife about seventeen years ago, and they had not adhered to Sudarite practice. They had kept the baby, who was now a strapping youth. How and why was that, he wanted to know. Who or what could Kandid use to win their trust and get the truth?

As he pondered how to unlock the confidence of the steward and his wife, he rested his gaze on a particular sconce that, at this angle, looked slightly newer than the others. He used a damp cloth to extinguish it, and jostled its bracket. He felt some movement. He yanked it. There was a graunching sound, but he could not work out where it was coming from, so he moved the bracket back and forth again. The noise was underneath the current floor, near the wall with the drain. He knelt down to examine the drain, which opened up onto a forbidding cliff.

He looked down. Whatever he had done had dislodged another chute, lower down. Fresh sludge had gushed onto the white rock of the cliff. He was sure that he could see a bone sticking out of it. Oh! This was a breakthrough! He surged with excitement, shouting to the guard on the door.

"Bring that wretched steward down here as quick as you can!"

The guard ran up the stairs.

Well, thought Kandid, there's no time for trapping him. I'll have the guard stick his head down the drain and I'll piss on his face till he tells me what happened here. He waited for the guard to come back. Time was moving on. Kallo was not a big castle. What was going on?

Eventually, the guard came back—without the steward. "We can't find them, sir!"

Well, if anyone knew of any secret passages out of this place, it would be the steward. Kandid had been too kind for too long. Squire Tallier was not going to like this.

Office of the Intelligence Minister, the Archive, Bankside, Nasrin. Late morning. The seventeenth day of the Sixth Moon, Year Fifty.

ALL-EARS' HACKLES WERE twitching. He was anxious to hear more from Kandid, who was on the trail of the errant steward and his wife's interesting son, and he was not good at waiting. So, he must distract himself with matters closer to home.

Everybody in Bankside was supposed to inform on each other, and the short walk to the Archive Building was regularly taken as staff dropped off their notes and collected new instructions. All-Ears received regular reports from Suki, the housekeeper in the quarters of Duke Yonnis. She had been recommended for

Bankside work by the Elder who ran the field hospitals where she had nursed. She had met Duke Yonnis during the war, and, like so many who had served, she openly admired him. Was she attracted to him? All-Ears supposed that some women must be. Although Yonnis was as pale as a ghost, his features were rugged in a very manly way. He was not tall, but he bore himself like a man with well-developed, well-sculpted muscles. His smiles were rare, but he had beautiful white teeth, and… he had better stop there. The scriptures did not forbid such thoughts, but they did not encourage them either. All-Ears reviewed what he knew about Mistress Suki. How solid was her commitment to the Republic? He could pound some holes in her story, but it seemed genuine enough. When something monumental like a war happens, anyone can reach out for change.

Suki was the only girl in a small family that eked out a living in village in the northwest. They had to live on the outskirts, near the stinking tannery, because Suki had a facial birthmark, so she was considered one of the flawed folk. When a few brave travelers brought news of the new Doctrine where holiness did not rely on beauty, Suki's family were keen to embrace it. They had to disguise their conversion and keep the old superstitions, year after year after year.

When the war came, Suki's brothers were drafted into Lord Sofon's regiment of the King's army—they had to wait for the right opportunity to turn their coats. Her father wanted to join the Army of Truth, and she wanted to help too. The mother, realizing that someone had to stay and face reprisals, offered herself as that hostage, so that her husband and daughter could escape. Alas, there was no remaining trace of her in the village.

The tanner was still there, and able to confirm his role in Suki's escape. He had been taking some skins to be made up into buff coats for Lord Sofon's cavalry by tailors in Daltor. Suki and her father hid in the cart, wrapped in the leather. The tanner took them as close as he could to the border with the North Middlelands, where Lady Charity had declared for the Truth. It was still ten leagues short of safety. They crept all the way to the Andel garrison through ditches, traveling only after dark. Suki claimed that they were in such a state when they arrived at the Truth garrison that they were more mud than flesh.

All-Ears checked the dispatch from Estlorn, the biggest and bloodiest battle of the war, in which the Healing Elder described his nurses plastered from head to foot in gore, running from soldier to soldier to apply bandages, hot water, or pine spirit, washing, feeding, comforting. All-Ears knew that Suki had served there, and at Grettin, Tinmoor, Inker, and more… Surely, she was deeply dedicated to the cause? How was she going to react to having a Glantar in her household?

"Good morning, Mistress Suki."

All-Ears smiled at her and indicated a plain upright chair by the fire where she should sit. She was dressed in a pale brown linen robe with an unbleached apron and a tight coif over her hair. He sat opposite her, stretching out his feet, close to the fire, always flickering in the grate. The weather could now be described as summery, but it had rained today, and he felt the damp as well as the cold.

"Thank you for your reports. You seemed to have settled in very well."

"Such as they are, sir," Suki replied. "The general's been spending time at the talking tent or with his dog. He keeps up with his combat training, reflects a lot, reads."

"A small correction, if I may, Mistress Suki. He is no longer the general. Arlo Clayhills is the general. You must learn to call

Duke Yonnis 'the Arbiter'. And 'the talking tent' is the Seat of Government, if you please."

Suki smiled, nervously muttering, "Sorry, sir."

"The Arbiter's very happy to have you as his housekeeper. He recognized your devotion to duty and your intelligence at Grettin, and he knows that Kimalloa needs those talents. I could've deployed you anywhere, but he knew that I'd continue to watch him in peacetime for his own safety, and he needs the very best person for that. I'm sure that you appreciate that the Sudarites still aspire to destroy him. You heard about the assassination attempt at Tamsit? That's the external threat. But I can assure you that he knows that he faces an internal threat. He knows that he's human and needs correction. I'm sure that he's confident that you'll be fair, honest, and correct in your reports to me of all external *and internal* matters that seem suspicious."

Suki beamed, blushed, and nodded.

Motivational speech over, All-Ears had to deliver his surprise. He coughed. "Mistress Suki, you're doing the job you do because you know that I need someone of the utmost integrity to watch over Duke Yonnis. He has agreed... for reasons of statecraft, he has undertaken to marry the woman called Esta Glantar—"

"A Glantar?!" Suki's eyes lit up with shock.

"It's a great sacrifice on his part, done for the peace of Kimalloa. But I'm sure that it will bring great changes in the household. She claims to have converted to our faith and to support the new constitution. I hope that's true, but I need you to watch this woman very closely, because she's a Glantar and she is not to be trusted."

"Y'reward him for winning the war for us by tying him— tying him for life—to a stranger from that terrible family of Sudarite monsters?!"

"Mistress Suki!" All-Ears chided her. "You really must be more discreet if you're to succeed in this critical assignment! There are Sudarites up and down the country who'll try to use her against us. We need her to be in Bankside and watched closely. You must be friendly and respectful towards her if you're to watch her well. I want to know her habits—what she eats, what she buys, what she says and to whom, how she walks and where, and even how she breathes. Can you do it?"

Suki stood up. She smoothed down her apron, then wrung her hands. She paced. Then she spoke. "What I understand is that I'm watching *her*, and I'm watching *out* for him. Oh, Squire Tallier, sir! Nowhere is so dangerous as a man's own household with a wife like that! And I must be his shield!"

All-Ears smiled. "Excellent. Go to it, brave lady."

Merchant Marsa's Cloth Warehouse, Exchange Street, Pornan, West Pozaria. Midday. The seventeenth day of the Sixth Moon, Year Fifty.

"WELCOME, DEAR FRIENDS!" Merchant Marsa and Madam Marsa greeted their neighbors, the Customs Officer and his wife. They were good people to know, and a fine spread of a midday meal had been prepared for them. Pink sea-fish, goose, and beef, followed by the first Besseman peaches of the season. After a good deal of handshaking, they wandered through the warehouse display room, which Madam Marsa had organized by color and texture of cloth, and into the dining room. Just as Merchant Marsa lifted his wine cup to his lips to toast his guests, an apprentice ran in, gabbling about a stranger at the counter.

"For Sudar's sake, boy, deal with him yourself!"

"He's some fancy foreigner. Says he can't understand me."

Merchant Marsa politely took his leave of his wife and guests, and followed the apprentice. In the display room stood a man who must be one of the so-called Kimalloan "court in exile", dressed in red doublet and breeches and an extravagant hat. No wonder he could not understand Pozarian. His sort were a burden on King Rolan. There had been dozens of them arriving in Pornan, week after week. Why did the king put up with them? No doubt the stranger would ask for credit and then not pay.

"Welcome to my display room, milord. How may I help you?"

"Good merchant, you speak slowly enough for me to understand you." The man spoke in truly awful Pozarian.

"I'm from Bessema," Merchant Marsa explained, even though his origin might be guessed from his very dark features. "I see that you're looking at the wools. What will you be using the cloth for, milord?"

"Servants' clothing. Nothing fancy. Kimalloan boiled wool would do."

"Sorry, sir. That trade is embargoed. And supply was very poor for years, anyway. I have boiled Osiranian wool. It's about the same." This man seemed to be trying to trap him, and with the Customs Officer sitting in the dining room!

The stranger looked up and down the rolls of cloth that Merchant Marsa had pointed out to him. "This blue—not the azure, not the indigo, this one. It looks like Deep Marine—the dye comes from plants that only grow in the woodland glades of Southwest Kimalloa." He pointed at a roll.

Merchant Marsa beamed with the confidence he had in his products. "It's *like* Deep Marine, but it's actually Osiranian Sapphire, and the dye comes from a mineral, not a plant. That color will last longer than anything you might have known in Kimalloa."

The stranger smiled back, indicating a degree of curiosity. "Pull the roll out for me."

Merchant Marsa was starting to feel irritated with his prospective customer, and not just because he had no manners. Was he here to buy wool, or did he just want to tittle-tattle to the King about the provenance of wools and dyes in Pornan?

Marsa drew the roll of woolen cloth carefully from its place. The stranger looked like he was just going to feel the cloth, but then he grabbed the whole roll and swung it forcefully, knocking the elderly merchant to the ground. As Marsa tried to kick his assailant, shouting for his apprentice and struggling to reach the dagger in his belt, he found himself looking up the blade of a long, thin sword, to a hand quivering with rage.

"I know the wool from my own estate, villain, and I know you work for the thieving god-killers!"

Marsa felt the burn of steel and the bubble of his blood as it spurted from his throat and spread over the well-scrubbed floor of his display room.

8

The manor house of Lady Deneesa of the South
Mountains, New Temple Street, Nasrin. Late morning.
The twentieth day of the Sixth Moon, Year Fifty.

HERE HE WAS, about to have a serious conversation about
the color of a dress. Yonnis had not thought, when he was
suffering deprivation to win a war, that within a couple of moons
of victory he would have his piety challenged over the color of
a dress. Even the everyday aspects of peace were a minefield to
him.

Lady Deneesa's Nasrin residence was a forbidding gray brick
on the outside and relentlessly brown on the inside. The drapes
and wall coverings were a variety of dark brown and light brown
checks. Where walls were left uncovered, they were painted a
pale brown, and where they were paneled, the wood was stained
as dark as peat. The rugs were woven from the undyed wool of
the brown-coated northern sheep. The servants blended into the
decor with their light brown uniforms and aprons of unbleached
linen. Yonnis had felt that he was tunneling under the earth like
a mole when he was admitted at the main door.

In the ochre-tinted light of the office of Lady Deneesa, where
she sat on a plain chair, wrapped in chestnut-brown robes and
veil, he made his case.

"Of course I agree that women should dress modestly and should not wear anything designed to deceive, such as corsets or face paint, but I do not read in the scriptures that any color is specifically prohibited."

"Perhaps it's difficult for a man to understand," Lady Deneesa responded. "Color *is* intended to deceive. Esta wants pink because pink enhances her complexion. That's vanity."

"I respect your interpretation of the scriptures on appropriate dress, my lady. Of course, as a woman, you perceive things that I could not." Yonnis tried to appease her. "But, in Yerallan, the word 'enhance' is a long way from 'deceive'. A pink garment does not change a lady's skin tone or deceptively cover a blemish or fault. Perhaps white silk—for purity—with a hint of pink could be tolerated. I would like my betrothed to feel special on her special day."

"Please don't flatter my faith, Duke Yonnis, especially when you don't mean it. It's vulgar." Deneesa spoke as if she were more hurt than offended. She fixed her small green eyes on him. "I know Esta Glantar. She's lived under my roof for four years and ye've only just met her. I can assure you, four years' encouragement and instruction hasn't been enough to undo her Sudarite beginnings. I'm advising you, as a friend, not to give in to this vanity, or ye'll have a tricky time in your marriage. If you signal to her that ye're willing to allow exceptions to rules for her, she'll not stop until she's overturned *all* the rules. A husband has a duty to save his wife from error. As a woman, she is always tempted, and, goodness me, Esta had a very poor start in her education at that lascivious court of her father's."

The matter of Esta's dress seemed like a small thing to Yonnis, and he wondered why Deneesa hadn't got more important things to get indignant about. He tried to consider objectively what Deneesa was explaining to him, but he was a man confused and driven by his unexpected lust for Esta, so he failed. "I thank you for your advice, my lady. I am sure that it is well meant. But I feel that this ceremony will be difficult enough for the Lady Esta. A pale pink dress would be a small thing to cheer her up. And I am concerned that it would be vain of me to flaunt my piety by denying her a comfort."

He convinced himself with this excuse, but not Deneesa.

"Well, Duke Yonnis, on your head be it. Y'know, I believe that you love the Eternal Spirit with all your heart, but d'ye fear It as you should? I see that you're smitten, and that can lead you to decisions that the Spirit mightn't want you to make. I wish you joy in your union, I really do. But please, please take care."

Deneesa sounded more sympathetic, but Yonnis did not want to be chastened by her. He merely nodded, and she changed the subject.

"We need to go over the security arrangements... "

Yonnis was barely listening. His first wedding had been a relaxed affair, an open celebration of a childhood friendship that blossomed into profound love. This marriage was just pieces being moved by All-Ears on the chessboard of the state. Afterwards, Tallier would tick off items on one of his lists. Risk of Pozarian invasion? Defused. Risk of Yonnis the Yerallan being able to rely on any support from the army? Defused.

"Thank you for your briefing, my lady." Yonnis bowed deeply and burrowed back through the brown and out of the door. Two green-uniformed guards flanked him as he strode away from New Temple Street back to Bankside. He headed for Squire Tallier's lair.

Office of the Intelligence Minister, the Archive, Bankside, Nasrin. Midday. The twentieth day of the Sixth Moon, Year Fifty.

YONNIS WAS ADMITTED immediately to the great man's office. The door creaked. Squire Tallier stood up from his desk and they shook hands. The spymaster looked very grim.

"Welcome, Yonnis. I trust this is urgent?"

"Sir, I am here to ask you to arrange, in all secrecy, as only you can, a pink robe and veil for the Lady Esta for her wedding."

Squire Tallier sat down at his desk with a grunt. Then he started to rave in a way that surprised Yonnis. "A dress. A dress! One of my best agents, a man I was with in Boriela, has been assassinated by a Sudarite exile in Pozaria! I have to find the worm—*the fucking worm*—who betrayed him! And you trouble me about a dress! For pity's sake, Yonnis!"

"I'm sorry, sir! Of course you must concentrate on the finding the traitor. It would be a case of blackmail, surely, or ambition?"

"Agh! Thank you for your banal insights, Yonnis. You may be interested to know that the prime suspect is his *wife*—his wife of fourteen years. Think about that as you marry Esta Glantar. Perhaps it's best if you get out of my way and go and fuss about pink somewhere else. You have my authority to ask your housekeeper to have an accident with some berry juice while preparing a white garment."

"Thank you very much, sir." Yonnis beamed his appreciation. "I realize that this is a complication that you could do without."

"It is indeed, but of course I'm grateful to you for taking on this unusual assignment." Squire Tallier smiled back, although Yonnis noted that it was a forced smile, lacking any warmth.

"Assignment? That is an interesting way to put it. What I do—I do for the peace of Kimalloa. Perhaps it is fair to say that I am marrying her to stop her becoming a focus for plots that would fracture the country again, but I hope to do that by respecting the marriage contract of our religion and doing my best to be a good husband."

"Oh dear." Tallier growled. "Are you falling victim to her wiles? Remember what happened to your one *true* love, Duke Yonnis. If you don't guard Esta Glantar closely enough, we'll be facing atrocities like your Day of Lamentation in Kimalloa. Guard her, you fool! Don't love her! Reflect! Reflect!"

Tallier's angry face etched itself on Yonnis's memory as he bid the spymaster a swift farewell.

North Gate Prison, Nasrin. Midafternoon. The twenty-second day of the Sixth Moon, Year Fifty.

ESTA WAS QUIVERING with fright at the sight of the roughly hewn stone and barred windows of the prison. No matter what Deneesa said, was this a trick? Was she going to be left here? There was the black-clad old spymaster, trying to look vulnerable with his stick, when he was the most frightening creature in all of Kimalloa. Yes, she should be grateful that he'd saved her from her uncle, but for what? What did he want with her, and why here? Hadn't she agreed to marry the ugly Yerallan?

Deneesa shooed Esta out of the carriage. They curtsied to Squire Tallier.

"Thank you for coming, my dear Lady Esta." Squire Tallier bowed. "I hope you understand that you didn't have to, but I am pleased to see that you're taking your future responsibilities seriously."

"Squire Tallier, sir, the Assembly voted me down—"

"I'm sorry for your disappointment, milady, but being the consort of the Arbiter will enable you to undertake some symbolic duties. I just want to apprise you of the risks. Once you are in the public eye, malign forces will want to use you for their own ends."

"What board game is this, where the queen can only ever be a pawn of other players?"

Squire Tallier smiled at her. His smile was as chilling as a grimace. He probably had not liked her use of the word "queen". So be it. He continued. "To hold any kind of position in any kind of society, you must be aware of threats and treachery—"

"I have experience of that—"

"Of course you do, milady. I apologize. But, please, humor me. I want to discuss some cases with you that I have to deal with. Let's go inside."

Esta was very reluctant to go inside, but Deneesa encouraged her to follow. The guards were big, intimidating, masked men who rattled with keys and weapons. The corridors were dark and forbidding, with metal doors either side. In each door was a small grille. Squire Tallier stopped at Cell 18, and urged her to look through the grille. The cell was small, but clean. There was a half-naked man, covered with the red tattoos that marked him out as a Raa, cowering and gibbering in a corner. She had never seen a Raa look vulnerable, and she was overcome with pity.

"By law, this man should die horribly. He was a Raa in the coven of Sudarite magicians who encouraged Navvan's war on his people. He incited Pozarians to join Navvan's army, which prolonged the war. We captured him at Tamsit, and he suffered straw fever on the journey here, which has not helped his state of physical or spiritual health, as you can see. He will get a fair trial, but the evidence against him is overwhelming. The judge will have to decide—should he suffer a painful public execution, when he might want to be a martyr, or should he just rot in prison? What do you think, Lady Esta?"

Esta offered a creative answer. "Has he not been offered the chance to convert and become an Elder? So many Raas have seen the light of the Eternal Spirit."

"May the Spirit bless you, dear lady. I see that your heart is full of mercy." Tallier gave her that menacing smile again. "He is determined to meet his imaginary gods. Should the judge help him, or make him wait?"

"Is a quick death out of the question?"

"It is. If we are to make a spectacle to frighten the public, they do expect cruelty. In this particular case, Lady Esta, if you were the judge, what would you do? One can look at this poor wretch, determined to suffer for his beliefs, and feel pity. But then we have to remember that he was determined to make others suffer for *their* beliefs."

Esta felt hot and flustered. What was the right answer? What did it say in the dreary scriptures of Yerobis the Liberator? "A long time in prison is a long time to reflect. That is surely what he needs."

"I tend to agree with you, milady." Squire Tallier turned then to her foster mother. "Lady Deneesa, I can see that you have helped Esta to understand the finer points of our faith. Now, let's move on."

They stopped at Cell 23. There was an unpleasant smell. Esta peered in to see a brightly dressed woman, who immediately spat at the grille.

"I'm not an animal in a menagerie, you god-killer vermin!"

"This is Madam Tervan, a Pozarian spy. This is the sort of person who might sidle up to you at an official engagement and try to promise you all sorts of things on behalf of her king. But, as you can see, she ends up here, and her promises end up here too... I doubt that she'll make her trial, poor lady. She has not adjusted well to prison food."

"I think Lady Esta has had enough, Squire Tallier," Deneesa suggested.

"Ah, but the adulteress in Cell 31—"

"Will the judge be merciful to an adulteress?" The words were out of Esta's mouth before it occurred to her that her interest might seem indiscreet.

"Only if her husband allows it. And is it mercy to spare her, when she would face a life as a beggar or a whore? These decisions are never straightforward, Lady Esta."

Esta nodded. Some things never change. Her great-grandmother Fillippa had been "taken ill" on a visit to Kallo Castle after being "too kind" to a court musician. Her husband, of course, had at least ten mistresses. They and their bastards were kept comfortable, by courtesy of Kimalloan taxpayers.

They returned to the gate of the prison, their shoes clattering on the stones, the moaning and pleading of prisoners ringing in their ears. Esta felt sick. She felt angry about feeling sick, because it was the effect that Tallier must have wanted.

He spoke to her as she was about to climb into the carriage. "Thank you for coming, Lady Esta. It was brave of you. And I can see that you are willing to learn. I wish you a happy marriage. I am sure that Duke Yonnis will teach you more about the ways of the real world."

Esta bristled at his patronizing tone. "Thank you, Squire Tallier. Perchance there are some things that I could teach him, too."

The Temple of Truth, Bankside Place, Nasrin. Daybreak.
The first day of the Seventh Moon, Year Fifty.

ONFRI HAD DRAGGED himself out of bed much earlier than usual. Defiantly, he wore a bright yellow doublet with gold brocade, yellow hose, and a bright red gown and hat.

"What an unwholesome time for a wedding," he had grumbled to his steward as he left his embassy. "It seems more suitable for an execution."

The protocols of state could be onerous, and he had been invited to be an international witness for the marriage of Squire Clayhills' son. It seemed churlish to refuse. Also, his curiosity was aroused by the opportunity to see the Lady Deneesa, because she did have a very famous foster daughter. His spies could not confirm whether that famous person was in Nasrin or not, but if she was in the capital, surely, she would be in attendance.

Onfri had been escorted to Bankside by four guards. He observed armed militia in their insipid pale green coats and army men in their dark green uniforms patrolling everywhere, which was attracting curiosity from citizens lucky enough to be starting their working day. He was marched through the imposing gatehouse at Bankside, just as the sun was lightening the sky and picking out the shapes of men with pistols on the ramparts. He was led to the temple and announced. Squire Clayhills came to shake his hand.

Onfri was dismayed by his surroundings. How could people of status be getting married in a drafty white shed? Why were they so suspicious of beautiful things? Many years before, he had attended a wedding at Pulkra Grove, a pilgrimage site in Bessema, where the backdrop was a blue-stone cliff spurting hundreds of little waterfalls. The sun shone on the water spray. It sparkled and created a web of mystical miniature rainbows. Light breezes caused waves of green shimmering through the sacred trees in the grove, hundreds of twisted evergreen willows. Now *that* was a suitable setting for a day of wonder, a day that the happy couple would cherish.

The other guests seemed to be the Clayhills' immediate family and some of the Clayhills cousins in the squirearchy. Or were they the new aristocracy? Time would tell. Onfri noted that Squire Tallier was not there—he was presumably orchestrating security and espionage from a safe distance. The South Borielan Ambassador, Mallan, was there, and Daggra from Osiran. Onfri nodded to them politely.

General Arlo Clayhills was not using a sling, so presumably his arm was a lot better. He wore a silk doublet that was dark gray with a hint of blue, under a dark blue gown. The gray reminded Onfri of the best hounds for dog-racing, something which had been banned by the Followers of the Truth, along with many other fun pastimes that encouraged gambling. Onfri watched the younger Clayhills intently. He was smiling so much that a hint of excess effort to smile could be detected. Most men with broken teeth did not display them so much.

Onfri would have expected the handsome war hero to find a prettier, younger woman as a wife. Of course, the Followers of the Truth postured that they did not care about external beauty, only the beauty of the soul. Onfri suspected that Lady Deneesa's beauty lay in her treasury. Was that enough to make the young Clayhills smile so much? The Followers of the Truth also postured about abolishing class distinction, but as he looked around at the fine-fabricked garments of true black—a costly shade—he felt that status was being paraded, regardless of the advice of their scripture.

Arch-Elder Yeramo called those gathered to stand. Lady Deneesa entered, dressed from head to toe in unbleached wool, as if she were wrapped in a shroud. The robes were completely shapeless and topped by a veil and wimple that almost completely covered her face. Behind her came Mistress Inga Clayhills, and the Yerallan Duke Yonnis, looking surprisingly smart in doublet and breeches of dark green wool decorated with white lace, under a black gown. The white hair on his head had grown somewhat, which introduced a degree of civilization to his features. There was a certain aura about him. Was it quiet authority, or the blessings of a god? These two guests must be the identity witnesses. Since the Followers of the Truth covered up so much, it must be essential to have them. Lady Deneesa's two youngest daughters followed. To Onfri's amazement, they were carrying flowers, albeit white ones for purity. He was frustrated that there was no sign of the foster daughter.

The exchange of vows was short, and there was little by way of a sermon to the happy couple and the assembled witnesses. Arlo lifted Deneesa's veil and dipped his head to kiss hers, and then their identities were confirmed by the witnesses. Onfri had done his research. He knew that the signing of a specific marriage contract was an important part of the ceremony. Unlike the open-ended ties of a Sudarite marriage, the Followers of the Truth had written obligations to each other, and financial ones were included. It was very businesslike.

There was applause after the signings. Onfri rose with the other guests to congratulate the happy couple, who shook the hands extended to them, but seemed anxious to get on with their day.

"If I could detain you a little longer, dear brethren," Arch-Elder Yeramo boomed, "we have another happy event to celebrate."

Guests were ushered back to their seats. Arlo and Deneesa left, walking hand in hand with the children, followed by several of the Clayhills' clan. Duke Yonnis, the Arbiter, lingered at the front of the room. Onfri was angry. He could sense that he had been set up to witness not the first marriage, but a second one, and his imagination was sizzling with suspicious indignation. Who might the second wife be? Surely not...? Oh, the poor girl!

As a tall figure in pink entered the storeroom, the excitement in the room was feverish. It had to be Queen Esta. Who else could get away with flouting the dress code of the Truth-Followers? Whoever had dyed the bleached white silk had produced swirls of varying depth of pink across the robe rather than a uniform color, which was very pretty and seemed so daring. It was like raspberries whipped into cream. Onfri was intrigued. Had she asked for a crimson tone to signal her martyrdom? Onfri looked at the Yerallan. He displayed more than a frisson of attraction. Indeed, Onfri was easily convinced that the fierce military genius was besotted with the girl. Her uncle's army could not even scratch him, but she had defeated the mighty general. Onfri began to smile, until he realized that Squire Clayhills was staring at him, anxious to gauge his reaction. He looked serious again.

Yeramo launched into a loud sermon about the need for reconciliation and healing in Kimalloa. Survivors needed to marry and be fruitful. The sacrifices of the past would be nothing if there were no sacrifices in the peace for the sake of the country. Onfri was reminded of ancient rituals, when the third sons and ugly daughters of noble families were sacrificed to bribe the gods to lavish their favors, such as a good harvest, on the country. But who was the sacrificial victim here? Certainly not Queen

Esta, who was getting a free pass back to the capital and some kind of connection with people who ran the country. She might have to dress like a bundle of laundry and pretend to enjoy being miserable, but these were minor matters. Squire Clayhills was taking a massive risk. Did he plan to use her to legitimize his regime? Perhaps he was trying to trap her. Or was he hedging his bets in case the republican experiment imploded? Whatever it was, it was going to introduce some excitement into Onfri's life, and he could not wait to write his report for King Rolan. He was also itching for the opportunity to congratulate Queen Esta. He was trying to compose his words, but his mind was jumbled.

With shocking irregularity, after vows were exchanged, the Yerallan threw up Queen Esta's veil and kissed her on the lips, causing some of the guests to cover their eyes. Ah, she was a beauty! Even when one could see so little of her! The glory of summer was in her eyes. Onfri forced himself to look away from her face to the wider scene. Yeramo was glaring furiously at Duke Yonnis, and Duke Yonnis returned an icy glare to the Arch-Elder which showed that he was still a fearless man. Just as their extended eye contact broke, a plaintive howl was heard at the door. The duke's dog was the obvious culprit. Onfri shivered, remembering the wolfish appearance of the hound. Was it a familiar? So it must be true that Marko cared for the Yerallan. Briefly, he thought he saw the red-skinned, ram-horned god peering through the open eaves.

Contracts were signed, there was applause, and witnesses moved forward to make their congratulations to the couple. Onfri waited for his turn. Queen Esta smiled in recognition; she had seen him daily at her father's court.

She chirped in Pozarian, "Excellency Onfri, what a pleasure to see an old friend such as you! I hope that you visit me—I mean, us—often!"

Instead of shaking her hand, Onfri bowed deeply and kissed it. He spoke very swiftly in Besseman. He looked up. She looked shocked. She gracefully withdrew her hand, without replying. Onfri sensed that all eyes were upon them, not least the penetrating gaze of the Arbiter. Onfri had heard that the eyes of Yerallans turned from blue to purple when they were angry, and now he was seeing it. It was not a pretty sight. Duke Yonnis extended his hand to Onfri as if to shake his, but then he yanked him close with his immensely strong wrist, and hissed in Pozarian, "Do not *dare* to endanger my wife!"

Onfri was deeply insulted by the assault. When he was released from the Duke's grip, his hand quivered over the pommel of his sword, but he did not want to escalate the situation, for the sake of the queen. He forced a smile onto his face and spoke quickly in Kimalloan, inviting the happy couple to dine at the embassy as soon as their schedule would allow.

The temple was empty of people before the next bell for reflection. Onfri was worried. His passion for the rights of the little princess he had known had made him reckless. Or was it guilt for not having done more to oppose Navvan when he'd snatched the throne from her? He wondered how long it would be before his message to Queen Esta was rattling Squire Tallier. Ten moments? Twenty? He had been foolish. He could have put her in danger. Why had he not composed something more ambiguous?

As Onfri was marched back to his embassy, news was passing by word of mouth in the curious Nasrinian crowd. He heard a lot of jeering and swearing. There seemed to be deep displeasure at a Glantar being in the capital. And marriage to the mighty general who had personified the rebels' cause? The citizens sounded baffled as well as cross. Even with the military out in such force, Onfri felt very uneasy.

Suddenly, a guffaw blew out from the crowd. Someone was having a belly laugh. Then another, and soon, as if to prove that laughter is infectious, "Ha, ha, ha" was drowning out the jeers and the grumbling. Kimalloans! The more serious that something was supposed to be, the more likely they were to find it funny. Onfri stopped to watch the tatty folk, still laughing, but also chatting and dispersing. Had he witnessed adroit statecraft in the temple, or some kind of delicious irony?

The manor house of Lady Deneesa of the South
Mountains, New Temple Street, Nasrin. Midmorning.
The first day of the Seventh Moon, Year Fifty.

DENEESA'S COOK HAD prepared a wedding breakfast of eggs and bacon. Arlo said grace for the first time in his new household, praising and thanking the Eternal Spirit for their food, and praying for support for those without food or shelter, as he knew they would be in Deneesa's mind as she ate. Whatever some people said about his new wife, she lived her faith, funding and helping out at soup kitchens in the east of the city. Arlo praised his new stepdaughters for their exemplary conduct at the wedding. They thanked him, calling him "Pa Clayhills", which he liked. They asked about the Arch-Elder's short sermon. At seven and five, they had barely known their father before he went off to subdue the regions to the south of the mountains, so they were curious about the references to Grakko's comradeship with Arlo.

One asked, "Were you with our pa when he died?"

Arlo felt a wave of pity for the girls who would miss their father forever, no matter how much he tried to be a good stepfather to them. "I was in hospital when your pa was killed. I'd been injured in the previous battle. That's why my left arm isn't very strong." The thought crossed his mind, Thanks to trying to keep that ingrate Duke Yonnis alive, but he suppressed it. Why did he think Yonnis was ungrateful? Maybe it didn't matter anymore. After three years in his shadow, Arlo was now the wounded war hero, the true Kim in charge of the army.

His new family had finished eating by the time that Esta's governess returned from her witnessing duties, with a look of relief on her face.

Deneesa laughed. "Well done, Tessa. What a happy day for you. Ye'll never have to teach that stupid girl again."

"Surely, dear wife, we should not make fun of those who are less intellectually gifted than we are? The Truth urges us to learn, but we can only learn according to our abilities." Arlo was not going to let Deneesa's legendary bitterness go unchallenged.

"Husband, that's a humane and pious thought." Deneesa acknowledged the correction. She turned to look at her daughters. "Girls, please note what Pa Clayhills has said." She turned back to Arlo to offer some defense. "Ye're right, but believe me, Tessa has suffered these past four years." Deneesa then changed the subject. "Tessa, do get yourself something to eat and then take the girls to practice some needlework. Mr. Clayhills and I have some business to transact."

Arlo noticed that Tessa was struggling to suppress a giggle, but she succeeded. She hastily consumed some bread and jam and a cup of tisane. The daughters started pestering her with questions about what exercises they'd be doing today, and when could they stop doing needlework and do some geography? The girls skipped off to lessons with Tessa, and Deneesa looked at Arlo.

"Our contract, husband? I'm not getting any younger while you stare at the tablecloth." She smiled.

Arlo was puzzled. The hint was clear enough to him, but he had not expected her to be at all interested in the physical side of marriage. "Of course, wife. Where do we…?" He had been in this house a few times now, but he still had no idea where the bedroom was.

Deneesa stood, took his hand, and walked briskly upstairs to a large bedroom with a large bed furnished with unbleached linen sheets and pillows. She closed the door and unwound her veil, revealing a mane of chestnut hair shot with wires of silver. She said sorrowfully, "Arlo, my body is well marked by childbearing and suckling, and I think that, for your sake and mine, it's best that you don't see too much of it."

Arlo sensed her unhappiness. He held her and kissed her. She drew the russet-brown drapes on the bed and disappeared behind them to undress, while he started to throw his fine garments onto a chair. It briefly crossed his mind how much better his arm had felt since Esta stroked it. When he was naked, he tapped one of the drapes on the bed and whispered, "May I?"

When she said yes, he got under the sheets and offered to hold her again. To his surprise, arousal followed. They rolled in each other, in the sheets, and then rolled apart, still panting.

"I know that I'm not all that ye'd have hoped for in the bedroom, Arlo, but I'll do my best to please you."

Arlo felt a wave of pity for Deneesa. He had done his duty, but he had been thinking about another woman, the lovely Esta, to sustain his passion. That seemed unfair and deceitful, but it was effective. Deneesa started to stroke his lightly haired, muscular chest, and then kiss it. No conversation with an Elder or a male relative had quite prepared him for what a woman might or should do as a wife, so he decided to let her continue.

"Arlo," she said softly, "I want as much of your seed today as you can make. You're a fine man and you deserve a son."

"There's no hurry, my love. There'll be other days." Arlo had managed one climax and he felt exhausted. How many more did she expect?

"Indeed, there will, but today's a good day for it... "

"Perhaps you know more than I do about... getting things going again?" Arlo sounded as sheepish as he felt.

Deneesa eased the sheets to one side. There was an unsettling hunger in the way that she gazed at his body, but he liked the admiration. "So this is why the Sudarites worship beauty," she murmured. "I think I might have to spend some time repenting tomorrow."

But this was today, and Arlo was all too happy to let her coax him to orgasm again.

A quayside inn, Nasrin. Midmorning. The first day of the Seventh Moon, Year Fifty.

"COMRADES! I HAVE some extraordinary news from Bankside!" Seemo rustled his papers as he roused the interest of the inn's customers.

"Get on wi' it then, Seemo!" cried an old man staring into the bottom of a mug as if it could not possibly be empty already.

"It's very short, and I s'pose it is intended to be sweet—"

"Make it even shorter and I'll stand you a drink, Seemo!" The landlady had her say.

"Very well, madam—it *is* your establishment!" Seemo bowed as well as he could with a crutch, and in a mocking way, flourishing his threadbare green cap. Then he noisily cleared his throat.

She took the hint, and brought him a mug of ale. He drank deeply from it.

"The Assembly of Commoners and the Senate of the Republic of Kimalloa are pleased to announce the wedding of General Arlo Clayhills, firstborn son of the Father of the People, Squire Yoshi Clayhills, to Lady Deneesa of the South Mountains, the widow of Lord Grakko, who heroically gave his life in combat at the Battle of Tamsit."

"Well, she didn't waste no time in findin' a young fella to warm her bed!" The landlady screeched, and then laughed suggestively. "I only wish I had her money, and I'd do the same!"

The drinkers laughed heartily.

"He'll be feeling up her wallet, Biddi, not her lady parts!"

Another peal of laughter rang through the inn. Passersby stopped to listen.

"Comrades, there's more."

"Oh, come on, Seemo, ya said it was short!"

"Also!" Seemo pronounced the word deliberately, and then paused to raise some tension. "Also, the wedding of the Arbiter at the Seat of Government, Duke Yonnis Krusa of North Yeralla, with Lady Esta *Glantar*, daughter of the late Rikko X."

At first there was a hush, then a flurry of:

"What?"

"Repeat!"

"Fuck me, did I hear that right?"

"I thought ol' Navvan did 'er in?"

"Are you takin' the piss?"

And similar expressions of confusion.

"That's all." Seemo said it almost teasingly.

"Us all'd love to hear what ya make of that, Seemo!" the old man at the front called to him.

Seemo smiled. "Well, since you ask, ol' Ullin… it sounds like a Sudo fairy story to me! The slayer of the dragon Navvan gets the princess that the dragon was going to eat. There's no denying that Duke Yonnis was a great gen'ral—much admired by those who fought with him—and I dare say the Elders have been urging him to marry. But the last of the Glantars? Mighty strange match for both of them, though—and I s'pose this is the clincher—the squires say she's following the Truth now."

"Well," one man with a scarred face shouted from the back, "I reckon most veterans wouldn't deny him planting his seed, 'ooever it's in!"

Raucous laughter broke out. A few tiny coins were thrown towards Seemo. A small boy gathered them up and brought them to him. Seemo ruffled his thatch of golden-brown hair.

"Thanks, Little Pollo! Time for us to move on."

The quarters of the Arbiter, Bankside Place, Nasrin. Midmorning. The first day of the Seventh Moon, Year Fifty.

ESTA KEPT REASSURING herself that it wasn't a real marriage. After all, a short introduction from that monstrous turncoat Yeramo and signing some parchment—what was that? Where was the ceremony, the pomp, the beauty, the wonder? No, it had no substance. She hadn't really made a serious promise to this strange god-killer. It was just a means to an end. She needed to be in Nasrin, and she needed to connect to people that could fund and drive the counterrevolution. This crazy republic idea was just temporary. Her people would soon get disillusioned with it and turn to her. In the meantime, she had to endure. To show that she was capable of trying to reconcile. And perhaps, before she would be taken seriously by some players, she had to show that she could produce heirs. His seed was not pure, but it was royal enough. This was the sort of compromise most princesses had to suffer after a war. Although, most princesses had luxury to console them. As Esta approached the distinctly ordinary door in the ordinary facade of the Arbiter's quarters, also known as Number 4 Bankside, she was underwhelmed.

A woman in a housekeeper's uniform was curtsying at the door, introducing herself, a maid, and two footmen. Esta was confused and insulted as this woman called Mistress Suki referred to her as "Mistress Krusa". She looked with disgust at Suki's birthmark. This was not a good start.

"Suki used to be an army nurse," the foreigner called Yonnis, now Esta's husband, explained cheerfully to her. "I first met her in a field hospital at Grettin."

So, the housekeeper was not just an informer of convenience, she was a spy of conscience, and deeply loyal to her master. Esta would have to be so careful.

The staff were leading them to the dining room, which had been prepared for their wedding breakfast. They would have to consume before they consummated. Esta would find out what a Yerallan ate. Dried fish, perhaps? Who was this man? She could only remember childhood stories of Yerallans—fierce pirates who looked like men but were snow bears crossed with eels. All the stuff Tessa spouted about the mighty Yerallan engineers who were modernizing the world had passed Esta by. Of course, this one was mixed up with Kimalloan and Osiranian bloodlines, so what did that make him?

Well, whatever he was, she was beginning to sense that she had some power over him. The kiss on the lips had been unexpected, and it had infuriated the Arch-Elder and shocked the grim-faced, black-clad god-killer women, so Esta decided to relish it. It was a gentle kiss and not at all slobbery, so perhaps she could tolerate Yonnis's physical attentions. They were going to have to come soon, as he was acting very nervously. Esta had to admit that she was nervous too. She could remember the lesson on "physical congress" in her queenship tuition. It had been acutely embarrassing. The Raias had told her how to subtly help a clumsy lover, and how to pleasure herself if her husband left her unsatisfied. The businesslike discussions with Lady Deneesa about wifely duty had left Esta convinced that *it* was painful and messy, but had to be done in order to have children and keep a man content, so that he didn't take risks that would involve catching ghastly diseases and passing them on to you. Her foster mother had promised her that it was highly unlikely that Duke Yonnis was infected with anything that would make her nose fall off. That was some comfort. Despite these discussions, she had no idea what *it* would feel like. Would he want to rut standing up, like soldiers with whores? Or would he be so pious that he wanted to lay a sheet over her so their bodies did not meet, as some Followers of the Truth did?

Esta just had to ask, "Husband, why did you kiss me on the lips? Arch-Elder Yeramo looked so cross."

Yonnis looked at the table and said, "Hmm." Then he looked up at her. "Esta, I must confess a vanity. We are the same height. I would have had to stand on my toes to kiss you on the forehead, or ask you to stoop. Either would have made me feel a bit ridiculous. And then I was entranced by your lovely lips. So, it happened. I am very sorry if I embarrassed you."

"No, you didn't. It was fine." Esta smiled at him.

He was about to move in to kiss her again when the door was opened and breakfast was served. Cold venison slices, boiled eggs, bread and cheese, fresh porridge, and her favorite food—plums pickled in mead. The maid also brought in a vase of freshly cut flowers that wafted a gentle scent over the table. And there was wine! It was almost a breakfast fit for a princess, assuming that the dreary porridge was for Yonnis. She was about to lift up her knife, but then remembered that there must be a reflection of thanksgiving first.

Yonnis closed his eyes, held her hand, and started to speak. He gave thanks for the food, blessed those who grew and prepared it, and then prattled away, thanking the Eternal Spirit for bringing him such a lovely wife and asking him to bless her today and every day. He made a point of asking for help in fixing broken Kimalloa. Ha—who broke it? His friends, the rebel squires... Esta kept her thought to herself. Then Yonnis asked for inspiration for "us" to work together on reconciliation and peace. Esta opened one eye and looked askance at him. That "us" was a big assumption.

Once the reflection was over, they started to eat. Yonnis was full of nervous chatter about the fuss over her dress (he hoped that she had enjoyed wearing it, but now it must be dyed a dark blue), the continuing good weather (he hoped that they would spend many sunny days together visiting the new craft sheds and hospitals), and an apology that the Arbiter's quarters might not be what she had hoped for in terms of decoration, but he asserted that they were very comfortable rooms. Hmm, she thought. Officers' Quarters, Number 4. White walls, dark paneling, unbleached linen, and dark green drapes. A man used to living in a tent might call that comfortable, but that is no recommendation to someone brought up in a proper palace, a proper palace in this fortress, which had now been desecrated. But there was hope! Concessions were stacking up. The pink dress was a big one, and the second was venison, plums, and wine for breakfast. What next? Perhaps her room could be decorated in blue?

Esta was relieved when he asked with a trembling voice if she was ready to retire to the bedroom. She nodded and rose from her seat, trying to signal her graceful resignation. Her chest was tight and her breath was very fast. Was that arousal, or was she just scared? He took her hand and led her to his bedchamber. She longed to see the old king's bed, a huge oak structure with ornately carved myrtle motifs finished in gold leaf, mattresses stuffed with soft swan down, and sheets of the rarest Besseman silk. But that magnificent piece of furniture had probably been dismantled, hauled out of a window, and dropped onto a barge to be sold somewhere, earning some paltry sum towards the upkeep of the soup kitchens. What Esta saw was a solid bed made from the unstained, cheap wood of a fast-growing evergreen. She wanted to groan. There were ivy-green drapes at the window and around the bed, the same army green as her husband's jacket. When she was queen, she would ban that dreadful shade. But there was a huge vase full of early roses. They were a deep crimson variety, with densely woven petals. They were waving a heady scent that was a delight to her nostrils. And the bed linen had been freshened with lavender water.

Yonnis latched the heavy wooden door shut and turned to gaze adoringly at Esta. "Dear Esta." He spoke softly. "I don't know what you have been told about the taking of seed, but the process can be... painful for the lady. Especially the first time. If you have any concerns, we don't have to do it now."

Esta responded by unwinding her veil and letting her bouncy black curls swish around her shoulders. Yonnis gasped and stepped up close to caress her face and to kiss her. To her surprise, she opened her mouth for his tongue. His aroused member was pressing into her belly. Yonnis was shaking, but Esta was energized by feeling in control. She loosened and dropped her clothing and then helped him out of his wedding suit. What could he see of her naked body in the soft light filtering through the drapes? Could he see the spotpox marks on her belly? Surely, her softly curved breasts and long legs would distract him from that.

Esta looked at her naked husband. His pale skin was pinkened by arousal. It was smooth, but of course, he did not feel soft. His muscles were as good as those on any sculpture of a god, and they must be as strong as anchor chains. Her eyes widened when she looked down at his erect penis. Oh, Afra, she thought. Is this your will for me?

Yonnis was hesitant. "We can still stop."

Esta shook her head. It had to be done. She climbed onto the bed and opened her legs. "Please do it." Her heart was pounding with dread.

He leaped onto the bed eagerly and knelt between her knees, then he stooped to kiss her nipples.

She moaned a little. "That was nice, but please put it in."

"My darling, it will be easier if you let me arouse you." He touched her where she had been taught to touch herself.

She gasped, wanting more of that, but she repeated her order. "Please, put it in."

Yonnis obeyed and she clenched her jaw and screwed up her face, determined not to cry out in pain, but a solitary tear escaped and ran down her cheek. He kissed it away, and continued to kiss her as he moved inside her. His fast and loud breathing indicated to her that his body was blossoming with exquisite sensations, but hers was not. She was relieved that it did not take too much longer for the urge to plant his seed to overcome him. His loud cry of ecstasy annoyed her. The whole house would hear it and be sniggering. Perhaps the whole house had been listening out for it. She felt the warm liquid spurting into her with faint disgust, but she smiled at him so that he would think that she was in some way satisfied. He smiled back, looking like a cat that had got the cream.

Yonnis rolled to her side and propped himself up on a pillow, continuing to kiss and caress her. "I'm so sorry that I had to hurt you, my sweetheart. It will get easier. Thank you, dear Esta. Thank you."

To Esta's relief, Yonnis soon started snoring gently.

She thought about pleasuring herself, but instead she sat up and looked between her legs at the mess of blood and seed-juice on the sheet. Oh well, she thought, that will give that ugly snoop of a housekeeper something to do. No doubt, All-Ears had asked to see the soiled bed linen after the marriage was consummated.

She noticed rags and a bowl of water on the bedside table, and squirmed to think that her discomfort had been anticipated and planned for. Nevertheless, she cleaned herself up and put her robe back on. Esta drew the drape at the window, which she discovered looked out over the river. She padded the window seat with a pillow and sat looking out at the neat rows of young fruit trees on the south bank. How the god-killers ranted about the value of fruit to keep the nation healthy. How practical. How regimented.

She heard a snort from the sleeping Yonnis. There he lay. So vulnerable. The man who had been feared by every Sudarite soldier in Boriela and Kimalloa. The warhound, the iconoclast, the puritan, the ferocious bear, the cool-headed strategist and reckless attacker, the man of blood, and the man of Truth. The man who was kind and who loved her. She could use him until the friends that Onfri had mentioned came up with a plan for her. But then what? A queen needs a loyal husband, and he would be that. His status as a foreign duke was no threat to her, and it was royal enough to make him a tolerable seed-giver.

Esta rummaged in her discarded dress and felt for a particular bead buried in a tiny, discreet pocket. Magnificent Afra, goddess of all the emotions between men and women, thank you for helping me to endure. Guide me. What should I do with this man when I'm queen? Should I keep him? Or should I kill him?

9

The Seat of Learning of Divine Crafts, religious house of Her Grace, Grand Duchess Kirina, Southwest Osiran. Late afternoon. The first day of the Seventh Moon, Year Fifty.

KIRINA HELD THE headdress of priesthood over the head of a young woman who looked up at her with enthusiasm and awe for her calling. The pink-robed students were singing beautifully. Every icon of every god lined the walls of the assembly hall, lit by hundreds of perfumed candles. The new priestess was resplendent in blue, eager to take the weight of the crescent moon. As she did so, Kirina cried, "The heavens have a new moon! All the gods are here to witness their new interpreter. May all their blessings guide you, Lady Nianna!"

The singing rose to a crescendo. Kirina presented Nianna with a divining wheel, which Nianna held aloft like a trophy of triumph. Then Kirina signaled for the singing to fade away, blessed all the students, and closed the ceremony. Nianna put her divining wheel on a stand, and went down from the stage into the crowd, to embrace the students as they trailed out of the hall. Kirina looked down in pride as Nianna thanked them for their support and offered words of encouragement for their learning.

Kirina had done her best to be fruitful for Yeralla, but thanks to the Borielan war, Navvan of Kimalloa, the coughing disease, and the perils of childbirth, she had lost children and grandchildren too soon. Nianna was one of the survivors—a white-haired, blue-eyed daughter of a daughter, loaned by the late consul Artoris of Yeralla on a diplomatic mission to Osiran to be a "big sister" to Ikra. Nianna had been a dutiful companion to the Crown Prince. She had also become fascinated by Kirina's craft and the power it gave her. She enthusiastically converted to the Osiranian Way, and learned everything that she needed to become a high priestess. She was Kirina's ideal successor.

Eventually, the hall emptied, leaving just Nianna and Kirina, breathing in the heady scent from the candles and gazing adoringly at the richly painted images of the gods.

"This is the great beginning, Nianna. I see it in my divining clouds. You will wield power through knowledge and prophecy. Your cousin Ikra will need you when I am gone."

"I promise that I'll protect him, Nanna, but I can only do that by making him ruthless."

"You must be ruthless for him. Don't spoil his delicate soul."

"And, to protect him, he needs loyal, strong sons. He will have sons, I know. But I am searching in my divining clouds for the fruitful woman who'll bear them. We must find one who will not plot with her sons against him."

"One step at a time, noble priestess." Kirina smiled at Nianna indulgently. "Fruit first—and that is difficult enough when all the great houses are as inbred as their horses, and powerful men kill off their families with cockpox." Then her face, and voice, turned to ice. "Fruit first, then, if the tree goes bad, chop it down."

Clayhills Place, the manor house of General Arlo Clayhills and Mistress Deneesa Clayhills, New Temple Street, Nasrin. Late evening. The first day of the Seventh Moon, Year Fifty.

"BROTHERS AND SISTERS! Welcome to Clayhills Place, as this fine house is now called."

The guests cheered Deneesa. She felt exhilarated. Was it the extended physical intimacy of earlier, or was it the prospect of a new power base, a national one rather than just a regional one?

"Brothers and sisters, what a joy it is to see you all. Thank you for coming. As you know, this morning I married the jewel of Kimalloa's future…" She paused for applause. "I married the brave, the handsome General Arlo Clayhills!"

Arlo stepped forward to receive more applause.

"It is a joy to have such a loving personal partnership…" She hoped that people had noticed the unusual glow of her cheeks. "But together, we are something more than that. We have a lot of work to do in this country. We two, we will be out there on the front line of our peace as we were on the front line of our war."

There was a round of rapturous applause. Deneesa smiled broadly, and then held up her hands to quieten the clapping.

"Thank you! Thank you and bless you! Enjoy yourselves this evening, brothers and sisters, old friends, new kin, and may the Eternal Spirit bless our beloved Republic of Kimalloa!"

The gathered folk raised cups of overly sweet South Borielan wine and cheered. Deneesa noted that Arlo looked a bit baffled as she took the lead that he perhaps thought was his to take, but his gray eyes were sparkling and he was happily shaking hands. Now she would do what she had learned to do to consolidate Grakko's power in his region. First, she honed in on Squire Coppermills and his young second wife. Deneesa asked polite questions, showed that she remembered details about them, nodded when either expressed an opinion, thanked them for the support and friendship that they might not yet have given, and emphasized every virtue that she thought Arlo had, and his great vision for Kimalloa. As soon as she detected a certain tiredness from these two, she moved on to Squire Beechwoods and his good lady, an attentive nurse to his many ailments. After some moments, they made excuses to find other people they needed to talk to. So on she went, from couple to couple, and eventually to the unique oneness of Arch-Elder Yeramo, who preached on the righteousness of marriage and fruitfulness, but had never found himself a wife.

"A wonderful party, Mistress Clayhills. I see that you are mustering your tribe already."

"We live in interesting times, Arch-Elder. One needs to hold friends close."

"Indeed. So why are your foster daughter and her new husband not here?"

Deneesa did not reply.

"It looks bad," Yeramo commented.

She now stumbled into an excuse that she knew would fail to impress Yeramo. "I wanted to spare them any… embarrassment. I mean, so many of our folk… would not have much to say to either of them."

"Very thoughtful, I'm sure."

A calculation skipped through Deneesa's astutely political mind. Yeramo's goodwill was probably worth twenty votes in the Assembly. "Thank you for bringing my omission to my attention, Arch-Elder. I do wish them well, really, I do. I'll visit them with the girls tomorrow and apologize, and invite them to supper."

"Bless you, Mistress Clayhills. Ye're a beacon of the Truth."

Deneesa moved away, trying to keep smiling.

Lord Ulfan sidled up to her. "Commiserations, Deneesa. It must be hard to be corrected by the Great Turncoat Raa," he said very softly.

Deneesa's forced smile cracked a little. "Greetings, kinsman. I thank you for your support."

Ulfan moved position to overshadow her and block the view of other guests. "It's not her, is it?"

Deneesa looked up at Ulfan. Should she trust him? Her late husband had. "Hmm. Well, I know how well you loved Grakko. I can't help wondering…"

"Why he was in the wrong place at the wrong time?"

"Ye've wondered too?"

"Well, let's wallow in the virtue of patience, Deneesa. Everyone is expecting Esta to ruin your father-in-law's Yerallan cuckoo. Sooner rather than later, I hope."

"What if she doesn't?"

"Did I say that she would know about it?" Ulfan grinned.

Deneesa shook her head and laughed quietly.

"I can tell that ye've had a… busy… day with the young Clayhills. D'ye think you can… guide him?"

Deneesa put her hand up to her face as if to adjust her veil, and mouthed something.

Maylan Castle, Eastern Region, Kimalloa. Early evening.
The third day of the Seventh Moon, Year Fifty.

SITRA WAS COMING round from a mushroom-induced trance in the castle gardens when the messenger arrived and collapsed on the floor of Lord Aldor's entrance hall. He had changed horses five times and ridden through the night, but it still took him two days to reach Castle Maylan. She had predicted the arrival of a messenger with news of difficulties, but she could not say whose. Sitra knelt to cradle his head and to bless him, calling for food and wine to restore him. Lord Rubin Aldor was already there and had seized the paper that he was clutching. As he read it, he made noises and faces as if explosions were going off in his head. Then he looked up from the paper to Sitra.

"Explain this to me, Raia," he fumed. "The Yerallan has been blessed by Lord Sudar himself on escaping the blast in his own capital, by Marko in every battle, he has also had the help of the weather gods, and now," he started to shout hysterically, "now he has been blessed by the goddess of love! What is going on in the Dome of the Divine?"

Servants were starting to peek round doors to see what was going on. Aldor twitched as every door creaked. He breathed deeply and calmed down.

"Let's discuss this in my office."

He stormed off and Sitra followed, still swaying slightly from the effects of her trance. Aldor shooed out his clerk and slammed the door.

"Tallier and Clayhills are playing some mighty strange games! Either they are making a parody of the old chivalric code, or maybe they are just extremely cunning." He paced for a few moments. He threw his head back and began shouting at the goddess of wisdom. "Feena, mighty Feena! Explain this to me! Or are you on their side too?"

"You must calm down, Your Grace," Sitra urged. "Goddess Feena does not engage with an angry mind."

"Well, make a potion for me to calm me down. Come back with it and read this letter to me. I'm not sure that I can believe my own eyes anymore."

Sitra scuttled off to the kitchen where she grabbed pinches of soothing leaves, roots, and flowers, scooped hot water from a cauldron over the fire into a large flagon, and stirred, muttering incantations over it. She then added some cold beer, as Aldor would be too impatient to wait for the drink to cool. She returned to the office and placed it in front of Lord Aldor, who was now staring blankly at the fireplace. Sitra picked up the paper. Onfri had not even bothered to code it. Aldor started to sip his drink.

Sitra read the letter to him. To begin with, it seemed hardly worth the urgency. "*Your Grace, I hope that my message reaches you before any other rumor from Nasrin. This morning, I witnessed the marriage of the son of Squire Clayhills, Leader of the Assembly of Commoners, to Lady Deneesa of the South Mountains—*"

Aldor interrupted. "No surprise there, of course. The Clayhills clan need her money. Gross hypocrisy! But good luck to the boy. He'll need it to get any pleasure out of dipping his member into that sour bitch's belly."

Sitra's voice now rose as her interest was piqued. "*No sooner had this brief ceremony concluded, but Duke Yonnis of North Yeralla, former general of the Army of Truth, stood by the Arch-Elder and was joined by a tall woman in a pink robe and veil who turned out to be our noble queen, Esta Glantar!*" She looked up from the letter and watched Aldor cringing. "*In the eyes of their religion, they are now married.*" Sitra watched Rubin shaking his head, then continued. "*The only hope that I can offer to you, as a man of the original and only faith, is that the color of her robe could be a sign that she has made a martyr-like sacrifice. The only advice that I can offer at this time is patience.*"

"Hmm." Aldor grunted. "That was what it said when I read it. Well, I suppose that if they didn't marry Esta to somebody, it would look like she was a prisoner, and in marrying her to him, they keep her a prisoner. What do you think, Sitra? What do the gods say?" Aldor sounded skeptical. "Was she wearing pink to give us a sign?"

"If she had become as zealous as Deneesa on her conversion, she would not have chosen it. It is a sign!" Sitra asserted.

Aldor was now looking as if he had smelled a bad egg. "I can't bear the thought of that ugly brute entwined with the lovely Esta. I know that she would have been brought up to expect to share her bed with a stranger for the sake of the country, but really, this is awful." He sighed, and tapped his fingers on his desk thoughtfully. "All-Ears is such a wily fellow. This isn't just about controlling Esta. Perhaps this was done to make Duke Yonnis unpopular with the veterans. Ha! They do that at their peril!" Aldor had done enough reflecting, and now felt driven to act. "Let's act on Esta's sign. I'm going to make contact with Lazzar, Sofon, and Fergan—"

"But, Your Grace, they supported the usurpation. Why not sound out Armon in the southwest first? He always supported Queen Esta."

"Because he double-crossed Navvan at Tamsit."

"And his eldest daughter is married to King Rolan's Grand Admiral."

"A good point, Raia Sitra. I will consider it. And now, it's back into disguise for you, Priestess. You've had a nice rest these past few moons. See if you can get into Bankside Place. I want to know if Esta will accept a holy kiss from a Raia."

Sitra offered some protest. "The vetting process for Bankside staff is extremely rigorous, Your Grace—"

Aldor rebutted it. "You can conjure your way past that. You claim to have spelled your way past bigger obstacles." He looked at Sitra as if he wondered what she was waiting for.

Sitra sank into a deep curtsy and said loudly, "Your Grace!" As she rose, she was reminded of her trance. "By the way, take care of your wife during this carrying. I had a warning from Afra."

Aldor frowned and grunted. "Do you ever channel any good news from the gods?"

Sitra went to pack her things, silently cursing Lord Aldor. She certainly could get into Bankside, but not by necromancy. She would get into Bankside, and close to Esta, because All-Ears also wanted to know if the new Mistress Krusa would accept a holy kiss from a Raia.

A barn outside Mersin, Southeastern Region, Kimalloa.
Late afternoon. The eleventh day of the Seventh Moon,
Year Fifty.

SEEMO HAD CHOSEN his location carefully. The territory to
the northwest of Nasrin had a long history of dissent. In the
long-ago era of the Besseman Empire, there had been the cult
of the One God, who was personified on earth as a poor man
who spoke of equality. A brave follower of the One God found
his way to this spot in the clay hills of Kimalloa. He was wise
and kind and a healer of hearts and bodies. Needless to say, this
much-loved man, Annan, and all those who listened to him,
were burned, and their own children were forced to start the
fires. The savagery of the Raas in that time was not forgotten and
it did not quell inquiring minds. Throughout the civil war, the
clay hills were known more for political and religious pamphlets
than for tiles. It was in this region that the light shone, or so the
writers claimed. So, it would be no surprise, in the aftermath of
victory, that new freedoms would be tested to the limit here.

Small groups of Nasrinian Distributors were making their
way out of the capital and into the countryside. Seemo sat in a
cart with Mistress Oona, whose husband had been killed at Kallo
Mill, and Little Pollo, who had been a drummer boy in the Army
of Truth, and wore his ivy green with pride. It was a quarter-
moon Day of Reflection in late summer in the rolling hills
crested with greenwoods, where grain crops waved their swelling
heads in a soft breeze. The local people would have been at their
temples in the morning, listening to the Elders praying for the
safe harvesting of the gifts of the glorious spring and summer.
Few had dared to hope in the bitterly cold rain of the first three
moons of Year Fifty, with the strongest men of the country still on
campaign, that a late sowing could produce such a bounty. It was
the blessing of the Eternal Spirit on their victory, Seemo was sure

130

of that. But he dared to ask more, not just from the Eternal Spirit, but from the commanders supposedly implementing Its will.

It was late afternoon now. Seemo's cart was starting to meet up and mingle with more groups of men, and a few widows, heading for the Great Barn at Annan's Cross, near Mersin. Seemo already knew some that would be there. Among the walkers were Sergeant Don, Pikeman Peet, and Gunner Moss. These three men had been at the first battle to defend Nasrin in Year Forty-Six, when Squire Clayhills led them to charge again and again to push back the King's forces.

They were enthusiasts, but Seemo knew that most of the men heading for the barn would be there for entertainment. He listened to the men marching behind his cart. They did not chat about land rights, but about which village would win the groundball tournament in the Day of Victory celebrations. One was convinced that the Borielan Gorak who had married a girl from Sillis would be unbeatable, but another thought that the ball skills of their own Kushno would be a match for him. Ah! Sport. How it diverted men from their problems.

Seemo turned his thoughts back to his own network, others displaced from faraway regions by the war, who had promised to bring their comrades. Walking from a village to the north should be Fillo the musketeer, whose family had perished from straw fever, and a pikeman called Barra who had lost an arm at Estlorn. From the south came Ross and Ponzo, formerly from the Middlelands, and from the east came Alfi, Fraz, and Aspri, carried on a mule cart by doughty muleteer Anti. Aspri was with his new wife, Dilli. What a tale that had been for the Distributors! He had taken pity on a dying Sudo prisoner, who offered him the buttons from his ragged shirt—all that he had left of any value—if he would take his prayer beads and love token to his wife in the northwest. After Tamsit, Aspri turned north, despite the dangers of entering Lord Sofon's region, and found Dilli and her hungry children. She declared that if the

Doctrine of Truth urged such kindness, she was converted. "In that case," said Aspri, "will you marry me?" *So*, the newssheets announced, *we poor men can do chivalry just as well as rich folk!*

Seemo did have some worries. This gathering, and all the others like it, would attract some troublemakers. There had been a few in every regiment, men who just enjoyed intimidation and violence. And there would be spies. Tallier's agents would not cause trouble. But what about lords like Lazzar? Rather than send men to break up the meetings in their regions and end up in a skirmish with the militia, they might just pay thugs to do the job.

On arrival at the barn, Seemo's helpers set up a makeshift stage from some barrels and boards. The barn had been patched up after years of decay, cleared, and cleaned, ready for new hay and straw. Today, it would shelter the cropped heads of a few hundred army veterans from the sun. This was his first chance to address a large crowd. Seemo—maimed newsman of the Nasrin docks, a nobody—was lifted onto the stage. He looked out at the sea of heads, bobbing like apples in a bowl, feeling energized by them. With rags, hazel sticks, and wool-markers, some men had made rough banners:

I am Maz the deaf gunner. Maimed for the cause.
I am Skotti—fought in six battles.
I am Yasu, homeless musketeer. Save the cause.
I am lame Ibbi—I need work.

And there was a banner with neat letters, sewn in desperation. *I am Ronya. My husband came back with a broken mind.*

Seemo managed to wave a wooden placard while balancing on one crutch. It said, *Seemo Shepherd. Maimed for the cause.* He wore his green army coat, but not his cap. He wanted to show his cropped head. "Comrades, welcome!" he shouted.

The crowd cheered him. Men continued to file in, and started pushing when it became clear that Seemo was about to speak.

"Comrades!" Seemo shouted again. Looking out at dozens and dozens of faces waiting for him to tell them something interesting, he couldn't help but feel blood pounding in his head. "It warms my heart t'be with you this afternoon. We are a fine bunch of men! We *are* the beating heart of Kimalloa. Didn't our commanders tell us so?"

The crowd cheered, heads bobbed, and placards were waved.

Seemo waited for the noise to subside and then continued. "A few moons ago, the Army of Truth—*our* army—won a great victory at Tamsit."

The crowd cheered again. "We beat the fat tyrant!" one man cried out. Some yelled that they were there and it was great to have been there.

After some exchanges in the crowd, Seemo raised his hand for quiet. "We were fighting for four years. Up and down the country, going where our commanders told us to, training to do what they needed us to do, and losing what we had to lose, like our limbs, our eyes, our minds, and many, many friends—our brothers in arms."

The crowd became somber, murmuring in sadness, remembering those lost friends.

Seemo continued. "Why did we do it? Why did we slog through mud 'n' blood 'n' guts 'n' disease 'n' hunger 'n' hardship? They promised us freedom. Better lives for our children. Opportunities! Well, have we got them?" He paused, sensing a bit of confusion in the audience. "What did we think freedom would mean, brothers? Of course, lords don't *own* us anymore, we're not their slaves. But what difference has that made?"

He paused again, and then let rip, trembling with emotion as he thought about the conditions of some veterans in the capital. "From what I hear, day in and day out, the freedom we have won is freedom not to have any work, or food, or a shed to live in! There are plenty of our comrades in *that* place of freedom, begging for help at the soup kitchens. There are still lines of hundreds at those sorry places every day!"

Some men cried, "Shame!" but others were still reticent, even cynical. They came to listen to the Distributor, not necessarily to agree with him.

"Wounded and widows got pensions though, Seemo!" someone shouted from the back.

Others shouted angrily that they were still waiting for their pensions.

"And craft sheds," said another.

And there was an element of aggression. "Ye're just a shit-stirrer, Shepherd-Man!"

The barn went quiet, waiting for Seemo to respond. He tried to shuffle closer to the front of the makeshift stage, to get closer to the audience, so that they could see the sincerity of his message in his face. He realized that many had expected nothing from fighting a war. After all, the common trooper had never been rewarded ever before. Rikko VII had famously let the navy sailors who saw off an armada from Bessema starve while he bought new jewels for his hats.

"Aye, we must acknowledge that our commanders' Assembly has *planned* some good things for us. Most are good men, pious men. But I put it to you, comrades—it is *not* ungrateful to expect them to keep *all* of their promises, all those hopes they raised in us when they wanted us to march into cannon fire. And keep those promises to all—I say *all*—of us. The squires, who said that we would have better lives, they've given us a few crumbs. They work very hard for us, talking at each other in that great tent of theirs… in that great Sudarite grove."

The crowd growled at the mention of the superstitious religion that had suppressed them.

"They sit there, our former commanders, with people who shot at us in battle! People who now say they are sorry for their mistake. Sorry that they shot at us and killed our brothers. Sorry? So! They should be bloody sorry!"

The crowd jeered loudly, and began surging forward to listen more closely to Seemo.

"Comrades, our commanders and our gen'ral, they were worth following in the war. They led us to victory and we have to be thankful for that. But do they have the right to dictate the peace? They're doing deals with king's men, before making sure that *our* needs're satisfied. They aren't involving us. But it was *us* that put them on the winning side. *We* made the sacrifices."

"Aye!" came a shout from Fraz, who was shaking his fist. "We've got a right to be heard!"

The crowd roared its approval.

Seemo continued. "So, we aren't serfs anymore. But if we're not owned by anybody, why are masters still making all the decisions about jobs 'n' trade 'n' pensions? We still have to dance to their tune! What's the point of thinking about things when they're not listening to our thoughts? We did not fight just to replace a single master with a whole bunch of 'em!" Seemo wagged his finger, and many men shook their fists.

One called out, "He's right—we haven't finished this!"

"You are good and loyal citizens, comrades, and of course we are grateful for the small mercies granted to us. Very thankful. May the Spirit be praised. But these're distractions. Only *twenty* people in each parish vote for the member of the Assembly of Commoners. Who are they? They are the folk who own some land, not the folk who walked into cannon fire. Squire Clayhills says—"

The crowd at this point growled a warning. "You lay awf 'im, Seemo, he's a good soul," a man with a very clear local accent shouted.

"I love him too, comrades, I assure you." Seemo knew that he had struck a nerve, but he had done so on purpose, so that he could quote the great man. "Squire Clayhills is the first man to say that we should have open minds, so please listen, and then disagree if you wish. He says that because we've no land, our identity can't be proved for votes. Well, that's convenient, isn't it? They could parcel the King's land out to us, but they don't, and we can't do anything about it because we can't vote. Do we want a say in running this country that we fought for?!"

"Yes, yes, yes!" The crowd now bayed like wolves.

"Do we want to make pots and pans in a shed and have no say, or do we want land and votes?" Seemo asked, holding his hand to his ear to hear the reply.

Most shouted back, "Votes!" and a few shouted, "Land!"

One shouted, "Ballbags! It's all ballbags!" and was jostled out of the barn.

"Where does all the power lie in this country, in every country?" Seemo asked them. "Let me tell you, comrades—it is land! Who's got all the King's confiscated land?"

"The squires!" shouted the crowd.

"Who's got all the leases on the Sudo lords' land?"

"The squires!"

"Who's got all the grange farms that the priests owned?"

"The squires!"

"What land have we got?"

"None!" The crowd shouted so loudly that the barn shook.

"Did we follow them for that?"

"No, no, no!" The crowd roared and waved their placards furiously.

"What's going on in Nasrin?!" some shouted.

But there was still some sneering dissent. "What are ya goin' to do about it, ya clodpolls?! Shoot all the squires?"

Seemo ignored the objector and asked again. "Do we want to make pots and pans in a shed and have no say, or do we want land and votes?" Again, he held his hand to his ear to hear the reply.

"Land and votes! We want land *and* votes!"

The chanting went on for several moments before Seemo held up his hand for quiet.

"Our commanders taught us to read 'n' write a bit—so let's use it. I've a petition here, asking the Assembly for land and votes for veterans. If you sign it, comrades, I will deliver it!"

136

Seemo flourished a large piece of paper. The crowd cheered and surged forward. The surge was barely contained by Seemo's helpers at the front. The makeshift stage was dislodged. Seemo toppled off, and was in danger of being trampled. He heard a gasp of dismay from those that could see the accident unfurl. Men at the front turned and tried to push back the crowd so that Seemo could be dragged out of harm's way, and they needed every bit of their strength to do so. Those being shoved backward got angry about it, and there was every chance of the rally descending into a brawl. Sergeant Don jumped onto a barrel and barked at them to ease off and form an orderly line if they wanted to sign. Seemo felt relief, and then he felt his bruises. Mistress Oona was fussing over him, which was wonderful. This was a happy and proud moment. People had heard him and responded to him. His voice rang out as he was being hauled to his feet by Peet and Aspri.

"Let me shake your hands, brothers and sisters, as you sign. Go back to your families 'n' tell them that you've made a stand for 'em today!"

There was more shouting and shoving into the line for the signing. The fit men made way for the maimed veterans to sign first, then shuffled forward in twos and threes towards the long piece of paper that Seemo had saved for moons to buy from Illio. The stink of homemade ink wafted from constantly replenished pots. Army of Truth men all knew how to form the symbols for their first name, and their trade or hamlet of birth for a second identifier. Only a few widows marked *X* and needed a neighbor to put a name next to it. Seemo watched with excitement as the signatures started to snake down the paper. No critical clerk could complain about the veracity of these signatures!

Skotti Brewer
Pollo of Priddin
Andis Reaper
Aspri Gunner
Ibbi Cowman

X (Ellina of Annan's Cross)

Fraz of Ettiash…

As the petitioners waited in line, they started to bawl out one of the chants that they had used to keep their spirits up when they had been tramping through deep mud in pelting rain, or sweating through sweltering siege days in the summer. All for the cause, and all so that their fellow countrymen could blast cannon into them. *"We are for Truth. We are for light. We are the free. We are true Kims. We have the right!"*

The organizers at the front of the barn repeated the message on the paper out loud, again and again. They wanted to be able to insist that everyone who signed it had understood what they were signing.

> *Dear and honorable Squire Clayhills, Leader of the Assembly of Commoners and Father of the People,*
>
> *We are veterans of the Army of Truth. We believe in the Eternal Spirit who gave us a great victory. We have made sacrifices to prove our commitment to the cause of freedom. We have lost brothers and comrades and suffered terrible injuries ourselves. Yet our former miseries are not yet relieved. We petition you to secure our future in our beloved country of Kimalloa. We petition you for land and votes for veterans.*
>
> *Signed by the following veterans, wounded, and widows…*

> *Dear and honorable Squire Clayhills…*

The Truth encouraged reflection, and now many more people were imagining a shared country. Seemo swelled with pride and hope. He was part of a dedicated band of devout folk who were determined to gather at least twenty thousand signatures and present them to the Father of the People on Victory Day. Surely, he would not ignore them.

10

Office of the Intelligence Minister, the Archive, Bankside, Nasrin. Early morning. The twelfth day of the Seventh Moon, Year Fifty.

From Brother Ronni of Market Square, Tinmas. His neighbor Siltin consistently fails to observe the bell for reflection more than once in a day.

From Sister Illia the grocer in Eastern Street, Daktor. Yulla, the baker's wife on the corner with Fish Street, called on Sudarite gods to curse a late-paying customer.

ALL-EARS SHUFFLED THE notes from his clerks and laughed at the unremitting urge of humans to report the perceived shortcomings of others, however banal, to "authority". It had its advantages. When people feel that they are being watched, they tend to behave better. Occasionally, even the trivial reports had to be followed up, because if people feel that they are being watched *and* there will be consequences, they behave at their best. Of course, a good spy would be on their best behavior all of the time. That was the worry. Who was out there, not being noticed by their neighbors?

Despite all the pettiness of a culture of informing, being a spymaster could be very rewarding when the stakes really were high. All-Ears had kept the report from his agent at the Pozarian court, dated the eighth day of the Seventh Moon, Year Fifty, in a special folder in a special drawer. After his daily sample from the tittle-tattle, he got it out to relish again. It was a short report, in a careful code. It began…

Dear friend, you may be interested to know that King Rolan laughed, seemingly with genuine mirth, about the marriage of his Kimalloan cousin to a bastard cousin from the faraway forests.

It had been a gratifying reaction to his statecraft. Rolan was too amused to be offended. All-Ears wanted to write down in large letters on the report, *Risk of invasion—defused!*, but he didn't. He must not get complacent!

Today, All-Ears had to consider something that had not been envisaged as a consequence of peace. The concept of "freedom" was whizzing off in all directions. The proliferation of radical sects in Nasrin and beyond was beginning to annoy and offend Elders, squires, and conservative citizens. The leaders of the sects all claimed to be Followers of the Truth, but they had some interesting interpretations of the words of Yerobis the Liberator. The Distributors were the ones who had some traction. They were gaining popularity among demobilized army veterans. There were a lot of them dispersed across the country. They were well trained, well organized, and well respected.

All-Ears had people at Mersin. Of course he did. They had briefed him as soon as they got back, so he had not slept well. The Doctrine of Truth allowed debate, but the fragile new republic did not need its own supporters undermining it. Something would have to be done.

There was a knock on the door. The door creaked. Yoshi and Arlo Clayhills entered, exchanged greetings, and sat down.

"It's very hot in here, sir," said Arlo. "I'm surprised that you don't melt. And that smell—it's worse than wood."

All-Ears was calling to a footman for small beer, and overlooked the comment. Hundreds of bell pits had been dug in the North Middlelands already, and he had some precious coal in a bucket beside the fireplace. Kimalloa had a new source of economic power, and his personal fireplace could stay hotter for longer!

"Are you worried about the Distributors, Ellis?" Yoshi opened the business.

All-Ears got to the point immediately. "As Father of the People, you're going to have to make a judgment call about where free speech ends and a threat to law and order begins." This was what troubled him. Where was the line, and how would people know when they were stepping over it?

"A bunch of veterans having a moan together in a barn does not breach the peace, surely? And they are being reasonable, because they're only signing a petition, they're not waving weapons around." Yoshi was slow to see wrong in others, especially the men who had delivered his dream of a free Kimalloa.

"I disagree, Father." Arlo jumped in. "They're ungrateful and excessively impatient! They've never been so blessed! We need to stop this dissent—nip it in the bud! Next Reflection Day we should have army and militia at all these barns—turning them away, at the point of a sword if necessary!"

"You seem very confident that the standing army and militia would happily use force against veterans, Arlo." All-Ears held his hands together as if in prayer, and then pointed them at Arlo to ensure his emphasis was noted. "I... am... not."

"Nor should we put them in that position," Yoshi added. "Let's be seen to be listening. There'll be room for compromise. We need to keep the radicals onside in the Assembly—for now, anyway. I shall accept the Distributors' petition on Victory Day, and then the Assembly can debate it—in due course. Isn't that how we always imagined it? Anyone should be able to raise an issue with their government. You are the general, of course,

Arlo, and you must make your own judgments about public safety with the Army Council, but surely our priority must be suppressing any Sudarite plot on Victory Day? That's a far more dangerous proposition. We must remember Yeralla..."

All-Ears responded to Yoshi's signal. "There are Sudarite sleeper agents in the army, militia, and administration, Arlo. I have information about *some*—we can root them out the night before. But we can't possibly know all of them. Every site where celebrations are taking place needs to be searched, and then searched again."

"Understood, sir," Arlo replied. "That is my priority, and I have very detailed plans for the searches. In addition, if the Distributors or any other sect starts disturbing the events with their ranting, they will be contained. And then detained."

"Obviously. We're having a party. We don't want anyone to spoil it." All-Ears paused, and quaffed some beer. "The short term is manageable. But we should have a longer discussion about these sects, particularly the Distributors. Let's have breakfast— the day after Victory Day, perhaps—with a few select guests. We who share the widest knowledge, and have shown the greatest commitment—we should decide what we want to recommend to the Assembly about the petition. We three, Deneesa, Ulfan, Yeramo, possibly Coppermills."

"Yonnis's ideas might—" Yoshi suggested.

"Absolutely not." Arlo's view was predictable. "Don't ask me to trust an oath-breaker with sensitive political matters. Anyway, he is supposed to arbitrate after discussion in the Assembly and Senate, so it would compromise him to involve him beforehand."

"Well, that's a fair point." Yoshi conceded, concluding the discussion. He left with Arlo, bidding his cousin a successful day.

All-Ears was glad to have Arlo's air of aggression out of the room. What was wrong with the man? His father had been brave and had righteous anger when he was young, but with Arlo— these days he just seemed to want confrontation whether it was needed or not. Did he need to prove that he was "the big man" now? Well, perhaps it was useful. All-Ears was the last person to want the people to think that the end of monarchy was the beginning of anarchy. Definitely not. Kimalloa must be governed with a firm hand if it were to prosper. Arlo would not just be a firm enforcer of the rule of law—he would be zealous.

What was next on his list? Perhaps he should review some notes from Suki. He skimmed:

> *Ninth of the Seventh. The sheets were soiled (again). The Arbiter rose early, washed, cleaned his teeth, had salted porridge for breakfast, and then went to the Seat of Government. Mistress Krusa slept late and wanted honeyed plums for breakfast. She sat on the roof terrace reading until Mistress Deneesa Clayhills arrived with her daughters. They stayed for midday meal. Early afternoon, the Arbiter arrived in a carriage and went with the mistress to see the digging of the new dry dock just east of the city. They came back pleased with what they had seen, and had a collection of cold meats and cheese for supper. They sat and talked about taking a trip to the north, the mistress having blue drapes in her room, and buying some paintings, which the Arbiter insisted must be "still life" (?). They retired after the last reflection bell.*

So far, so good, thought All-Ears. Was it right to tempt fate with the installation of Agent Pia, also known as Raia Sitra, as a "companion" to Esta? He would do it anyway.

Western Watchtower, Bankside, Nasrin. Midmorning. The twenty-first day of the Seventh Moon, Year Fifty.

ARLO FELT THAT it was good for morale to chat to his men from time to time. He had watched Yonnis do it to good effect, and if Yonnis could do it, then Arlo could do it. But perhaps things were different in a tent in the mud of a Middlelands plain. When Arlo dropped into sentry points and field bases, the men seemed nervous and awkward, and that in turn made him feel awkward. Things were a bit better in Bankside. He was often in Bankside for meetings and his personal guard were stationed there. He knew them well. He felt entirely relaxed as he headed to the western watchtower for a beer. The clatter of his footsteps alerted the men in the guardhouse, but the sentries on the battlements were not so alert, and, it being a hot day, the door up to the top of the wall was open. Arlo could hear their banter quite clearly, which was interspersed with boyish giggling.

"The old gen'ral's makin' up for lost time with that new young wife of 'is, so I hear. They're at it virtually ev'ry night, I've been told—on good authority…"

"Go on—what've you been told?"

"She purrs when they're shakin' the sheets!"

"Purr? How can a woman purr? Only cats purr. You're a simpleton to believe that."

"No, really, pal, that's what Kushno said, and he has to try and sleep in the next room with it goin' on. And he—old Yonnis, I mean—he grunts as loud as a prize boar when he comes!"

There were gales of laughter from the men at the thought of the pious general in the throes of ecstasy. Arlo felt a rush of anger, but he must not show it. He walked as quietly as he could up the stairs, under cover of the laughter. The banter continued.

"That I *can* believe—those Yerallans take their rutting seriously. Ask any of our girls who married an Adventurer."

Then Arlo announced himself as loudly as he could. "Pay attention to your duty, soldiers!" He loomed in the doorway.

They jumped to attention and looked very fearful. "Sorry, sir!" they chorused.

"Brothers, remember that gossip is the playground of evil. What on earth are you thinking of, to discuss other people's most private matters when you are on guard?! Just concentrate on the job in hand. People are relying on you to keep Nasrin safe."

"Yes, sir!"

Arlo could feel the soldiers' fear of him, and he enjoyed the moment. "Now stop gazing at your feet and watch out for wrongdoers in the streets!"

"Yes, sir!"

The soldiers returned to their watch posts and Arlo stomped back down the steps, inwardly fuming. There would be no comradely beer-sharing today. It was not the lack of discipline of his men that aggravated him. They would talk about the mating act, wouldn't they? It was hearing that Esta might be enjoying taking Yonnis's seed. Twice already, he and Deneesa had endured supper with the pair, and he had been comforted by their awkwardness. If they were not estranged, what could he do to change that?

He loitered in the courtyard, wondering if he could catch the footman Kushno on an errand. He would doubtless trade a favor if Arlo offered not to denounce him to his master or to an Elder for entertaining his friends with intimate household secrets. Surely, Kushno would soon be carrying a message, or taking the dog for a walk. But to Arlo's surprise, it was Esta and another woman who emerged from Number 4 with the dog. He wandered over, removed his hat, and bowed deeply.

"Dear Mistress Krusa, what a lovely surprise to see you. And this is…?"

The women curtsied.

"Good morning, General Clayhills. This is Mistress Pia," Esta's lovely melodic voice informed him. "Squire Tallier has appointed her as a companion to me, so I can do more things when my husband the Lord Arbiter is at work. Isn't that nice of him?"

"May the Spirit bless good Squire Tallier. I shall look forward to seeing you out and about more often, Mistress Krusa. Welcome to Bankside, Mistress Pia. What an easy job you will have—companion to someone so companionable!"

"Thank you very much, General Clayhills," Pia replied.

"I like your colorful sash, General Clayhills—such a dashing effect!" Esta commented.

She was paying him a compliment! Arlo felt a flutter in his stomach. Was she flirting with him? What was he supposed to say back? Were those big eyes bigger when she looked at him? Purr? Ha! He would make her roar like a big cat of Bessema!

"Thank you, dear lady. It is nothing compared to the beauty with which you grace the earth."

Esta looked down, knowing that she should rebut such excessive flattery, but not quite sure how to do so. She fluttered her long black eyelashes nervously, which excited Arlo all the more. He stared at her, longing for her to look up at him again, hoping to see her eyes wide with desire. She continued to look down. He started to reach out to her chin—

Pia's voice snapped into his reverie. "General Clayhills, may the Spirit bless you for your kind greetings. We'll let you get on with your duties. You must be a very busy man. Good day, General. It's been a great honor to meet you."

Arlo raised his hat in farewell, wished them a pleasant walk, and continued smiling while thinking how much he would like to strike Pia. He went to collect his horse to ride home. He started wondering whether his uncle was losing his grip. Coupling Yonnis with Esta had been a crazy idea. When would that cough get the better of Uncle Ellis? The cause needed new blood, and a stronger hand.

A place that does not exist – officially. Midnight. The twenty-fourth day of the Seventh Moon, Year Fifty.

"UNBURDEN YOURSELF, NESKA. Then you can sleep." The man in the mask smiled at Neska, who could barely remember her own name, and was convulsing with the shock of more cold water being thrown over her. Her robe stank because she had soiled it several times since they had tied her up in this bare, stone room. Her long, gray hair dripped and dripped. She was no longer sure who she was protecting or why. The gods were testing her, but she was close to the end now, and she would be free. Visions came into her head of the golden gate at the entry of the Dome of the Divine. She could smell something now, something familiar from the great rituals of worship in the sacred grove. Yes, there was Raa Erren, she could see the snake on his neck, he was ready to kiss her head in blessing.

"Atakiri, my child—"

"The child lives… " she gasped.

"Whose child?"

"The child of Her Highness… "

Nasrin. Early morning. The twenty-seventh day of the Seventh Moon, Year Fifty.

YONNIS WOKE TO the sun streaming through the drapes. Just as he, and all of Kimalloa, had hoped, the weather was clear and warm. Esta turned over and tried to snuggle down for more sleep, but he gently shook her awake. Today, of all days, they both needed to be up and alert early, ready to do their duty. Crowds had been gathering in towns all over the country to honor their veterans first, and then to enjoy themselves—to the degree that the law now allowed. The militia were on full alert in case of protests or plots.

In Nasrin, the program began with veterans marching and waving their regimental colors. Their green coats were worn with pride. Special open carts had been made to enable maimed veterans to take part. There was a parade by the standing army in full armor, showing off their arms and artillery. Assembly ministers, senators, and other senior officers of the government, visible above the crowds on a platform outside the gates of Bankside, held their caps to their hearts as they passed. Wives stood somberly next to their husbands. An enormous Kimalloan flag hung behind them, a simple tricolor of ivy green, white, and purple. When the last soldier had saluted the dignitaries and the flag, the Arch-Elder conducted a service of thanksgiving. The fallen were remembered with funereal drumrolls and wailing trumpets. Yonnis had been remembering and reflecting throughout, and at this point, he started to cry. Esta fussed to find his handkerchief for him.

After the commemorations, sports and entertainments were to take place at Victory Park, and some members of the platform party, including Yonnis and Esta, were going to walk with the crowd. They were closely guarded. They could smile and wave, perhaps occasionally stop to gently shake an outstretched hand, but the militia were there to parry any thrust from a knife. There were agents in the crowd looking out for any suspicious activity. A space had been cordoned off thirty strides from the procession, where a few long-haired men chanted "Not our party!" and "Sudar will return!"

Yonnis's sleep had been disturbed by flashbacks to the explosion in the capital of Yeralla. His joy in connecting with so many people distracted him from his worries, until he suddenly felt a claw grasp his ankle. He tensed in horror. He looked down, expecting to see the red talons of Marko.

An old woman in rags had sunk to her knees and crawled through the legs of the guards. "Please cure me, my lord, please cure me!" she begged.

Yonnis crouched down to speak to her. "I am sorry, mistress, I am not a healer. But the men at the back of the procession, the ones in the white robes, they are. Let this guard take you to one, and may the Spirit bless you."

By this time, a guard had hauled the woman to her

feet. Esta reached out to pat her shoulder, and smiled at her sympathetically.

The woman looked at Esta as if struck with ecstatic awe, and held her hands up above her head, causing her sleeves to slip down. Curious red marks, which might be burns or sores, were disappearing from her arms. She yelled, "I am cured! I am cured! God bless Your Majesty!"

Yonnis looked at the expression on Esta's face. She looked like a kitten intrigued by its first sight of a bouncing ball of wool. The guards struggled to hold back curious bystanders.

Yonnis turned back to the guard who had hold of the old woman and ordered him to take her to the Healing Elders, "Perhaps they can work out what trickery has been done here."

Esta was bubbling with excitement. "I didn't realize that it was really true that I could cure diseases because of my royal blood. Isn't that wonderful?"

"Darling Esta, I wish that you could cure all manner of diseases with a touch. If it were true, I think we would have seen evidence of it before now. We have been to hospitals, and this has never happened. Now, sweet wife, forget this incident. You just have to keep smiling and waving for ten moments or so, if the crowds will allow us some progress."

As soon as they reached the gates of Victory Park, Yonnis hurried to the side of Squire Clayhills to witness the presentation of the Distributors' petition. The ceremony was carefully orchestrated on both sides. Squire Clayhills stood where the foundations of the gates to the new Debating House had been laid, flanked by many Assembly members and clerks. Militiamen formed an aisle for the petitioners to approach. The Distributors looked suitably humble as they slowly paced forward. They had tied the pieces of paper from around the country into one roll, which they unraveled as they progressed, so everyone could see how long it was. They had exceeded their target of twenty thousand signatures. Then, as the men at the front bowed to the Father of the People, they rolled it up again. Squire Clayhills shook their hands and took the heavy roll of paper. There was a roar of approval. Cheering and clapping continued as the roll was passed to a nearby clerk and Squire Clayhills waved both hands to the crowd. Then everyone peacefully moved on to watch the sports.

Younger men were keen to show their prowess at groundball, handball, unarmed combat, swordplay, stick-fighting, running, jumping, throwing, rowing, and swimming. Older men showed their skills at archery and bowls. There was even softball for women. After admiring something of everything, Yonnis settled down to watch the swimming finals. Standing on the riverbank in the comforting warmth of the sun reminded him that it was a very long time since he had been swimming. He allowed himself a brief pang of nostalgia. The Binar might flow gently this side of Nasrin, but it could never be as inviting as the pure ice-melt lakes where he had learned to glide through the water like an eel.

The Ladies' Enclosure, Victory Park. Midday. The twenty-seventh day of the Seventh Moon, Year Fifty.

ESTA WALKED THE rows in the Ladies' Enclosure, smiling and shaking hands. She had to move so quickly from widow to nurse to wife of a sergeant or daughter of a gunner, but these women smiled widely at her, making her feel that she was special and that she was giving them something special. She had learned her part from Deneesa. She was to thank everyone, and in specific cases say, "Thank you for your sacrifice, sister."

Most of the children present were over four years old. The birth rate had plummeted during the war, but now it would surely boom. At one point, Esta found herself shaking hands with a woman who had a toddler clinging to her robe. She looked down from the woman to the boy and started to say, "Oh, he's so little—"

The woman seemed to understand immediately that Esta was curious. She spoke plainly. "I was raped when King Navvan's troops came to raid my village. But I couldn't blame the baby. I love him."

Esta tried not to look horrified. She had been brought up to expect that a baby born of rape would be taken out into the forest to die. But of course, the Truth had abolished all the rules about "the flawed". "I'm s-s-so sorry." Esta was taken aback by the woman's bluntness, and her overwhelming love for her child. "May the Spirit bless you, and your sweet boy!"

The commander's wife who was guiding her program moved her quickly away.

The Groundball Arena, Victory Park. Late afternoon. The twenty-seventh day of the Seventh Moon, Year Fifty.

DENEESA WAS SHOOING Esta to her seat for the groundball final. The one beside it, intended for Yonnis, was empty.

"Where is he?" Esta asked. "He likes sport. He wouldn't miss this."

Squire Clayhills leaned over. "Last thing I saw of him, Mistress Krusa, he was kicking a ball himself, with some drummer boys—"

The general noise and chanting for different teams subsided, and Esta heard a roar of "Whoa, General Yonnis!" It was repeated again and again until an arm was raised and waved above a white head, mingling among the pink and brown ones. The crowd clapped. This was popularity! She had seen crowds cheering her father, but he had been finely dressed, seated on a stage or in a carriage, not in among them. Oh, if only she could inspire the people to chant *her* name! She started to hear a whisper from Afra, the goddess who wove spells for the power of love over another. "This man, this man that they salute, is yours. Use him."

Arlo interrupted her daydream, barking at a militiaman, "Get him out of the crowd and bring him to where he should be sitting!"

Squire Clayhills raised his hand to indicate to the militiaman that he had something to add. "Just send a footman to deliver a discreet message."

Just before the kickoff, Yonnis sat down next to Esta and took her hand. "I am sorry if I embarrassed you by being late. I was waylaid by some men from the ninth battalion."

The noise of the crowd was immense with expectation as the game started.

Deneesa leaned over. "You didn't embarrass *her*, but you embarrassed all of us Clayhills! How do you think my husband, the real general, feels about that stupid chant?"

Yonnis immediately apologized, but Deneesa flicked her hand to dismiss it.

"You are always sorry, Duke Yonnis."

Esta wondered why Deneesa sounded even more bitter than usual. Then she felt the sad eye of Squire Clayhills fix upon them, and turned to watch the game.

The Groundball Arena, Victory Park. Early evening. The twenty-seventh day of the Seventh Moon, Year Fifty.

AFTER THE PRESENTATION of the trophies for the sporting events, which were wooden tankards carved in the new craft sheds in the east of the city, Yoshi beamed at the crowd, raised his hands, and started to speak.

"Citizens, brothers, sisters, I hope that you have enjoyed yourselves this afternoon. It's been a wonderful day to celebrate the new Republic of Kimalloa."

The cheering lasted several moments before he could continue.

"Our scriptures urge us to learn and to work, but from time to time, wholesome recreation is justified."

More cheering. It was gratifying to have their approval, but were they going to cheer every sentence? This speech might take longer than he expected.

"Now, please indulge me for a few moments. I know that we reflected this morning on the war and all that we lost, but I want to remind you of all the peace-building we have achieved so far."

Yoshi went on to list several reconstruction projects. Each was cheered in turn, and many of the crowd were now holding clenched fists high in salute.

"I want to thank you, the people of Kimalloa, for all that you have sacrificed to make this happen. The war years were hard for all of us. We fought long and hard for the promise of a better future. We will have a better future."

The crowd roared in agreement and waved their hands and hats.

"It will take time, but we are building the foundations, and they will be sound. The Eternal Spirit has blessed us with a good summer so far, so if we take care of the harvest, we should manage through the winter and forge forward again next spring."

He paused. As he did so, cries of "Spirit bless you, Father!" were yelled from the crowd.

Yoshi was starting to feel lightheaded with the power that the crowd was pouring on him. He must stay humble. He looked around him at a sea of people. So many, from rich and poor and everything inbetween, had come together today in a special way. He had always longed for this, a Kimalloa of harmony and opportunity. His emotional rapture came through as he concluded his speech. "May the Eternal Spirit inspire and bless us all and our beloved Kimalloa, brothers and sisters! Go in peace to your homes."

As the crowd started to disperse, Yoshi found himself enveloped in a congratulatory hug from Yonnis. Almost instantly, Arlo's hand was on Yonnis's shoulder, pulling him away.

11

The quayside, Nasrin. Sunset. The twenty-seventh day
of the Seventh Moon, Year Fifty.

"A IN'T IT LOVELY how pink the sky is?" Mistress Oona
remarked.

"It's lovely, but it ain't as lovely as your sweet face, Mistress
Oona." Seemo was feeling bold. His landlady had been so full
of pride when she saw him shake the hand of the Father of the
People when the petition was presented. Surely, she now thought
him worthy of some affection.

"Seemo Shepherd! If you wasn't one-legged, I'd kick you for
yer forwardness!"

"Dear Mistress Oona, I mean it. You are the light of my life. I
know that I'm no great prospect as a provider, but have I any hope?"

She hesitated to reply, and looked away from him. Seemo's
heart sank. They were walking back to their humble huts from
the Victory Park celebrations. Little Pollo lagged some way
behind, looking at every boat and ship, and what the sailors and
porters were doing. Hundreds of citizens were milling around,
looking for places to eat or drink, or just to sit and watch the
sunset. Seemo was just about to press Mistress Oona for an
answer when a well-dressed woman, possibly the wife of a clerk,
approached her.

"May I ask, sister, where did you get that veil?"

"I made it myself, sister."

"Where did you get that color cloth? It's so unusual—sort of… mottled."

"I made the dye myself, sister."

"Oh. Well. May I admire your skill?! It looks very nice."

"Thank you, sister. May the Spirit bless you."

"You too, sister."

Mistress Oona turned to Seemo. "That's about the twentieth lady who's asked me about the veil. I could've sold it so many times. Then I wouldn't have to worry about money."

"Could you make the dye again?"

"No one could make two the same of this. It took a lot of time. I had to dye it pink, but messy pink, not a single tone, and then dye it blue to get the purple. It's not a true purple, of course—"

"You've *invented* something! Clever lady!"

Mistress Oona laughed. "Not really. I got the idea from the Bankside laundry gossip 'bout the Glantar woman's wedding dress changing from white to pink to a blue that was a bit purple."

"And I thought we were done with fashion nonsense. But if ladies would buy it…"

"So what? I can't stop working for Ol' Karna to make veils. Not without a husband to keep me."

Seemo's heart now lurched down to his boot. From his despair, an idea bloomed. "I'm going to ask Illio. He might give us a loan."

"What's this 'us'?" Mistress Oona sounded quite aggressive.

She looked up and down at Seemo, frowning. He wondered what she saw. A cripple who couldn't do any decent laboring job? A shabby green coat? But his shiny brown head was clean, his eyes were bright, and his heart was true. Suddenly, she leaned towards him and kissed his cheek. His emotions soared so much that he nearly fell over in surprise.

"Mistress Oona," he wailed. "You can't do that in public!"

"I just did. Did you like it, or are you going to denounce me?"

"Of course I liked it!"

"Hmm…" Mistress Oona huffed. "Well, let's see how things go, ol' soldier. Elder Yerandal's urgin' me to marry again. I dare say I could do a lot better than you if I tried hard enough… but I could make an awful mistake and do a lot worse. Mebbe the Elder could find a loan for 'us.'"

Seemo's arms had been getting very tired after a long day swinging about on his crutches from the procession to the tournament and back. He now had the strange sensation that his arms were wings, and he was gliding on a warm breeze, wrapped in the pink sky.

The garden of the Pozarian Embassy, Nasrin. Sunset. The twenty-seventh day of the Seventh Moon, Year Fifty.

RUBIN ALDOR SAT in Onfri's beautiful garden, where red roses were blooming and the fruit on the trees was ripening. It was a perfect evening for watching the sunset cascading a red-and-pink radiance across the sky, promising more warmth tomorrow. Instead of thanking the weather gods, he felt like chiding them. They had given the god-killers a glorious day. Up and down Kimalloa, people would remember in years to come what a good time they had at the first Victory Festival.

Rubin and Onfri raised their wine glasses.

"To what, Onfri? What can we drink to? One pathetic trick with an old woman! That was all we could muster to spoil their show of dominance."

"Small symbols it will have to be—for now—and you can thank Sitra that there was even that. Twenty-seven of our loyalists were arrested in Nasrin alone last night. Let's drink to the future, Rubin. Our time will come."

Rubin drank some wine. It tasted as soft as velvet. "Yes. I believe there's hope. They sat me almost on Clayhills' lap at the groundball—to deter assassins, I suppose—but it gave me a close-up view of their reactions. The new general and his old wife were furious about the crowd chanting for the Yerallan. That was very amusing! They're falling out with each other so soon."

Onfri smiled. "Therein lies our salvation, Rubin. Power corrupts and power divides. There'll be jealousies and there'll be factions. We should do what we can to drive wedges between the god-killer elite."

"Well, you're the expert on that. Do your utmost. I can't help thinking that we'll have to wait for a catastrophe, like a great plague. Even so, we are divided and weak. The Lords of the North won't follow Esta, even if she declares for our faith." Rubin took another mouthful of the gorgeous Pozarian wine. "Poor Esta. She admired Nolli's uncovered hair, you know—she must long to show off her lustrous curls. I'm going to donate a new craft shed or three in some godforsaken villages of inbreds on the fens—for *our* veterans—and invite the gracious Lord Arbiter and his wife to visit them. Then I might know more about who she is now."

"They will be overwhelmed by your generosity, I'm sure. But don't get her hopes up. King Rolan has had a gutful of Kimalloa—"

A scream of agony escaped from an upstairs window.

Onfri's face opened wide in anguish. "Blessed Lord Sudar, the child's coming early. We must fetch a Healing Elder or they'll accuse us of neglecting her."

"She needs your Raia!" Rubin had heard the howls of childbirth before. Somehow, this one was different.

Fifteen moments later, Elder Yersil arrived to find the ambassador's Raia muttering incantations over a stillborn baby and Lady Aldor dead on a mattress drenched in her blood.

There was nothing he could have done to save them. Rubin was on his knees, shaking with shock and begging Yersil for a Sudarite burial. Yersil took pity on him, and put his hand on Rubin's shoulder.

"Your Grace, I know that you heard your wife's anguish, but she must have very soon slipped into unconsciousness and I'm sure that she died peacefully. I'll go and ask Squire Tallier about the burial."

When Yersil left, Onfri gazed with curiosity at Rubin. "That was a fine performance, Your Grace."

Rubin got to his feet and, although there was not much power in his fist as he was still shaking, he punched his friend. "How dare you? I've lost a good wife—and a child!" Then he turned in fury on the Raia. "And you, Raia, explain why Afra has done this to me!"

The young Pozarian Raia took a great personal risk, and replied, "Your Grace, Afra sends you comfort for your loss, but reminds you of your surrender to the god-killers."

Rubin snarled back at her. "Oh, so the gods have to keep punishing me?! Poor Nolli. Caught in the crossfire between the gods and a coward. Well, I love my family, my household, my regiment, and my region like a good lord should, and we'd all have been obliterated if I hadn't surrendered. We live to sustain our faith and fight another day. If the gods have forsaken me, so be it—but, Raia, ask Sudar to find some pity for my sons!"

Clayhills Place, New Temple Street, Nasrin. Early morning. The twenty-eighth day of the Seventh Moon, Year Fifty.

As YONNIS WAS about to knock, the door of the Clayhills' earthy home opened.

"Yes, sir?" The footman looked at him expectantly.

"May I see General Clayhills?"

"Alas, no, sir, he may not be disturbed."

"May I see Mistress Clayhills?"

"She is with him, sir."

Yonnis wondered if the footman was telling him that they were still in bed and enjoying the comforts of married life. He smiled. "Please tell them that I called."

"Of course, sir."

The footman bowed and slowly closed the door on Yonnis, who turned and walked towards the gate. And who should be at the gate, but Lord Ulfan?

Yonnis tried to exude bonhomie. "Your Grace! What a pleasant surprise to meet you. May I thank you again for the loan of your lodge in the north for my summer break? I have not seen much of the north, since my campaigns were mostly south of Lady Charity's region."

"Ye're welcome, Lord Arbiter."

Ulfan looked conciliatory, but swept past him and up the drive. He had been so keen to offer his lodge when he overheard Yonnis reminiscing about swimming. Why was that? A peace offering? Yonnis did not want to be so obvious as to watch him and see if he was admitted to the house, but as his guard closed the gate behind him, he glanced back. Ulfan was hastily ushered in. At the corner of the street, Yonnis saw Squire Tallier's carriage. It was so dusty, as if it had been on a long journey. It stopped, and Squire Tallier called to him out of the window.

"I'm so glad that I've seen you, Yonnis. Please would you go straight to the Pozarian Embassy and give our condolences to Lord Aldor? Alas, his poor wife died last night."

"Of course, sir." Yonnis nodded and bowed. So, he was the diplomatic errand boy while there was an important meeting going on. Yonnis felt a quiver of disquiet pass through his gut.

Clayhills Place, New Temple Street, Nasrin. Early morning. The twenty-eighth day of the Seventh Moon, Year Fifty.

ALL-EARS STAMPED HIS boots on the rush mat before he entered, to clean them and to let off some frustration. "Well, that was close. I've sent him off to Onfri, but he'd noticed that he had been denied entry and Ulfan had not."

"Well, what's he going to do about it?" Arlo growled. "It's up to us who we let into our home."

"Come and sit down, Squire Tallier." Deneesa escorted him to a well-padded settle.

"Ah, Mistress Clayhills, how kind you are!"

Lord Ulfan was already calling for his beer to be filled up. "Before we start on the long piece of paper—"

Yoshi Clayhills cut in with uncharacteristic annoyance. "It is not just a long piece of paper, Lord Ulfan! 22,344 citizens of this country put their name to a request to their government. It is a petition! We have a duty to treat it with respect."

"A duty laid out in the scriptures, Lord Ulfan," Arch-Elder Yeramo added.

"My apologies, brethren," Ulfan conceded. "But before we discuss the petition, and I know that was the main point of our gathering, can Squire Tallier enlighten us about the 'miracle' of the old woman's healing arms?"

"Don't trouble yourself with a simple herbal trick! I have grave news from Kallo. The steward's wife has made some preposterous claims about the parentage of her son."

"Hmm." Ulfan nodded. "And you believe them?"

All-Ears bristled with discomfort. She had been tortured. She was having delusions. But how could she make up something so bizarre? "No. But if she could utter them, others must believe them. The steward and the boy have crossed from

160

the Edgelands to the Greenlands. It's possible that they're going to seek protection from Lord Fergan."

Deneesa sighed, and All-Ears felt pity for her. Fergan was a rabid Sudarite, but he was still her younger brother. "What are these claims? Why would he bother with them?" she asked.

All-Ears spoke carefully. "You remember the Princess Anna-Louisa, supposedly dead from the sweating sickness about fourteen years ago?"

"A baby? Oh, how convenient for him to be found now."

"Dear Deneesa, your brother will be as skeptical as we are. He will have them interrogated for weeks. Even if he believed the boy to be hers, he can't be an heir if she had been violated…" Yoshi suggested, sounding hopeful.

"And who do you think protected this child all these years, if he were flawed?" All-Ears asked.

"Please stop the guessing games, dear Squire Tallier. Who do you think did so?" Deneesa stood up and starting to pace.

"We know what Navvan's urges were. What if *he* 'forced a promise' on his thirteen-year-old sister?"

The room went quiet for several moments.

"The veterans will soon drop their pens if Fergan kicks off." Arlo declared. "Perhaps it's in our interests to provoke the Sudos."

The quarters of the Arbiter, Bankside Place, Nasrin. Early evening. The twenty-eighth day of the Seventh Moon, Year Fifty.

YONNIS AND NESSI had got caught in a cloudburst. They arrived home soaking wet. He dropped his gown and hugged and kissed Esta. She noticed that the damp had penetrated to his doublet and breeches. He was just going to sit on the settle, smelling of wet wool. It was one of the many strange things that he did. She called Footman Kushno to light a fire and bring warm ale.

Yonnis started pontificating as soon as he sat down. "I think that I need to do some research on the route of the north–south canal when we take our break there. Every time they check expenditure it is clear that it is escalating beyond what had been planned. But no one has built a canal like this before, through this particular terrain, in these weather conditions, with unskilled men. Of course it is going to have problems, but it must continue until it is finished. It is prevarication that is costly with such a project!"

What kind of destiny was it, to have to care about digging a canal? Was that what government was all about?

The bell for reflection rang. Yonnis jumped to his feet. Esta rose too, grumbling inwardly about the relentless calls to think. She let Yonnis do the praying.

"Eternal Spirit, shine light into our darkness. Let us discover more ways to improve our world…"

After the reflection finished, she said, "A big ball thing arrived today. Can you explain it to me?"

"Aha!" Yonnis jumped up with delight and went to spin the globe. "This is a present for you, as you said you would like a bit of color in our apartments. This is a model of our planet. Our whole planet! Well, what we know of it. Look at all this beautiful blue sea! You may have seen maps before, but this globe puts us in our place." Yonnis pointed out a large mass of white, brown, and green. "We are so small compared to this at the top. This is Osiran, which is where my grandmother Grand Duchess Kirina is regent for the Emperor."

"Why did your grandfather marry an Osiranian? I thought Yerallans hated them?"

"It was a marriage to try to stop that hate, to ensure peace. It is still working. We tolerate each other rather well these days." Yonnis started to quickly spin the globe, and gazed at an area where blue blobs of water spattered a large green reach of land, with brown smudges of mountains in the north. He pointed. "Here is my homeland. Sometimes, Esta, I miss it. Not so much now. It was worst when I heard, several months after it happened, that my uncle had died. I was on campaign in the Middlelands. I did not even have time to grieve for him."

"I can't understand how you could suppress it. I was devastated when my father died. I knelt at the foot of his coffin howling with grief while horrible men like Navvan mocked me by bowing and calling me 'Your Majesty' when they had no intention of respecting me as queen." Esta let a few tears of bitterness escape.

Yonnis held her and kissed her. "I cannot imagine how hard it was for you at such a young age to have your world tumble down. It must have been so frightening." Yonnis stroked her hair. "I am so sorry, Esta." Nervously, he twirled the globe, and then stopped it and focused on her. "Well, let us leave geography for another time. I think that it brings sadness to both of us. I know what you have now, with me, is not what you dreamed about as a child. I had losses too, Esta. Life is hard, and difficult to understand. Let us just enjoy what we can."

Esta nodded. She clung to him and the smell of wet wool. Her mind wandered. Surely, she was still destined to be queen. It had been ordained at her birth by the Raas that she would sit on a throne. Onfri had told her to wait. How long? The old woman at Victory Day had been a sign. What should she be doing to prepare? Pia had been telling her stories about a great queen of the Glantar dynasty, Anna-Afra, who sacrificed her own right to rule to support her infant son. Oh, she must find out more about being a regent. Perhaps those who thought of her as a silly, spoilt girl would change their minds if she were a mother of a healthy baby boy. Yerallans were a robust people with all their swimming and rowing, hunting and fishing and fighting. So perhaps Yonnis had been sent by the gods to help her? The gods work in mysterious ways...

She started to kiss Yonnis gently, and pressed herself against him. Of course, he responded.

"Dear husband!" she gasped. "Please forgive my urgency. I would like some time with you in your chamber before supper!"

"Dear wife! I forgive you!" His blue eyes opened wide with joyful anticipation. "Let's hasten to my chamber. I need to get out of these wet clothes—*very soon!*"

The Main Square, Sakarias, Central Osiran. Late afternoon. The second day of the Eighth Moon, Year Fifty.

GRAND DUCHESS KIRINA sat by the grand coffin of her younger brother and shed tears. Death comes to us all. She knew well enough that in his last few years, her precious Zanda had been tired of life, and frightened by it. The gods of the afterlife had finally reached out their mercy to him, but she was going to miss him—so much.

The heavy coffin was carved from the blackest wood, lined with white silk embroidered with silver thread. Emperor Zandalian IV, embalmed, wrapped tightly in linen and dressed in his military uniform, lay within it, under a lid of leaded glass. The priests of the underworld had done their best to paint the death mask as he had been in his prime.

Kirina traced her fingers over the carving on the coffin of her brother as a young boy, with her, and their mother and father, under the arch of the capital city. She would remember him so throughout this marathon journey. It was as well that it was long. She needed time to think. Young Ikra was listless and withdrawn. Kirina wondered—was he mourning his grandfather, who had not recognized him for three years, or was he mourning his loss of freedom as he transitioned from Crown Prince to Emperor?

"Come, Your Majesty," she said. "Let your people see you. Just a glimpse."

The massive gold carriage carrying the coffin, pulled by eight white horses, had stopped in the town square of Sakarias. The coffin was propped up, so that the late emperor could be seen. The local duke had corralled all of his serfs into the town to welcome the funeral procession. The smell of roasting sacrificial oxen and deer for the public feast to honor the old and new emperors was hanging heavy in the air. The haunting voices of priests and priestesses were singing the praises of their dead ruler, and blessing the new one.

Kirina and Ikra, two short figures in black, handed purse after purse from the windows of their carriage to cavalrymen who rode out into the crowds, throwing small copper coins and yelling, "Hail, Ancestor Zandalian! Hail, Blessed Kirina! Hail, Emperor Ikra!"

The serfs rushed to catch what they could, and shouted, "Hail, Ancestor Zandalian! Hail, Blessed Kirina! Hail, Emperor Ikra!" in reply.

Kirina had planned this great journey, town by town, from the southwest to the great cave in the northwest where emperors made their final journey into the underworld. It would serve to settle the Osiranian nobles. They had bad habits, like jostling for favor and plotting for revenge when there was a change of emperor. So long as they could see that Kirina was the constant, and they were reminded that she had goddess-like status with the poor wretches whose endless toil kept their lazy aristocratic hindquarters covered in fur, Ikra was safe. Oh, how Kirina needed to eke out a few more years of life, despite the pain in her hips and her hands, her failing eyes and ears. If she could see Ikra to twenty, with some healthy sons and good advisers, she could join her brother Zanda and they could play again in the lush gardens of Larriklias. Of course, Ikra might make his own crazy decisions, like Yonnis. Children, grandchildren, great-nephews... they were like naive opponents in a board game, wanting to make bold moves. But Kirina was experienced enough to get the game back on her terms, eventually.

She held out both hands, lowering and raising them, to encourage the crowd to cheer louder. Listening to this in every town on the long journey would surely strengthen her magic.

The lake at the hunting lodge of Lord Ulfan, in Grannit in the Northeast Region of Kimalloa. Midmorning. The third day of the Eighth Moon, Year Fifty.

YONNIS CARVED SMOOTHLY through the water, stroke by stroke. Fed by an awesome waterfall that cascaded tunefully down twenty strides of rock, Ulfan's lake was cool and clear, and Yonnis relished being immersed in it. The hazy heat of the summer sun was reaching its peak. As he reached the shallows, he bobbed up and threw water at Esta, who was sitting naked on the bank where they had nuzzled each other and the buttercups.

"Stop it!"

"Esta! Please come into the water and let me teach you how to swim. It worries me that you don't know how to. We use the Binar wherries often—what would you do if one capsized?"

"The wherrymen know what they are doing. Or you would save me. Anyway, sailors don't learn to swim—they say that it is better to drown quickly than to struggle against the water and drown slowly."

"Ha! No one has come back from the dead to confirm that. Anyway, Kimalloan sailors may say what they like, but Yerallan sailors, being men of reason, know that most shipwrecks happen near to shore, where those who can swim have a chance to make it to land and live."

"Husband, you have an answer for everything."

"Yes, I do." Yonnis smiled, allowing himself a moment of self-congratulation. "I can see that you are hot. So, you could at least come into the water and cool down."

Staring at him defiantly, Esta strode into the water. She

stumbled, shrieking as she plunged into the soft shingle of the shallows. Yonnis quickly picked her up and held her up. He urged her gently into a position where she was lying on her back in the water and his arms were doing very little work.

"Even if you could just float in the water, that would enable others to rescue you. Just relax and let the water push you up." Just as he thought that he was making progress with the swimming lesson, Yonnis caught a movement out of the corner of his eye, and as quickly as he caught it, he pushed Esta behind a rock, whispering urgently, "Hang on and stay low!" Then he plunged back out into the water, blood pumping in his temples, yelling at the bushes, "Hey! Show yourself!" They were completely vulnerable, but an assassin with a pistol had one chance, possibly two, and if he were hurried, he might miss.

Two children stepped sheepishly out from the bushes. A boy with a crude fishing rod, and a smaller girl with a bucket.

Yonnis was so relieved. He wanted to laugh, but he had to be stern. "Now, children, you know that you can't fish here. You are on Lord Ulfan's property."

"Are ya a water sprite?" the little girl asked.

Yonnis shook his head. "I am a guest of Lord Ulfan. I am here by invitation, and you are not. You should go back to your village before the guards catch you."

"Can't go back without a fish," the girl explained. "Mam's got nothin'."

"Wait, then," Yonnis ordered. He plunged back into the water. The ripples started to settle where he had plunged. After a moment, he made a furious splash near the bushes where the children waited. They jumped back. Yonnis stood waist-deep, clutching a large, squirming fish, which he threw onto the bank. "Take it as my gift and go. May the Eternal Spirit bless you and your family."

The wide-eyed children nodded and scrabbled the fish into their bucket. Then they ran off, giggling.

Yonnis swam back to Esta, who was peeking over the rock, gasping and gabbling.

"I was so frightened—I thought we were going to die—and then it was just little children—and then you disappeared in the water—and I was frightened again—and then that fish—that fish! Yonnis, how did you do it? Magic?"

"Tut! Esta, I do not do magic! I have skills. The son of a Yerallan duke never knows when he is going to have to feed himself."

"Skills. So you say. It looked like magic."

Yonnis did not correct her again, but he had a flickering worry that she still believed in things that she claimed to have left behind.

The Great Hall of Lord Lazzar of the Northeast Region of Kimalloa. Early evening. The tenth day of the Eighth Moon, Year Fifty.

ESTA TREMBLED, AND could barely stop herself whimpering. Four men to the right of Lord Lazzar, and four men to the left of him, were aiming pistols at them. Her eyes were drawn to the muzzles of the guns. All she could see was black circles in gray metal, pulling her in. The black circles were getting bigger and bigger, pools of nothingness that she might fall into. How did they keep their arms so still for so long, with such heavy guns? Well, if she must die, at least it would be quick. Why would Lazzar do this? She remembered him from court—way back when she was five years old. He'd bowed and said, "Your Highness." She'd put her arms up to him and commanded, "Take me to Papa!" He had. And now he was pointing guns at her. Was it because he thought that she had betrayed their faith?

Yonnis strode forward, swept off his hat, and bowed deeply. "Your Grace." He made no mention of the gunmen, and he was not looking at them. He looked straight at Lord Lazzar, a large man dressed in red and yellow, with long dark braids and a waxed beard, standing on the platform in his hall.

The Lord of the Northeast did not smile, and he did not return any greeting. Eventually, he growled at Yonnis, "You have no idea how much I would like to murder you and kidnap your wife!" Lord Lazzar drew his sword, and held it high, ready to cleave Yonnis's head.

Esta was suddenly jolted away from the guns to look at the big blade glinting in the sun streaming through the windows. "No!" The word blew itself through her lips, and then floated on the air like a leaf. Where did it come from? Was it from Afra? Lazzar was now staring at her. Kidnap, he had said—*kidnap*! He just wanted to control her, like everyone else! Esta dug deep for a bit of queenly dignity. "Please don't do that, my lord. If you ever loved my father, please let us be. We came here at your invitation, to honor you."

"Honor me?!" Lazzar looked like thunder, but he sheathed his sword, and he did bow. "Princess Esta. Forgive my manners. I did love your father. It's an abomination that you have been forced into this sham coupling. Let me get rid of this unworthy husband for you and spirit you across the sea to Pozaria so you can bring us back a real king of the true faith."

Oh dear. Her head started to pound. He was offering what Esta had dreamed of, so many times, when she looked out along the black water surrounding Whiteleaf Castle. She hesitated. What did she want? Could she bear the consequences? She tried to cover up her indecision by turning to gaze in wifely devotion at Yonnis. He had noticed the hesitation, and his eyes were full of sadness. She looked back at the angry eyes of Lazzar. "Please don't do that, my lord," Esta replied. "There would be terrible reprisals on your family and your people—they have already suffered—"

"Oh, Your Highness!" Lazzar laughed. "You show yourself as your mother's daughter rather than your father's, to care about families and poor folk! Well, shall we talk about the piles of burnt cinders where there were villages? And the desperate women and old men trying to till the land? And the new orphanages full of copper-haired infants? Ulfan's savages did all that in the name of the Doctrine of Truth."

"I am sorry to hear that. Very sorry," said Yonnis.

"Sorry? My Lord Arbiter? Sorry? Yes, we have heard about your penitence in the north. And we had a good laugh about it! 'Sorry' does not help a region that has been harried into destitution!"

"I am willing to listen, Your Grace."

"But you might want me to listen to you in return, and I couldn't stomach that!" Lord Lazzar paused. He turned to Esta. "Your Highness. Out of love for your father, I will let you go, but be assured he will be fuming like a volcano in the Dome of the Divine to see you shackled to this… creature." He waved his hand at Yonnis. "You seem to be pleading for him. Are you sure?"

Esta felt drawn into the muzzles of the guns again. She nodded nervously.

Lazzar laughed at her again. "I'm sorry to say it, Your Highness, but Navvan was right—you would have been a useless ruler. There's not a sliver of ruthlessness in you. Well, you may go. Apart from your weakness, which you are asking me to indulge, there's whispers that Ulfan would be pleased if harm came to the Arbiter, so—much as it sticks in my gut—it suits me to let him live."

Esta practiced a blank face. Behind it, she was brimming with disgust at Lazzar's sneering. No wonder he had supported her burly, brutal uncle. All men like him wanted was to be in the gang of the biggest belligerent.

Lazzar sat down and shouted at them. "So—off you go! I lied about supper. I just wanted to see the whites of your eyes. There's a place in the next town run by your lot if you want to eat safely. Just do your sanctimonious observation and reflection while you are in this region, Lord Arbiter. Then push off back to Nasrin and tell them we need more money spent up here."

"Your Grace, I promise you that I will observe, and reflect, and report. I am committed to the rebuilding of Kimalloa—all of its regions. Perhaps you could suggest where I should observe?"

Yonnis's polite persistence was received with an ironic smile.

"I'll send you a list. Now fuck off." He turned to Esta and bowed. "Pardon my language, your Highness."

Eight pistols remained trained on Yonnis and Esta as they left the hall.

As they got back into their carriage, Yonnis praised Esta. "Well done, my darling! You spoke so well."

Esta was now trembling visibly, and he put his arms around her.

"What *was* that? In there?" Esta found some energy to be indignant.

"If you will excuse my soldier's language, that was Lord Lazzar waving his cock around."

"So, it was just some kind of... gesture?"

"Surely, it was. He didn't kill us, and he did agree to list his grievances."

"Were you confident that he wouldn't kill us?"

"I confess that I did not expect such hostility, particularly not with you at my side."

"Well, he didn't show *me* much deference." Esta reflected with bemusement—how sheltered her life had been!

"Did you want to take his offer? To go to Pozaria?" Yonnis's voice was edged with anguish.

"I would not leave you to be tortured to death by him." Esta realized that her answer begged more questions. She looked at Yonnis, who opened his mouth to speak and then shut it. Of course he was going to let her off the hook. He had heard what she assumed that he had wanted to hear. "I would not leave you."

She sighed inwardly as Yonnis suddenly switched from gentle accusation to humility.

"Oh, Esta! I am sorry! I am so ungrateful! You saved my life, and I am quibbling. You have a beautiful soul, and I love you. Thank you, thank you!" Yonnis grasped her hands and kissed them. "It's starting to work, Esta. Our partnership. Do you feel it as I do? We are going to heal Kimalloa!"

12

Office of the Intelligence Minister, the Archive, Bankside, Nasrin. Late evening. The ninth day of the Tenth Moon, Year Fifty.

ARLO KNEW THAT he was a good general for peacetime. Planning the defense of ports, naval patrols, training maneuvers, and the rebuilding of forts inland—it all suited him. But he was itching to flex his muscles with some kind of action.

"I think that the army should break up the next Distributor meeting. The people of Kimalloa need to be protected from anarchy."

He noted with annoyance that his announcement caused flickers of concern on the faces of his father and Squire Tallier. It was late in the evening and the sun had set. Squire Tallier had piled up the coal on his fire. Arlo sat in a hard, uncomfortable chair as far back from the fire as he could be while still leaning into the conversation. He would have preferred to pace the room, because he felt agitated, but as a tall man, there was barely room for him to stand.

"The scriptures are clear, Arlo," his father replied. "We must allow protest. We must answer it with logic."

"Father, we've said that we'll give them some of what they want," Arlo argued. "The only purpose for further meetings must be to cause trouble." Was there nothing he could say to shake these old men from their complacency? "We need a show of force to disperse them before that ludicrous Seemo stirs them up." Arlo slapped the arms of his chair.

His father tried to defend the veterans. "These were our men just a few months ago—"

"And we might need them again if there is trouble in the Greenlands... " Tallier warned.

Arlo snorted in derision. "Agh—send Yonnis up there to woo the Raas! He seems to be sticking his nose into quite a lot of things."

"He has a prior engagement. He has offered to explain our compromise to the Distributors." Squire Tallier seemed content with that.

Arlo laughed. "I'm sure that a lecture from him will make all the difference! Well, let's see what happens at Mersin. If they tear him limb from limb, let's hope that the militia can pick up the pieces."

Arlo rose to leave as Squire Tallier pronounced the last words of their discussion.

"Hmm. 'Esta the grieving widow' is a spectacle that I don't want to contemplate."

Arlo bade a respectful farewell to Squire Tallier and his father, and daydreamed all the way back to his command post in Bankside. Impure calculations were rushing into his mind. Deneesa was carrying his child. She was old. Anything could go wrong, as it had with Lady Aldor. And Yonnis was courting assassination again and again...

A barn outside Mersin, Southeastern Region, Kimalloa.
Early afternoon. The twentieth day of the Tenth Moon,
Year Fifty.

THE BARN NEAR Mersin was full of hay and straw, so the Distributors met outside. The enterprising farmer had erected some makeshift canopies, but it was an exposed spot, and the men were warmed only by their collective breath. It was the afternoon of a reflection day. The sky was heavy with gray clouds but, mercifully, it was dry. Yonnis had walked out to the barn with his dog, but no guards. He had told Squire Clayhills that he would defend the new voting arrangements to the veterans. After all, the purpose of an Arbiter was to arbitrate where there were entrenched views. The Assembly had debated the Distributors' petition long and hard. They had come up with a compromise, but the lords in the Senate had blocked it. Controversially, as it was the first time he had to do so, Yonnis the Arbiter made a ruling. He decided, with no hesitation, in favor of the Assembly compromise.

Yonnis was soon recognized and introduced to Seemo, who shook his hand and then shouted to the crowd, "We are honored, comrades. The Arbiter has come to explain to us what has been decided in Victory Park."

The men stood, arms folded, looking defiantly at their former hero as he climbed up onto the barrels and boards that passed for a stage. In the war, to taunt their opponents, the men had chanted, "Under General Yonnis, we are the Army of Truth. We've never lost a battle—hey, hey, hey, how about you?" or even just "Whoa! General Yonnis!" when they wanted to praise him after a successful day. He was getting no cheers today.

"Comrades," Yonnis started. "May I call you that?" It was more of a challenge than a question.

Some men spat on the ground and growled. One shouted, "You're no comrade of ours!"

Yonnis continued confidently. "That's not how I remember it. I slept under the same canvas as you, and I remember the smell of mold because our shelters never dried out." He allowed a small pause for the men in the crowd to remember the smell. "I ate the same food as you—slurping soup made from some sort of vegetables, chewing hard biscuits and dried eel. The chewing

175

helped us to think that we were not still hungry." He paused again for the men to remember the bland tastes, the feeling of eating but not feeling full. "I pissed and shat in the same holes in the ground as you."

At this point, there was a ripple of laughter. Yonnis judged that it was time to get more serious.

"I comforted the wounded, and prayed with you for the friends that we lost."

The mood changed again, as the men remembered their lost friends.

"And I was in the thick of battle with you. I never asked you to do anything that I was not prepared to do. I fought as hard as you did for our cause. So I think I *do* have a right to be considered your comrade."

The crowd grunted in acceptance.

Yonnis continued. "You went through great suffering to gain freedom."

"Aye, we did."

"You have that, comrades—you do *have* freedom. Just imagine if, five years ago, you had wanted to come together at a meeting and demand something from King Navvan. What would have happened?"

He waited. No one replied.

"You do know what would have happened! His soldiers would have opened fire on you, slashed at you, chased you back to your villages, and burnt your houses, whipped you, or maimed you, raped your wives and daughters—they might even have fed your children to their dogs in front of you." He paused. "Is that not so? Have you forgotten what it was like before the war?!"

The men muttered and shuffled.

"Now, thanks to our victory, you are free to speak, you are free to meet. You can petition the caretakers of the country. That is what we do in the great talking tent in Victory Park—we are taking care of Kimalloa. You have brought your demands to the

Assembly. The Assembly has debated them, and has made some provisions. That is how the Doctrine of Truth works. Nobody's whim or vanity drives policy."

Yonnis reminded them of the rebuilding of the country and the creation of jobs. He had memorized a long list of projects in Nasrin and the surrounding counties that these men would know. Some might even be working in them. Each one drew a murmur of approval from somewhere in the crowd.

Yonnis then paused and paced. "Let's think of some more good news. Oh, our wounded and widows have pensions! The first casualties of war in Kimalloa ever to have pensions!"

There was a muted cheer of acknowledgment for the pensions. Now Yonnis would explain what the latest law had given them.

"Oh, and I take it that you have heard that all Army of Truth veterans, whether they have land or not, provided that they can present a letter of identity from their Elder, veterans... now... have... the... vote. This is revolutionary for Kimalloa, comrades, and for the whole world. It is progress. You have made your point, and you have your votes."

Enthusiastic cheering broke out.

"So, when the election comes in the spring, you can decide who you want to represent you. So why are you still discontented?"

Yonnis did not have long to wait for the obvious, and expected, reply.

"Land! We asked for land!"

"Comrades, we are human. Equal in our potential for eternal peace with the Spirit, but on earth we have different drives, different luck, different outcomes, deserved and undeserved. It is hard to work the land. What do you do, as a family with a smallholding, when the crop fails? You have choices now, comrades. You can stay in your village and work on a farm. Or you can go to a craft shed and learn a trade. You can build roads and canals and buildings. You can work in mines or quarries. There are loans if you want to set up a business. But the land that was owned by your commanders is still owned by your commanders. You will gain nothing by impoverishing the men who have empowered you. They will manage the farms like they managed their regiments, and they will pay you a fair wage for hard work. And the land that was owned by the Raas, that now belongs to hospitals and orphanages, and they need land to feed the sick and the orphans—surely that is fair? But you can work on those farms too. The Elders will not cheat you."

Yonnis pressed on. "If you still want to own land, there is some land on offer. But where do you think that the King had land? It was land that he could not gift to his cronies—sandy scrubland, moorland, salt flats and bogs. Only the scrawniest of sheep can graze there. But if you truly want your own land, you can try it. And by the way, if you take some land, you have to pay your taxes."

The crowd laughed at the idea of any of them being rich enough to pay taxes.

"Truly, comrades, we are making progress. But each man has to find his own way forward. You had no choice five years ago— you were *owned*. Now you have choices. That is the freedom that you fought for."

Yonnis paused. The crowd was quiet. He wondered what they had expected. They had never been promised land. The promise had been freedom.

One man forced himself to the front, quivering with fury. "You've sold us down the river, you damned foreigner with your damned whore Glantar wife!"

Yonnis so wanted to kill this man with his bare hands. He could certainly deliver a serious injury. A blow under his chin, forcing his head to whip up, a punch to his temple... but this was not war. He was Yonnis the peacemaker. So, he squatted down to be nearer to the face that was twisted in anger. From the corner of his eye, he noticed that Nessi's ears were flat against her head and her lips were curling. "I don't think that you learned those foul manners in the Army of Truth! Article Number 26—*No soldier shall use abusive language towards a senior officer. If he does, he will be subject to immediate solitary confinement and punishment as the army court sees fit, up to and including hanging.* Maybe you could have been lucky and got two moons' privy duty."

There were a few ripples of laughter generated by memories of privy duty for misdemeanors, but the mood in the crowd was tense.

Yonnis spoke again. "Bad words are easy, my friend, but it is not the way of men of Truth. Many 'damned foreigners' have made sacrifices for Kimalloa—sacrifices beyond your understanding—and they have as much right to be here as anyone born here. And even if you don't like me, you commit a *heinous* sin to abuse my wife. I haven't met your wife, but I assume that she is a pleasant and dutiful woman. You do the same for mine."

The crowd was cowed. Someone accused of a heinous sin by a neighbor must be marched off to the nearest Elder to account for themselves. Who was going to do it? The man backed off, still snarling like a juvenile wolf who has been warned off the prey by the alpha male. A few men came forward to persuade him to go with them quietly to see an Elder. He was jostled as he was led away from the crowd, with some men shouting, "Blockhead!" at him.

Yonnis stood up, feeling that he had humiliated the hostile man enough to have sustained respect, but still wishing that he had killed him. He quietly called on the Eternal Spirit to bring him back to his senses. That interruption had probably been intended to trick him. There were such players among the Distributors. The heckler might even have been a Sudarite spy. Yonnis distracted the crowd's interest in the removal of the man by speaking again.

"Please, comrades, reflect like the good Followers of the

Truth that you are. Remember that you have freedom, just as your commanders promised you, and you have exercised your freedom to petition, and you now have votes! I pledged myself to win our war, as you did, and we succeeded! Now I have pledged myself to our peace, as you have. Brothers and sisters, go back to your homes to build that glorious peace for your families to enjoy. May the Eternal Spirit bless you."

There was a ripple of applause, and some cheers. It did not sound wholehearted to Yonnis, but it was progress. Yonnis helped Seemo back onto his crutches, and led him from where he had sat listening at the side of the stage to stand at the front.

Cheers greeted Seemo, and the crowd chanted his name. "Seemo! Seemo! Seemo!"

Seemo waited for them to calm down, then cleared his throat to speak as loudly as he could. "Thank you for coming to talk to us, Lord Arbiter. Maybe we'll give these minor concessions some time to work. But this isn't over."

Yonnis nodded to him.

As he strode back into Nasrin, unguarded apart from Nessi, some men and boys ran after him. Yonnis did not fear ambush and he did not turn around. They caught up with him.

"We do understand, sir."

"We know the Assembly has a lot to do."

"We heard you backed us, sir."

"It's not personal 'gainst you, sir."

Then he felt a little tug on his sleeve and looked down to see a drummer boy.

"May I shake your hand, Lord Gen'ral?"

Yonnis offered his hand, which the boy took and shook vigorously. He thought about the awful things that the boys who followed their fathers into war had seen and should not see.

"What is your name?" he asked.

"Pollo, sir," the boy replied. So many boys had been, and were still, named after the sun god.

"I am pleased to meet you, Pollo."

The little troop walked with Yonnis back to the capital, peppering him with questions.

"I served in the Fourth—d'you remember us, sir?"

"Yes, you fought very bravely at Grettin."

"An' what 'bout us—North Middlelanders at Tinmoor?"

"You attacked the enemy's left flank and broke through within a few moments."

"An' us musketeers in the rye fields at Estlorn?"

"Excellent coordination—solid volleys of shot that mowed down the enemy."

Yonnis was grateful for his memory for detail. These men were hungry for recognition.

When they got to the dock area, Yonnis looked for the boy Pollo. He had been feeling a heightened sense of care for children since seeing Arlo's pride that Deneesa was carrying his baby.

"I have to turn off for Bankside now, Pollo. Which man is your father?"

Pollo shook his head. "My pa died at Kallo Mill."

The words landed heavily on Yonnis's ears. "I am sorry for your loss, Pollo. I am sure that your pa is at rest with our Eternal Spirit. Is your mother working?"

Pollo nodded.

"And you?"

Pollo shook his head.

"You should think about an apprenticeship with a cloth merchant." It was the safest trade Yonnis could think of. "If your ma has problems finding one, go to your Elder and he will know how to contact me."

Pollo nodded and whispered, "Thank you, sir."

Yonnis stood up and shouted out to the men who were still milling around. "May the Spirit bless you for accompanying me back to the capital, comrades, but it is time for us to go our separate ways. Before we do, I have a question for you. We passed a soup kitchen, about thirty strides back. Did you notice anything about the men queuing there?"

They shrugged.

Yonnis tutted. "Come now. You are men of Truth. You should be observant. I noticed something about the men in the line. I noticed long hair. It is not your comrades who are destitute. It is the poor wretches who fought on the other side who have drifted into Nasrin looking for work. They were unlucky—born in the wrong place to the wrong serf-owner. Their wounded get no pensions and the fit men get no jobs. Please think about them before you next claim that the Assembly does not give you enough."

The men stared at their shoes.

"Right so, Gen'ral."

"We'll think on."

"Nice to meet ya."

They slunk off. Yonnis watched them for a few moments. A few passed the soup kitchen line again and offered a small coin each to the donation bowl, perhaps hoping that their consciences would be clear next time the bells rang for reflection.

A holding cell at the Bankside Garrison, Nasrin. Early morning. The twenty-first day of the Tenth Moon, Year Fifty.

"GOOD MORNING, GUNNER Kellin." All-Ears stood as tall as he could, but was leaning heavily on his stick. "I am Squire Tallier, the Minister for Intelligence."

Gunner Kellin jumped to attention. "Sir!" He saluted.

All-Ears cast his critical eye over Kellin, who was wearing faded, ragged clothes. It seemed like a clumsy effort to underdress; even a gunner should have better attire for a day off. The man's lined face and baggy red eyes suggested a sleepless night. Then All-Ears looked around the cell. It was as clean as he would have hoped. It was small, but there was room enough for a big man like Kellin. There was some light and ventilation from a grilled gap between the back wall and the ceiling. The cell was cold, but he had rough blankets and a straw mattress. There was a large bucket for the necessary bodily functions.

"You know why you are here, Gunner?"

"Yes, sir."

"What do you have to say for yourself?"

"Yesterday, I was off duty. I attended a veterans' rally near Mersin. I spat and swore at the Arbiter, and I insulted his wife. He accused me of a heinous crime, sir."

All-Ears tutted. "Those are the facts, Kellin. I know the 'what' of your behavior. I want you to explain the 'why'."

"Yes, sir." Kellin looked slightly less confident. Perhaps he was nervous at the prospect of more in-depth questioning.

"We can sort this out amicably, Kellin." All-Ears tried to smile reassuringly, but he knew that his smiles and grimaces could be mixed up. On this occasion, he didn't care if they were. "First of all, as you are a serving soldier, why were you attending a *veterans'* rally?"

There was a pause, and pauses, as far as All-Ears was concerned, generally meant lies. Lines were being remembered, or made up.

"I was there out of interest, sir. I'll be a veteran someday."

All-Ears grunted. "Sooner rather than later, if you don't satisfy me in the next few moments, Kellin. Does 'being there out of interest' urge you to make an intervention that could have caused trouble? Your own comrades in the militia would have had to sort it out, and could have been injured in the process. That's hardly fitting behavior for a soldier in the Army of Truth— one in the Clayhills regiment, no less!"

"Sorry, sir!"

"I'm sure that you have claimed to be sorry! I'm sure that

you repented with the Elder of Mersin, and sent an apology, of sorts, to the Arbiter. Your repentance is not my concern. I want to know why you wanted to stir up the veterans against the Arbiter."

Kellin shrugged, which enraged All-Ears.

"If you think that you are a man of Truth, tell me the truth or I'll have you whipped in front of your comrades and sent back to your village with a brand on your face!" He didn't mean it, but he had to say it.

Kellin was trying to look defiant, but All-Ears also noted lines on his forehead, and eye movements suggesting complete confusion. Kellin was trying to work something out. What was it?

All-Ears calmed down. "Who gave you the words, and who paid you?"

"I wasn't paid, sir! I was obeying orders, as a soldier should. I didn't know that it might offend *you*, sir." Kellin looked utterly miserable.

All-Ears was satisfied that he had an answer. Now, he had to back off. "Well, I commend your loyalty to your commander. You can go back to your barracks now, Kellin—get your uniform on, and go to work. But I do urge you to reflect. Discipline is important in the army, and you are clearly an orderly man, but there may be rare occasions—*very* rare occasions—when the consequences of orders have not been as fully explored as we might hope. On such occasions, all of us—me, you, all Followers of the Truth—have to call on the *Eternal Spirit* for guidance and, if It so prompts us, ask questions."

Kellin looked even more confused, but clicked his heels and saluted. "Yes, sir!"

"Hmm." All-Ears banged on the door to indicate that he wanted to leave. He turned back to Kellin, still at attention. "You're a good man, Gunner Kellin. May the Spirit bless you."

All-Ears returned to his office, very angry with himself, but even more angry with Arlo.

13

The quarters of the Arbiter, Bankside Place, Nasrin.
Midmorning. The twenty-fifth day of the Fourth Moon,
Year Fifty-One.

SUKI GLIDED FROM room to room, unlatching every window in Number 4 and welcoming a rush of fresh air into the house. The weather was sunny and breezy, offering an excellent opportunity to reduce the lingering smell of smoke from the fireplaces. She bruised and scattered fresh herbs on the floors.

Suki relished her job as a housekeeper in Bankside. She felt as if she were in love with the place, despite its past. It was now the headquarters of the Republic that the men she had tended had been fighting and dying for, where the Doctrine of Truth was observed every day. Although she chided herself for pride, she allowed herself credit for keeping the household well-fed, well-watered, well-dressed, and clean. Having come to the joy of letters and numbers quite late in life, she was also constantly grateful for her new skills in record-keeping. She relished the monitoring of expenditure, and managing the stock of provisions, from bed linen to cheeses. And she did her duty in keeping Squire Tallier informed about everything that she could possibly think might be useful to him.

She had discerned what was routine in the household, and what was not. The Arbiter's nightmares, his fastidious hygiene routine in the morning, his return from training at the combat school after his work at Victory Park, and even his noisy giving of seed that amused the footmen and maids—this was normal. Mistress Krusa's indolence and boredom during the day had been addressed by the appointment of her companion, Pia, who was full of suggestions for something to read or sew, or where they might take a walk. Oh, how happy Suki was when they took a long walk. It gave her a chance to inspect Mistress Krusa's room in detail.

It was the morning after the Arbiter and his wife had departed for a trip to the Eastern Region. Suki was checking Mistress Krusa's dressing room. She thought that she would check that Konni the maid was putting clothing away in drawers neatly. She patted some veils in the bottom drawer of the clothes cabinet, and felt something hard and round. She carefully fingered through the veils to find it. It was a small bracelet of beads, each from a different type of wood, and each marked with a tiny drawing of a plant. Suki knew exactly what it was. It had been compulsory to have them before the war. Now, it was almost compulsory not to have them. She was dismayed. This could have awful consequences. Had it been hidden in a hurry, or was it just carelessness to leave it where Konni could easily have found it? She made haste to Squire Tallier's office.

"My dear Mistress Suki," he complained wheezily. "Please make more effort to disguise your moods. People will have noticed you coming from Number 4 to here with that look on your face and there'll be gossip all over Nasrin by lunchtime."

"I'm sorry, sir." She curtsied. "But I'm so worried 'bout what I've just found!"

He motioned with his hand towards the chair where she was accustomed to sitting during their longer meetings. He sat in his favorite chair, close to the fire. "Is it to do with her moon bleeds?" he asked.

"Still no sign. I think she has now missed three. She's been asking for calming tisane ev'ry day this quarter-moon. She's almost certainly carrying." Suki twisted her hands in her apron. "That would be good news—if I hadn't found what I found this morning!"

Suki dipped into her pocket and offered him her find. Squire Tallier's face was blank. She had expected surprise or dismay or anger. She was frustrated. Why was he so calm?

He took the beads and examined them, muttering, "Myrtle for Afra, olive for Feena, pine for Pollo, willow for Reena, beech for Esta, and oak for Sudar. Love, wisdom, sunshine, serenity, home, and strength. An interesting mix." Then he exclaimed, "This is sad news indeed!"

Suki stared at him appealingly, waiting for words of wisdom and instruction.

"Well," he sighed, "she is not doing anything illegal. There are many people up and down the country who are outwardly observing the Doctrine of Truth but calling on the old gods when they want something foolish like good luck. Perhaps she had been getting desperate to conceive. But the Arbiter must find out. I don't know how he will take it, but he must find out."

"He'll be so upset, Squire Tallier. He's a pious man. He won't want superstition under his own roof." Suki had been appointed to guard the Arbiter from threats within his household. She had found one, and now she wanted backup. She started to sob. "Can't you do something? We can't have that Sudo stuff tainting the household and undermining the Arbiter!"

Squire Tallier went back to his desk to retrieve a handkerchief. He offered her the cloth. "I'm distressed too, Suki. Let me do the worrying for you. There could be a simple, and innocent, explanation. Perhaps it was a gift from her mother that she cannot bear to lose. Let's hope for the best. I'll tell him, be assured of that, but it'll have to wait until they're back from the east. In the meantime, you had better put this thing back where you found it." Squire Tallier gingerly returned the prayer beads to her.

Suki, handling the beads with equal disgust, dropped them back into her apron pocket. "Aye, sir." She stood up and hurried back to Number 4. Of course, she had to trust Squire Tallier. Perhaps he would set a bigger trap for Esta Glantar, after the baby was born.

The solar of Maylan Castle, Eastern Region, Kimalloa. Early evening. The twenty-fifth day of the Fourth Moon, Year Fifty-One.

L ORD RUBIN ALDOR was still not his usual colorful self. He was dressed in a black silk suit with a black lace collar and cuffs, still grieving for his wife. He had always taken Nolli for granted. She had been arranged for him by his father because of her money, which he had appreciated; but she was also gentle, affable, cheerful, and a good mother. He was very sorry that he had lost her. Her sudden death had shocked him into long days of reflection, and he was still not at peace. A white streak had appeared in his hair, and new lines creased his face. He had commissioned a plaque which was placed next to her portrait in the great gallery at Maylan Castle:

> *To my beloved wife, mother of my fine sons. Nolli Aldor, blessed of the goddess Afra. Transcended to the Dome of the Divine on the twenty-seventh day of the Moon of the Elm in the year of the Empire 1876. Always in my prayers. Rubin Aldor, Lord of the East.*

And he did pray by the portrait and plaque, even though he felt the evidence stacking up, day after day, that his prayers were not heard.

But he did have some hope. Like most of the old aristocracy who had been forced to live at court, Rubin had rarely seen his sons when they were very young. His house arrest by the Army of Truth had meant that he saw much more of them, and he liked what he saw. Now, he took an interest in their horse-riding, fencing, and falconry; he played with them, ate with them, and read with them. And here they were, his fine boys, after supper on a wet spring evening, sitting attentively in the purple velvet, cross-framed armchairs of the solar, wondering how to behave when the visitors from the god-killer government came to stay.

Rubin had to brief them carefully. "He is a foreign duke, but he is from the new government, and although we do not like the new government, we must be polite. His wife is here supporting the new government, but she's really our queen, so we must be even more polite to her."

The boys looked puzzled.

"Yes. Politics is complicated. Just talk about the weather, what you're learning, and what you know of our lovely region. Do not on any account mention religion. They have some very strange beliefs that we have to tolerate. For the time being."

"Will you ever be king, Pa?" the younger boy asked.

Rubin hesitated. His family tree included several legitimate minor royals and one very notable illegitimate prince. He had never aspired to kingship, but if anything happened to Esta, he might be a candidate. What should he say to his dear son? "No. That isn't my destiny. And, please, if anyone approaches you in years to come, maybe after I've died, and says that they want to make you king, refuse it. It's not fun, being a king. It's a lifetime of hard work and worry. You think that you have power, but you don't. People want to take power from you, and you have to be a horrible person to hang on to it. People will fawn in front of you—and plot behind your back. They expect you to make brilliant decisions, and then they undermine the implementation of them, or whisper that they are flawed. Royal blood—and we

189

have a bit of it—may come with some magic, but it doesn't mean that Lord Sudar will bless you with loyal subjects."

The boys looked wide-eyed with dismay. Perhaps he had said a bit too much for them to take in.

"Sorry, boys. Let's get back to the rules for the next few days. Don't swear at the Greencoats or militia as you've heard me do. I will have to bite my tongue as well. Let's enjoy the food and sport, and," he crouched close to them and put his forefinger to his mouth, "shhhh! Keep our secrets!"

The boys nodded, and then laid out pieces for a game of taffle, squabbling about who was to defend the King and who would attack him. Rubin sat with them and watched them, whispering move suggestions to each of them in turn, to help them improve their skills.

Chambers of Her Grace, Grand Duchess Kirina, the Doretsi Palace, Lonikipia, capital of Osiran. Early evening. The twenty-fifth day of the Fourth Moon, Year Fifty-One.

KIRINA'S DIVINING WHEEL almost leapt off the rim of its bowl as the elements below it rose and fell, to and fro, as if they were in a gale. The blues in the water flickered so rapidly, she struggled to keep up with the images.

Her concentration was shattered by a loud banging at the door.

She went to the door and wrenched it open herself, pulsing with anger. "So?"

A large bald man wrapped in black fur was kneeling on the threshold. "Your Grace, I pray you, forgive me for disturbing you."

"Come in." She strode towards the fire and sat down by it, but gave him no leave to sit. "It's good that you are here promptly, Chancellor, but I have already read the signs. The Grand Dukes of Orguizin and Nor are squaring up to each other over the succession."

"They are also questioning your right to continue as protector of the Emperor. You were, of course, the only person who could reach the late emperor, your divine brother, but… they say that Ikra is a young man who might benefit from the advice of men."

"Ha!" Kirina spat into the fire.

The chancellor stared at the sizzling sputum, then bowed deeply. "Should I come back later for your orders, Your Grace?"

"You can have them now. When have I ever procrastinated?! Treason has to be snuffed out decisively. Poison them both. They have competent wives to run their regions. Bring their eldest boys to court as hostages."

"Your Grace." The chancellor bowed again. "It might help if there were a plan for the Emperor's wedding?"

"I know that, Chancellor. And I do have a plan. And because I'm an old woman—a very clever old woman—instead of an ambitious middle-aged man keen to pimp his daughters, it's a plan that will stop these succession crises once and for all. Negotiations will start soon. Tell that to the whisperers. Hurry to do your work, Chancellor."

The chancellor backed out of her sanctuary. Kirina swished across the room to a finely carved desk laden with all types of paper, pots of a deep indigo ink, and quills made from the glossy feathers of ravens. She wrote in small, neat hieroglyphs on a delicate fragment and rolled it up into a tiny canister made of polished shell. She left her chamber and walked to the loft where the messaging birds were kept, seeking out the pure white plumage of the one she called the Nasrin envoy.

Maylan Castle, Eastern Region, Kimalloa. Late afternoon. The twenty-seventh day of the Fourth Moon, Year Fifty-One.

A CLOUD OF dust announced the arrival of the guests. Rubin waited at the castle gate, ready to conduct the meeting and greeting with due formality. The carriage that must contain the Arbiter's wife was soon visible. What should he call her? He had known her as Her Royal Highness the Princess Esta. Briefly, she was Her Majesty Queen Esta, then the Lady Esta, and now Mistress Krusa. He didn't like "Mistress Krusa". Given that her husband's official title was "Lord Arbiter", would he object if Rubin called her "Milady Esta"? He could try once, and find out. As the carriage got closer, he examined its features with interest. The wood was covered in a dark varnish that was highly polished and reflected the rays of the sun. No doubt, the varnish was a waterproofing compound of some sort. There were some curves in the design, but he supposed that they were for efficiency rather than aesthetics. No carving, painting, or gilding adorned the woodwork. A man in a gray gown and cap on a black horse rode behind the carriage with the uniformed guards—that had to be the Lord Arbiter.

The carriage drew to a halt and three ladies stepped out. All were fully robed and veiled, but status was obvious. Milady Esta was wrapped in a fine silk of indigo and mottled purple, her companion was in blue-gray wool, and her maid was in unbleached linen.

Rubin's cook had been devastated to learn that a lavish feast involving swans stuffed with ducks stuffed with larks was not appropriate for these guests. He had promised to put all the imagination he could muster into roast beef with root vegetables, followed by a plum pudding. Rubin had merely pondered with relief that the Followers of the Truth were much cheaper to entertain than royalty, who would happily bankrupt their hosts with extravagant demands.

Castle Maylan's great hall was prepared beautifully for the dinner. Its glorious color and tapestries, paintings and stained-glass windows, richly tiled floors and marbled fireplace were picked out by blazing sconces and candelabras. The dining table was a solid oak piece with intricate carvings of myths relating to the god of feasting, some involving his excessively large member. A large plain linen cloth had been draped over it to avoid offense to the guests. The tableware included the novelty of forks as well as knives and spoons, plain ceramic plates sensitively ordered from a new craft shed, and in contrast, finely cut glass goblets from Bessema.

Rubin permitted the Lord Arbiter to offer thanks for the food, and while the god-killer loudly addressed his Eternal Spirit, Rubin silently thanked his goddess of the hearth. During the meal, Rubin talked about the local provenance of the food and briefed the Lord Arbiter and Milady Esta about the projects they were to visit. He had been quite open with them in the invitation that his craft sheds provided work for veterans of the losing side. It was his money that financed them and so he chose who benefited. He thanked them for showing an interest, assured them that he was a great supporter of reconciliation, and noted graciously that the new regime had "some good ideas".

When the eating was over, Rubin dismissed most of the diners, including Sitra (now posing as Pia), who had sat well away from the top of the table. He had ignored her. Whatever she had to tell him could wait.

He embraced his sons and wished them goodnight, saying pointedly to Milady Esta, "These boys are my heart and soul now. It has been so hard for us since poor Nolli passed away."

The visitors looked concerned about his lingering grief, and said how sorry they were for his loss. Rubin invited them to sit with him for a while before retiring, and he took them to a parlor with well-padded chairs and a roaring fire.

"Lord Arbiter, just think—last time we met here, you were telling me how you were going to vandalize my castle."

"And what repairs would be allowed, Your Grace. I am relieved to see that you have been able to adapt so well." The Lord Arbiter had the good grace to look embarrassed. Old Squire Clayhills had been general then, but the Yerallan had been the commander in charge of the slighting. "I am sorry for the past, Lord Aldor. I hope that we never get into such a state of discord again."

"Yes, we can both pray for that, sir. I feel, having spoken to you at some length this evening, that you are no bigot, despite some of your pronouncements during the war." Rubin was inviting the Lord Arbiter to be flattered.

"Your Grace, be assured that I do despise your religion and its superstitions. But just because you follow it, does not mean that I despise you. Anyone who has the capacity to love and be loved is loved by the Eternal Spirit."

Rubin laughed politely as if the words had been intended as satire. Was this the Yerallan style of diplomacy, or was it just this Yerallan who was odd? Then he quickly turned his head to Milady Esta, having noticed out of the corner of his eye how she winced. Perhaps she thought that her husband spoke clumsily. Perhaps she fundamentally disagreed with him. She sat, looking demure and modest in her robe and veil, but she was delicately stroking the soft velvet upholstery on her chair, as if she missed such comforts.

"Well, milady, this is quite different from the chivalric conversation we were used to at court."

Milady Esta smiled and twiddled her goblet of wine.

"My uncle had the Convocation, like the Assembly, instead of a court," the Lord Arbiter explained. "It was focused on getting things done for Yeralla."

"Of course, sir. Yeralla is the very essence of efficiency. Wonderful engineering. Wonderful administration. Wonderful at everything military. Wonderful at water sports. I do admire these things, sir. But what about beauty? Is there beauty in Yeralla? Are there wonderful pink sunsets, the green of trees, the blue of the sea, the yellows and reds of flowers? Are there melodic sounds, like birdsong? How do you honor them, if your faith focuses only on knowledge and usefulness? Surely, Lord

Arbiter, creativity makes a nation strong? What is wrong with appreciating beautiful things?" He waved his hand around the room, to draw his guests' attention to his own taste in decoration.

"Creativity is not banned, Lord Aldor," was the rebuttal. "Not in Yeralla, and not here. It is just that certain subjects and forms are... absolutely unacceptable. Followers of the Truth would never have themselves painted surrounded by naked children."

Rubin felt the tension in the room heighten while the atmosphere plummeted. There was an awkward, long pause.

Esta reached across to touch her husband's arm. "Dear husband, I am so tired after our journey. May we retire?"

Rubin called a footman and a maid to guide them to their quarters. He wished them both a good night's sleep, and sat back down. Did that sad young beauty still want to be Queen of Kimalloa? A year ago, that might have excited him, but now...

Some moments later, as lights were being extinguished around the castle, Rubin heard a tap at the door of the parlor. Somebody had approached very quietly. He knew who it must be.

"Sorry, Sitra," Rubin said without looking at her as she closed the door. "I do congratulate you on spelling your way into the Arbiter's household so effectively, but I sent you on a wild goose chase."

She swept into a curtsy. "Your Grace? It was no wild goose chase! Queen Esta is with us. She's still of our faith."

"Really? Well, that's good to know, but—we shouldn't get her hopes up."

"Pardon, Your Grace?" Sitra must have heard him clearly. He perceived that, rather than a question, she was firing an accusation at him.

He shrugged at her. "Raia Sitra, pray for me! Since Nolli... I just don't know what to do. I can't afford to lose anything else in this life for... for some futile gesture against the tide of history. Sudar may call me a coward, and perhaps I am. But I hear Nolli's voice in my dreams, urging me to cherish my sons. I'm sure that the time will come for a rebellion. We must just wait for the right time, the right leader."

"Don't you fear being cast from the Dome of the Divine into the fire at the center of the earth? That is your destiny if you fail Lord Sudar again."

Rubin shuddered with fear as the Raia's green eyes fixed on him. He could almost see the flames of the underworld in them. His skin was getting hotter. Could he feel the hairs on his arms burning? He rubbed his sleeves to extinguish the prickling. Then he exploded. "I feel that I am damned, whatever I do!"

"Your Grace." Sitra left briskly, not bothering to curtsy, and without a backward glance. Rubin poured himself a strong drink.

Clayhills Place, New Temple Street, Nasrin. Late evening. The twenty-seventh day of the Fourth Moon, Year Fifty-One.

WHY CAN'T I arrest her?!" Arlo raged at All-Ears. "She's laughing at us! Prancing around the country on missions of 'reconciliation' when she's praying to those awful gods? She has got to be up to something. Plotting with Aldor, no doubt."

Crumbs of bread and cheese and the stalks and stones of fruit were scattered over Deneesa's best white tablecloth. The cabal always ate simply and well before putting Kimalloa to rights. Dozens of candles were lit in the ample parlor, but they cast plenty of shadows to challenge old eyes. Yoshi's gray curls were distinctive, as were Deneesa's ample brown veil, Yeramo's green eyes, the copper hair of Ulfan, and the brown baldness of Coppermills. Arlo's luxuriant hair and beard were punctuated by his contorted face. All-Ears did not want to think ill of Yoshi's son, but evidence was piling up that Arlo's personal and political grudges were driving him into a state of unreason.

"The difficulty is, General, that we have to catch her 'up to something'. We've said that, provided they are discreet, the Sudarites can continue to worship in their own homes. If she is sanctioned only for possessing prayer beads, well, I can tell you there are thousands of households up and down the country where they still have them to rub for 'a bit of good luck', and it doesn't look good to crush what's widely regarded as a harmless bit of hope in the darkness." All-Ears was equally angry with Esta, but he had learned the value of patience. However, religious observance was not his specialty, so he looked at Yeramo, expecting a ruling.

"Tallier's right, Arlo. We'll stoke up resentment if we try to confiscate every set of hidden prayer beads in the land. Pia's got to get more evidence—genuine evidence, not planted evidence. Don't be distracted by the Esta sideshow. We need to worry about the new pretender! And there is still no whisper from Fergan's castle."

Deneesa drew away from the table. All-Ears could feel her anxiety wafting across to him. "I can believe that Fergan would give them shelter, but to take that story seriously? Surely, he wouldn't..."

Of course she had to hope for her younger brother, but it was All-Ears' job to assume that Fergan was gullible.

Yoshi Clayhills, who was looking thoughtful, opened his mouth and uttered an "Er" which hushed the cabal. "Deneesa, you know your brother better than any of us. I know that you want to think the best of him, but what do you, in your heart of hearts, expect of him?"

Deneesa sighed. "He always loved a good romantic legend as a little boy—perhaps he's still a romantic."

"Spirit save us!" Ulfan groaned, reaching for his mug of beer. "I'd rather have silly Esta as consul than a monumental fraud as king!"

"Steady on, Ulfan! Or Arlo will have you arrested for treasonous thoughts!" Yeramo laughed.

"Don't digress, brothers!" All-Ears snapped, which brought on a fit of coughing. "Help me—make a decision—about—the pretender. It's not Fergan's reaction we need to worry about, it's the Raas. They will decide if the pretender is genuine or not. If we assassinate the steward's boy, it could provoke trouble where none might've been planned. What say you all?"

A craft shed in the village of Sakkor, Eastern Region, Kimalloa. Midmorning. The twenty-eighth day of the Fourth Moon, Year Fifty-One.

RUBIN LEAPED INTO the Lord Arbiter's plain carriage and sat beside Duke Yonnis and opposite Milady Esta and her maid. The Lord Arbiter was warm and polite, and Rubin wondered if Milady Esta had protested about his excessive frankness of the previous evening. As the carriage bounced along the basic road to the craft shed, they discussed the crops sprouting in the large flat fields of the east, and how thankful they were that food was now growing where blood had been spilled.

Rubin felt some pride as they disembarked. The craft shed was a hive of productive activity, which surely must impress any Yerallan. Widows and children were clustered together, braiding lengths of straw which were then stitched into hats. Maimed veterans were making rush and straw mats, sometimes demonstrating ingenuity, such as a man with only a left arm combining with a man with only a right arm to twist and tighten the fiber. Straw was a plentiful by-product from the fields of wheat and corn, and the rushes grew vigorously in the streams and ditches. The workers looked well-fed and content. The spring sun came out to bless the event. The veterans seemed sheepish about speaking to these well-dressed people, but the friendly approach of the visitors put them at their ease. The hat-makers and mat-makers spoke to the Lord Arbiter and his wife about what they did and about the weather. Rubin smirked as some of them thanked Pollo for his warmth that day, without realizing that they were making the pale man cringe.

While the Lord Arbiter was deep in conversation with a Sudarite veteran from the Maylan siege, Milady Esta asked Rubin to accompany her back to the carriage to pick up a box of honeyed dried fruit for the children. Her maid protested that that was her job, but Milady Esta insisted that she and the host should distribute them together. She opened the door of the carriage from one side, and Rubin from the other.

Speaking in hushed Pozarian, which he hoped would help to confuse the guards, Rubin joked, "You know, milady, I fear that even the horses might report back to All-Ears."

Milady Esta cut across Rubin's frivolity. She grabbed his arm. "How are you going to help me to free our country from the iron-heeled boots of these puritan ranters?" Her eyes flashed with expectation.

Oh dear. He had dreaded this scenario. His stomach lurched in self-disgust for deserting his best friend's daughter, but he had to put his own sons first. He took a deep breath. "Be assured that I know that you are the true queen, Your Majesty, but let me advise you, as I would have advised your father, the last true king. They—the puritan ranters—have the gods on their side at the moment, even if they don't recognize them. The tide *will* turn, but it could be many years. In the meantime, we just have to make the most of a bad situation. I have sons, and I have to protect them. When you have children, you'll understand. I'm... very sorry." Rubin picked up a box of dried fruit.

Milady Esta looked at him in horror. She must have put so much hope into this encounter, and he was just urging her to endure. "Sorry? You're sorry? You will be when your head is on a spike on the Great Eastern Gate. Now I see why you surrendered Maylan Castle so easily."

Rubin had to try and quieten her, and quickly. "Your Majesty, I surrendered because I live in the real world! Might is right—and it is they who have the well-organized, well-trained, well-paid, motivated army," he hissed. "Of course it irks me to see what they're doing to Kimalloa! But some of this change will stick and we have to adapt!" Rubin indicated that he was ready to move. There is only so long you can rummage around on the floor of a carriage without arousing suspicion. "Are you coming to share out the fruit?"

Milady Esta was glaring at the floor of the carriage. "Tell my maid that I feel sick."

Rubin had thought when she first showed her anger that she might be a true Glantar, but now she just seemed like a thwarted toddler. He muttered to her, "Madam, men do not follow petulant girls into battle. Come and smile, like a queen who loves her people, if you think you are one."

Milady Esta suddenly withdrew from the carriage door and vomited by the wheel. She retrieved a cloth from a pocket in her robe to wipe her face, and leaned into the carriage again, groaning.

Rubin handed her one of the small pieces of dried fruit to sweeten her breath. "So, you really are sick. You're probably carrying a child. Now, Majesty, this is hopeful! A son of yours might attract a following. It's such a shame that you can't save him from becoming a puritan ranter... or can you?"

On that note, Rubin was relieved to see Milady Esta's eyes brighten. They emerged from the carriage and walked back to the craft shed, smiling at the children clamoring for the sweet tidbits.

14

Eglin, a small town in the eastern Greenlands. Early evening. The third day of the Fifth Moon, Year Fifty-One.

OUT OF THE dark streets came pinpricks of light. Like glowing insects, they hovered and clustered. Agent Kandid merged with them as they turned from insects into ghoulish shapes, gliding quietly to the west of the town. He could see the twisted willows swaying in the distance. As they entered the grove, the ghoulish shapes became a crowd of torches, held aloft by masks. The masks had no emotion painted onto them. Kandid was grateful that he could not see the emotion behind the masks, and the other masked folk could not see the emotion behind his. He could feel evil creeping among them. There was tension, expectation, and bloodlust in the air. Kandid listened carefully to the chanting of the Raas. It was beautiful and rousing. They were wafting pungent smoke around, which he feared. He started to wheeze like a man with a weak chest, and tried to snuffle into a cloth to avoid its effects. He chanted responses in the right places, and got louder as everyone else got louder.

Then the Chief Raa, resplendent in red robes and a golden helmet with ram's horns, made a pronouncement. "Loyal disciples of Lord Sudar, this is an auspicious day! A grandson of Rikko IX has been delivered to us in the Greenlands. We have been chosen! He waits with Lord Fergan for us to show our commitment. Children of Sudar, our gods have decreed it—they will smell the sacrifices in the Dome of the Divine tonight!" He took a deep breath and boomed. "The time for retribution has come!"

The crowd roared its approval, then broke into gangs, running back into the town, shouting and swearing. Kandid ran too, silently exhorting the Eternal Spirit to save him from having to do what the masks were expecting him to do. Staves and knives were being pulled out of the black robes. Particular houses were stormed, and all the occupants dragged out. Where were the militia? They were shooting, and running into the masks with swords drawn. This was his chance to let out a visceral scream and drop to the ground, spilling the bag of pig's blood that he had hidden under his robe. Much as he longed to jump up and help the militiamen, his duty was to observe, survive, and get news to Squire Tallier.

He crawled into an alleyway. The mob was in such a frenzy now. Their faces were hidden, but their callous laughter and jeering displayed their twisted hatred. One by one, the militiamen lost their lives trying to push back the masks, who were dragging their prey to the temple. Three Elders had taken cover behind an upturned cart in front of the doors, and emerged in succession to fire pistols. Within moments, the cart was moved, the Elders were captured, and the temple doors were barged open. The trussed citizens were separated from their screaming children and thrown in, then buckets of pine spirit, and then all of the torches. Every last one. The masks barricaded the doors. Who screamed louder? The anguished cries of the terrified victims were heartrending. The howls of triumph of the crazed torturers were sickening. Kandid knew that he had to stay for the inevitable—he had to be sure of what he witnessed. Soon, smoke started billowing from the roof and he smelled the roasting flesh. His guts quivered like jelly. Then he ran until his lungs were ready to burst. Kandid headed for the garrison stables and wrenched open the door. He grabbed a simple rope bridle, and leapt onto the largest steed he could see. Quickly and quietly, he urged it out of the building, over a fence, and into a cross-country beeline for the safety of the North Middlelands.

After reaching the garrison at Andel, Kandid gave his testimony to the commander and to the clerk who managed the word-birds. As the birds took flight and the garrison readied itself for action, he took a pistol, walked to the back of the privy block, and shot himself.

Clayhills Place, New Temple Street, Nasrin. Early evening.
The fifth day of the Fifth Moon, Year Fifty-One.

YONNIS ARRIVED EARLY, embarrassing Arlo with excessive hugging and expressions of joy to see him and to celebrate the arrival of Yoshi Junior. He apologized for Esta's absence, explaining that she had been feeling unwell for some days. They sat in one of the brown reception rooms, drinking stronger beer than usual. Arlo asked about the trip to the east and what Yonnis thought of Rubin Aldor and his projects for his own veterans. Yonnis replied with some enthusiasm.

Arlo smiled as if he were joking and commented, "I think that you are getting a little too sympathetic towards our enemies."

Yonnis looked offended, but brushed the statement aside. "Please tell me about your son. I am so happy for you and Deneesa. It is truly wonderful that the Eternal Spirit has blessed you both."

Arlo was keen to oblige, and to start at the beginning. "To be expecting a child—it's a whole new wonder! I fretted about Deneesa's food, her exercise, her rest, and how much the baby had kicked every day. But she just told me to concentrate on keeping the country a safe place for children. She's so *devout*." Yes, thought Arlo, I have the good wife, and Yonnis does not yet know that he has Esta the Sudarite. Tallier's revelation about the prayer beads had made Arlo's plans easier. He didn't have to bother about finding a way to marry Esta. He just had to find an opportunity to have her. Quickly, he switched his mind back to explaining his exemplary fatherhood. "Anyway, I was in the house when her labor started. The cries of pain! Ugh. Yonnis, we've heard men cry out in pain, but this was quite a different thing. I paced and paced for nearly half a day, and then I heard the lusty cry of a newborn infant. In fact, let me say a newborn boy—I could tell straightaway that 'twas a boy with a fine pair of lungs. I leaped up the stairs and banged on the door of the bedchamber. 'Let me in! Let me see!' It was a messy baby that sat and screamed in my arms as the cord was cut!"

"What an amazing feeling that must have been!" Yonnis's eyes were wide in awe.

Arlo detected a whiff of envy and relished it. "It was indeed."

"I am so pleased for you!" Yonnis beamed a big smile, showing his impeccable white teeth.

"You next, my friend?"

"Well, the delay is not for want of trying."

Arlo wished that he had not raised the subject. That awful image of Yonnis and Esta entwined jumped into his head again. He tried to move the conversation on. Yonnis might be doing his duty in the bedroom, but how did he perceive his union? "You took such a great risk, taking on Esta. How's it going?"

"It was my obligation to Kimalloa. And things could have been so difficult between us, but I am blessed! She's adorable. Well…"

Arlo leaned forward to listen more closely. Was the hesitation going to be revealing?

Yonnis shrugged. "She gets frustrated from time to time. Obviously, she has had so much frightening change in the past few years."

"Is she not grateful for the mercy we have shown her? For the home comforts that she has? For the love that you lavish on her?

Does she complain?" Arlo could not stop himself twisting the knife.

Yonnis frowned, and changed the subject. "May I have a few moments with Yoshi Junior?"

Arlo hesitated. "Well, Deneesa'll only let us in if she isn't feeding, of course. There's some kind of routine with the little master—sleep, cry, feed, pee, shit, cry, and then sleep again. But that's all so very healthy! I even like it when he's cross—he looks at me, frowns, grabs my beard, and screams."

Yonnis laughed with him. "He'll grow out of that—by the time he has sixteen years!"

They were allowed in, as the baby was in the "sleep" mode of his routine. Deneesa stood back and let them peer into the cradle. Yonnis gushed with a sentimentality that irked Arlo.

"What a fine little man! Oh, the innocence of a sleeping baby. If only we could protect them more, Arlo. If he were mine, I could not suffer the rain to fall on him or the wind to buffet him. Think of Yeribbi, how much he loves his sightless daughter. It is overwhelming! You know, after that meeting with the Distributors, I walked back with a young drummer boy whose father had died in the war. He was such a character. I wonder whether I should have brought him back to Bankside? I have made so many fatherless children, Arlo—"

Arlo butted in. "Yonnis. You can't take in a boy like you took in that dog."

As Yonnis turned his gaze back to the sleeping baby, Arlo glanced at Deneesa and raised his eyebrows in disdain. Yonnis could be reckless even in his mawkish repentance.

Clayhills Place, New Temple Street, Nasrin. Late evening.
The fifth day of the Fifth Moon, Year Fifty-One.

ARLO FELT SO good when he saw his father with Baby Yoshi. He loved them both, and he loved how much his father had been excited and cheered by the arrival of his new grandson. Baby Yoshi was also shown off to the guests, which he clearly found terrifying. He wailed, then shrieked, but immediately stopped and gurgled with joy when he was taken into the welcoming arms of the Father of the People again, to everyone's amusement and delight.

The guests sat down to a late supper and talked about the latest bills and petitions, infrastructure projects and debates. Squire Tallier had sent a messenger to say that he was delayed, which was clearly worrying Arlo's father. Arlo was irritated. It must be a very serious matter to keep his kinsman away from celebrating the arrival of Baby Yoshi, and if it was *that* serious, why didn't he say what it was?

After the last reflection bell of the day, when the ladies had retired to their sitting room and the men to theirs, Squire Tallier arrived and was hastily helped into the room where the men were in teams playing taffle on a large board. Squire Tallier was breathing heavily and his face was red and puffy. It looked like he had been sobbing.

He broke the horrified silence. "Brothers, I have just had news from the Greenlands. There have been several attacks by Sudarite mobs on our people. They have been thrown into temples, and the temples have been burnt to the ground."

Arlo yelled at a footman, "Get our swords! We haven't a moment to lose."

Squire Tallier held up his hand. "Wait, Arlo, let's just understand the gravity of this. Whatever we do, it cannot be done in panic. Who here remembers Marlbek? Some of you will. I do. The stench hit me first. I have hated to be near roasting pork ever since. There was such a huge pile of charred bodies, they were spilling out of the temple and into the main square. I was the regimental clerk with the Kimalloan Expeditionary Force in Boriela. I had to document it all. A town of five thousand people had been reduced to twelve hundred, and with a savagery that was beyond anything that we might see from beasts. Friends, never underestimate what butchery the Raas of Sudar are prepared to inflict when their power is threatened. Brothers and sisters, this is our Marlbek."

The listeners were stunned. Arlo felt bile rising in his throat. He shouted out his frustration. "This is what comes of waiting, delaying, holding back!" He was about to blame his uncle for the deaths when his father spoke.

"Do whatever you have to do to suppress this, my son. Make an example of the perpetrators, but make sure that our men do not sink to depravity, however much they are provoked. Ellis, is Lord Fergan implicated?"

"This couldn't happen without his implicit involvement. But it was the Raas who stirred up mobs."

"Well then, we know what the endgame is. His castle must be pounded to dust, and let's hope that we can take him alive, and all his wretched priests."

Arlo was feeling dizzy as thoughts galloped around in his head. This was his campaign, and he was going to win it. "Let's get messengers out to every garrison to send men to gather at Andel. We must look like a wall of steel when we charge into the Greenlands—and act like one from town to town until we reach the sea."

"Arlo, may I join you?" Yonnis thrust himself forward.

"No!" Squire Tallier butted in, denying Arlo the satisfaction of saying it. "You must be at Victory Park at first light, arbitrating. You will need to stop the radicals taking out their fury on the monarchists."

Arlo bade a brief farewell to Deneesa and rode to the Nasrin garrison, full of anticipation. He had craved such action ever since his left arm had healed. He would be at the front of the mighty Army of Truth, crushing the Sudarite scum. Yonnis hadn't finished the war. He would.

Onisbi Street, Nasrin. Late morning. The twelfth day of the Fifth Moon, Year Fifty-One.

MURDERIN SUDO SCUM.

IN WHITE LIME, on red brick, across small leaded windows, which were broken. The mob had obviously hijacked a soilman too, as there were globs of fresh, stinking excrement all over the front of the house.

"Oh, Seemo! Look at Mistress Sibberin's house!" Oona had dragged him here from his last reading stump. "That broken glass will have shredded those lovely drapes I made for her. Oh, my best customer! And she was the first! She helped me so much!"

"What happened to her? Is she safe?"

Oona took a deep breath and wiped her face. "May the Spirit be praised, they all got out the back and the Elder took 'em in. The mob weren't goin' to have a go at him. The militia arrived in time, just for a change. But she's not right in the head this mornin'—she's gibberin' and wailin'. She was so frightened— she's still frightened! The ol' man's talkin' 'bout going to Pozaria."

"Feelings are running high! There's a curfew tonight, after the early evening bell."

"Good! People should mind their own bizness, and not go attackin' their neighbors just because of somethin' happ'ning a long way away."

"Is she... a Sudo?" Seemo was curious. It didn't excuse the nastiness, of course.

"Well, yes. But she doesn't make a thing of it. None of the fam'ly do. It's a law-abidin' household. And they're nice, Seemo. They're nice! I don't understand." Oona shed some more tears and sniffed. "It's not helped by that stuff you spout ev'ry mornin'!"

Seemo did have to read some lurid headlines these days. He learned his calls by heart, and bellowed them confidently.

"Limbs of children fed to dogs!"

"Charred remains of fifty-six true Kims found in temple ruins!"

"Survivor tells harrowing tale of escape through sewer!"

Bulletins were coming back thick and fast from the Greenlands. It was blood-chilling stuff, but people wanted to hear it. Just once he had a story about Sudo neighbors hiding Truth neighbors, but even regular customers walked away as he read it. The bad news always drew a crowd. Some people got wound up, and wanted to have a go at easy targets. Like Mistress Sibberin.

"It's my job, my sweet. Folk have a right to hear the news—"

Oona was not listening. "The footman said that the militia have got children as young as eight years in the lockup! Runnin' amok and throwin' stones at people they don't know! Can we stop Little Pollo gettin' involved? I bet some of his pals were out here. Oh, Seemo, can't you get Pollo a proper job? I'm only gonna marry a good step-pa to my boy! Now come with me to the temple. I've got some bonbons to cheer up the children— and mebbe mistress too—although I fear she could be beyond cheerin'—ever! Oh, it's a scandal that folk who say they follow the Truth can do stuff like this! Sometimes I think we'd be better off with the old king back—"

"Oona! Don't say a stupid thing like that! They'll be throwing shit at us next!" Seemo could tolerate so much of her chatter, especially as she was upset for a good reason, but careless talk about the old ways—no way!

Office of the Intelligence Minister, the Archive, Bankside, Nasrin. Early morning. The twenty-fifth day of the Fifth Moon, Year Fifty-One.

"AH, YONNIS." ALL-EARS greeted him with a hearty handshake. "Let me pour you some beer."

"I would prefer to drink tisane this early in the day, if you have some. I must get to Victory Park. Many squires are back in armor, but the work of government must press on."

"I think that you will need the beer."

"Oh no!" Yonnis groaned. "Has something terrible happened in the Greenlands?"

"You know that the conduct of that campaign is very secret. I cannot share anything. Be assured that the Army of Truth is in control, as you would expect. Anyway, please sit down and take some beer. I must tell you something I have been meaning to tell you for some time, but events overtook me. I do apologize."

All-Ears had been desperately trying to find the hole in his network in the Sudarite priesthood. He could not bear losing control and losing face. He had twenty new suspects to interrogate, but he also had to deal with Yonnis. His wife's indiscretion seemed more sinister now.

"What is it?" Yonnis sat on the edge of his chair, leaning forward, looking worried.

"My agents in your household have told me things that you should know, that your wife should have told you." All-Ears watched Yonnis starting to crumple, as if he had punched him in the stomach.

"How ill is she?"

"She's not ill. She's carrying your child. She has missed four moon bleeds."

"Four?! Why has she not told me? Perhaps she is worried because her mother lost so many children?"

"I'm sorry, Yonnis. There's more." All-Ears made the unusual move of getting up out of his chair nearest the fire, stepping across to Yonnis, and grasping his shoulder. Did he do it to reassure him, or to gauge how shocked he was from the movement of his body? Perhaps both. It had been unexpected and inconvenient that Yonnis had taken his duty to his wife so seriously that he had fallen in love with her. How deluded was he? "You know that my agent, Pia, is a converted Raia. She has confirmed that your wife follows her old superstitions under your roof. She longs for what she thinks is her destiny as queen. I fear that she has been waiting... so that she can use the child to blackmail you in some way."

Yonnis stared into the fire in the grate for some moments. All-Ears felt him twitching. As the twitches developed into shudders, Yonnis shrugged off All-Ears' hand. "Your agent has trapped her! She observes the Truth. She saved me from Lazzar. Of course she dreams about what might have been. But they are just a girl's dreams."

All-Ears braced himself. "Alas... oh, my dear Yonnis... I can barely suffer to tell you... she has done a bit more than dream! When you were in the east, under Lord Aldor's roof, she asked him for help to overthrow the government. To be specific, she asked him to help her to free Kimalloa from 'the iron-heeled boots of these puritan ranters'. That's what she thinks of us. There's no doubt."

Yonnis looked as if he was going to be sick. "I can talk to her. It was... a moment of madness. A joke, perhaps? They had some strange ideas about humor at her father's court. Or perhaps Lord Aldor was trying to trap her?"

"Yonnis, he told her that he wasn't interested. He's wiser than I thought. She, on the other hand, is more foolish than I feared. I would've arrested Esta by now if I didn't know that she was carrying your child. The other mitigating factor for her is that I'm confident that she had nothing to do with the evil in the Greenlands. She probably fears the pretender. Nevertheless, she has tried to incite rebellion, albeit in a very desperate and ineffective way. Do you want to divorce her now, or after the baby's born?"

Yonnis looked horrified. "No, no, no! I am pledged to reconcile Kimalloa, I cannot divorce her! We are bound together—the old regime with the new. I gave my oath. Sir, I can never allow her to be harmed. I can reason her bad beliefs out of her, I am sure."

All-Ears had tried to be nice. Now he was angry. "You test me, Yonnis. You test me to the limits of my forgiveness—again! She's a danger to you and everything that you believe in! A pregnant queen is worth twice as much to a kidnapper as one without a child, and just imagine how valuable she's going to be to our enemies if she has a boy! Yonnis, please! Don't forget poor Marsa! A lying wife leads only one way for the husband!"

"Squire Tallier, it was your plan. Marry the last one of the old dynasty, and our enemies will see that the only way forward is to accept the new power in the land, as she has. It was what happened in history, according to your research. What has gone wrong?"

All-Ears paused. Yes, the plan. A plan with good historical precedent. But he had not told Yonnis which precedent. He had always expected that he would have to execute Esta sooner or later. He ignored the question. "For the time being, Esta's confined to Bankside. She may not leave. Not at all. She may not accompany you to visit a hospital or to an embassy dinner. If she even tries to take a walk on the south bank, the guards will stop her. Pia will stay undercover to get her to concentrate on the baby. You should compose a letter of retraction for her. If she signs it, well, these things are usually not worth the paper that they are written on, but we might have some kind of respite. But you have to make her understand that there will be no more chances."

"Thank you, Squire Tallier. Thank you! May the Spirit bless you." Yonnis looked dazed.

All-Ears felt glad that he had never experienced the aches of the soul that lust and love can bring. His soul was aching enough from the pain of failing to deal with the new pretender.

The quarters of the Arbiter, Bankside, Nasrin. Midmorning. The twenty-fifth day of the Fifth Moon, Year Fifty-One.

ESTA WAS ROUSED by a door slamming. She had not slept well. Discovering that she had a cousin had been bewildering. Discovering that Raas would declare him king, despite his questionable conception, had flung her into despair. Pia tried to comfort her, telling her that Sudar still had a plan for her and her baby, but Esta was tired of hearing "wait", "endure" and "patience". She felt the swell in her belly and decided that today, she had to tell Yonnis. She donned a dressing gown and walked into the parlor, where her husband sat with a wet cloth clasped to his face.

"Husband? I thought that you were going off to work? What's happened?"

Yonnis peered above the cloth. "I have a terrible headache. Have your breakfast, and then would you take some fresh air with me?"

"Of course." Esta called Konni the maid and asked for toast and the same tisane as yesterday.

"What tisane is that?" Yonnis asked Konni, rather than Esta.

"Arrowroot and ginger, sir."

"To calm the stomach? Well, I think I will have some of the same, please, Konni."

Esta started to feel a cold shiver gripping her spine. Had he guessed? Was he angry with her for not telling him? He would soon forgive her. She would tell him how terrified she was. Memories of her mother's lost babies had been swarming through her dreams. The circumstances of Lady Aldor's death also troubled her. In the afternoon, they had been chatting merrily at the Victory Festival, Esta admiring Nolli's gall in displaying her chestnut ringlets. Within half a day, the poor woman was dead on a mattress soaked through with her own blood. That was what unborn children could do to their mothers. "Shall we go to the south bank to see how the fruitlets are doing in the orchards?" she suggested.

"No. Let's just go to the bowling green. I would like to admire the oak tree that grows there."

Oak was Lord Sudar's tree. Why did Yonnis want to admire it?

Yonnis and Esta headed out to the former bowling green. There were some off-duty guards and footmen playing groundball, but they were absorbed in their game. In the far corner, behind the bank that had been raised to protect the green, was a special tree. It inspired awe. Children did not try to climb it, and men did not piss on it. Even the dourest of Elders could not propose to fell it. It was over a thousand years old. Its name had been changed to defuse its religious significance. There were plenty of features on this tree bark that were smoother than they should be because, over the centuries, thousands of worshippers had stroked it as they prayed. Sudar's Oak had become Ten-Man Oak, because its stout trunk was very broad and looked like ten burly men writhing together to hold up the tree's massive crown, which had been formed by nature alone. Dozens of branches reached out in every direction, and each was laden with hundreds of delicate eight-fingered leaves which waved in the breeze. The nubs of acorns were forming on every twig. This tree alone could keep a fine hog fed for days.

Yonnis strode up to the tree and placed his hand on its gnarled trunk. "Esta." He said her name softly, but Esta could discern a trace of accusation in it.

"Husband, do you have something to say to me that cannot be overheard by the many ears of Bankside?"

"You call me 'husband'. Sometimes Yonnis. Never 'darling' or 'sweetheart'. You saved me from Lazzar, but then you try to incite Aldor. What exactly are your feelings for me? Can you at least be honest with me while Sudar is listening to you?"

For a moment, Esta hoped that Yonnis was showing some respect to Lord Sudar. But that seemed so unlikely. She started to feel hot and nauseous. She stared at the roots of the tree.

Yonnis railed at her. "You have been fooling everybody so well, Esta! You fooled Squire Clayhills. You fooled your foster family. You even fooled Arch-Elder Yeramo... and you certainly have made me a fool." Yonnis had started calmly, but now his darkening eyes betrayed his anger.

Esta trembled. "Please, Yonnis—husband, darling—I'm sorry, I—"

"You have no idea of the things that I have seen!" He spat his words bitterly at her. "I have pledged myself to the peace of Kimalloa, and you—you, who I thought to be my partner in encouraging peace—I find that you have tried to provoke another round of war! So, you want more war, Esta. I should take you up to the Greenlands so that you can see the charred remains of children, hear the cries of half-dead humans as dogs chew on their limbs, smell blood running in the streets! And the young pretender, the pawn in all of this? He will be dragged back to Nasrin in chains for a horrible death."

Esta had her hands hovering by her ears, ready to shut out any more details. When she realized that Yonnis had paused, she looked up defiantly. "So, did Squire Tallier save me from my uncle just to order my death himself?"

Yonnis's face screwed up in frustration. "Esta! You committed treason! I have defended you to Tallier, but we are on a fine knife-edge here! You *must* listen to me and stop this folly, so that we can both just survive. You may not love me, but if you value your own being, your own possibilities, do not challenge the Doctrine of Truth. I am frightened for you, Esta. Why are you not frightened for yourself?"

"My faith is not folly! My royalty is not folly! It is me. It is who I am and what I must do!" Esta let her pent-up frustrations flow. If Yonnis loved her so much, he would help her.

Yonnis was punching his hand into his palm, and his tone was menacing. "Did you pretend to convert in the hope that if the Assembly won the war, they would give you the crown? And would you have then renounced the Truth? Would you have had your foster family burnt alive for their beliefs?"

Esta looked straight at him. "Burning saves the souls of unbelievers. It means they can enter the Dome of the Divine, despite denying the gods."

She saw that she might as well have hit Yonnis in the face with a rock. His face contorted in bewilderment and tears rolled down his craggy cheeks.

"Oh, Esta. How can you? How can you believe such... such... *evil* nonsense? So you think the mass burnings in the Greenlands are *merciful*? I don't know what prayer I can offer to the Eternal Spirit to mend your corrupted soul."

"Dear Yonnis—and you *are* dear to me, I swear it—let me teach you about the old ways, which are a real faith and the only faith. If you renounce your Doctrine, I can save you and your friends from the flames in this world and the next! I will save you, dear husband, if you save me now. And there is such a good reason to do so, because I am carrying our child!"

He slumped and sat on the roots of the great tree. He let loose a sob which squeezed Esta's heart. She knelt down to try to comfort him, but he pushed her away.

"Oh yes. Our child. When did you know? Because Tallier has known for two moons! I should imagine all of Bankside knew before I did. I am only the father."

"I was going to tell you today, but then this happened. I swear it, I swear it with my hand on the oak of Lord Sudar— does that convince you?" She grasped the tree with her right hand. "Remember what you said to Rubin Aldor? You can despise my faith, but you don't have to despise me." Esta was panicking, wondering if she had overestimated her power over Yonnis.

He gasped through his tears. "I don't despise you. I love you, and you know it, and instead of giving me some kindness for it, you torture me with it."

Esta decided to try some humility. "I know that I have broken my oath to you, and you can divorce me—"

"Oh really, Esta, you know that I cannot! Because I will not break the oath *I* made to *you*, which I meant with all my heart."

Esta felt her hand tingling where it rested on the oak, and drew it away. She stood up and shook, as a breeze from the river rippled her robe and veil. She looked at Yonnis, and eventually, he looked up at her. He dragged himself to his feet and managed a strained smile.

"Well, wife, you have all the best cards. You have my oath, my heart, and my child. I have to collaborate with you. But please, you should kill any silly dreams you have about sitting on a purple-and-gold throne with your little prince on your knee. Tallier would hang you as a curse-maker before allowing that."

Now Esta started to cry. She had been dreaming about having it all—this realm, this man, this child, and the comfort of the ways of the past. Why could she not make it happen by wishing it so? Where was the destiny that the Raas had predicted and promised her?

Suddenly, Yonnis put his arms around her. "Oh, Esta. What a mess! I expect that you are meant to be living another, more glamorous life somewhere. But you are trapped in this place and time, just as I am. I wish I could countenance otherwise, but I do not imagine that there is a happy ending in this for any of the three of us."

Yonnis started to guide her back towards their quarters. After a few paces, he stopped, drew away from her, and stared, as if trying to reach into her soul.

"Here is one possibility for you to think about, Esta, as you prepare for motherhood. If, in years to come, you are chosen as queen and you return Kimalloa to your faith, but I do not convert, will you—in order to save me, of course—will you tie me to a stake and send our child with a brand to light the tinder?"

15

Office of the Intelligence Minister, the Archive, Bankside,
Nasrin. Early evening. The fifteenth day of the Sixth
Moon, Year Fifty-One.

I T WAS SO warm that All-Ears had even ventured to edge open one
of his narrow windows. An urgent knock on the door surprised
him. All-Ears did not like to be surprised, and the announcement
that the Osiranian Ambassador was at the front door, without
having sought an invitation or being given one, filled him with
curious dread. It was a rare occurrence. The official residence
of Duke Daggra was called the Embassy of Shadows. The few
Osiranians in it were only very occasional diplomats. If all was
quiet on the border in the far north, they would sit and drink,
play cards, and take mistresses, in that order.

All-Ears asked his footman to prepare refreshments and
then forced his aching joints to hobble to the door to greet the
visitor in person. It was certainly His Excellency Duke Daggra.
Tall, broad, and wrapped in the softest of black bearskins despite
the warmth of early summer, his big feet accommodated in
boots made from a fine dark red leather. His face was as red and
saggy as anyone might expect of a heavy drinker in later life.
His bushy beard was pure white. Above his bulbous nose were
narrow black eyes.

"Excellency Daggra!" All-Ears exclaimed. "What a welcome surprise to receive a visit from you. Please come through to the reception room."

"No, Mr. Tallier." Daggra was always blunt. "Your office, please. This is private business. No clerks to take notes. Just us."

"Of course." All-Ears was usually a calm man, but this situation was making his heart thump. He prayed behind his smile. Please, Eternal Spirit, no war in the north. Please, no war in the north when we haven't finished in the Greenlands...

As Daggra entered the office, he swept off his cloak, revealing a gaudy silver doublet and breeches. He sat down first, as if the office were his, and pointed to the chair opposite for All-Ears. He glanced at the banks of narrow, locked metal drawers. A flustered footman entered with a tray of dried fruit, dried meat, and cheeses, two glasses, and a bottle of the harsh rye spirit that Followers of the Truth associated with treating wounds, and Osiranians regarded as something to quench their thirst. The footman poured the spirit into green-glazed cups from Nasrin Craft Shed Number 48.

When the door was shut again, Daggra said, "We can make much finer tableware in my country. We should do more trade. Which is why I am here."

All-Ears could breathe properly again. This was not about military threats. But why turn up unannounced to start trade negotiations? Why come to the Intelligence Minister rather than the Trade Minister? "That sounds like a very interesting idea, Excellency. Trade's very good for prosperity. What do you have in mind?"

"We are well known for our furs... and our reliable summers produce nice grain... our wood is very good for papermaking... you rely on our silk, of course... and we do have big guns. You have little guns for battles, but now you need to defend your ports and there is nothing better for sinking enemy ships than big guns. And then there is the tableware, very fine tableware.

Oh, and perhaps we could send you some of our enclaves of the people of the One God? Their neighbors are resentful, as ever, and I know that you need to repopulate the Greenlands."

All-Ears' brows knitted in concentration and puzzlement.

Daggra had a straight face for a little while, and then he laughed loudly. "I am sorry. My joke!"

"So, you are not here to talk about trade?"

Daggra shrugged and then went off at a complete tangent. "You must be aware that in his latest letter to his grandmother, Duke Yonnis—the man you call Arbiter—he told her that his wife was carrying their child?"

"It's early days, Excellency, but yes, they're hopeful."

"They are hopeful? But they are not happy. Indeed, he is very unhappy. You know that Her Grace Kirina is particularly fond of this grandson. She is a very old lady. And she would like to see him before she dies and advise him in person. Perhaps there is some chance that they could meet? To reinforce our peaceful relationship?"

All-Ears nodded. Perhaps it would be a good idea to take Yonnis off on an international mission for a moon or two. It would distract him from wanting to risk some peace-keeping in the Greenlands.

Daggra leaned closer. "Now let me explain the trade we can do. We have a new young emperor. We are finding it hard to recruit an empress. The usual stable of mares, well, we have noticed that they can have weak offspring. It has come to His Majesty's attention that the woman he calls Queen Esta and you call Mistress Krusa is a beautiful young woman and now a fruitful one. In return for Queen Esta, he is prepared to offer a treaty of perpetual peace on your northern border, and a very attractive trade and aid deal."

All-Ears wondered if the new emperor suffered mental distress as much as the previous one. "Your Excellency, she's not mine, or anyone's, to trade with in this way. What does your emperor propose to do about her marriage and the child?"

"Squire Tallier, we keep a closer watch on that household than you do!" Daggra wagged his finger. "You and I know that she took her marriage oath under false pretenses. She clings to her old faith, which is not ours, but it is not a problem to us like it is to you. We can absorb those gods into our own Divine Host. So she could be divorced easily. And I think that you might like that to happen."

All-Ears barked back quickly. "Duke Yonnis would never do that."

Daggra laughed again. "Don't tell me that you can't engineer a situation in which he *has* to do so."

"And the child?"

Daggra shrugged. "This child is the father's. By the way, your Healing Elders must confirm to us that the child has not damaged the mother. We need her to have lots of healthy babies with Emperor Ikra. The deal is off if mare or foal prove faulty."

All-Ears heard what Daggra had said, but was having problems processing it. He wondered if the cook had put a dreaming herb in the spirit. "Your Excellency, this is an extraordinary idea. There must be other princesses that would appeal to your emperor."

"None as desperate as her. Being the wife of the Emperor of Osiran has never been an easy prospect. And, alas, mothers of princesses remember what happened to Empress Kloda."

All-Ears wondered whether he cared about that happening to Esta. He would prefer it not to, but there would be no more rescues if she left Kimalloan soil. "Now, I can see why you are interested in her, but I can't take the risk of Esta Glantar persuading Emperor Ikra, or a future child of theirs, to restore her to the throne of Kimalloa by force."

"I see your problem. But we can arrange for the Highest of All the Raas in the Holiest of Sanctuaries in Bessema to tell her that Osiran is her destiny, not Kimalloa."

"You can?"

"Her Grace Kirina can."

All-Ears raised his eyebrows. "You think that she would willingly agree to your plan, with this… this spiritual guidance that you can arrange?"

Daggra nodded. "Fine clothes? A big palace? His Majesty might even employ a company of Kimalloan actors for her."

Spirit be praised! Perhaps the Esta problem could be resolved without a messy trial and a martyred husband. That canny curse-maker Kirina was an unlikely ally, but a promising one.

"Why don't I organize a discreet dinner party while he is in Osiran? You can give her the High Raa's ruling and the proposal. Let's see how she reacts."

Daggra smiled broadly, showing big yellow teeth.

All-Ears continued. "And Her Grace can convince Duke Yonnis?"

Daggra winked at All-Ears. "Her Grace has a way of making people see things her way. Even a stubborn grandson. Of course, the Grand Duchess expects you to send him back to Yeralla a very rich man after all this is over. As you should have done when he defeated Navvan for you." Daggra rose to leave. "And by the way, you must keep faith in this. Remember that we helped you rebels because some of Kirina's kin were killed in the Yerallan Day of Lamentation. All was quiet on the northern border so your mountain lords could charge south." Daggra added, "It seems so strange that Navvan should blow up the Yerallan ruler's womenfolk, something that was not in his own long-term interests, and while he had a civil war on his hands at home."

All-Ears' hackles rose. "Are you forgetting? His target was Yerobis the Liberator, and he got him."

"And those fishermen caused that convenient riot that delayed the King with the money and the nephew with the brains." Daggra smirked. "A counterplot worthy of your genius, Squire Tallier."

All-Ears forced a laugh. "Your Excellency! Another joke? If only I were half as clever as you think."

Indeed, if only, he thought.

On the outskirts of Lord Fergan's castle in the Greenlands. Late afternoon. The sixteenth day of the Sixth Moon, Year Fifty-One.

A CRACK LIKE the dawn of time rocked the earth under their feet, and the gunners cheered as a huge hole opened up in the mighty wall of the castle. It had been a long time coming. It was a difficult castle to surround, and there were few suitable sites for gun placements. The ramparts were so covered in clinging, creeping greens, the gunners had started to wonder if the plants were absorbing the shot. They just kept pounding the cannons, waiting for them to find a weak spot.

This was day twenty of the siege. Gunner Kellin was in the spot he had agreed with an engineer who estimated the range and advised on the angle of the shot. His assistants worked tirelessly, preparing the gun, cooling it, and cleaning it, then loading the gunpowder, wadding, and the heavy lump of metal. Then more wadding, and they rodded it all down tightly in the barrel. It was his job to aim, step back, and wait for the sergeant's signal so that the battery was coordinated, then light the priming powder with a long linstock. The noise was painful. They blocked their ears with wool and opened their mouths, but still it was so loud that it hurt, and the shudder of the earth shook their bones. This time, after nearly a day of this tiring routine, Kellin was so delighted that it had been *his* cannon that had dealt the mortal blow! His sergeant yelled at him to report to the officers' tent while they waited for the rubble to settle. Kellin was thrilled to do so, and ran as fast as he could.

The general, resplendent in his finely polished armor, purple sash, and dark green plumed helmet, was already out of the tent, with a triumphant grin on his face, showing his broken teeth framed by his glossy beard.

"General, sir!" Kellin bowed so deeply that, after the exertion of his run, he toppled over.

General Clayhills pulled him to his feet. "Kellin! My man! I know that I can trust you to bring good news!"

"It's a big 'ole, sir. The dust might take a little while to clear."

The general turned to the commander at his side. "Send the local militia in first."

The commander saluted enthusiastically. "With pleasure, sir!" he barked in a strange accent.

Kellin looked at his boots. He did not like this commander called Norro, from the North Mountains regiment. Kellin had heard things about him in the past few weeks that he would rather unhear.

The general gave Kellin a hearty slap on the back. "Back to your post, Gunner. Get the horses ready to move the cannon."

Clayhills Place, New Temple Street, Nasrin. Late morning. The twenty-first day of the Sixth Moon, Year Fifty-One.

A LETTER HAD arrived for Deneesa. It was a proper letter, rather than a note from Bankside translated from a short code sent by word-bird. She cherished the feel of the smooth paper, the smell of the ink, and the shapes of the words. Baby Yoshi had taken a long feed, and was sleeping. She could sit in her office and relish reading the letter.

Darling Deneesa,
I wanted you to know it from me first, and I hope that you
will understand the reasons for this, and forgive me. I am
sorry to report that the home of your childhood is now a

ruin. But I know you will be delighted to learn that the rebellion is crushed! Like a snail under a hobnailed boot!

Fergan will soon be in a carriage to Nasrin to stand trial. I have to tell you that, although he eventually surrendered, he is defiant. As a result of his intransigence, there have been many deaths. The scavenger teams will be here for a long while cleaning up. There is no sign of the pretender. We have been told that he died from straw fever during the siege, but there is no evidence. It seems a suitably pointless end. We should have taken him out earlier!

I am jubilant in our victory, which was ABSOLUTE! Our men were all deeply revolted by what they found when we arrived here, and we fought like an unstoppable machine. We must never let these Sudos get out of hand again, not even one of them! I will make the country a purer place, fit for our son! Tell him that his father loves him and misses him. The recent time has been very hard, but it is a comfort to know that I will soon be back in your loving embrace, dear wife!

Arlo

SHE HOPED THAT the last phrase was true. But she had started to ask herself, after two moons of calm in the house, did she look forward to the return of her husband's feverish temper? Would it be better or worse now that he had this great victory under his belt? Well, he thought it was great. There were some whisperings around Bankside that it was tainted. That chilling word "vengeance" had whistled down corridors and across hearths. And while Yonnis had been repentant of his revenge, Arlo was wallowing in his bloodlust. What was that doing to his soul?

16

The Great Hall, Bankside, Nasrin. Early morning. The nineteenth day of the Seventh Moon, Year Fifty-One.

THE DAYBREAK WAS difficult to discern, as the sky was dark with dense cloud, suiting the gloomy occasion. Lord Fergan was to be held to account for the atrocities in his region. Yonnis, Squire Tallier, Squire Clayhills, and many other officers of the government were making their way across the Bankside courtyard towards the Great Hall. On a high platform at the front of the hall, Squire Coppermills wore a fixed expression of benign gravity. He was presiding as judge over a packed courtroom. All the important men in the country, and some important women, were there to see Kimalloan justice at work.

Lord Fergan sat in a raised box, flanked by armed guards. He was a short man, about the same age as Yonnis, with the chestnut hair, olive skin, and green eyes common in his region. He wore crimson silk, and kept his tall black hat on. Although haggard, Lord Fergan wore a countenance of proud defiance.

Yonnis noticed that Arlo was seated on the top bench with Judge Coppermills and the prosecuting lawyer. He had subdued the Greenlands and he had brought Lord Fergan to trial. He had his place in history. Yonnis had congratulated him, but was troubled by the rumors of a great loss of civilian lives in the campaign. Squire Tallier's newssheets had claimed that the Army of Truth had not killed a single non-combatant. But of course, they could have stood by and let the local militia loose to avenge their families and neighbors. And he, Yonnis the Kingslayer, could say nothing, because he had admitted to vengeance. Arlo was the new hero, and because he had brought Lord Fergan to trial, the depopulation of the Greenlands was not up for discussion. For sure, Lord Fergan had started it, by giving free rein to malevolent priests who whipped up mobs to commit mass murder, but Arlo did not seem troubled by his contribution in the aftermath. He had even joked to Yonnis, "Good news for your Distributor friends! There is now plenty of land for them to bid for in the Greenlands."

Yonnis sat on a raised bench for government observers, situated behind the jury of thirteen gray-haired squires. He had been allocated a seat next to Mistress Deneesa Clayhills. What must she be feeling, since Fergan was her younger brother?

"Good morning, Mistress Clayhills," he greeted her, bowing before sitting. "This must be a difficult time for you."

Mistress Clayhills looked very sad, but she spoke with calm composure. "Thank you for your concern, Lord Arbiter. How is my foster daughter?"

"She is starting to get big. It is wonderful for me, Mistress Clayhills. I love to feel the baby kicking. Unfortunately, my dear wife is often worried, because of her mother's difficulties."

"I must reassure her. I'll visit when you are away, Duke Yonnis."

"Thank you, Mistress Clayhills. How is Master Yoshi?"

"Growing strong, for which I thank the Eternal Spirit every day."

Judge Coppermills called the court to order. "Brothers and sisters, we are here today for the trial of Lord Rikko Fergan of the Greenlands for incitement to mass murder."

Lord Fergan interrupted. "This is not a court that I recognize. It's not a king's court. Who are you commoners to judge a lord?"

Judge Coppermills seemed to relish the challenge. "You're going to sit and listen to the charges against you, prisoner, or I'll have you gagged and bound." He turned back to address the jury. "I hardly need remind you of the gravity of the proceedings. Please listen carefully and pray to the Eternal Spirit for guidance. I call on Arch-Elder Yeramo to bless our deliberations."

Lord Fergan jumped to his feet and spoke up again. "Judge, please excuse me from the room while that turncoat Raa speaks!"

"Be seated, Lord Fergan, address me as 'Your Honor' if you want my attention, and turn your face to the wall if you wish to exclude yourself from our reflection." Judge Coppermills was resolute.

Yonnis tried to understand Fergan. He must be so frustrated that the world had changed around him, and he was on the wrong side of history. Yonnis had never had to face such a challenge to his sense of self. Would he cope if it ever happened? He would probably be as angry as Fergan if it did.

Yeramo offered a brief blessing, and Judge Coppermills called the prosecutor to explain the charges. This prosecutor, a well-known, up-and-coming young lawyer, rose to address the jury. Yonnis admired his style. He was eloquent, explaining horrors in detail and without emotive elaboration, although his pauses were crafted to land his verbal blows. He described bands of masked and armed men going from house to house in ten towns, rounding up citizens who were Followers of the Truth. They were marched to the nearest temple, where they were locked in, and the buildings were set ablaze.

The mood in the Great Hall was somber. Faces that had been a blank canvas before the prosecutor started speaking were now lined with despair. There was silence for several moments after his speech, which finished with a list of over a hundred names of those who perished and the ominous words "and many, many more, whose remains were unidentifiable". Yonnis could not fail to remember similar words from the trial of the zealots who attacked Yeralla. How much of Farida had he been able to bury? Just a charred foot in a shoe.

The prosecutor started to call witnesses who could not be eloquent, and who found it difficult to recount what they had seen, heard, and smelled. Those listening in the courtroom started to turn red with anger or white with disgust. Tears were shed, a few fainted, and a few ran out to vomit.

The dark gray sky was getting darker as Lord Fergan was finally invited to offer a defense.

"Have you chosen a lawyer to speak for you, Lord Fergan?" Judge Coppermills asked.

"I'm not going to give credence to this charade by using one of your wordsmiths. I'll speak for myself... Your Honor." Lord Fergan rose, looked around, and when he was sure that everyone was watching him, he began. "This country's no longer recognizable as Kimalloa. Some disgruntled Yerallan Raa made up a few epigrams five decades ago, and a way of life which had its roots in the dawn of time has been attacked by men on the make. The so-called Truth is not religion, or even philosophy, and it is certainly not Truth. It's an excuse for rich men to rape Mother Earth to make them richer still."

Judge Coppermills interrupted him. "I didn't ask you for a political speech. Just answer the charges, Lord Fergan."

"I don't have to answer to you, impudent squire! I only have to answer to Lord Sudar, and we all know that whatever I say, I'm going to be with him soon enough. It was not me in a mask who rounded up god-killers, but I'll not condemn those who did. To have died by fire means that your coreligionists are now safe in the Dome of the Divine, realizing the error of their ways. 'Twas the kindest thing that their neighbors could've done for them."

Yonnis joined in the collective groan that reverberated around the Great Hall. Lord Fergan had condemned himself. The jury would go through the motions of retiring to reflect. To no one's surprise, they returned with a guilty verdict within fifteen moments—just 1,500 heartbeats. Yonnis watched Judge Coppermills as he carefully and deliberately prepared himself to pronounce the verdict.

"Prisoner, you are condemned to death. Since you think that death by fire is a kindness, we'll see how you feel when it's done to you. That shall be the method of your execution—"

"Wait, Your Honor!" Mistress Clayhills cried out.

"Yes, Mistress Clayhills?"

"Our law allows an appeal from a close relative, and I am the sister of this man. Guided by the wisdom of the late Lord Grakko, my first husband, I've long been a Follower of the Truth. I gave loyal service in the war of liberation. If my service has been valued, I beg that, if my brother must die—and of course, given the evidence, he must… , Your Honor, please grant him the mercy of beheading by sword."

There were murmurs and gasps around the Great Hall. Yonnis was relieved. Deneesa Clayhills might seem bitter at times, but she must believe in the value of love, even for those who are difficult to love.

Lord Fergan growled in frustration. "Ha! Don't be impressed by my sister's claim to love me as her brother when she shares a bed with the man who destroyed our home and our land, and she wasted no time installing her second son as the new lord of my region. Listen to *my* wish, Your Honor. I am ready to die by fire!"

Judge Coppermills shouted back. "In which case you are mad as well as bad! I agree to Mistress Deneesa Clayhills' request. Not as a mercy to the prisoner, but as a mercy to *her*. Commander Magg, find the best swordsman in the garrison to dispatch Lord Fergan on the bowling green at first light tomorrow morning. Bring a Raa from the North Gate Prison to pray with him tonight. Only officers of the court and the jury are to be allowed within thirty strides of the site of execution. The head will be displayed on the Binar Bridge Gate for six moons. Court dismissed."

There was a flurry of flapping black cloaks as the observers rose from their seats to leave.

Yonnis, Yeribbi and Squire Beechwoods were waiting by the great door, urging them to donate to the Greenlands' orphanages.

The quarters of the Arbiter, Bankside Place, Nasrin. Early morning. The twentieth day of the Seventh Moon, Year Fifty-One.

THE CLOUDS HAD scattered. A glorious full moon hung above the battlements in a dark blue sky, and shone soft silver beams through the casement windows of Number 4.

"Luna is blessing your journey," Esta had whispered to him as he turned to say goodbye.

Yonnis had replied with a passionate kiss. Would she be sensible while he was gone? Surely Pia would make sure that she was. Fergan's trial was still fresh in his memory, and his sleep had been disturbed by a particular memory of Boriela.

Yonnis was in a posse of men sent to clear the streets in the west of the town after the gate gave way. They went from house to house, hauling out any man with a weapon. The Yerallan Army rules were that a captured enemy combatant could turn their coat or hang; women, children, and the elderly should not be harmed. The South Borielan Army of Liberation had some rules too, but they were crazed with bloodlust after the enemy had thrown the charred bones of children over the walls at them as they laid siege to the town.

As his back was turned to the house he had been searching, he spotted a woman running into an alley on the far side of the main square. She was grabbed by two soldiers. One of them snatched her prayer beads and dangled them under her nose as he leered and laughed at her. Then he tugged at her skirt. Yonnis started to run towards the scene, but soon felt the weight of several men blocking him and holding him.

"This is a war, boy!"

"Look what they did to us!"

"The Sudo whore had it coming to her."

"No! We are Followers of the Truth! We are better than this!"

Esta had woken him out of his nightmare, as she often did. She seemed to be having a few of her own these days, triggered by memories of her mother's failed pregnancies. Yonnis felt a strong pull to stay with her, to indulge the aching joy he felt about the bump in her belly. But he also felt a strong sense of duty to respect his grandmother's request. She had made him feel special, ever since he was jostling to be noticed among his uncle's large brood of children and foster children. This might be his last chance to see her.

Four guards were waiting outside to escort him and his small entourage to the docks. Nasrin was waking up. Bakers were starting to waft sweet smells into the streets as the soil carriers made their last trips over the bridge to the south bank with their noxious cargo. Blacksmiths were firing up their forges, and the trundle of carts to and from the fruit, fish, and meat markets was building up. Men were queuing at the docks for work as they rode past. The ship taking Yonnis northwards was small and should be swift if the winds were kind. There was nothing to do but read and talk for a few days.

Yonnis's party was led by Commander Colmo, a former ploughman, who was very excited to be in charge of an international expedition. At Yonnis's request, Little Pollo, the drummer boy, was also included. He had ignored Yonnis's advice about the wool trade, and turned up at Bankside begging to work for the army. Colmo tried him out as a messenger. Pollo ran fast and he was both quick-witted and hardworking, so he got the job.

Kimalloans did not know much about Osiran, so Yonnis was peppered with questions every mealtime.

"How long 'ave you spent there before?"

"Eight moons in Year Forty. I went there to help my grandmother when she became regent for her brother."

"Are they Sudos?"

"No. Their gods are very similar, but they don't really matter. They have to worship the Emperor. That's why most of the emperors go raving mad."

"How much bigger is their land, compared to Kimalloa?"

"About ten times bigger, but much of it is too cold for people to live in."

"What do they eat?"

"They grow very good grain. We will eat nice bread."

"Do the women show their hair?"

"No. They cover up. Rich women in colorful and decorated silk, poor women in linen and wool. Don't even look at them, else their fathers or husbands will kill you horribly."

Yonnis also had long conversations with his companions and the sailors about their experiences during the war and their hopes for the peace. In particular, he reflected with Colmo, who was troubled by his time in the Greenlands.

And one day, Little Pollo cornered him in his cabin and asked, "Should I ask Mistress Suki to marry me?" He was shooting up now, his voice was high and low in the same sentence, and he was suffering all the pains of turning into a man.

Yonnis smiled at him. "What an honorable young man you are. You know, I asked my first wife to marry me when I had only eight years!"

"Did ya?!" asked Pollo. "And she waited for you to be a man?"

"She did. We married when I had sixteen years and she had twenty. I assure you, the wait was worth every moment."

"But the Elders are urging our women to get married soon, and there are loadsa soldiers, real men, in Bankside that might fall for Suki's lovely eyes and pious ways."

"Well, dear Pollo. If you don't ask, you will never know. There are three possibilities, and you must be prepared for all of them. She might say yes, and then it is just a matter of taking the Elder's advice about how long you should wait. You can build your friendship in the meantime. She might say she wants time to think about it. My wife did. In which case, you just have to be patient. But remind her from time to time—persistence always pays off. Bear in mind that Mistress Suki has a much better job than you—she might not want to give that up lightly. Of course, she could say no and marry someone else. Which will be hard for your true heart to take, but you must endure it. There will be other ladies for you, Pollo, I'm sure of it!"

Pollo nodded, and then asked a lot more questions. Yonnis relished the experience of playing the role of secondary parent to him. How long before he would be advising his own son? Esta's bump kicked so much, it must be a boy.

The winds were as kind as they could be. The voyage was smooth and quick. They scudded out of the mouth of the Binar into the Pozarian Strait and past the northern stretches of the Southeastern Region on day one. On day two, they tracked close to the coast of the Eastern Region, looking out for trouble from Pozaria on the starboard side. Yonnis watched Maylan Castle as they passed it. He remembered that, when he had been chatting to the Sudarite workers in Lord Aldor's craft shed, he had fondly imagined that peace in Kimalloa might be possible. Then came the Greenlands disaster, and he realized that it would take generations to heal the country's wounds. His quest would outlive him. At best, he could lay some foundations. On day three, the ship glided past the Northeast Region of the dangerous Lord Lazzar and the South Mountains of the loyal Lord Grakko Junior. On day four, they disembarked at the most northerly port in the Northern Mountains, where they were greeted by Lord Ulfan, who was to join them. Ulfan was the guardian of the borderlands, eager to broker some diplomacy with the new emperor. Yonnis found it challenging to put aside the memory of Ulfan holding a sword to his throat, but he had to work with him.

The small party were to meet the Osiranian royals at the nearest palace to the Kimalloan border, Larriklias. The ship's journey from Lord Ulfan's northern port to the Osiranian coast took another day. As the Kimalloan party docked, they were met by stone-faced Osiranians who were both guides and guards.

Yonnis was now apprehensive. It was over ten years since he had seen his Osiranian nanna. He remembered her as graceful, mysterious, and a lot of fun. Of course, he had always thought of his grandmother as old, but what could seventy-one years look like?

Osiran stretched out as far as they could see. Settlements were few and far between. They crossed plains rich with waving, black-seeded, full-eared grain, but the people working in the fields looked very thin. The Kimalloans were absolutely forbidden by the Emperor to offer alms to any of his subjects, so they just had to turn their heads away and travel onwards.

Larriklias, Osiran. Midmorning. The first day of the Eighth Moon, Year Fifty-One.

YONNIS HAD NOT been to Larriklias before. Osiranian cities could be so different, according to climate and the taste of the local feudal lord. It looked more cheerful than Nasrin at first glance, but it lacked the zest for progress which made the Kimalloan capital buzz. Larriklias was a cluster of white-walled buildings with glazed, blue-tiled roofs which reflected the glare of the sun. The streets were paved with a soft ochre rock, and were well drained. The people in the streets might as well have been wearing blinkers. They ignored the party of foreigners, focusing on their own tasks. After some confusing twists and turns, Yonnis saw a long building with large windows, surrounded by many soldiers and enormous metal gates, which were ornamental as well as defensive. After much shouting between the guides and the men behind the gates, they were opened and very swiftly closed again after the last of the rear guards passed them. Yonnis hadn't spoken Osiranian for many years, and it took a while to understand the instructions being barked at the party. Eventually, they dismounted by the steps to the door of the palace, and waited.

Within a few moments, the mighty bronze doors were pushed open, each needing three men to do it. Flanked by two senior military men in lavishly adorned deep red uniforms, and a tall-hatted, black-clad priest, were an elderly woman in a shimmering blue robe and veil topped with a gold coronet, and a small young man dressed almost entirely in gold brocade who also wore a coronet, although he seemed too delicate to bear the weight. His hair was light brown, straight, and thin; his eyes were a soft gray, and he smiled warmly at the visitors.

"Welcome, kinsman and friends," said the young emperor, in faltering Kimalloan.

Yonnis was excited to see his grandmother, and he wanted to rush and embrace her, but in Osiran, that would never do. The party all knelt, and waited to be told to rise. Emperor Ikra did not allow their knees to gather dust. He waved at them to stand up. Yonnis slowly recited a speech of thanks. The Emperor nodded, and then Yonnis carefully embraced his grandmother, who wept joyful tears. He held her gently, as she seemed so frail, but she clung to him fiercely.

"Oh, blessings of our ancestors!" she cried. "Is this grizzly warrior truly the little scrapper that used to make me laugh with his antics?"

A warm feeling of being loved washed over Yonnis. He beamed and turned pink, feeling glad and proud that she had fond memories of him. As a child, he had always run first to Nanna Kirina to demonstrate any new skills he had been taught, shamelessly showing off. "It's been too long, Nanna. I'm sorry. I have been trying to put the world to rights."

"Hmm," she muttered. "Let's discuss that later. Now, we must make you comfortable after your long journey. It's time to eat."

While most of the party were escorted to the kitchens to enjoy the legendary Osiranian bread with some very strong cold meat, Yonnis, Lord Ulfan, and Commander Colmo were served lavish roast dishes on finely decorated silver platters, and vintage wine in glasses that shone like crystal in a room that seemed to be all windows and mirrors. The ceiling swirled with gold plasterwork and colorful paintings. The opulence made Yonnis feel uncomfortable. Lord Ulfan demonstrated his diplomatic skills, wading in to thank and praise the Osiranian nation for their goodwill at the border during the war, and for the opportunity to talk about improved trade and communications. Yonnis watched him with curiosity. Lord Ulfan could be fierce and hotheaded, but could also be so charming when he chose to be. Which was the real Ulfan?

Office of the Intelligence Minister, the Archive, Bankside, Nasrin. Late evening. The first day of the Eighth Moon, Year Fifty-One.

ALL-EARS SLAPPED HIS cousin on the back and hugged him. "Bravo, Father of the People. You've done it again! Why were we ever worried about letting the veterans vote?"

Yoshi smiled ironically. "It's a relief to have their endorsement of the constitution."

"So now we can get on with things again—but..." All-Ears grumbled. "Yes, there is always a 'but'. The Distributors have a new petition for land reform, an even bigger one this time. I am going to need a bigger Archive Building if they carry on like this."

Each dealing gingerly with their own stiff limbs, All-Ears and Yoshi sat down slowly.

All-Ears started to summarize the work of his agents. "There's nostalgic chatter in the inns—in the countryside inns—for the 'good old days'. It's a folk memory, although a false one, of vast swathes of common land where even the lowest of the serfs could graze their cow and pig all year long. The Distributors tell them that the evil bastard Rikko VIII gave—yes, we know he sold it, but people have been led to think that he *gave*—the common land to lords and squires to graze sheep to boost the wool trade and his tax coffers, while his people were left to starve. So, in the minds of the petitioners, a return of common land is theirs by ancient right—"

All-Ears noticed Yoshi grimace in pain. He had pushed back into his chair, closed his eye, and twisted every muscle in his body for several heartbeats, his skin turning a deathly gray. All-Ears leaned forward in panic and grasped his hand. "What is it, Yoshi?"

"I'm sorry to disquiet you, Ellis. Please do go on."

"Not until you tell me what Yersil makes of your complaint," All-Ears demanded. "I take it that you have consulted him?"

"Ellis, we're not getting any younger—"

"You don't need to tell me. I get less able to move day by day. But my decline has been very slow and gradual. You were as energetic as a man half your age just a season ago, and now—well, I must speak frankly. You look frail. And that's not right, my little cousin."

All-Ears cast his mind back to Yoshi as a boy. Yoshi had been fostered with the Talliers while his father endured imprisonment, and the loss of his right hand, for challenging Rikko IX over one of his many arbitrary taxes. Young Yoshi had been vigorous, although also very thoughtful and studious. The young All-Ears had not been gifted with athleticism—he had always been destined to spend his life with paper and ink—but Yoshi had encouraged his elder cousin to play indoor games, and All-Ears often wondered whether his reluctance to let Yoshi, or anyone else, win at hide-and-seek had determined his career.

"Well, to save you torturing a confession out of Yersil, I'll tell you." Yoshi joked, but he did not smile. His face was a picture of defeat. "I have the wasting disease. I've several months of increasing pain and incapacity to endure, and then, if the Spirit is merciful, I may pass."

All-Ears burst into tears. His sobs were loud enough to solicit a knock on the door from a footman. Yoshi sent the footman to find cloths and stronger beer, then he dragged his chair closer to his distraught friend.

"It's bad enough to be facing the pain myself, but I also bear the burden of knowing that my pain will cause distress to my nearest and dearest. But you can prepare, Ellis. By the time I go, you'll be relieved that I'm at peace."

The footman arrived with supplies and left rapidly. All-Ears wiped his eyes and blew his large nose noisily. He was shivering.

Yoshi leaned forward to shovel some coal onto the perpetual fire in the grate. "I don't want immortality—"

"Well, you have it, Clayhills!" All-Ears snapped back. "You are the hero of the revolution, even if you are modest about it. It was you who did all the thinking, all the planning, and took the stand in Nasrin to trigger the mutiny! And the wasting disease is not a fitting end for you! It's cruel, and… it tests my faith! It tests my faith. How can the Eternal Spirit be the force for good in the world if It allows this? As if you hadn't suffered enough in your lifetime." All-Ears sat back in his chair, closing his eyes and clenching his fists.

"Ellis, no!" Yoshi chided him. "Any of us might get it. Our scriptures free us from ideas about curses and illnesses being deserved or undeserved. They just happen. I must endure. And, although I've had times of despair, I've been blessed. I've seen a transformation in Kimalloa that was unimaginable when I was a boy. I feel that I've done something to improve the world."

All-Ears looked at his cousin's eyepatch and his twisted leg, and reflected that perhaps it was a miracle that Yoshi had made it to fifty years. But he couldn't accept that the end was in sight.

"You must have an Elder in the house at all times to tend to you. Are you staying here or going to your manor?"

"There's still so much to do. But I will take longer spells at the manor, and I do want my last days to be there. Please make sure that I'm buried at the temple in Clayhills Town—without a marker, I want no fuss."

"You might not want fuss. But the country will want to mark your passing."

"Well, maybe we can turn our minds to that nearer the time. For now, we need to deal with the land reform petition. Let's get Yonnis to do a bit of arbitrating with the radicals when he gets back."

"Yoshi! Don't change the subject when I am not ready for it. I'm sorry to ask—but you know that I *have* to ask—who will hold the country together when you're gone? I know Ronni Coppermills is your deputy, but he's even older than us."

Yoshi looked surprisingly defiant. "The Assembly should elect a new leader, when I've gone. There's a process in place."

"But we must consider—"

"No, Ellis. We shouldn't fix things for the next generation. They must make their own decisions. Please, let's not discuss this again."

The Father of the People promptly left, leaving All-Ears in turmoil. If he lost Yoshi, could he carry on? His dedication had been inspired by Yoshi's. Why did he have to live on and watch Yoshi die? He wanted to be free from the pains in his joints, his wheeziness in winter, his fragile stomach, cold feet, failing eyes and ears and bladder, and innumerable other daily challenges, but above all to be freed from the gaping hole of loneliness in his life that would appear when Yoshi was gone. Maybe there were other brilliant, skilled, kind, wise men to carry the banner of Truth when Yoshi passed, but they would not be All-Ears' extraordinary little cousin. There was only one of him.

The Palace of Larriklias, Osiran. Midmorning. The second day of the Eighth Moon, Year Fifty-One.

WHILE LORD ULFAN managed the talks about trade and security, Yonnis sat with his grandmother in a room with finely woven tapestries on the walls and patterned carpets on the floor. The chairs were large, amply stuffed with soft wool, and covered with thick velvet. A huge silver pot, full of the finest camellia tisane, stood ready for its refreshing contents to be poured into delicately painted cups. Yonnis was dressed in his best suit of ivy wool and white lace, but he still looked shabby and out of place. His grandmother was robed in bright blue silk and dripping with silver jewelry.

"Is the tisane ready to drink yet, Yonnis?"

He checked the pot and poured it, then placed the cup on the table beside her. Nanna Kirina beamed at him and grasped his hands.

"What a joy it is to be with you. You know, I was sending you as much positive magic as I could to get you through those battles, but I always worried that it was not enough, and I would never see you again." She paused, and lost her smile. "The curse of long life is that so many of my children and grandchildren have died before me." Tears began to roll down her wrinkled cheeks. "I hope I last long enough to see a great-grandchild from you, and young Ikra secure on his throne."

Yonnis leaned across to hug her, as gently as he could.

"Thank you, Yonnis. It's so good to feel you as flesh and blood! I know that you've never forgotten me, despite being so busy. Every letter has been a relief that—thanks to miracles from whoever we choose to worship—you're still alive, and loving me, as I love you. But to be sitting here with you—it's a privilege to have the company of my dear boy again." Kirina kissed his hands and sighed. "Sometimes I miss Yeralla. Such a beautiful country with all the roaring waterfalls and bright blue lakes and silver-barked woods. Don't you miss it?"

"Yes, I do. Not just because it is beautiful. I do think that, despite that horrible day, Yeralla is a fair and rational place, a safe place to live."

Nanna Kirina sighed. "Can't you ever think of your homeland without thinking of the atrocity? Surely, we can now close that chapter? I was proud of you when I heard that you had killed Navvan Glantar. I knew then that you have some of my Osiranian blood in you."

"Please, Nanna—in my faith, avenging is not a duty, it is wrong—"

"But him?! You knew that he had to *pay*. For Farida. Anya and Merutis too, but mostly Farida. Your lovely Farida. Do you remember how you used to run after her? You were eight and she was twelve, but she never dismissed you as a baby. She was under your spell, as I was. And when you fought off those boys who teased her, with your wooden sword! It was so funny! Of course, not so funny when you stole a real dagger from the combat school and lunged at one of them for pulling at her veil. You got beaten for that. But you did not mind, because you had shown Farida that you were her knight."

Yonnis heaved with regret as he was flung back in time, remembering adventures with Farida, Merutis, and his cousin Anya. Carefree years before he got dragged off to the Borielan war. He had hoped in some way that he was keeping his friends safe, and he hadn't. They were all gone.

"I don't understand your mad religion that makes you feel guilty for doing a natural thing."

"Didn't you learn about it—with Grandpa?"

She laughed. "I think that your grandfather was a true Yerallan pirate! Welcoming the creed of Yerobis was about seizing the riches of the priesthood!" Then she became serious. "A spirituality based on logic... It's not possible. We humans need magic. I was loyal, of course, and I wore those dreary robes and veils. I think you can see that it did not take me long to lose that." Nanna Kirina waved her hand over her bright attire and decoration. "But..." she whispered, and winked. "I did bring some of those thinking processes back—I want to know what magic works every time and why. That will help to keep Osiran ahead of Bessema." She leaned forward. "Now, my favorite boy, let's take this rare chance to share in conversation what we can't share in letters. On the subject of putting a queen in dreary robes, tell me what is really going on between you and your second wife. I know that you must love her. Does she love you?"

Yonnis looked at the swirling patterns on the carpet. How they reflected his swirling emotions about his wife. "I know that I married for a reason you must find strange. I had disappointed Squire Clayhills... No, I must be completely open about my wrongdoing—I had betrayed his trust. I needed to make amends to him, and to Kimalloa, so that the men who followed me into battle could enjoy a prosperous peace. So, I committed to a quest for the peace of Kimalloa, and to do penance for wreaking my personal vengeance on Navvan. Squire Clayhills wanted me to marry the enemy's niece. It was supposed to be a gesture of reconciliation—but really, I am her jailer. The most that I can hope for from her? Some recognition that I am trying to be kind about it, perhaps? Anyway, when were women ever supposed to love their husbands? We must be grateful to be tolerated."

Nanna Kirina's eyes narrowed, and then she sighed.

"Do you understand, Nanna? I did think about your situation. You were married to Grandpa for peace, and it worked very well."

"Oh, Yonnis. What a mess. I am proud that you care so much for peace and people and progress, but really, do you think that you can do it single-handed?" Nanna Kirina shook her head. "And Esta—did *she* marry to make this peace work? Or does she still want to be queen?"

Yonnis felt dread forming in his gut, but perhaps Nanna could help? She had been the one who taught him so much when he was turning from a boy into a man. Without embarrassment, she had explained how women's minds and bodies worked, and the joys and miseries of relationships. "Yes, she does still think that it is her destiny to be queen. The death of her brother and father put her in a position where she might be expected to rule as queen in her own right in Kimalloa, but being deposed, disappeared, and then a protected... guest... of the revolution, well, she has suffered shock and disappointment. I think she is still in the world of her father's court—in her head."

Nanna Kirina straightened her back and winced with pain. She stared straight at Yonnis, her eyes full of concern. "But you will never be her knight restoring her to the throne, because of your beliefs, and your hatred of her faith."

Yonnis leaped to his own defense. "But on a personal level, I *am* saving her. I am saving her from herself and the people who would manipulate her. If she tried to launch a rebellion, she would fail and be executed. So, I am her knight."

"Not in her eyes, Yonnis." Nanna Kirina took a sip of tisane. "You are standing in her way. I know what it is like to be a queen, a wife queen, and then I had much more power when I returned here as regent. It gives you a zest for life. People have to listen to you and do what you say—how rare a privilege is that for a woman? I can imagine how awful it would be to have it taken away. Of course she would want it back. She will never stop wanting it back."

There was an awkward silence between them. Yonnis examined the patterns on the carpet again. Was there enough reasoning, or even magic, in the world that could persuade Esta that there was more joy in modesty and motherhood than in beauty and power?

After some moments, Nanna Kirina spoke. "If she had the chance to realize her dreams, in a way that did not compromise the peace of Kimalloa, would you love her enough to let her go?"

Yonnis felt his stomach churning. Of course, if his love were true, it would mean letting Esta go. That was painful enough— but how could he lose another child? "But, Nanna, we are a family now. We are tied forever by a new life. Of course I can't let her go." He reflected on his words, knowing that the very different worldviews of mother and father would be played out year after year as they tried to commandeer the soul of the child, who would probably hate them for the confusion and strife. He didn't want that. He stared appealingly at his grandmother. "Can I?"

17

Queen Reena's Hospital, the Great North Road, Nasrin. Midmorning. The fifth day of the Eighth Moon, Year Fifty-One.

DENEESA'S SLEEP HAD been interrupted by extraordinary noises from Arlo. She tried to wake him, but he seemed to be in the grip of some kind of trance. He was raving about the time that was coming, the reckoning for the superstitious hordes, his destiny to save Kimalloa. She went to get cold cloths from the kitchen to reduce his sweating. Eventually, he had come round, and looked at her as if she were a complete stranger.

"Arlo?" she asked. "Are you back in the land of the living?"

"What's happening?" He looked frightened.

"You just had a bad dream, darling. Again. Try to go back to sleep. Ye'll forget it."

Arlo shut his eyes and did seem to drift off into more peaceful sleep. Dawn had broken, the first reflection had come and gone. Deneesa slipped out of the house. Two guards followed. First of all, she went to the flower market and bought a whole cartload of flowers, ordering the flower-seller to push it to the Queen Reena Hospital. Deneesa walked alongside. The poor woman kept looking at the fine dark brown wool of Deneesa's robe and veil.

"May I ask who you are, Yer Ladyship?"

"I am Mistress Deneesa Clayhills, wife of General Clayhills, daughter-in-law of the Father of the People, Squire Yoshi Clayhills."

"Oh my!" gasped the flower-seller. "What an honor it is to meet you! And to 'ave sold my flowers to you! Oh, just wait till I get home to tell my little 'uns!"

"At least you will be home early today, sister. Where do you live?"

"Near Mersin. I buy from lots of diff'rent folk as I walk into the city. The women and children cut flowers from the field edges 'fore sun-up."

"Excellent! It warms my heart to hear about such hard work and keen enterprise. Mersin, you said? So d'ye attend the Distributor meetings?"

The flower-seller took a while to answer, and her answer sounded defensive and deliberate. "Only to sell pies."

"You make pies too! May the Spirit bless you, sister, for sharing your skills."

"Thank you, Yer Ladyship."

Deneesa asked no more questions. She started to tell the flower-seller about her children, focusing on the younger ones living in Nasrin. When they got to the gates of the hospital, she gave the flower-seller a generous bonus. Once inside, she walked with a nurse, from ward to ward, setting up the flowers where they might cheer the poor sick folk. She had really come here to see Elder Yersil, and after the last vase was put in place, he appeared, unwrapping a bloodstained apron and handing it to a nurse. Another nurse brought a bowl, and to Deneesa's relief, he washed and wiped his hands thoroughly before shaking hers.

"Thank you so much for bringing so many flowers," he said. "They cheer those who work and volunteer here as well as the sick and the dying. How can I help you, Mistress Clayhills?"

"I wondered if ye'd treated men returning from the Greenlands with swamp fever?"

"Yes. Of course. Any particular bout of it is usually not very serious, unless the person is already weak. But unfortunately, it does recur, and as the person gets older, the fever can be more of a threat."

"What're the symptoms?"

"Well, feeling very hot, sweating, trembling, fainting. Loss of appetite. Sometimes the sufferer has delusions. It lasts for about three days."

"Three days." Deneesa thought hard about her next question. It was going to be easy for Yersil to guess that she was inquiring about symptoms that Arlo had, but she expected that he would be discreet. If Tallier found out... well, he probably knew already. Her household staff were as obliged to inform as any others.

They started walking back to the front gate of the hospital.

"Is it ever shorter than three days, but recurrent within days?"

Yersil hesitated. So, she must assume that he had guessed. Now she had to deal with the honest answer he was duty bound to give. "That's unlikely to be swamp fever, Mistress Clayhills."

"What's it likely to be?" She waited.

"It sounds like... well, the scenario is usually this. When men have serious wounds, we have to treat them with dream-inducing plants to reduce their pain during operations—those very plants that the Sudarites use to induce their so-called religious experiences. Sometimes, the wounded like the effect and feel driven to experience it again after they've healed. Those plants can be procured, if you're keen enough to find them. Especially in regions like the Greenlands."

Deneesa struggled not to show her dread. "Oh, I see. And does that drive for the plants last long?"

Yersil's brow was knitted with lines of concern. "Mistress, we know from those dreadful superstitious practices that the plants can make people mad. Some people can control their use of them—the Raas were expert at that, of course. But that's quite rare."

"How sad… Have Healing Elders developed the knowledge to help the sufferers?"

"There is someone. But the sufferers have to want to go to her. No treatment is easy, nor is it guaranteed to work."

"Perhaps I could fund some research?"

Yersil smiled at her. "Thank you for your generous offer, Mistress Clayhills. I am sure that it would be helpful."

Deneesa thought that she could detect pity in the Healing Elder's demeanor. She did not like the feeling of being pitied.

The orchards of the south bank, Nasrin. Early afternoon.
The fifth day of the Eighth Moon, Year Fifty-One.

ESTA WAS HORRIFIED by her big belly, and even more horrified that Pia urged her to exercise, claiming that it might make the birth easier. After lunch one day, when the sun was high and the sky was cloudless, Pia had waved some paper at her with unprecedented enthusiasm.

"I have passes from All-Ears himself!" Pia chirruped like a bird trying to attract a mate. "We can enjoy the clear air of the south bank orchards! He wants us to be refreshed for his special supper tonight."

"I'm not sure."

"Esta, I know that you must be uncomfortable, but please don't deny me a change of scenery."

"You can go where you want. I'm the one under house arrest."

Pia waited.

Esta gave in. "Alright. Perhaps I can get some plums fresh off the tree and enjoy them before All-Ears poisons me."

Pia laughed. "Oh, Mistress Misery! What am I to do with you? Let's look at it that way, if you like—our last taste of beautiful plums. We'll enjoy them all the more!"

Two guards followed them across the busy Binar Bridge,

recently paved with mottled gray stones, where travelers and traders from the south were arriving, noting with gruesome interest the heads on pikes over the gate into the city. Everyone with a cart going in and going out was subject to clumsy searches from surly militiamen. They checked passes and wooden identity tokens, then peered invasively into the faces of those that they checked, so that they might remember them.

The green-coated guards ensured that Esta and Pia would be waved past the line, but of course they had to chat with their comrades in the process. Esta heard one of the guards ask the militia about the fresh heads on the gate.

"What did they do?"

"Forgin' coins, stealin' from a hospital, murderin' an innkeeper—and the woman was an adulteress."

The guards and the militiamen shrugged and nodded, as if to say, They got what was coming to them.

Then a militiaman added, "Fergan's rottin' well—a bit of 'is cheek fell on a wherryman yesterday!"

The men laughed. Esta shivered as she took a brief look at Fergan's rotting head. It could have been hers.

Within a few moments, Esta and Pia were on the wide public footpath through the orchards, which enabled citizens to admire the fruit. This was Lord Ralf's land, and his able Squire Cherry managed it well. The sight of rows and rows of ripening fruit on neatly espaliered trees and the colorful carpet of wild plants between them cheered Esta. Bees buzzed among the flowers that grew between the rows. Their honey-rich hives were another income source for the resourceful managing squire. Children, supposedly there to chase birds off the ripening fruit, were running up and down the rows in sheer joy in the sunshine. Esta wished that she could join them.

"Look how full the apples are already! And they are such a nice mix of green and red. Perhaps we can find someone to explain what variety they are. And maybe there will be a sorting station where we can buy some plums?"

Pia's face darkened. "I can't see any fruit-pickers around. But I can see some horsemen crossing at the junction of the paths ahead."

Esta followed Pia's eyeline to the riders. "D'you know, that man in the middle looks like Arlo Clayhills. His beard is so distinctive."

"It is General Clayhills," Pia noted. "I wonder where he's been this morning that requires him to take the path through the orchards."

They waited to politely greet the general. He rode ahead of the other soldiers and stopped in front of them. He dismounted, swept off his hat, and bowed. Esta's guards saluted him. Esta and Pia curtsied. As Pia rose, she waved the passes at him.

"Mistress Krusa. Mistress Pia." Arlo smiled. "How nice to see you. I hope that you're well."

"Yes, thank you, General." Esta was thinking of keeping the conversation as brief as possible, but curiosity got the better of her. "What brings you to the orchards today? Other than the cheerful sight of fruit that'll keep us from hunger in the winter?"

"This fruit has to be guarded, madam. There have been several attempts by organized criminals to steal cartloads of it from the stores and from the craft sheds where it's dried or bottled. The militia need help from the army at this time of year."

"It is such a blessing from the Eternal Spirit that the Army of Truth are ensuring the security of our food." Esta commented, with false cheerfulness.

"It's quite a change for our intelligence services to be infiltrating apple gangs instead of an opposition army's regiments. But we can take on any challenge." Arlo was clearly proud of everything he supervised. Then his tone changed, it became softer. "Mistress Krusa, may I speak to you without your companion—?"

To Esta's relief, Pia butted in quickly. "No, you may not, General. Mistress Krusa may not speak with any man privately, except her husband."

"If you had let me finish, insolent woman, I was going to say, 'so close'. I suggest that you take some steps back and I will keep the official distance away."

Pia retreated, but stared with intent at the space between Esta and Arlo. It was the required three strides, just.

"I haven't had a chance to congratulate you on your fruitfulness, Mistress… Esta."

Esta did not like the familiarity, but she did not correct him. "Thank you, General Clayhills. Of course, you have been away on duty." She was not going to offer him any congratulations for his ruthless suppression of her people. "Please convey my blessings to Mistress Clayhills. It's so kind of her to be visiting me and helping me to prepare for my child." Esta felt her heart beating faster. She knew from her very first meeting with Arlo that he was attracted to her. At the time, she had been quite attracted to him, but now, she found him frightening.

"I wish you a safe delivery." This was polite enough. Why did it need to be private? Then Arlo lowered his voice. "I'm sorry that you have to bear the child of yesterday's man. But things can be different. I am the man of the future, my lady. There will come a time when you need my support. Because when you're in prison—and you seem determined to end up there—I will be able to do what I like with you. Think about what you're going to do when that time comes. Be assured of my…" Arlo paused to make sure that he had her attention. "Be assured of my admiration."

He did look at her with admiration, but it was of the cynical kind offered by a man with power over a woman. Esta saw lust, and a desire to do her harm. She imagined that it was the look that men give women they intend to use, abuse, and then accuse. The tension between them was broken when Arlo's horse whinnied and stamped.

"It seems your horse is ready to go," she said, turning her gaze to the ground, noticing the horse dropping a pile of fresh manure on it. She lifted her pomander to her nose.

Arlo mounted the horse and put his hat back on. "Safe journey home, mistress."

She thanked him. He rode back to his soldiers.

Pia stepped quickly to Esta's side and clasped her hand. "Calm down, Esta, breathe deeply."

"Curse him for upsetting me when I'm carrying an innocent child! What happened to the charming, wounded war hero?"

"Shhh! You must not use that word. Do you want to get us both hanged?"

"I think that he threatened me, Pia, but I couldn't work out what he meant."

"Let's talk about it later. We must make sure that he has no opportunity to harm you."

"Let's go back," Esta decided. "The smell of that horse poo has put me off buying fruit. Should I tell Yonnis how much I fear his friend?"

"Perhaps. Let's pray to Feena for guidance."

Esta looked at Pia and knew that she had heard more than she was supposed to hear. She suspected that Pia could hear a pin drop at forty strides.

A quayside inn, Nasrin. Early afternoon. The twenty-fifth day of the Eighth Moon, Year Fifty-One.

SEEMO HAD JUST finished reading out a newssheet about the new tax inspectors who were going to make sure that the greedy lords and merchants paid their dues. The drinkers in the inns had uttered the occasional muted cheer, but were soon bored by the subject. It was not one that sold well. Seemo sat at a table on the outer frontage of the inn, on a roughly hewn bench.

He watched the activity in the ships and the relentless flow of the Binar. As he gazed aimlessly towards the west end of the quay, where a large Borielan ship was being unloaded, he noticed a black cap on a pale man, a gray dog, and—Spirit be praised— Little Pollo, who was no longer little. Seemo waved. Pollo broke into a run and arrived, enveloping him in a huge hug.

"My, my, it's good to see you, scamp! And I dare say that your ma would love to see you too! Are you on your way there?"

Pollo looked towards the Arbiter, who was now standing by the table. He had taken off his cap, as if he were going to stay.

"Go and see your ma, then, Pollo. Take Nessi, if you like."

Seemo noticed that Pollo responded as if he had received an order, and trotted away with the dog.

Then the Arbiter turned to Seemo. "May I join you, brother? I need your professional advice on land reform. Will you spare me some time for a pie and a mug of beer?"

"Oh." Seemo had not been expecting this. He laughed. "It sounds like you're taking the piss out of me, Arbiter, but if it's worth pie 'n' beer, you go ahead."

They talked about Little Pollo's adventures on the Osiran trip until the landlady appeared with two mugs of Nasrin's favorite dark beer and two pies consisting of dry pastry with questionable meat as a filling. Seemo quaffed some beer, bit into the pie, and waited for the Arbiter to get down to business.

"I know that you are suspicious of me, but I think that you also know that I supported votes for veterans out of respect for the men that I fought with, and I have no vested interest in blocking the aspirations of the Distributors. I am a foreigner after all, with no land in Kimalloa."

Seemo gave him a wry smile. "That's as may be. But you earn yer comforts from the Assembly's coffers. And you're an aristocrat. Your pa had land."

"That's how I know what an onerous responsibility it is. And the weather can be against you, especially in Kimalloa, which is why you need an alternative product to grain so that the country can buy grain elsewhere when harvests fail. A pig or a cow on the common is not the answer."

Seemo wondered who was giving the advice. He took another mouthful of beer, savored it, and then took another. Then he replied with heartfelt truths. "Some of the people who signed that petition have seen their children die from hunger. And you can't imagine what that feels like, till it happens to you. A cow or a pig on the common might be the difference between life and death for innocent little ones."

Seemo knew that the Arbiter's wife was carrying. Had he had struck a nerve? The Arbiter looked very thoughtful. Eventually, he answered.

"You are right—I cannot imagine how that feels in my heart. I can only work things out in my head. Hunger comes from different directions. When food is taken from you. When you can't afford it. When it is not there because the harvest failed, or the animals got a disease. A country like Kimalloa, that has trouble producing a regular food supply, has to have something reliable to trade with others in return for their food when we have none. Maybe in time it will be coal, or metals, or bricks and stone. But for now, the country needs wool, and sheep need space to graze. You used to be a shepherd, Seemo—surely you know something about it."

Seemo grumbled cynically. "What you mean is that landowners won't give up the profits from wool. Let's get down to the crux of the matter, Mr. Arbiter. Is the Assembly going to refuse to sign off the proposal?"

The Arbiter leaned across the table to make closer eye contact. Seemo did not want a staring match, but he was prepared to endure one, if he must.

"I've come to you at some risk, brother. You know that. In certain quarters, they do not like me standing up for veterans."

Seemo had to acknowledge that that might be true, but he

was not swayed by it. "Very brave of you, I'm sure. What's your answer, Arbiter?"

"Kimalloa survives on borrowed money, and we pay back with wool. We cannot default on those loans, given to us by allies to support our cause. Your proposal, as it is currently worded, will fail. Do you see why?"

Words. These fancy folk twisted them into riddles.

"You're looking to approve some different words to the ones people signed up to?"

"The best I think possible is that lords and squires are obliged, without seeking compensation, to restore one tenth of the land enclosed in the time of Rikko VIII to common land."

A tenth?! So that was the most that was on offer.

"One tenth?! I can't go back to my men and say that's a good deal!" Seemo's face twisted in indignation, and he banged his pot of beer on the table.

"It is a lot of land for most squires to gift back to the people, and a huge amount for lords! Their forefathers did pay the King for it, even if it wasn't his to sell. There will be a lot of opposition, even to one tenth. Is it better than nothing?"

A tenth. Not much room for cows. A few chickens and geese, perhaps.

"You men born to rule! You protect your own land and trade and give the men who fight for you crumbs—just crumbs! You make me sick."

The Arbiter did not react. He did not appear to be angry, and he was not getting up to leave.

Seemo sighed in frustration. "When this proposal's debated, there'll be a huge crowd in Vict'ry Park. We'll let the Assembly know which way they should vote."

Now the Arbiter looked at him with a hint of desperation. "If we don't find a way forward on this vote, the issue will go back in the line for a very, very long time. Please, Seemo. I am committed to the peace of Kimalloa—I know that you and the

Distributors are too. Don't risk a backlash from landowners! There are many who would soon turn their coats and invite in a Pozarian pretender if they feel that the Assembly asks too much of them."

Seemo finished his beer. "Don't threaten me, Arbiter. If the lords want a fight with us, we're up for it. We beat the King and we'll beat them."

The Arbiter just would not shut up. "Being a leader is not just being a dog who barks for others. Leaders sometimes have to ask their followers to do difficult things. I urge you to be gracious about a tenth. See how it works out. You can always petition again after five years. Remember your scriptures—even small steps of progress are blessings."

Seemo placed his hands on the table and rose carefully, reaching for his crutches. "Arbiter, you said you'd come to ask my advice. It is—you do what you have to do to survive in yer job, and I'll be the judge of how I survive in mine. Thanks for the pie 'n' beer." He swung away from the table and headed home, burdened by what he had heard.

The office of General Arlo Clayhills, Bankside. Early morning. The twenty-sixth day of the Ninth Moon, Year Fifty-One.

"UNCLE ELLIS! YOU'RE like a ghost that haunts this fortress!" All-Ears smiled at Arlo, as if his presence there at such an early time were completely normal. He was sitting in the general's office, at the general's desk, and he had been rummaging in it, and wanted Arlo to know that he had been rummaging in it. It was the power he had. He looked intently at Arlo, his big frame looming in the doorway, the worry on his face, and at his sunken eyes and blotchy skin. He looked like he had been on the poppy juice again. "And good morning to you too, Arlo. I'll take that as a compliment. Did you have a good breakfast?"

"Yes, thank you, sir. Look, I'm busy. What's the purpose of your visit?" Arlo moved into the office, closed the door, and opened a window.

All-Ears winced at the prospect of a draft of fresh air. "Your pa's illness—"

Arlo grabbed All-Ears' gown with both hands and pulled him to his feet. He pressed his face close to his. "Shut up! Just… shut up!"

"Arlo, if there is anything that I can do to help, I'm your secondary parent…"

"Help? How can you help when the Elders say there's no hope?!"

"Of course, I understand that. But I want to help *you*, Arlo. We all need help when we face the loss of loved ones—even if it's just someone to listen."

Arlo released his grip, and All-Ears reached quietly for his stick for balance.

"Sir, it would be no privilege to have you listen to me—you listen to every conversation in Kimalloa. But as my secondary parent, you may do something." Arlo's ire seemed to slip away. His expression became thoughtful, anguished, even sheepish. "Please, if you are talking to me as Uncle Ellis—please would you remind my pa that I am his *heir*?"

All-Ears nodded. "Well, Arlo, I can do that. Let me leave you to your duties. I hope that you have a productive day."

He noticed Arlo's eyes flashing with hope, and his stomach rolled.

18

The quarters of the Arbiter, Bankside Place, Nasrin.
Midmorning. The twenty-sixth day of the Ninth Moon,
Year Fifty-One.

"WHY IS THIS happening to me?!" Esta wailed.
It had started just after Yonnis left for work.
She had been lying in bed, trying to drift back off to sleep. The
agonizing twist between her hips shocked her wide awake. She
sat up and groaned, then saw her belly move and felt a gush of
liquid between her legs. Dampness spread across the mattress.
She screamed, and Suki and Pia had run in. Of course, she had
been told about childbirth and had seen what it had done to
her mother, but this had barely touched her imagination about
experiencing it for herself. She shrieked at every contraction
and sobbed in between.

"This is torture! My back is breaking, my parts are burning—
they are burning! Can't you do something?" Pia was a Raia—
where was her magic?!

"The only thing that can be done now is to encourage the
baby to be quick," Pia replied. "You need to keep calm and keep
moving. Breathe slowly, please—in for three... hold... out for
three... wait... in for three..."

Suki and Pia walked Esta around and around, but it was not
easing the pain. Occasionally they would stop and sit her on

the birthing stool to help the baby move downwards. Every few moments, Pia would check for signs that the baby was ready to be pushed out.

"*Argh!* It's like a sword shredding my innards! Pia, ease the pain, please, it's unbearable—is there something evil inside me for it to hurt so? I wish that I could faint!" Esta felt her belly tightening like a corset of hot metal. "I need to pass water!"

Suki placed a chamber pot between her legs and said, "Let it go, mistress."

Esta did.

Pia then offered her some warm beer. "Now drink, mistress. This should help."

Pia flashed her green eyes at her, and Esta believed that there would be something special in the liquid now warming her throat.

The reassurance did not last long.

"Agh! There's something like a cannonball pushing down into my parts! Oh… it's agony! When is it going to stop?" Tears burst forth again, and Esta whimpered.

"Breathe!" Pia snapped, and then sat Esta on the birthing stool again, pushing up the skirt of her smock and parting her legs. "It's looking good, Esta. Can you try to push?"

"Push? What the fuck d'you think I'm trying to do?!" Esta yelled at Pia.

Suki covered her ears and looked sour.

Esta felt that time was crawling. How long had it been? She had heard bells, and Suki and Pia muttering reflections— how many times? At some point, Konni had come in to change the mattress and bed linen. Other times, she brought food or drink, or took the chamber pot to be emptied. Esta had helpers, but none of them could help her. She was alone in the world with something that had grown enormous in her body and was now fighting its way out. She was so tired. Now she knew why women died trying to give birth. She knew that she wasn't dead, because she was still in pain. But it loomed. Out there in the streets of Nasrin, of all the women in the same state as her right now, one out of every three would die. Would she be one of the lucky two? Did she even want to be one of the lucky two?

Her helpers walked her around and around, sat her on the stool, walked her around... now... oh gods! What on earth was happening? Esta felt compelled to push really hard this time, every muscle in her body was tensed, and her head throbbed with the effort of it. She roared like an angry bull. She was sure that she had pushed all her guts out from between her legs. The searing, scorching pain overwhelmed her. She barely noticed that Suki and Pia were fussing over something small that was making a piercing noise. Suki handed a squirming, messy lump to Esta while Pia dealt with some bit of gut that was attached to it. Esta was unimpressed. All that agonizing effort, all that damage to her poor body, for this?!

"It's covered in blood and slime!" She glowered at Suki.

"Yes, mistress. That is normal. We will wash her soon. But let's see if she is ready to feed."

Suki guided the baby's wailing mouth to Esta's nipple. The baby was ready to feed, but this was also a shock to Esta.

"That feels horrible! It really hurts!"

Suki tried the other side.

Esta writhed in pain again. "No, please. Don't make me do this. I'm not a cow. Can I have a wet nurse?"

Pia intervened. "If you leave her hungry, she will scream at you even more. She will only take a little at a time to start off with. Please, Esta. Endure. You will come to like it. Aren't you pleased to see your little girl?"

Esta was baffled. She was supposed to be overwhelmed with love for the odd little creature that had caused her such pain and was pulling on her sensitive nipple, but she was not. Was she unnatural? Surely not. Perhaps she was just tired. "I'm very pleased to see her, but... I'm so very tired. And it stings a lot down there. Can you clean me up and let me sleep?"

"I need you to sit in the stool until the afterbirth comes out. Then we can clean you up and let you sleep."

Suki eased the baby away from Esta after a few moments. To Esta's horror, something yellow was still seeping from her nipples. Pia wiped them quickly while Suki washed the baby. Esta started to feel nervous. Where was the other stuff that was supposed to come out? Why was Pia looking on edge? Esta gasped with relief when a blob of something came out and Pia declared it to be whole. Konni arrived with warm water, a honey salve, and some clean smocks for Esta and the baby.

Esta had just drifted off to sleep when crashing doors reverberated throughout the house, announcing the arrival of the baby's father.

"Did no one think to send a messenger to tell me that the baby was coming?! What's happening? Tell me at once!"

Esta was jolted awake, and heard Suki in the dressing room, appeasing Yonnis.

"My Lord Arbiter—sir—there's no cause for concern. The labor was quite quick and the mistress 'n' the baby're both well. You've a beautiful baby girl with your big blue eyes and the mistress's black curls."

Esta heard a thump on the floor—Yonnis had either fainted or he'd dropped to his knees. Now he was praying loudly. He thanked the Eternal Spirit with passionate intensity. Then he apologized to Suki.

"I am sorry for being angry. I am sure that you and Pia, and everyone, have been concentrating on the mistress and the baby, as is right. Please send for Elder Yersil, and General Clayhills and Mistress Clayhills. We must have a naming ceremony as soon as possible."

What was he thinking?! Esta did not want Arlo Clayhills anywhere near her or the baby.

Now Suki was asking what name she should call the baby.

"Well, had she been a boy, I would have wanted Merutis in honor of my friend who died on the Day of Lamentation. So, I name her Merita. Let's call her Merri for short. Let me see her." Yonnis barged into the room and went straight to the cradle. He held the crying baby with a look of wonder on his face and tears in his eyes. Eventually, he turned to Esta. "She's so beautiful! Like you, Esta. Thank you! Thank you for this precious gift!"

Esta grunted in reply. "Is she crying again? What a noise."

"It's what babies do, my darling. It is the melody of new life!"

But it would not be Yonnis who had to put up with it, day in, day out.

"Shall I bring her to you? Perhaps she is hungry." Yonnis spoke to Esta, but his eyes were fixed on the wrinkled little face in his arms.

Esta accepted the baby without smiling at her. Merri attached to her nipple and Esta did her best to endure.

Yonnis kissed her forehead. "My poor darling. Was it really hard for you?"

She nodded. "Like passing a cannonball—while being trampled by a horse."

He winced. "The Eternal Spirit will bless you for your bravery. Elder Yersil is coming. He will prescribe what you might need. And Arlo and Deneesa are coming over for the naming. I've decided on Merita."

"Oh," said Esta, her face twisted in pain as Merri gripped and sucked. "We hadn't discussed names."

Yonnis shrugged. "It is the father's choice in Yeralla."

"Hmm." Esta felt indifferent, but muttered, "A pretty name." This baby was not her destiny. Esta only had to make sure that she survived long enough for Ikra to be satisfied that Esta was a healthy mother.

Merita coughed up her last mouthful over Esta's breast. Esta quivered with disgust.

"Phwoar!" Yonnis noticed smells coming from both ends of the baby with the pretty name. "Help, Suki! Konni! We need clean cloths in here."

Yes. Thank goodness for the servants. Esta could not imagine how poor women coped with babies. Suki and Konni took over. Then Yonnis sat with Esta, kissing her gently.

"Thank you, Esta. You have given me my heart's desire. She is our hope. And she is a beacon of hope for the peace of Kimalloa! We will find a way around our problems—and we will do it for her. You are an amazing woman, Mistress Krusa."

Esta felt a wave of guilt. She found the energy to kiss him back. "I'm so tired, Yonnis. Can you get them to find a wet nurse for the baby so that I can sleep?"

Yonnis looked puzzled. "Not yet, Esta. She needs to draw her strength from you."

Esta grunted and changed the subject. "Why are Arlo and Deneesa coming to the naming? We weren't the witnesses to Yoshi."

"It's our army brotherhood," Yonnis replied. "It still means a great deal to me."

"If I were not so tired," Esta replied, "I'd argue with you about making all these decisions without asking my opinion, after I've gone through half a day of agony to deliver your child!"

Yonnis hugged her. "Sorry, Esta. I will try to do better next time."

What "next time" was he talking about? Esta felt another pang of guilt. Their flawed partnership was over. Hadn't he noticed?

There was a knock at the door and Elder Yersil stepped in. He had on a clean apron over his unbleached linen robes. Esta gave him an uncensored and detailed list of pains that she was experiencing. He listened politely and promised salves and potions to help her, but she knew why he was really there. She prayed urgently to Afra that her womb was not damaged.

The quarters of the Arbiter, Bankside Place, Nasrin. Midmorning. The tenth day of the Tenth Moon, Year Fifty-One.

ESTA CAME ROUND slowly. She had just managed to drop off to sleep, and now the baby was shrieking again. Everyone was nagging her. Feed the baby. Get up and walk around a bit. Drink more. Pass more water. Rub the baby's back so that she can puke all over you. Cuddle the baby. Sit in the chair for a bit. Lie back while we apply the salve. Try this tisane. Eat this chicken. She had been too exhausted to object to the nagging. It was presumably well meant.

The household seemed concerned by her lack of interest in her baby. Why should she be interested? Queens gave their babies over to the care of others almost immediately after birth. But in the miserable Doctrine of Truth, mothers' milk made stronger babies. Esta's nipples were cracked and bleeding, but still they brought the hungry wretch to pull and pinch them.

Suki was attending to the baby, and, having checked that she was not wet, she turned to Esta. "I think that Merri needs another feed, mistress. She's a hungry baby!"

Suki approached the bed with the baby in her arms. Esta had been feeling gloomy since the birth. She felt a sudden wave of resentment and anger break over her. She sat up and pushed Suki away. Suki staggered and screamed as she toppled over, trying to shield the baby. Esta gasped in surprise. Had she really pushed *so* hard? Merri's secondary mother had just arrived at the bedroom door, and saw the disaster unfold. Suki had kept a safe hold of the baby, but she had landed on her back on the floor and hit her head. Deneesa knelt down to help Suki to sit up, and she took the baby, who was wailing in shock.

Suki gasped. "Oh, Mistress Clayhills, thank goodness you're here! Did you see how she pushed me?! She pushed me away when I tried to give her the baby. Oh, how could she reject her lovely baby?! Is Merri alright?"

Esta now felt the full force of her foster mother's thunderous green-eyed glare.

"I saw it, Esta. What is wrong with you?!"

"My teats are cracked and bleeding! I'm in pain! I can't sleep for more than five moments at a time. But she keeps bringing the child to feed! I need help, Milady Deneesa! Surely there must be a healthy wet nurse somewhere in Nasrin!"

Deneesa fumed back at her. "D'ye think that endangering your baby and injuring your servant are the best ways to get help?! You unnatural woman!"

She unbuttoned her robe and took out a lined, leathery breast to offer to Merri, who greedily took it. Esta looked in disgust at Deneesa's well-sucked breast. Deneesa looked contemptuously back at her.

"I will feed her today if you will not. And I will enjoy it, Esta, like a real woman. And there will be consequences for your assault. Just imagine what trouble you might have been in if the ancient penalties for endangering a Glantar heir had not been repealed. Really, Esta! Your father would be appalled."

Esta burst into tears so overwhelming that she could barely breathe, let alone protest to Deneesa about her threat. Her pappa would have got a wet nurse for her!

Deneesa looked towards the open door. "Konni! Come and help Mistress Suki. And, Kushno, bring this cradle into the main reception room, and then you can take a horse to Victory Park and ask the Lord Arbiter to come home." She was taking charge, and she was secondary parent. Esta wondered what that would mean for her, the sad, bad real mother?

Pia appeared in the doorway.

Deneesa nodded towards Esta. "Deal with her. Make sure that she gets the sleep she craves—we all know that you know how—and make sure that she wakes up ready to apologize. As if she wasn't in enough trouble already."

Pia nodded and muttered, "Yes, Mistress Clayhills."

Esta realized that a version of this episode would soon be on All-Ears' desk. Would it give him more reason to deal with Daggra, or would he think twice about sending an "unfit mother" to a powerful country that he needed to keep happy? The High Priestess Kirina would know every detail. She had a magic window into her beloved grandson's household. She, who had endured her husband's conversion of his country to the miserable Truth and had still supported him and given him four children. Would she curse Esta for endangering her great-grandchild? Oh, she might indeed!

By the time Pia came back with a sleeping drink, Esta's mind was in a dark place. She drank quickly, and slept deeply for some time. As she came round, she became aware of Yonnis trying to wake her up. There was someone else in the room, in the robes of an Elder. Eventually she recognized the Army Elder, Yeribbi. Everyone admired Elder Yeribbi's love for his own children. Was he here to give her advice on how to do it?

Yonnis was babbling to Elder Yeribbi. "You see, dear Yeribbi, my wife is tired and ill. She could not possibly have pushed intending harm."

The Elder asked him to be quiet and wait while he established the facts. Esta slowly looked around, and realized with dread that her small bedroom was full of people. Elder Yeribbi spoke to Suki, who said that Esta had pushed her over when she was carrying the baby to her for a feed. Konni confirmed that Suki had a bruised back and a cut on her head. Elder Yeribbi then spoke to Deneesa, who was holding Merri. Deneesa used the word that filled all Followers of the Truth with deep shame.

"I saw what she did, Elder Yeribbi, and I denounce her for the *heinous* sin of endangering her baby. I will not let go of this child until all of you can assure me that Merita will never be left alone with her mother."

Now Elder Yeribbi had to speak to Esta. "Is this true, Mistress Krusa?"

Feverish memories of what they were talking about were running through Esta's head. Heinous sins usually meant punishment. But it would be worse if she responded to the accusation with excuses. "It's true, Elder Yeribbi. I'm very sorry. I'm sorry for pushing Suki and I'm devastated that I put my baby at risk." Then Esta unashamedly ripped open her smock to show them all her sore, cracked, bleeding nipples. "I'm in pain and I'm tired! I'm sorry—"

Yonnis sighed heavily. "Oh, Esta!"

The next voice she heard was the Elder's. "So. There's no doubt. I'm sorry to say that I think some sanction is necessary. Parents get frustrated with babies up and down the land and we have to let them know how serious a matter it is if they let that frustration get the better of 'em. We must be patient with our little ones. And Merri is, of course, a special baby. The peace of Kimalloa in human form."

Esta started to cry. Life had turned sour in so many ways, and she seemed unable to sweeten it, whatever she tried. She had hoped that being a mother might give her some power, but now she felt utterly humiliated, and very much at risk of… something bad.

Elder Yeribbi sighed and closed his eyes to reflect. Then he looked at Esta. "Mistress Krusa, have you no regard for your reputation? Or for the trouble you cause to your husband? You must reflect, and you must listen to your foster mother! For the assault to your servant, you must apologize in public in the temple. And for endangering your own baby, you should receive ten strokes of the thumbnail cane from your accuser, Mistress Clayhills, but not before you're recovered enough to bear it. A suspension of two moons should be more than enough. During that time, of course, you may wish to persuade her that you've repented enough to not need chastisement."

Esta wailed in horror and reached for Yonnis, who put one arm around her while his other hand was clasped tightly over his mouth. Esta knew that Elder Yeribbi did not have much choice. Any less a punishment, and there would be complaints about leniency for the privileged wife of the Arbiter.

He spoke to her again. "In the meantime, perhaps absence from the child will make you realize what she means to you. As you can afford a nurse, put one in charge of Merri. But you're not excused all feeding, Mistress Krusa. You'll do a mother's duty. You may see her at other times, but only with another person present, preferably your husband or Mistress Clayhills. You do realize that this matter has to be documented and read out at the temple?"

Esta nodded. If she had learned anything about the Doctrine of Truth, it was that it delighted in naming and shaming. It was a punishment considered especially useful in dealing with those who thought that they had some social status.

The Elder left, and Esta's accusers followed him. Esta was convulsed with sobbing. She felt quite unable to do anything else.

Yonnis hugged her. "Esta. You need to calm down. I'll send in Pia. I have to sort out the nurse. Then I will stay with you tonight. I don't know what sort of spiritual sickness you have, but I will try to help. Don't worry about the beating. I will not let that happen."

Esta wondered if he could understand how trapped she felt. Was now the right time? "You know about Ikra's proposal, don't you?"

He stared at her like a sick puppy, and nodded.

"I know how much you love me. You love me so much... you will let me go. Won't you?"

Clayhills Place, New Temple Street, Nasrin. Early evening. The twenty-eighth day of the Thirteenth Moon, Year Fifty-One.

ARLO DREW BACK a drape to admire the winter sky—deep blue with splashes of stars and a full silver moon casting soft light that made the frosted grass sparkle. How cold it must be outside. But inside, the fire was blazing, their bellies were full of good food, and the drink was flowing. The close brotherhood at the top of the Republic of Kimalloa was together to celebrate the end of the shortest day—without decoration. The walls were as brown as ever.

"Well, gentlemen. Before we start the critical rematch of our taffle tournament, let's raise a toast to the year gone by, which has seen the Republic build on its success, and to the year to come, when we will make even more progress."

Arlo raised his beer mug. His father, Squire Tallier, Squire Coppermills, Lord Ulfan, and Arch-Elder Yeramo did the same, pronouncing their own cheers and drinking deeply.

"If I may delay the sport for a few moments…"

All heads turned in expectation to the Father of the People. Arlo wondered what was coming. Please, not some reference to his illness. Couldn't they just enjoy themselves for the evening?

"As you all know, I will not see all of Year Fifty-Two, and we might as well be practical about it."

"Please, Father, not now—"

"As the year closes and another one begins is as good a time as any, Arlo. I know that you are all anxious about what will come next—"

"All Kimalloa is anxious about what will come next!" Squire Tallier grumbled.

"Enough, Ellis. I have to be quite clear about what I want, with you, my closest kin and allies. You're the people that I know will understand my thinking and fulfill my wishes. What I want to say is, I don't think that there should be any assumptions about who takes over as Leader of the Assembly. Brother Ronni," Arlo's father nodded to Squire Coppermills, "will deputize, of course, but after I go, the Assembly must have a free and open vote on who they want to succeed me. If it's Squire Glass, so be it."

There was a ripple of laughter, but Arlo was aghast, confused, dismayed. What was his father saying? Where had this come from? He knew how much Arlo wanted to follow in his footsteps, and he was talking about a vote? Nobody had thought a vote was necessary for Yoshi Clayhills to be declared Head of State.

"This is not a joke, brothers!" Arlo's Uncle Ellis declared. "This is the future of Kimalloa! We must consider who is best suited."

"Do we have a gap in our thinking here, brothers?" Lord Ulfan asked. "If the Leader of the Assembly is to be Head of State, shouldn't the Senate have a say too? The Assembly has been riding roughshod over our interests—"

"Father, I am ready…" Arlo tried to butt in, but the words died on his lips.

"If you want to follow my wishes," Arlo's father insisted, "commoners only to decide—and no secret fixes. Do we follow the Doctrine of Truth, or are we scheming courtiers?"

Arch-Elder Yeramo answered. "We are men of Truth, and we love you, Father of the People. We love you enough to want to preserve your legacy to Kimalloa."

"Only the elected commoners can do that, dear Yeramo, by exercising their choices wisely."

The Father of the People expected to have the last word, especially since everyone was deferring to his frailty now, as well as his reputation. However, his statement only caused everyone to speak loudly at once, so much so that Deneesa swept in from the ladies' parlor and demanded to know what they were arguing about.

"Dear Deneesa," Arlo's father replied. "Our friends think that only they are qualified to choose the next leader of Kimalloa. What vanity is that?"

Arlo looked to Deneesa for help. Perhaps what he wanted to say would sound better coming from her. He knew that he could trust her. She walked over to hold the hand of his father and fixed her green eyes on him.

"My dear father-in-law—y'know how honored I am to call you that—can you see this as I see it? It's not vanity to

271

acknowledge that the Republic is young, and to lose you, the one so loved by the people, so soon, could cause a crisis. Some anchoring, with the Clayhills name—"

"What? Didn't we fight against dynastic rule?"

Was everyone supposed to nod in agreement? Deneesa did not. "In Boriela and Yeralla, there are the preferred families," she persisted.

Something seemed to dawn on his father's face, and he turned to look in puzzlement at Arlo. "My dear son. You have been a great general for our cause. You should build on your military success that has been so well earned. But if you want to resign your position and run in the Clayhills when I vacate the seat, I'm sure that you'll win."

Arlo felt battered. His dear pa was disappointing him, rebuffing his hopes, his expectations, in front of others. Why? Was he losing his reason? He looked around the room. Everyone seemed embarrassed, unwilling to make eye contact with him. They were trying to distance themselves from the tense atmosphere. Lord Ulfan was setting up the taffle board, Arch-Elder Yeramo was pouring some more beer, Squire Coppermills was moving some chairs. Squire Tallier was shooing Deneesa back to the wives in the next room. She looked back at Arlo, trying to mouth something like "Give me time", while looking at him with some kind of concern that irked him. "Could cause a crisis"? There *would* be a crisis.

19

The quarters of the Arbiter, Bankside Place, Nasrin. Early morning. The tenth day of the First Moon, Year Fifty-Two.

NURSE TANSI WOKE up suddenly, feeling troubled. There was a little gasp in baby Merri's cry that was different.

Beyond the thick stone walls of Bankside, the city was quiet. The dreary rain that marked Kimalloa's winter had been heavier than usual. The Binar frothed and rippled rapidly between the banks, lapping over them in some districts. Ships had difficulty docking. The wherrymen could not operate their ferries. The poor could not keep their fuel dry. They could not keep their clothes dry either, so they shivered into all types of sickness. The newest threat was the most feared. The spotpox was on the rampage. After two years of mildness and plenty, the grim claw of want had returned to the capital.

Despite the efforts of Elders to gain knowledge about spotpox, hope and prayer were still the main remedies. People had to take risks to work, to get food, and to tend others that were sick. The specter of death was a clinging companion. Elders worked night and day, tending fevered bodies and anguished souls. Mass graves had been dug outside the city gates, and carts driven by hooded men took bodies out to them, again and again. The city waited for the crisis to pass. The spotpox had come and gone before. Many would die. Many would live, although they could be disfigured or disabled by their scars. Children were most vulnerable, particularly the very young, those gurgling bundles of hope from happy reunions and new unions at the end of the war. The solid gates of Bankside could not keep out the spotpox. How it got through physical barriers was not known. Like an invisible tide it crept into the guardhouse, the kitchen, the laundry, and the accommodation of servants, soldiers, clerks, and officers.

Tansi jumped up to tend Merri. She could tell that the baby had it, although the spots had not yet formed. Merri felt hot. Tansi quickly poured cold water from a jug into a bowl and dipped some cloths into it. She started to pat Merri with them.

It was very early morning, but the Arbiter was up. He had heard the plaintive crying. He opened the door of the nursery, looking paler than usual. "Is it the spotpox?" he asked.

Tansi nodded.

Tears started to well in his eyes and run down his face. "Give her to me. If she is to die, she will do so knowing that her father's heart beat for her to the last. What do I have to do?"

"Keep her cool. Bring her for a feed as often as you can. Perhaps Mistress Pia can suggest some herbs to dry out the spots when they develop. Oh—and burn drying herbs on the fire." Tansi gazed at him in surprise. He really did intend to nurse his child. She had never seen a man who believed that a baby girl might need her father in her sickness. Merri was still crying, but as she nestled in Yonnis's strong arms, the intensity of her cries reduced. "Have you had the spotpox, sir?" Tansi asked tentatively, wary of explicitly warning him of his own risk.

"No." His reply seemed gruff, implying that her question was irrelevant. Well, she had heard that he had been fearless in battle, but did he understand what a foe like spotpox could do?

The quarters of the Arbiter, Bankside Place, Nasrin. Early morning. The tenth day of the First Moon, Year Fifty-Two.

Esta was dragged from sleep by Yonnis barging into her room carrying the wailing Merri. He was gasping at her through tears. She realized that the worst had happened, took the baby, and cuddled her. Was Merri going to be snatched away to the Dome of the Divine, just as Esta had grown to love her? Yonnis opened the window. A cold blast of winter air cleared the mustiness of woodsmoke. Then he sat down, took off his doublet, and opened his shirt. He took Merri back from Esta and held the feverish baby to his chest, hoping that the beating of his heart would comfort her. He started to pat her with cold cloths, just as he had seen Tansi doing it.

Esta complained. "When I was a child, it was said that fresh air was not good for the sick."

Yonnis had an answer, of course. "I suppose it depends on the quality of the air. Logically, coolness must help a fever."

Esta still got up and pulled the window in, leaving only a narrow gap, as the winter wind had quickly chilled the room. She put on a dressing gown and wrapped a blanket around Yonnis. She sat beside him on the settle. "She's so tiny." Esta's eyes filled with tears. "How can she survive it when my poor brother didn't? He was a strong boy."

"You survived it, Esta. Can you remember anything— anything at all—about having it?" Yonnis had asked her before about the scars on her belly, and she had been acutely embarrassed about even admitting that she had what she regarded as a flaw.

"I had only three years. I can't remember it. I do remember when my brother had it. The Raas prayed and sacrificed day in, day out. His room was draped in red, and incense was burned by his bed to help him heal. He had a raging fever, and the maids struggled to stop him scratching his spots. He rallied, he seemed to be getting better, and then... some of the spots went green and smelled awful. He got another fever, and then he just… he just… stopped breathing. You can't imagine my mother's desperation, and my father swung between fits of anger and deep black moods. It was a great loss to me too. I sat there crying, and I had to listen to a Raia trying to defend Lord Sudar's will. She said that Little Prince Rikko was sleeping with the gods who wanted his loveliness for themselves. They couldn't share one so precious with Kimalloa."

Esta watched Yonnis patting Merri repeatedly with the cloths, changing them as soon as the coolness was absorbed by the baby's hot skin. Any other woman might long for such a husband, devoted to her and her child. But Esta Glantar was not any woman, and still, he loved her enough to let her go. She prayed for magic from the goddess of love, Afra. Please find a way for us to part that won't hurt him too much.

"That awful smell you mentioned—was it like rotten eggs?"

Had he no idea how a princess lived?

"I've never smelled a rotten egg. But it was a smell of… decay."

"He may have died from reeky rather than the spotpox itself. It happens. Was it quick?"

"Once they went green—a lurid, livid green—yes, it was quite quick." Esta sighed so deeply, as if she wanted her whole being to disappear through the floor. She had been at her little brother's side when he drew his last breath. She traced her misfortunes, and Kimalloa's, to that tragic day.

"So. The maturity of the spots will be the main point of danger." Yonnis the strategist was planning ahead. "Esta, please go and check with Pia what herbs she needs to dry the spots. We will be prepared. And please tell Konni to come to do the swaddling cloths. They are wet with sweat as well as pee."

Esta went to the door. Something occurred to her, and she turned back. "Yonnis, have you had the spotpox?"

"No," he replied. "But I was around horses and cows when I

was small, and that is supposed to be protective, or so we believe in Yeralla."

"I hope so." Esta felt a strange tightening in her chest. It would be so awful if something happened to Yonnis.

Clayhills Place, New Temple Street, Nasrin. Early evening. The thirteenth day of the First Moon, Year Fifty-One.

"LISTEN, ARLO."

Arlo switched his attention to his uncle, trying to suppress his frustration that it always seemed to be him who had to do the listening. Were any of his cabal listening to him? Their plan was for *his* vigor to take Kimalloa forward, after all.

Uncle Ellis continued. "If there is one thing that we know about the wasting disease, it is that it is slow! We will be with your father just before the end. All you have to do is ask him if he is happy for you to follow in his footsteps, and if he says yes, which he surely will, that is enough for us to put things in place."

Squire Tallier sounded so confident. Arlo appreciated that he appeared to be trying to be a true secondary parent to him, trying to build a bridge over the chasm that had suddenly opened up between him and his beloved pa.

"But you yourself, Arlo, you need to be preparing—dare I say, wooing—support," declared Arch-Elder Yeramo. Well, it was his job to preach.

"I know," Arlo replied, as blandly as he could.

"Otherwise, we can't be sure that there won't be some opposition," Lord Ulfan butted in.

"Of course there'll be opposition," Squire Tallier observed. "It would look suspicious if there were not. It should be arranged..."

"I am surrounded by the best of the country's leadership and my clever wife. The Spirit has blessed me. I thank you all for

your help and guidance." Arlo praised them, but he wondered—
was he just a pawn in someone else's taffle game?

"We're all on your team, husband."

Deneesa would say that, wouldn't she? Arlo was sure of
Deneesa's desire to have power. Just so long as she didn't want it
more for herself than for him. Uncle Ellis—he would twist and
turn every which way. But he did regard himself as one of the
Clayhills clan. Arch-Elder Yeramo had a history as a turncoat, but
the upside of that was the zeal of a convert. Lord Ulfan was most
interesting. He was Grakko's cousin, one of Deneesa's many friends
with land, status, and money. He was committed to the Truth, he
had been ruthless in the north, he was a formidable Leader of the
Senate. Arlo couldn't succeed in the Seat of Government without
him. But what was in it for Ulfan to have Arlo as Leader of the
Assembly of Commoners and Head of State? The right of veto for
the Senate, so he said, and no Arbiter to support the Assembly and
force their will through. Ulfan hated even the remotest possibility
of advancement for Squire Glass, that was for sure. Perhaps he
was the most trustworthy, because he was the one who had made
a political calculation and decided that Arlo was his best prospect
for getting what he wanted. Arlo sought eye contact with Ulfan,
and smiled. They could be a great partnership.

"Let's go over the plan again," Ulfan suggested. "No surprises,
no omissions—the smoothest political change in the history of
the world. We're the great minds that can do it!"

"It's simple enough, brothers and sister! Ronni will declare a
state of transition after the funeral enabling the Father's *chosen*
successor to take control."

Why was Uncle Ellis using such emphasis? They had
gone through a lot of scenarios, as they should. In the heat of
the debate, had Arlo slipped up? Perhaps he had. Something
stronger was needed.

"We must back it up with the threat of a Pozarian invasion.
They would be stupid if they didn't think about invading after

Kimalloa loses its guiding light. There will be evidence. I'm sure that you can make it so, Uncle."

"Not necessarily. They haven't forgotten what they call the 'hiding light.'"

Arlo's hackles were rising. His nostrils flared. "And where is he hiding? In the sheets with their puppet queen! Our republic would be a better place without either of them—"

"I agree," Ulfan cut in.

"I have plans in place, brothers," Arlo's uncle declared.

"Well, share them with us!"

"I can't. You'll just have to trust me."

The quarters of the Arbiter, Bankside Place, Nasrin. Midmorning. The eighteenth day of the First Moon, Year Fifty-Two.

SUKI WORKED HARD to keep the household functioning. She demanded more cleaning of everything, especially the linen. Konni and Kushno fell ill as well, so Suki and Tansi were stretched to cope. Pia was some help, but Suki argued with her about the food order.

"Surely, more strong meaty broth is needed," she insisted.

"No." Pia's reply was calm but definite. "Stomach-soothing herb tisane with salt and honey is needed. Really. It's obvious, isn't it, Suki? Spotpox vomiting is no different from the sickness women have when carrying."

Suki did not trust Pia, no matter how many times Squire Tallier told her that she should. She was a former Raia who whispered with Mistress Krusa in the priest-tongue. That could not be right. Of course, Mistress Krusa wanted Pia's way with the food and drink, so, in desperation, Suki delegated the kitchen to her.

Day after day, she watched the Lord Arbiter hold his daughter to his heart. He patted her with cool cloths, guided her little hands away from the poultices on her spots, and chatted to her to keep himself awake. Although he was exhausted, he did his duty to the country too. He reviewed papers that were brought to him, after insisting that they were read out three times so that he absorbed their content before doing so.

One morning, as Suki was brushing the step, she heard the Assembly clerks approaching. They were gossiping with disgust about the increasingly unkempt, unshaven, and unwashed man clutching a sick and smelly baby, who was too tired even to hold his pen properly.

"Is that smell him or the child?"

"I wish they wouldn't send me! I don't like to see an old soldier behaving like a woman."

"He's not the man he was during the war."

"Someone should tell him that lots of babies die in their first year, and he can't stop it happening to his."

Suki chided them. "Are you Followers of the Truth? You know what the scriptures say about cherishing our children. That applies to fathers as well as mothers, y'know!"

"Apologies, Mistress Suki." They doffed their caps and looked sheepishly at her.

Suki admired the Arbiter's devotion to his daughter, but she was utterly sick and tired of his devotion to his wife. If Merri survived, would Mistress Krusa poison her mind with Sudarite superstition? Suki could not sit by and let that happen.

The quarters of the Arbiter, Bankside Place, Nasrin. Early evening. The twenty-second day of the Second Moon, Year Fifty-Two.

MERRI HAD BEEN one of fifty-four small children in Bankside who had caught spotpox. After three weeks of jangling nerves in the Arbiter's quarters, Merri's spots had healed and she was once again happy and hungry. Everyone in the household had felt a growing relief and confidence as she improved day by day, and then one morning when she let out a loud, gurgling baby laugh, they were exultant. They dared to cheer. They had all contributed to saving the baby. Esta felt particularly proud. She congratulated herself on producing a strong baby. Surely Ikra would be impressed?

Then, just as it was assumed that the spotpox crisis was over for Number 4 Bankside, Yonnis complained of a headache. He was sweating profusely, and his pale features had turned a vivid red. Another vigil with cold compresses, tisane, and poultices came and went successfully, and Esta willingly took the lion's share. He might be a puritan ranter who had helped to thwart her ambition, but he loved her, and in some small, strange way, she was fond of him.

One evening, as Yonnis was recovering, and sitting up eating some soup, a scream of anguish was heard through the open window. It tailed off into a low, strangulated wail. His face sank into an expression of pure sadness. "I think that some poor family has lost a child."

Esta nodded. "Pia said there've been forty deaths so far in Bankside. Twenty-three children. But most who've had it are recovering. Look at Konni and Kushno. They were back up on their feet in two weeks. She said that it's far worse in the east of the city. Over three thousand gone. It must be difficult for the Elders who have to keep count of the misery."

"Yes. I am sure that it must test their faith. We were so blessed, Esta, that our baby survived."

Esta could not stop herself saying, "It was my prayers that saved her, Yonnis. I am sure of it. My Sudarite prayers to my namesake, the goddess of the hearth."

Yonnis carried on slowly eating the last of his soup, and then slept, snoring softly. A few moments later, Suki knocked on the bedroom door. Esta opened it to her, offering the tray with a bowl and cup on it, assuming she had come to collect them.

"M-Mistress Krusa." Suki spoke with difficulty. Tears were rolling down her cheeks. She bobbed a little curtsy. "I'm sorry to bring bad news. We've just heard that Little Yoshi passed away. Mistress Deneesa's footman brought the message. He insisted that the Lord Arbiter should be told."

Esta was entranced by Suki's eyes, which were boring into her. There was a message there—was it an accusation? She shut her eyes quickly and hung on to the ivy-green drapes of the bed. She tried to offer silent prayers of sympathy for the parents. Much as she had come to despise them both, she could imagine how desperately sad they were. Eventually she gathered her thoughts to speak. The bearers of bad news always expected an appropriate response, even though they spoke of situations for which words made no difference at all. "Poor Little Yoshi! How awful for my foster mother and the general. I pray that the Eternal Spirit will comfort them. What a terrible, terrible loss. The Arbiter will want to know, and to send a message. I'll wake him. Thank you, Suki." Esta closed the door, hoping that Suki had not seen that she was now shaking with fear. Was Suki suspicious of her? Did she imagine that she was a curse-maker who had harmed Yoshi? She had certainly cursed Arlo!

"What is it?" Yonnis was waking up.

Esta sat on the bed and held his hand. "I am sorry, Yonnis. Suki brought a very sad message. Little Yoshi has died."

Yonnis held his face in his hands and prayed for the Eternal Spirit to let the innocent Yoshi rest in peace, and to comfort Arlo and Deneesa. He muttered his prayer again and again, for several moments. Then he looked at Esta. "What can I do for my poor friend Arlo? He was so delighted to be a father, and now his pride and joy has been taken away from him. What can I say, when our child has lived and theirs has not?"

"I don't know." Esta wondered whether she should share her fears about the consequences for her of such misfortune for the Clayhills.

"Send Kushno for Yeribbi," Yonnis demanded.

"I think that he'll be with them." It occurred to Esta that there was spiritual guidance closer to hand. "But if you want help to compose some words from both of us, perhaps Pia could help?"

"Perhaps she could. Please fetch her, and paper and ink. I want to write now. I want it delivered tonight."

Office of the Intelligence Minister, the Archive, Bankside, Nasrin. Late evening. The twenty-second day of the Second Moon, Year Fifty-Two.

SUKI HAD NOTED with contempt that Pia was helping to compose the condolences to the Clayhills family. She should desist, but the shock of the news about Yoshi heightened her fears for Merri. She decided to put on her cloak and pay a late visit to Squire Tallier.

She braced herself for the heat of his office. Here he was, at his desk, pen in hand. He must have heard the door creak, and he had not put it down. He must be signaling to her to be brief.

"From the lateness of your call, you must be agitated, Mistress Suki. Please don't tell me that the Arbiter's health is failing?"

Suki shook her head. "First of all, can I reflect with you for Baby Yoshi?"

"Of course." Tallier put down his pen and struggled to his feet.

They reflected for a few moments. Suki was still praying for the soul of the baby to be granted eternal rest, and for the Clayhills to be comforted, when Squire Tallier interrupted with some irritation.

"Excuse me, Mistress Suki. Why here? My dear friend and cousin Squire Clayhills has lost his grandson, and I am trying to compose some words to take to him—"

"Squire Tallier, I'm so sorry to disturb your grief, but

I'm in turmoil. I don't believe that the Arbiter's quarters are spiritually… clean… enough." Suki stood stiffly, proud to be the pious housekeeper in her practical brown robe, her hands clasped together on her unbleached apron. "Sir, I know that you've told me just to observe, and that law is not being broken, but she's working away at him, bit by bit. And now she's got him listening to that Pia about their condolence letter! You say that Pia's working for you, but I hear 'em whispering in the priest-tongue—she's a Raia! And she's making spells under the roof of pious folk—how can you be sure she didn't curse Mistress Deneesa because she denounced Madam-Who-Thinks-She-Should-Be-Queen?!"

Squire Tallier shuffled from his desk to his seat by the fire and lowered himself into it, indicating to Suki to sit opposite. He sighed. "Really, Mistress Suki. You disappoint me. You are giving credence to the Sudarites' faith if you believe that their spells and curses work, and you are disrespecting me if you think that one of my top agents would utter one."

Suki jumped to her feet. "I'm sorry to persist, sir, but I have to live in that household! We all know that Esta Glantar prays to false gods and that Mistress Pia helps her! It's bad for all of us, and most of all, surely it's not right for the baby. And remember, sir, you tasked me with defending the Lord Arbiter from threats in his household. Ev'ry day I wonder when she'll drag him to the scaffold with her."

Squire Tallier leaned forward. "Suki, what would you have me do?"

Suki frowned. She had heard about the purges of the old kings. When they decided that there was some treachery going on, the guilty and the innocent would be rounded up and burnt or beheaded. She did not want that. "Can't you send her into exile?" She gazed hopefully at Squire Tallier. She knew that he didn't trust Esta. She knew that he must have plans for getting rid of her.

"Mistress Suki. Listen carefully. Without definite evidence

of definite plotting, there is no legal reason to exile a petulant aristocrat. After the Greenlands, my sleep is not troubled by Esta Glantar."

"Really, sir? You must have heard the gossip—people are sneaking back to the trees to pray to the false gods because they say the Truth does not have an answer for the spotpox."

Suki waited. She realized that she had rattled Squire Tallier. It was difficult to discern his mood from the way that he looked at her. His face could be as blank as a snake's. Eventually, he coughed and spoke.

"The old world is not yet dead, and the new world is only just born. People used to the old world are infants in the new one—it is hard for them to adapt, especially when we ask them to accept that we have no magic to stop personal tragedies. If I thought there was any chance that magic could have saved Baby Yoshi, I would have hauled every Raa out of prison to cast spells. Wouldn't you?"

Suki's eyes widened and she opened her mouth and shut it several times, breathing unevenly.

"You see the complexities I have to deal with?" Squire Tallier asked her. "For all we know, Sudarite prayers are as well meant as ours. I can't police the souls of every citizen. They can pray for a return to the old ways if they like, it is only when there is action that they break the law."

Suki processed his words. "Definite evidence?" she asked. "What would that have to be? A letter? A reliable witness?"

Squire Tallier frowned at her, as if he were about to issue a warning, but he did not. "Mistress Suki, I think that you've had enough of the Arbiter's household. I will see if there are any better jobs for you in Bankside, with a more pious family."

Suki nodded. "Thank you, sir."

They parted with smiles. As she was ushered out of the door by a footman, Suki's imagination started to whirr with possibilities. She had not seen Ambassador Onfri in Bankside for a while. Perhaps she could invite him to congratulate the Arbiter on his recovery, and drop a letter into his coat. Was her lettering good enough for a forgery? Probably not. Suki strode back to Bankside, sad but resigned. As she crossed the vast Bankside courtyard, she saw Kushno hurrying out, presumably to General Clayhills' house with the Pia-crafted letter from the Arbiter and his wife. Suki huffed. Instead of marching back to Number 4, she decided to extend her absence from the tainted household and offer her own condolences to Mistress Clayhills, in person.

The quarters of the Arbiter, Bankside Place, Nasrin. Early evening. The sixth day of the Third Moon, Year Fifty-Two.

A CLERK ARRIVED at Number 4 with a written note conveying Squire Coppermills' displeasure that Yonnis had not attended the Seat of Government at Victory Park for six weeks and three days. In particular, Coppermills felt that the Arbiter should have attended the discussion of flood defenses in person. The clerk stared at Yonnis. He looked curious, with just a hint of fear. Yonnis had made the mistake of using the looking glass when he was washing, and he knew what the clerk could see. He was more haggard than usual and his skin looked grayer than usual, apart from his right cheek, which was a vivid pink with spotpox scars. He tried to make his refusal easy for the clerk to deliver.

"Please tell Squire Coppermills that I look even more like a corpse than usual, and I remind him that it would be difficult to clean vomit from the fine leather of the Arbiter's chair. I need a few more days at home."

The clerk left Yonnis's parlor, and Esta walked in. Yonnis thought that she looked particularly glorious. Whenever she entered a room, he was always catapulted back to the first time he saw her—the regal swish of the robe, the imperious look, but above all, the self-confidence of beauty. She was wearing her favorite purple-blue mottled robe that had once been her wedding dress. She let her veil slip, revealing her mane of black curls. Her face and her eyes were glowing. His gaze was drawn to her luscious lips.

"What news from Victory Park?"

He watched her lips move. She asked the question in her usual breezy way, as if she were interested, but not that interested, in any answer he might have.

"Squire Clayhills is too ill to run the Assembly and Coppermills is throwing his weight around. I feel no desire to rush back."

"Has your lunch stayed in your belly?"

"Spirit be praised, yes, it has. Toasted bread and honey—they seem to soothe. But I am still such a weakling. I tried to pick up my sword this morning, and it feels so heavy. I will not be doing combat training for some time."

"But that's two small meals you have kept down today!" Esta seemed pleased, excited even. "Progress! Yonnis, you must recover. When the warmth from the food gets to your muscles, your strength will return. Now, will you try something a bit stronger for supper? I'll cut it into tiny bits for you."

"Esta, will you at least stay here with me until I am fully better?" Yonnis still longed to believe that he could find a way to make her happy to be his wife. Her departure for Osiran had been delayed by the spotpox outbreak, but, having been delighted by the survival of the child, Ikra was now getting impatient.

Esta paced. She looked at him with guilt in her eyes, then she looked away, then she shot the guilty look again. After a few moments, she moved towards him and rubbed his arms. "Yonnis, we've said before—in another time, another world, we could have been twinned souls. But in this time, this world, I have to go. I want to go. Please bless me for my new life. Maybe I can stay a few more days… I need to think—"

"Think about this." Yonnis buried his hands in her hair and kissed her.

The manor house of Lady Deneesa Clayhills, New Temple Street, Nasrin. Early morning. The seventh day of the Third Moon, Year Fifty-Two.

ARLO WAS SITTING at the table, staring blankly at a plate where an egg and slice of ham stared blankly back at him, when Deneesa arrived for her breakfast. She leant down to kiss him. She wished that she could console him. She had lost children before. This was his first time, and he was suffering.

"You must eat, Arlo," Deneesa commented as she sat down opposite him. "I know that you miss him—so much—but starving yourself can't bring Yoshi back."

Arlo banged the table. "Don't talk about him like that—like he was just some friend who came to stay for a while!"

Deneesa snapped back. "Y'know, my heart is breaking too! More than I can describe!"

She had hoped that he might consider comforting her. But no, it was anger all the time with Arlo these days. He went off on a new rant.

"I'm going to denounce her as a curse-maker! Or maybe it's him."

Deneesa felt her heart pounding with anxiety. What Arlo was suggesting could put the quality of his judgment into question. What would the Army Council think? What would the Assembly think? Magg had already protested to Tallier about Arlo being a man of "unreason", and only held off from denouncing him in the temple out of respect for his father. She spoke quietly, trying to appeal to whatever sense of reason he had left. "Darling, we are Followers of the Truth. We know illness is not caused by curses."

"But we know Sudarites still *cast* curses, and it is a heinous crime, and bad words are harmful even if they don't carry the disease itself."

"I thought that you rather liked Esta, from some of the things that you say in your sleep. Surely you don't think that she would try to harm you?" Deneesa tried to stop herself letting him know that she had heard his fantasies when he thought that he was safe in unconsciousness, but perhaps it would make him think twice about the warps and inconsistencies in his outbursts. It hurt her, but she was sanguine about the drives of men.

Arlo did not question her or defend himself, so she carried on.

"Rest assured, Arlo, she's not clever enough to cast spells."

"Pia, then! She could!"

"She works for our own dear All-Ears. She has the knowledge, but no motive."

"And what's your excuse for Yonnis? Does nobody question how he managed to survive the Day of Lamentation and innumerable battles, why his misjudgments are always forgiven, why his child survived illness and mine didn't?! You know the Sudarites think he's their god of war?"

"He was brought up in the Truth, no one questions his piety."

"Which is what would give him such an excellent cloak to cover his true identity—he is the familiar of that curse-making Osiranian bitch Kirina!"

"Arlo?" Deneesa looked at him in amazement. His imaginings were getting ever more rampant. She knew that she had to confront him. She had been putting it off for a long time, out of pity for his grief. "Arlo, I know what's talking, and it's not you. It's the poppy juice! Your nightmares, your behavior during the day—it's getting worse and worse. Please, dear Arlo, there's a special healer that you can go to—"

"How dare you?!" Arlo was spluttering, raving. "You're defending my enemies, enemies of Kimalloa, and you're accusing *me* of needing healing! Pa is ill and it's my duty to take charge of this country and drive it forward, faster than he has, and you? You are supposed to be helping me. We've been planning what to do—and the time is coming. Soon!"

Deneesa was remembering those plans with regret. But she had made them, and could not unmake them. "Arlo, really—I love you, and honor you! Haven't I given you all the money, resources, and influence that you have asked for? Haven't I talked and talked to everyone who matters on your behalf?"

"Alright! Just don't criticize me like that ever again! Can't a man grieve for his son without being accused of madness?"

Deneesa took his hands and started to kiss them gently. He allowed it, for a few moments. Suddenly, he withdrew, grabbed her wrists, and squeezed.

"Ow!" she cried. "Arlo! Please stop!"

"You see, Deneesa. You may be powerful, rich, and clever, but it's the way of the world that might is right. Even with my weaker arm, I could break your wrist... quite easily." He stared intently at her. Then he smiled. The smile broke into a laugh. It chilled her—how much he seemed to be enjoying her alarm. "Be the wife I need."

20

The Seat of Government, Victory Park, Nasrin.
Midmorning. The tenth day of the Third Moon, Year
Fifty-Two.

YONNIS HAD BEEN impressed to see, as he had approached Victory Park, that some magnificent roof beams had been put in place, soaring above the canvas still protecting dozens of padded benches for the members. Progress outside—but what of inside?

Frania, the widow of Lord Dalmo of the South Middlelands, was the first to welcome Yonnis back and congratulate him on his recovery when he took his seat for a Senate debate. It should have been Ulfan, but at least Yonnis felt that Frania was sincere. Lord Ulfan had not forgiven Yonnis for the land reform compromise. He had sworn that the land he gave back would be the most inhospitable, and there was plenty of rock and scree in his region. The rumble of approval for Frania's words was gratifying. Today, Yonnis would try to enjoy the debate about the plans for a transport hub in the Middlelands, where five roads and three canals were to meet. This was a transport hub that was so obviously a good idea, but it generated heated exchanges. By midafternoon, Lord Ulfan had steered the debate to a dignified conclusion. The scribes noted what amendments had been passed, which had failed, and the final wording of the resolution. Lord Ulfan brought it to Yonnis for his signature.

"The Spirit has blessed you again, Lord Arbiter. We weren't sure that we'd see you back."

"I have been blessed indeed, Your Grace, and I am very grateful," Yonnis replied.

Lord Ulfan was hovering, eager to say something else. Yonnis looked up to his face from his paperwork.

"D'ye have a plan—for when the Father of the People passes?" Lord Ulfan asked quietly.

Yonnis did not trust him, and would not share a plan with him if he had one.

Ulfan persisted. "Can you imagine how fragile the Republic started to feel with both of you at death's door?"

Yonnis was puzzled. Why was Ulfan trying to engage with him in this way? "Graveyards are full of indispensable people," Yonnis responded. "I am sure that you would be able to manage any scenario, Your Grace."

"Walk back to the Assembly, Lord Arbiter, and see how the factions are jostling and squabbling. Perhaps you could talk some sense into them."

Yonnis wondered if Lord Ulfan was fishing for something, trying to provoke him to test his authority. But perhaps a bit of arbitrating from the Arbiter could help Squire Coppermills. He decided to walk down the corridor to the Assembly. It was noisy. Squire Coppermills' voice was at a fever pitch, shouting down first radicals and then monarchists, then moderates complaining about the other two groups. There was even a bit of pushing and shoving in one corner of the chamber.

"Brothers, be warned! Those of you who can't observe the rules of debate, and who keep shouting down other speakers, making farmyard noises, and whatever, I swear that I shall call in the militia to haul you out of here!"

The members erupted with more angry noise and fist-waving. Was the Acting Head of State really proposing the use of militia? Yonnis could see why. Tempers were so frayed there was a risk that punches would be thrown.

"Gentlemen!" Yonnis shouted, although it hurt his throat, swollen from weeks of vomiting. He moved swiftly, grabbing the ceremonial mace of authority from its stand.

The attention of the unruly men on the benches was instantly his. The Arbiter was back, and he was doing something that had not been done before. The mace was usually just an ornament indicating that the Assembly was in session, but Yonnis cradled it as if it were a far more potent and precious symbol of Kimalloa's ideals. The sound in the room petered down to grumbling and shuffling. Some members smiled, perhaps pleased to see him back. Others, perhaps those who nicknamed him "the army clerk", looked surly, annoyed to be called to account.

Yonnis took up a very visible stance at the front of the platform of the chamber. "What would the Father of the People think if he could be here to witness this? Reflect on what he went through so that you could have your say." He had invoked the right image. "Men of Truth do not bray like donkeys and brawl like rats. We are building the peace of Kimalloa! It helps if we are peaceful in manner ourselves. What are you debating to get you into such a fever?"

"An extra halfpenny per mark on land tax, Lord Arbiter," a clerk replied.

Yonnis paced for a few moments, intending the Assembly members to use them to reflect on how small the proposal seemed. Then he shrugged. "And will an extra halfpenny cause any taxpayer to starve? Because—surely—only a threat to life and limb would cause such bitterness. There could be no proposal of exceptional harshness in this body because it is your government—it is of you, and you are it." He held the mace out towards them, and then cradled it again. "Your minister, Squire Beechwoods, knows what he is doing, gentlemen. I urge you to listen to him again, and to think before you shout. Remember the principle of Squire Clayhills—we must all aspire, in debate, to say less and to say it better. I hope that you can decide on this bill today, using reason and reflection, and pass it to the Senate tomorrow."

He looked around at them, now passive, although still grumbling. He tried to make eye contact in particular with the leaders of groups who could calm down their cliques. When he had waited long enough for complete silence to grace the gathering, he spoke again.

"May the Eternal Spirit bless you, gentlemen. Remember that you are the guardians of fair government, Kimalloa's beacon for the world. Now, please excuse me—I need to rest."

The grumbles and shuffling returned as Yonnis returned the mace to its stand and left, but the howling and shouting had stopped. He was starting to feel sick again. Maybe it was the illness, maybe it was the bad behavior in the Assembly. He had never witnessed anything like it in Yeralla. His uncle had often sent him to give his answer on questions raised by the Convocation, where the members were so quiet and thoughtful. Were the Assembly members really so aggressive about a halfpenny on tax? No, he concluded, they were already angry with grief for their leader, and fearful of what might happen next.

He noticed Ulfan watching him like a hawk as he headed to the catering area for some tisane. Ulfan had suggested the intervention. Had he expected Yonnis to be humiliated? It looked like he hated him for succeeding. So be it. Yonnis did not need the man who devastated the north as a friend. The respect of Assembly members was a greater comfort.

The manor of Squire Yoshi Clayhills in the countryside northwest of Nasrin. Late morning. The fifteenth day of the Third Moon, Year Fifty-Two.

THE MANOR WAS as peaceful as ever, sitting proudly on a clay hill, surrounded by trees whose translucent new leaves were now open, bathing all beneath them in gentle green. Yellow and blue flowers were springing up in the garden, the lawns were lush, and the red-clay bricks of the manor shone in the sunshine. Birds were singing joyfully.

All-Ears ordered footmen to carry Squire Clayhills out onto the terrace with a number of blankets, and to bring a chair and blankets for him. He had made the journey every week since Squire Clayhills had "retired to recover". It was six weeks now since the Father of the People had been seen at the Seat of Government.

"How is Ronni doing?" Yoshi asked.

"Well enough, with some timely help from Yonnis." All-Ears was reluctant to tell him how fractious the Assembly members were.

"I pray every day for Baby Yoshi. My condition is such now, Ellis, that my body is returning to babyhood. Somehow those smells—they remind me of him. I know that sounds awful, but it's the way my mind is working now. Dear Inga and Andia and Piria—they comfort me and clean me, but when I think of what poor Piria has to do... these are not the memories that I want my granddaughter to have of me." Squire Clayhills wept quietly.

All-Ears was fuming to himself. Where were Arlo and Deneesa when their help was needed? Yonnis had visited as soon as he was recovered. Beechwoods visited. Lady Frania visited. So many friends offered support, but Arlo and Deneesa were conspicuously absent. They might claim to be grieving their son, but All-Ears was sure that they were still furious that the Father of the People would not anoint Arlo as his successor.

Yoshi's wife, Inga, came out onto the terrace and fussed around them, bringing beer and cheese. All-Ears could tell that she was working hard to keep her husband cheerful, but her cheeks looked red raw from salty tears shed in private. All-Ears urged her to join them, but she declined and went back inside.

Yoshi and All-Ears sat on the terrace, sipping beer, nibbling cheese, and reminiscing about their long lives, reassuring themselves that progress was now underway again, despite the floods and the spotpox. They exchanged banter about their roles. People loved the Father and feared the spymaster. Perhaps it was a necessary combination. All-Ears had always been ready to do the dirty work so that Yoshi could not be tainted by it. Then Yoshi cut across the conversation.

"Ellis. We once talked about the potions."

All-Ears felt a chill of apprehension. "We did. And you haven't been taking them. Your bravery is as remarkable as ever, my dear friend." All-Ears, whose ailments, although they had been aggravating him for years, were relatively minor, felt humbled.

"I'm surprised to have lasted so many moons since Yersil told me that I had the wasting disease. I've been ready—ready for whenever my body decides to surrender. But perhaps we should control things. The extension of uncertainty won't be good for the Assembly, and therefore not good for Kimalloa. You, if anyone, can make sure that there's no trace? I don't want the poor souls who have so many hardships to manage in their lives to think that I was giving up."

"Oh, Yoshi." All-Ears' heart sank. "I'll do my best, if that's what you want."

"And you must make sure that you are full of energy when I go, Ellis. Keep Kimalloa peaceful!"

All-Ears moved from his seat to hug his cousin, tears welling up in his eyes. "Let me go and fetch the Healing Elder from his lair, we'll need his advice," he whispered.

All-Ears turned, and grabbed his stick. Crack! He smelled smoke and felt blood spatter onto his arm. With a surge of energy, he turned around to make a hopping, stumbling lurch at the gunman who was just a few strides away on the lawn. This renegade soldier was now aiming at him, shouting some

Sudo nonsense. All-Ears half-hoped that he would shoot. Crack! Crack! Crack! From the roof, two stories above. Body shots. The gunman dropped to his knees. He was not yet dead, but he was not far off.

All-Ears ripped open his collar to show him a tattoo that had reassured many Sudarite prisoners that they could talk to him. "Atakiri, my son." He spoke as quickly as he could. "How did you serve?"

Through the blood gurgling out of his mouth, the gunman chanted, "All... hail Lord Sudar! I avenged... the holy trees!" His eyes closed and his body went limp.

Screaming and yelling were engulfing the house. Inga ran out, wailing as she cradled Yoshi's blood-soaked head. Andia was on her knees at her father's feet, gasping for breath through her sobs. Guards and their sergeant ran to All-Ears.

"Who was this creature?" All-Ears asked.

"Man called Kobi, sir, origin'ly from the east, but he arrived here from duty in the Greenlands just a few days ago. He came to us with a long record of service in the war and the recommendation that he was a good shot, which he was when we tested 'im, and he seemed so devout! Why would he do this?!"

All-Ears knew that no network of informers could be perfect. He had been double-crossed in the Greenlands, and now this lapse, which was so utterly devastating. A Sudarite zealot had slipped unnoticed into the Army of Truth, and wormed his way into the country home of the Father of the People. Yoshi's hope for a planned, peaceful passing and a dignified continuation of the country's business was over. People were now running from the fields to see what was happening, and an avalanche of half-truths would soon be rumbling across the land.

"Bring Elders to take Squire Clayhills' body to the temple and help the family. Find the best legal clerk you can to help me gather evidence. For now, nothing goes to Nasrin. I'm not going to make a hasty statement." All-Ears spoke quickly and then turned to vomit beer and cheese onto the lawn.

In due course, a clerk arrived. They flicked away flies from the blood as they removed the buff coat of the assassin, and then examined his outer clothes. Inside overlarge sleeve buttons, they found prayer beads. As the clerk was set to make sketches of the scene, the position of the bodies, and the probable trajectories of the pistol balls, All-Ears started to question the staff, making his own notes.

"I 'eard a shot, then more shots." That sounded honest, but it wasn't very helpful.

"I heard a shot, then he shouted something about Sudar, then there were much louder shots."

"There was a shot... then a shout about Navvan... and then a muffled shot."

How extraordinary it was that several people could hear the same things, but hear different things. All-Ears thought hard about what he had heard. He had heard an excited man, surprised by his success, jabbering. If he had to write it down it would be, "Sudar be praised! I've done it—I got him!" And, as shots pierced his body, "The... god... ki..."

Then one of the guards told him confidently, "There was a shot. Then he screamed, 'I did it for Queen Esta', and then there were two more shots."

All-Ears asked, "And where were you when you heard this?"

"By the stable block."

"And yet people much nearer the house could not distinguish his words. How do you explain that?"

"Perhaps their hearing's not as good as mine."

"Indeed. So it might be." All-Ears then turned his face to one side and muttered quietly, "How fortunate you were that exposure to gunfire and cannon fire in battle did not affect your hearing." Then he looked back at the guard, who nodded to him, not having heard a word.

Kobi's bunk was searched for clues. Nothing. The other guards explained what they knew about him. Private Kobi was annoying. He prattled. His protestations of piety were relentless. He would talk back and disobey housekeeping orders. He boasted that he had spent a good proportion of the war on privy duty. He said that he regarded it as glorious labor, a message from the Eternal Spirit about the holiness of humility. In some ways he was the perfect spy, because no one suspected him of being capable of anything big, dramatic, or disloyal.

As he had arrived fairly recently, Kobi might have been the only person in the household who did not know that the Father of the People was already dying. Or perhaps he did know, and was driven to make his point quickly—the point he had been waiting for so many years to make.

All-Ears felt a surge of panic. His heart was wracked with the agony of losing his lifelong friend. His eyes could not unsee the blood pouring from Yoshi's head. But Inga, Andia, Piria, the household, and the guards expected him to take control of this awful situation. How he wanted to mutilate Kobi's body, which was still on the lawn, being examined for clues. Well, he would commandeer a crane in Nasrin Docks, raise that body on high in a tight cage, and it would stay there for citizens to hate until the crows had eaten their fill of his flesh and the weather had pounded his bones to dust. All-Ears was convinced that this man was the type of enemy that he most feared—a fanatic prepared to get deep underground within the enemy, able to be patient for years, waiting for a lucky chance. Notably, Kobi had been a fanatic working alone, absolutely alone, aware that as soon as another person knew the plan, his risks of exposure started to multiply.

However, so many of the people of Kimalloa would find it very difficult to believe that there were such single-minded fantasists. There must be a conspiracy. And who would be top of the gossips' list of suspected conspirators? Esta Glantar.

The quarters of the Arbiter, Bankside Place, Nasrin. Late evening. The fifteenth day of the Third Moon, Year Fifty-Two.

YONNIS WANTED TO weep for Yoshi Clayhills, but he found himself out of control, howling at the intelligence officers who were searching Number 4 Bankside. They had brought the saddest of news and then immediately intruded in the most brutal way on his grief.

"Squire Clayhills and I fought together, gentlemen. Have you any idea what that was like? We stared through the gates of hell together! Where does the idea come from that I would betray him? It is a monstrous lie! Tell me!"

The investigators said all they could say, which was that they had orders to search the premises in connection with the assassination. At this point, Yonnis knew very little, but he feared that Esta was being framed. They searched every room, including the privy, checking laundry, cupboards, drawers, and floorboards. They were looking for letters, and found some. All of them had the censor's stamp, or were papers from the Assembly or Senate. There was nothing here that had not already been read. Just as Yonnis thought that they were ready to go, they asked to search Merri's cradle.

"No!" he yelled, drawing his sword.

"No, sir!" Suki cried out. "I'll do it. They won't see anything!" She quickly checked the blankets in the cradle, blocking the view of the investigators. "I'm so sorry," she gasped. "I had no idea." She spoke directly to the investigators as she handed over what she had found. She avoided eye contact with Yonnis.

The investigators looked from her to Yonnis, who had sheathed his sword and put on his hat.

"This is my household, and I take responsibility for this… anomaly. Take me to Squire Tallier, then." Yonnis pointed to the door.

"We must ask that Mistress Krusa comes too."

Esta appeared with her cloak on. "Of course. There's nothing I'm not ready to discuss with Squire Tallier."

Being escorted across the courtyard to the Archive, flanked by investigators and guards after a very obvious house search, was bound to be unpleasant. Yonnis and Esta showed as much dignity as they could muster. Their steps were confident and their heads were held high. There were faces at every window, watching and then shouting to others. The Arbiter and the Glantar woman were under arrest—so they must be guilty of something. What connection could there be with the death of the Father of the People? What had she done to the hero of the war? What would happen to them? Beheading or burning? Who would decide?

Squire Tallier crammed Esta, Yonnis, his two tired clerks, and two guards into his stuffy office.

Yonnis tried to remember all he could of the Kimalloan codes of law. "Sir, please can you explain what happened to cause my house to be searched? It is a tragedy for the whole nation that Squire Clayhills has died, and we are both horrified to hear that it was at the hands of an assassin. We would like to be able to grieve. You must be aware of the bond of comradeship we had."

Squire Tallier coughed. "One witness claims—and I do emphasise that it's a claim, not a fact—to have heard the assassin shouting that he did it for Queen Esta." He looked directly at Esta. "Mistress Krusa, do you know Private Kobi of the Army of Truth, lately stationed in the Greenlands garrison?"

Esta answered adamantly. "No, I do not."

"Of course you would deny it."

"How dare you suggest that my wife is lying?"

Squire Tallier sneered at Yonnis. "You of all people know how well she can lie. She has been lying about her conversion to the Truth, and you have been covering for her. I think that only you would have hidden her prayer beads in your child's cradle."

"She has not broken the law. It is not illegal to worship the Sudarite way in private. In public, she has been discreet. Of course, I accept it was stupid of me to hide the beads."

Squire Tallier nodded. "Mistress Krusa, it is a mystery to me why your husband is so loyal to you, when I hear that you do not deserve it or value it."

"Squire Tallier!" Esta was crying. "You and your agents risked your lives to save mine, and I know that Squire Clayhills stood up for me in Parley Square at great risk to himself. Please believe me that I could never, never, *never* support any harm coming to him. I'm shocked at his loss, and it's a great loss to Kimalloa. He was perhaps the greatest natural leader we ever had."

"Greater than any of your Glantar forefathers! He certainly was. Or was he just another 'puritan ranter', Mistress Krusa? Oh—how painful it is—that word... 'was'... " Squire Tallier's face turned from anger to grief.

Yonnis waited while Squire Tallier took some moments to collect himself, then he quietly protested. "I know that some fanatics do write to my wife. I know that you intercept the letters, sir. You must have them to check. Do you recall a man called Kobi? If he was good enough to get into the Clayhills' household guard, he was good enough to know not to involve anyone else."

"It'll be days before we can assess whether he had any support, and if so, where from. And in the meantime, I can't sit around listening to your predictable denials. If I don't take time for my own grief tonight, I'll explode. Of course, we're old comrades. I'm inclined to believe you, but it's my job to keep an open mind. Treason comes from the most unlikely sources. Lord Arbiter, you may carry on with your duties, but I suggest that your wife stays at home—and I mean in the house. No strolls around the bowling green... for her own safety."

They rose to leave. Despite the heat in the room, Esta was shivering with fear. Yonnis knew that even if she had not done anything to encourage Kobi, the fact that the assassin had shouted her name, or that a witness chose to claim that he did, was a terrible threat to her.

Squire Tallier spoke to the guards. "Take Mistress Krusa home, and take the Arbiter to the Osiranian Embassy. He has some urgent business there."

Office of the Intelligence Minister, the Archive, Bankside, Nasrin. Early morning. The twenty-second day of the Third Moon, Year Fifty-Two.

ALL-EARS WAS WRITING up his journal when the first reflection bell rang.

"Eternal Spirit, giver of all comfort and refuge of those in need, please look after my dear cousin in his rest, and bless all of us who mourn him. Reach out to us in the darkness of our grief and bring the light of consolation. Inspire me to do better in my work for you and your people. Please keep us safe today."

When the finishing bell rang, he returned to his writing, in the book that was usually under triple lock. He would choke on the third key rather than let anyone else have it. This was his version of events. The one that he wanted future generations to read.

The Father of the People was buried as soon as his close family could gather in the gentle hills. This was a family already broken by the death of Baby Yoshi. I feel particularly for Yoshi's dear wife, Inga. I last saw her reeling from the bare-knuckled blows of grief on the day of his death. I cannot say much about the ceremony. General Arlo barred me from the family burial, despite me having been his father's closest cousin and friend. I was told to concentrate on finding evidence about the assassination. I felt such anguish and hurt, but I had to endure it. I spent the allotted time of the burial remembering Yoshi—the sweet boy who played hide-and-seek and taffle with me, the brave young man standing up to Rikko and Navvan, the visionary who launched our revolution, the soldier, and the statesman who brought us together again in peace. The Spirit knows how big a hole there is in me now that he is gone. A hole that will not heal.

It is a tribute to the citizens of Kimalloa that their grief has overcome their need to lash out. Newsmen have been sent out again and again to relay the message that the assassin was deranged, and not part of a plot. There have been no reprisals—so far. The Assembly decided the day after the assassination that a monument to Squire Clayhills should be placed in Parley Square, where he had stood his ground while Navvan's agents threw manure at him, starting the revolution. Citizens were asked to bring small stones as tokens of their respect, which might form a base for the monument. As soon as the appeal was made, dozens and then hundreds and then thousands of tear-soaked stones were brought, forming piles which grew into cairns. Some brave Sudarites turned up, bringing distinctive red stones, which they hold to be special tokens of esteem. Elders worked long shifts to help mourners with their prayers.

Now, today, a procession will take place from the East Gate of Nasrin to Parley Square. It was in the east of Nasrin that the Truth was first embraced. A wooden model of Squire Clayhills has been built by some enthusiastic woodworkers in one of the craft sheds. Another craft shed produced a fine cart for it, and the local muleteers thought that their beasts should pull it rather than fancy horses. The people of Nasrin have been making up their own minds about what they want to do, like Followers of the Truth should do, and they do not care about protocol or operational logistics, other than working with the militia and army to ensure the safety of the event. There has been great anxiety about further acts of zealotry, but I am confident that the spontaneity of the people will counter against anyone trying to plan when or how to blow members of the government to bits. The Distributor Seemo and the other newsmen know their stumps and will be alert to any unexpected faces. They even have their own informal ticketing system to track people's movements, involving ivy-green thread. I will be there, not as the Intelligence Minister, not as a squire, not even as Yoshi's cousin. Today, I am just a grateful citizen of Kimalloa.

By midday, All-Ears was waiting at the East Gate. It had been opened to allow people traveling to the city to join the procession, and the line was now stretching out along the Great Eastern Road for a long way. Dockers were plentiful, but so were construction workers, carpenters, bakers, brewers, butchers, fishmongers, clerks, cooks, laundry girls, tailors, waiters, market stallholders, coalmen, millers, and many more professions and those of none. Men and women of all ages thronged the streets with children in tow. It took a quarter-day for the whole procession to complete the mile from the East Gate to Parley Square. The crowd then stood in Parley Square and packed the streets feeding into it. They were praying and reflecting, encouraged by innumerable Elders, as it would not have been feasible for them all to hear one speech from Yeramo, despite his enormous voice. When the evening reflection bell rang, a collective wail of grief hung in the air. A great life had been celebrated; respects had been paid.

All-Ears noticed a small gathering around an uncovered white head. Some veterans had heard the distinctive accent of their old general reflecting loudly when he heard the bell, and flocked to him. They had not forgotten him; they had not turned against him. And he had kept faith with them—votes, land reform. It was popularity that should help the country heal, especially at a time of collective grief and forced change. But to some, Yonnis the penitent was a fraud and a threat. Tallier felt heavy with grief, responsibility, and anxious anticipation. He called for a carriage, and groaned more than usual at the effort of getting into it.

The quarters of the Arbiter, Bankside Place, Nasrin. Late evening. The twenty-second day of the Third Moon, Year Fifty-Two.

WHEN YONNIS RETURNED from the funeral, Merri was brought to him. She smiled and laughed as he bounced her on his knee. The innocent baby was happy, but the household was tense. Yonnis had not forgotten Suki's deference to the investigators. He and his wife had always been watched, but when would watching become interference, or even action, such as poison? He had some vestige of faith that those who claimed to follow the Doctrine of Truth would care about the truth, but it could not be taken for granted. However, the bread smelled like bread. The butter and cheese were fresh. The smokiness of the ham seemed usual. He had been insisting for the past week that they drank only tisane, as small beer could easily be tainted. Yonnis also insisted on Esta sleeping in his room, and he kept his sword close by. He wondered how much they could sleep tonight.

Today, she had shown her grief for the Father of the People at the Bankside Temple with other folk unable to attend the procession. She had made a statement for the evening newssheets. "I mourn the passing of the Father of People, who risked his life to save others, including me, and to save Kimalloa from tyranny. He was a hero beyond all words of eulogy. May the Eternal Spirit bless him with the sweetest of peace in the afterlife." If she had left before the funeral, many would claim she was escaping from her guilt. She was not guilty, and she had loved Squire Clayhills, in her own way. Now she had earned her right to leave without a cloud of suspicion hanging over her. This was her last night in Kimalloa.

Yonnis wanted to stay awake and hold her. If he did fall asleep, he expected nightmares. It was very late when they lay down, only partially undressed, ready to rise early to go to the docks. Yonnis dozed, but dreamed about Esta being tied to a stake and burned while he was chained to another and forced to watch her pain before his began. He woke up screaming, then collapsed back on the bed and dozed again.

The quarters of the Arbiter, Bankside Place, Nasrin. Early morning. The twenty-third day of the Third Moon, Year Fifty-Two.

IT WAS AT the darkest time, just before dawn, when the bedroom door burst open. Yonnis fumbled for his sword. Esta was wailing with fear. The room was very dark, but Yonnis could not mistake the faint glow of the muzzle of a pistol aimed at his head.

"Esta Glantar, you are under arrest for aiding and abetting the assassin of Squire Clayhills, Leader of the Assembly of Commoners." Arlo spoke to Esta, but his pistol was pointing at Yonnis. "Put your sword down, Yonnis," Arlo commanded, but Yonnis did not.

Yonnis could hear more bodies piling into the room, Esta screaming, and Nessi growling. Something flew across the room. There was a deafening crack. Pain seared across his head just before he heard a pistol ball thudding into wood above him. There was another gunshot, amid shouts and yowls of pain. A strange smell of spirit wafted into his nose. Something wet and salty was dripping from his hair. He could see the glint of swords clashing, he felt the air quiver as clubs were swung and bodies slumped to the floor. The foul smell of dense pistol smoke added to the chaos. Yonnis felt a strong tug. He was being dragged off the bed. Something told him that the person doing the tugging was on his side. He dodged and parried the flying metal with his own blade as best he could, while Pia and Little Pollo guided him out. Their escape was covered by Colmo and his men, who were fighting Arlo's men hand to hand throughout the house.

In the courtyard, Esta and Pia were quickly lifted onto horses. A soldier's hand was reaching out to help Yonnis to mount another.

He gasped, "I can't leave Colmo to deal with this. I have to help. I never retreat!" He shook his head to try to stop the blood running into his eyes, and sprayed the cobbles. "What about Merri?! I can't leave her!"

"Suki took her!" Pollo piped up. "She rushed out with Merri when she let the men in."

"She did what?! Suki? Oh, how could it be Suki? She was so... so loyal."

Pia reached down and grabbed his chin, very hard. She looked straight into his eyes and tried her hardest to enthrall him. "Whatever madness possessed her to work with Arlo, she is loyal enough that she would not harm your child. And you must get your wounds treated if you are to see Merri again. Come on, Yonnis. Get on the horse!"

She let go, and Yonnis let himself be shoved onto the horse by one of Colmo's men. Pia slapped the horse's side. It started trotting towards the gatehouse.

He heard Pia shouting, "Pollo, tell Seemo to help us!"

The inky sky was splitting, spilling dawn over the battlements. The garrison was in confusion—some soldiers were already mounting their horses or grabbing their weapons ready to follow Colmo's orders, while others were trying to stop them. The force of Pia's will and the single-mindedness of the soldiers escorting them got them out of the fearsome gate.

21

Queen Reena's Hospital, the Great North Road, Nasrin.
Early morning. The twenty-third day of the Third Moon,
Year Fifty-Two.

YONNIS FELT LIKE a hammer was landing on his head again
and again, thumping out a rhythm that shot shocks of pain
down his face. Blood was seeping through his hair, down his
neck, into his shirt, and sticking to his skin. He was aware that
someone had tried to shoot him, that there had been chaos, and
then he had been dragged out of his house, slung onto a horse,
and brought to the hospital. He was aware of being in danger,
aware of Esta being in danger, and feeling frantic about the
whereabouts of Merri. But he could not reduce the danger, or
find his daughter, unless he had his head stitched.

Elder Yersil applied pine spirit to Yonnis's wound, which
made him yell.

"You're fortunate, my Lord Arbiter, the damage is quite
shallow. The skin's split and the bone is grazed, but only very
lightly. After I've stitched it, you should live. I'd offer you malt
spirit to drink, but—"

"No. I need a clear head. Give me the wood." Yonnis chewed
hard on a piece of wood and grasped the arms of his chair as
Yersil stitched his head.

Pia was picking splinters out of Esta's cheek.

Esta squeaked, "Ow!" as the splinters came out, and, "Ow!" as she was cleansed by the pine spirit. "That stuff stinks," she complained.

"Not as much as reeky," Pia replied, "which you can get from a small cut as well as a big one. So, dear Esta, wear the pine perfume and give thanks for it."

They were in a small room with large windows looking out onto the hospital garden. It was a sunny day, and the natural light of the early morning was enough for the Elder's work. The tiled floor had been recently mopped with crushed herbs, leaving a strong astringent smell hanging in the air. There were solid wooden benches stacked against the walls, with ominous metal instruments lined up on them. Yonnis tried to breathe and sweat his tension out into the room. Elder Yersil concentrated on mending Yonnis's head. Pia was now assisting him, alternately tapping the wound with pine spirit and snipping the finished stitches. Yonnis clutched the chair. Esta sat opposite him. She was an anxious observer, one hand holding a cloth to her damaged cheek and the other laid reassuringly on Yonnis's right knee, which jolted as Yersil's needle pierced again and again. Eventually, Yersil seemed to think the embroidery was complete, and he reached for a poultice and a bandage. The room was spinning around Yonnis, faster and faster. He felt sick.

"Apply the smelling salts, Pia! Quickly!" Yersil barked.

Pia snatched the glass of reviving salts and wafted it under Yonnis's nose.

"Honestly, my Lord Arbiter," Yersil tutted, "it was just ten stitches. Perhaps you should grow your hair. You're going to have a grim scar to cover."

"I have got a dreadful headache," Yonnis slurred.

Yersil offered him a sliver of the bark of the Sudarites' most holy tree. "Chew this."

Yonnis chewed the willow bark vigorously, and as he did so, he was swamped with the sounds and smells of the debacle in his bedroom. He started to feel panic. "Where is Merri? Did Pollo find her?"

Esta stood in front of him, offering an unconvincing smile. She bent to gather his hands into hers and kiss them. "We don't know, darling. We just have to trust that Suki is keeping her safe."

Darling? She called him "darling". But it was too late to relish the endearment. "Arlo would not have killed me and arrested you without a plan for our baby. Deneesa would not allow that."

Yonnis tried to think, but it was painful. He noticed Pia peering out of the window.

"Elder Yersil, do you have the authority to keep armed men out of the hospital?" she asked.

The Elder shook his head. "I know that they're already squaring up to each other in the front yard—Colmo's men from the Bankside garrison, and that snake Norro from General Clayhills' personal guard. I've sent a messenger to the Arch-Elder, as you suggested. If he comes here in person, we've a chance. I used the name Sitra, as you asked. Who's she?"

Yonnis felt the room spin again. Suddenly, Yersil's fingers were in his mouth, searching for the sliver of bark. Yonnis lurched forward. The bark, and a fair bit of bile, were spat at great speed onto the floor and the bottom of Esta's robe. Now Yersil was yelling for tisane and bread. He was trying to look into Yonnis's eyes. Yonnis detected a look of concern passing across the Healing Elder's face.

Queen Reena's Hospital, the Great North Road, Nasrin. Early morning. The twenty-third day of the Third Moon, Year Fifty-Two.

PIA WAS GETTING nervous about the standoff in the courtyard. How long would Norro wait? She had stunned Arlo and thrust a sleeping draft into his face, but it might not last for more than ninety moments. She looked at Yersil and Esta fussing over Yonnis, who was starting to look a little bit revived. Really, he should be tucked up in bed and helped to sleep for a quarter-moon, but that could not happen. Perhaps Pia would survive today, and perhaps she wouldn't. Had Squire Tallier failed? Had he compromised her for the sake of some other scheme? Just in case, perhaps now was the time to seek pardon.

She took a deep breath. "Yersil, you asked who Sitra was. I'd hoped that there might be a better time to explain to you all. Yonnis, Esta, you've every reason to hate me. I've made some errors of judgment. Yonnis, you should strike my head off."

"Why?" they asked in unison.

"We should've all sailed to Osiran days ago. If it had not been for our love of Squire Clayhills, perhaps we would've done. What I did do... I persuaded Colmo to be ready for an attempt to kidnap Esta. As soon as Arlo and his guards moved, they were on their tail. It's not the first time I've done too little, too late."

If Yonnis's head hurt from the physical wound, he obviously had a spiritual one too. "Arlo was my friend once. How could he invade my house at dead of night, point a pistol at me, and try to take my family away from me? And what happened to Nessi? My poor dog!"

"If dogs have an afterlife, the Spirit will grant her the best one. She crouched and growled until the critical moment. He couldn't see her. And then she must have sprung like a big cat. It was Nessi grabbing Arlo's arm that spoiled his shot. Then some worm shot her."

"Why didn't you kill that horrid man? Norro wouldn't be after us if you had cut his throat!" Esta demanded.

"Esta—"

Elder Yersil shook his head. "Not now, Pia! You three need an escape plan. Take some nurses' robes and go out the back gate."

"What then?" asked Esta. "Our horses are with Colmo at the front."

Pia knew a thing or two about hiding in plain sight. "Perhaps we could go to a ward where there's infection that the soldiers would not want to risk—then we could wear the full veils with the nosebags."

Yersil nodded.

They donned brown robes, and unbleached veils with face coverings fitted with small pouches stuffed with herbs to protect the wearer from foul miasma. Yersil led them to the back of the hospital, where fevered bodies lay on straw mattresses on the floor, covered only by loosely woven, rough cloth. Long windows opened out onto the garden, circulating cool air to relieve the smell. It was clear that these poor souls already had reeky, and were on the threshold of the afterlife. A cart was positioned in the garden, ready for fresh bodies to take out by the back gate.

"Tie up the body sacks," Yersil ordered. He turned to the tired sisters already on duty. "Reinforcements for you, for a short time, so you can take a food break."

They hurried out.

Pia grabbed some string. "Let's start by the window," she whispered.

The first poor wretch they checked had already breathed his last. Pia worked with Yonnis to wrap the body. Pia glanced with concern at Yonnis's disguise. His bandaged head distorted his veil, and he was sweating profusely, which looked suspicious.

"What were you saying earlier?" he asked. "Why should I want to kill you?"

"The work I do—sometimes I do some harm for the greater good."

Yonnis seemed to be chewing over her words as his fingers crafted strong knots for the wrapping of the body bag. Pia noted with relief that his hands were somewhat more delicate than might be expected for ones which had spent long days in armored gloves. He might just pass for a nurse if soldiers burst in.

"So, you are more than an informer? Whose version of 'the greater good'?"

"Therein lies the problem."

The Seat of Government, Victory Park, Nasrin. Early morning. The twenty-third day of the Third Moon, Year Fifty-Two.

THE SUN WAS creeping upwards, shooting rays of warmth across the large expanse of grass that was Victory Park. Spring flowers were bursting with joy and color. The dark green ribbon leaves on the ancient, twisted willow trees shimmered in the faint breeze. All-Ears would have lingered to admire the scene—spring was his favorite season—but his heart was as heavy as a cannonball. His attention was focused on soldiers—lots of them. They were performing drills, trampling the grass and flowers. Near the door of the Seat of Government, he spotted Commander Magg.

"Magg!" he called.

He noticed instantly that Magg seemed reluctant to engage with him, half-pretending not to hear. All-Ears hobbled as fast as he could towards him.

"Magg!" He repeated his call, and sounded as irritated as he felt.

"Squire Tallier, sir!" Magg replied at last.

"Commander, I don't remember the Army Council advising the Assembly of maneuvers in the park today. Why is this needed?"

"Orders from General Clayhills, sir. We have to be ready for the worst today." Magg paused. "The general will be here soon, but he had to deal with the Sudos at Bankside."

All-Ears noticed that Magg's eyes were twitching. No doubt he desired a break in eye contact, an opportunity to look away, because he was a man of Truth and he must be lying. "Ah, that. I'm sure that it won't take him long. Thank you for the explanation."

All-Ears responded as quickly as he could to cover his own dissembling, and turned his head to look at the soldiers, who, for the time being, were marching up and down in a square formation. His heart was not just heavy now, it was thudding enough to break his ribs from the inside. So, Arlo had broken ranks and was chasing his own fantasies. Which should have been thwarted before they began. All-Ears noticed the Arch-Elder's carriage approaching the gate and being turned back by a messenger on a white horse, waving a red pennant. Something important must be happening at the hospital. That could be a good sign, but it might mean disaster. All-Ears felt panic slip round his neck and squeeze his throat.

Queen Reena's Hospital, the Great North Road, Nasrin. Early morning. The twenty-third day of the Third Moon, Year Fifty-Two.

"IN YOUR HEART of hearts, are you Pia, a woman of Truth, or this... Sitra, whoever that is?"

Pia and Yonnis had respectfully wrapped a second still-warm corpse, and were moving on to the next. It was as good a job to do as any while they were waiting for the jaws of the trap to close around them. If they went out the front, they would be easy targets for Norro's musketeers, and if they went out the back, they would be run down by horsemen. Yeramo's help was not guaranteed. Pia might have only a few moments to tell Yonnis what she needed to tell him if she wanted peace in the afterlife.

"I have to serve many masters."

"That's no answer." Yonnis complained. "I know that

dissemblers are necessary in times of war—I depended on their information to decide on tactics in battles and sieges—"

"And you relied on them even when you didn't know they were there. Remember Tamsit? You had some help from the firecracker that I aimed at Navvan's horse's backside and the saddle I'd loosened."

"A firecracker? Was that all it was, when people said that they saw lightning? What were you doing at the battle? Camp followers were far behind the action."

"I was Navvan's Chief Raia, Raia Sitra, and I was an agent for the Truth."

"But you were a Raia to me..." Now Esta, who had been lifting a cup of dreaming herb tisane to the lips of a dying man, turned her head towards Pia to hiss her confusion.

"I'm sorry, Esta. I believed that it was for your own safety. I hope that revisiting the old ways with me brought some comfort to you, but really, I was converted a long time ago, in Yeralla."

Esta looked bewildered. "What kind of trick is it, to be as dead-eyed as... as a *snake*... behind smiles of friendship and loyalty?"

"Esta, I've just helped to save you from prison, or worse! I hope that you'll come to realize that I've been a loyal friend—to you both."

Yonnis kept working away at wrapping the dead. "And when exactly were you in Yeralla?" he asked. "Were you involved in the gunpowder attack? Now I know why I should kill you!"

Pia now knelt to look Yonnis straight in the eye and confess. "I was not a rebel agent then, just a Raia who wanted to convert. But I was trapped. I was supposed to bless the zealots that Navvan sent, and predict for them—times, places, and so on. I used fake trances to give them false information. But they had bloodlust, ambitions for glory, and a ship full of gunpowder—"

Yonnis tied a knot so hard that he broke the string. He spluttered with anger. "Pathetic! Pia, Sitra, whoever you are!"

Yonnis's eyes had turned purple. "All those beautiful people blown to bits because you could not try harder to stop it—or was it because you thought that the Kimalloan rebels needed it?"

Pia was still holding eye contact, even though she knew that the color change in Yonnis's eyes did not bode well for her. "My conscience whips me every day. I failed to stop an awful tragedy. Just as you have nightmares about the deaths that you've caused, I do too. We live in dreadful times, Yonnis. After it, I was determined to learn how to be a better spy. All the embassy staff were sent back to Kimalloa, where I rode on the success of the plot to get close to Navvan, and I found a way to feed information to Squire Tallier." She paused. "You still have your sword, Yonnis. I've confessed to you as a Follower of the Truth should do. I know that I failed to stop the death of *Farida*. You must decide."

Pia used the emphasis to try to get Yonnis to think what Farida would want. Yonnis did reach for his sword, concealed by his loose robe. For several moments, Esta and Pia were transfixed, watching his arm tense and relax, tense and relax.

The Ministry of Intelligence Printing Company yard, Words Street, Nasrin. Early morning. The twenty-third day of the Third Moon, Year Fifty-Two.

STATE OF EMERGENCY DECLARED!
Last night, an attempt was made by Sudarites to kidnap Esta Glantar from Bankside Place, and to restore the monarchy and their superstitious creed. This assault on our beloved Republic of Kimalloa was swiftly dealt with by General Arlo Clayhills. Following the attack, General Clayhills has pronounced a state of emergency and will take direct control of the Seat of Government.

During the attack, our respected Arbiter and former general of the Army of Truth, Duke Yonnis Krusa of Yeralla, passed into the hands of the Eternal Spirit. The Republic of Kimalloa extends our sympathies to his family in Yeralla and to the loyal comrades who served under his command. For citizens' own safety, unless they are involved in essential work, they are advised to stay at home until the uprising is completely suppressed. Obey all commands from the militia at this critical time!

Seemo snatched the paper from the printer. "What?! Well, this is a bloody shock. With Squire Clayhills barely cold in his grave. State of emergency? Who could've seen that coming? I didn't always agree with him, but it grieves me that the Spirit has taken our great war leader. So why did such a kidnap get so far? Surely, that's more than suspicious?" He paused. "Last night? Today has barely begun. All-Ears' clerks must do a night shift."

The print men and the apprentices were working as hard and as fast as they could. The meaty reek of tallow candles was evidence that they had been working before dawn. The morning was young, but messengers would soon be dragging other newsmen into the yard to line up for their quota of the "special message" for the great Kimalloan public.

Illio grumbled, "There's no point pepperin' me with questions. I just print the stuff. I haven't got time to chat, Seemo. Are you going to take this out to your readin' stumps and get out of my way? There'll be dockers gatherin' on the wharves for their breakfasts by now. What are you waitin' for, brother? I'm givin' you first pickings."

Seemo was rereading the newssheet. "Illio, the print is not proper dry, it's going to smudge."

The printer shrugged. "And what don't you understand about 'state of *emergency*', eh? Some guards dragged me out of bed long before dawn and told me to get it out at once! So, I'm a bit tired and grumpy, Seemo. Why don't you hop off?"

"Just one favor, brother, before I go—may I see the scribe's original?"

"For fuck's sake, Seemo, you're a pain in the butt. D'you think we'd be workin' this hard if it was a hoax? It's on my desk out the back if you must see for yerself."

Seemo made his way to the printer's office, looked over the paper, and shouted back to Illio. "That's General Clayhills' personal stamp, it's not from All-Ears."

Illio answered, "It's good enough for me and it came with the cash, so I don't care either way. Now fuck off!"

Seemo swung onto his crutches and did as the printer suggested. He hopped out of the small yard, away from the smells of the printer's trade, and into the more varied smells of Nasrin's busy streets—stewing vegetables, fetid breath, stale sweat, and horse manure. He had to contain himself. If he started causing panic now by shouting about a state of emergency, he would never get to his first stump.

It took him ten anxious moments. It seemed as if a cart was blocking his way at every turn, but his cry of "Please, brother, let an ol' crippled soldier through!" smoothed his passage. The docks were busy now and the dockers were drifting into the inns looking for sustenance before queuing for work.

As Seemo began his announcement, heads buzzing in conversation or buried in mugs of small beer were raised. They slowly turned to stare at him, as if he were crazy. The inn fell silent. What would be the reaction to this news? Seemo finished, and waited.

The stillness was broken by a beer mug smashing against a wall and the man with a cropped head who threw it crying, "What the fuck's goin' on?!"

"Stay home when there are Sudos running wild?"

"We need to get out there and stop 'em."

There were more cries of frustration and confusion about the loss of their old general.

"Is that it?"

"Is that the best they can say for a great man?"

After a hubbub of several moments, the man who threw the beer mug yelled, "I'm goin' to Bankside to find out what's goin' on. Anyone else comin'?"

The landlord looked annoyed as several customers swigged back their drinks and marched off. The men were immediately noticed by two militiamen. One followed Seemo and the other rushed to find a cavalryman to catch up with the curious dockers.

Seemo swung himself as quickly as he could onto his next reading stump, and then his next, creating similar havoc. Word of mouth soon stripped ahead of him as men poured out of the inns and shouted to the craftsmen working on the ships. The message that the Sudos were in revolt and the war general was dead was received, and then, Seemo noticed from the cacophony of chatter, whatever was in people's heads that they wanted to believe was added into the mix.

"So, the Sudos got their own back on him at last."

"Poor old Yonnis, eh? I bet he took a few of 'em out with 'im."

"They must have skewered him when he was still asleep! Cowardly bastards."

"Perhaps he were already dead—poisoned, don't ya think?"

"All-Ears'll have the bastards on the rack already, I reckon."

"Hey, Seemo, will there be another newssheet today?"

Seemo stood to watch the dockers marching off to the west. Carts and lifting gear on the wharfside were abandoned, leaving ship captains shrieking in frustration. Seemo stood in the street for a few moments and shouted a general message. "Bankside attacked by Sudos! General Yonnis dead! State of emergency!" Illio would be furious with him if he didn't complete his round, but how could he, as a Distributor, not try to help the garrison to catch the Sudos?

He glanced at the disappearing dockers again and noticed

someone trying to push through them. Seemo broke into a broad smile as he saw that it was Pollo staggering towards him.

"Pollo, you little truepenny! I'm glad to see you, boy. Have you come from the guardhouse? What's happened?"

Pollo had run home, and then to the printer's yard, and then to the wharf in pursuit of Seemo. He was gasping for breath and was obviously in a state of high anxiety. "He's not dead, Seemo!" he gasped out. "You mustn't believe it. They weren't Sudos who attacked him."

"What?" Seemo felt entitled to be confused. He was skeptical about some of the details in the announcement, but it was unthinkable in the Kimalloan Republic of *Truth* that the government would print completely wrong information.

"Some of Colmo's men have taken them to hospital, but there's others..." Pollo gasped again, "...trying to arrest them." He grabbed Seemo's coat.

"What others?"

"Gen'ral Clayhills' guards. Gen'ral Clayhills tried to shoot the Arbiter this morning and take away his wife. Oh, Seemo! Nessi's dead and Baby Merri is missing."

Seemo realized that the time for asking questions was over. He assumed his loudest speaking voice and boomed sonorously at the backs of the dockers heading westwards. "Comrades! Comrades! Here's the latest news from this honest boy! He works in the garrison. Sorry to say, this announcement I've been given is hogwash! There's a plot to harm ol' Yonnis, but it ain't the Sudos. Run to the hospital! Run!"

Seemo wondered how much he could ride on his reputation with the workers of East Nasrin to get them to question an official newssheet. He was not sure if they pitied him or admired him, but they listened to his speeches, they followed him to protests.

To his relief, four big men turned back. One hoisted Seemo onto his shoulders and another took Seemo's crutches and held them high, yelling, "Oi-oi, brothers! Let us through! Turn north for Reena's!"

Seemo hollered to anyone who would listen as they passed through the crowds on their way to work or market. "Gen'ral Yonnis attacked in his bed! Split in the Army of Truth! Rally at the hospital!" Others started to repeat the message as the crowd following the big dockers swelled its ranks.

The weight of numbers crammed into narrow streets slowed their progress. Shivers of fear trembled through the citizens of Nasrin as they observed the clusters of strong men heading with a purpose to somewhere. Storekeepers closed their shutters and housewives rushed inside to bar their doors. Braver souls decided to follow the men. Wherever they were going, something interesting must be happening.

From fifty strides away from the hospital, Seemo, high up on the docker's shoulders, could see two groups of armed men in the courtyard—some mounted, some on foot. There were two commanders shouting at each other, and the men on foot were poised to lower their halberds for action. A Healing Elder, wearing the white robes of his profession with an apron and long gloves stained with blood, stood defiantly in front of an inner wooden gate, closed across the entrance to the hospital building. As the protesters got closer, Seemo could see a distinctive yellow sash. It was Commander Colmo who was defending the Elder, and the inner gate, with his men.

The commander of the other group was noting the approaching bare-headed veterans, and it seemed to anger him. "D'ye hope to frustrate the will of the Republic of Kimalloa by calling out a mob, Colmo? Ye'll be next for a charge of treason."

"I'm not the traitor here, Norro."

The crowd started to rumble, but they were confused—both groups of soldiers had green coats. Some had heard Norro call them a mob, so they started to shake the railings and jeer at him.

"Brother Colmo!" Seemo bellowed. "What truth do we know?"

"The Arbiter's quarters were raided by these men. Whoever gave the order to 'em intended him to be dead, but we got him out. He's injured, but alive."

The crowd shook the railings vigorously, cheering.

"Tell them the whole truth, Colmo, if ye're a man of Truth." Norro was poised to lay down his trump card. "This hospital is also harboring Esta Glantar and her Sudo curse-maker, implicated in the murder of Squire Clayhills."

A gasp rippled around the crowd. Some had heard the gossip that the murderer of the Father of the People had said that he did it for "Queen Esta". They grumbled and growled. Seemo hesitated. He did not know how to handle this. He offered up a quick prayer for inspiration, and as he did so, he heard the clatter of horses' hooves. Some strangely dressed men were now approaching the scene and trying to edge through.

The largest strangely dressed man on the largest horse now shouted to Commander Norro, waving a paper. "I am Daggra, Ambassador of Osiran. These papers are signed by Squire Tallier, if you need to look. As of fourteen days ago, Mistress Esta Krusa is under the protection of the Emperor of Osiran. If she is going anywhere, it is to our embassy. And we take a great interest in your treatment of Duke Yonnis Krusa, as do the Ambassadors of Yeralla and Boriela. Let them out."

Most of the crowd had never seen or heard an Osiranian before. As they jostled to get a clear view of Daggra in his bearskin cape and silver hat, the wooden gate behind Elder Yersil creaked open. Behind it stood three women in nurses' brown robes and plague veils. One pulled her veil off, revealing the bandaged head and gray face of the "late" Duke Yonnis. Seemo heard gasps, wails, and cheers.

From the west, a choking cloud of dust and the pounding of hooves announced the arrival of someone else important. The carriage skidded to a halt. A big man with a huge gray beard and fierce eyes stepped serenely out of it. He was enveloped in flowing black robes and sported a tall hat and some kind of staff. One of Colmo's men opened the gate for him, and a few of the crowd spilled into the courtyard at the same time, wanting to be in the thick of the action. The new arrival pointed his staff at Norro.

"We are Followers of the Truth, and we'll not solve this mystery with weapons—we'll do it with words. Norro, retire with your men back to the barracks. Colmo, follow my carriage to Victory Park—there is trouble there and we must attend to it. Get those three into it first." He waved at the brown-robed figures. "Yersil, may the Spirit bless you for your devotion to your duty as a healer."

Elder Yersil bowed to the man—perhaps he was the Arch-Elder? No one else moved.

"I've orders from General Clayhills," Norro stated. "Who are you to override them?"

The Arch-Elder glared at him. "I am the spiritual leader of this country and the man who is going to make General Clayhills examine his conscience."

The crowd cheered, and waved their fists at Norro.

The Arch-Elder opened his left palm to salute the gathered citizens, then pointed his staff at Norro again. "Did you hear that? Remember your oath to the people of Kimalloa, and withdraw."

The Arbiter shouted to the crowd. "Thank you! Thank you, brothers and sisters!"

The crowd roared with approval.

The Arbiter came over to Seemo, who was still sitting on the shoulders of a tall, strong man. "Seemo, you are a devout man of Truth. May the Spirit bless you, and dear Pollo for bringing you. Something strange is happening today, and we have to stop it, to save the peace of Kimalloa."

The crowd started chanting, "Whoa! Seemo the shepherd!"

Seemo then saw the Arbiter protesting to Commander Colmo. "I don't want to go in the carriage. I want us to walk with Seemo and…" He fainted.

Elder Yersil handed a vial of smelling salts to one of the other robed figures. She had caught Yonnis's arm and was showing notable strength in holding him up.

Elder Yersil turned to Commander Colmo. "Just sling him in the carriage with Yeramo and make haste, please. I've got a hospital to run."

Seemo wondered why the Arbiter was suspicious of the carriage. "It's not over yet, comrades!" he shouted. "Let's follow this carriage. We don't want any more kidnap attempts."

Norro's horsemen disappeared down one street, only to reappear on the main road, galloping towards Victory Park. The man carrying Seemo hoisted him onto the platform beside the driver of the horses, then hung on to the side of the carriage and yelled, "Make haste!" Seemo looked behind to see Colmo's men, the big Osiranian, and a long trail of people, some running like hares.

22

On the way to the Seat of Government, Victory Park, Nasrin. Late morning. The twenty-third day of the Third Moon, Year Fifty-Two.

YONNIS HAD FEARED that the real purpose of the carriage was to whisk them away to the Edgelands to disappearance and death. So often, what he had thought was going on was something quite different. Truth was ironically elusive in the Republic of Truth.

Esta fretted. "He is still ill, you know, and now he has this great wound on his head." She looked at the bandage and fretted some more. "Will he make it?" she hissed to Pia.

"Of course he will," Pia hissed back. "He is tough."

"Hmm. *Was* tough." Yonnis grunted, chiding himself for self-pity. If only he could recover enough to see that Merri was safe. "Arch-Elder, do you know where our baby is? When can we have her back?"

"My belief is that your housekeeper has taken her to Mistress Deneesa." Yeramo smiled, which cast a strange light over his usually stern countenance.

Yonnis groaned.

Pia said, "Deneesa is her secondary parent—don't forget, she has even suckled her. She loves her, and—"

"And she wants her in place of Yoshi! I will never get her back." Yonnis knew that he sounded bitter, and he didn't care.

Esta sighed. "I shouldn't have kicked Suki."

"It wasn't the kick." Pia seemed so sure. "She's a devout Follower of the Truth. She's one of the flawed folk. You can't imagine how much she hates Sudarism. She was convinced that you'd contaminate your daughter with your beliefs. And she's not the only one suspicious of you after all the gossip of the past few weeks. When we get to Victory Park, you must stay in the carriage!" Pia finished, and Yonnis watched Esta's face twist with indignation.

Yeramo leaned towards Esta with a misty sparkle of concern in his green eyes. "For your own safety, dear lady, you must go to Osiran."

"I'm going. Daggra will make sure that I get out of here. What about Yonnis?"

Yonnis was breathing hard, trying to suppress an agonizing sense of loss. "I'm still the Lord Arbiter of Kimalloa. I have my duty to do at the Seat of Government. Let's see if I survive it."

The Seat of Government, Victory Park, Nasrin. Late morning. The twenty-third day of the Third Moon, Year Fifty-Two.

SEEMO WAS RESTLESS as the houses of the city thinned out and the great grove that was now Victory Park loomed in the distance. The new, majestic Seat of Government Building towered above the swaying willow trees, and the vast expanse of soft green lawn reached down to the sparkling river. As the wheels of the carriage rolled closer, it was clear that something was wrong. Up with the coachman, Seemo could see through the railings that there were lots of well-dressed men surrounded by soldiers. The usual early morning collection of women taking children to play and older folk taking the air were moving away from them. He could hear some angry shouting.

The carriage and its mounted escort entered the park and tried to make progress towards the frontage of the building. Seemo turned his head to check for the folk running behind. "What's going on?" he shouted to anyone that could hear. There were soldiers trying to shut the gates on the veterans, and women trying to block them. "Oh, brave ladies! Stop them, sisters! Stop those renegades! This park is our park, and we've a right to be here and have our say!"

The sisters were doing enough, and the citizens of Nasrin were starting to pour through the gate. Seemo then tried to take in what was happening ahead of him. The well-dressed gentlemen, who must be members of the Assembly and the Senate, were on the grass outside the Seat of Government Building, being jostled by soldiers. The Arch-Elder opened the door and stepped down from the carriage, now in the middle of the throng that had run with it. A throng that was curious and fearful. A few of them had picked up stones along the way, some carried small knives, but that was no match for guns and pikes.

The Arch-Elder raised his staff in his right hand, as if in blessing, and acknowledged the crowd. He was interrupted. Four soldiers came out of the Seat of Government Building carrying a body dripping fresh blood. They dumped it at the Arch-Elder's feet. Seemo recognized Squire Glass. It looked like his belly had been ripped open by a large sword.

"Wh-what evil is this?" His breaking voice told the listeners the depth of his dismay. "Comrades, Squire Glass has been murdered—by our own men!"

The crowd roared angrily, and started to surge forward. The soldiers stood defiantly, hands on their swords, while other soldiers marched up behind. A bearded man on a tall chestnut-brown horse emerged from the open gatehouse of the Seat of Government, and walked the horse at a leisurely pace towards the Arch-Elder. There was an uneasy quiet, and Seemo noticed that the Arch-Elder was staring in disbelief. Then he looked back at the rider, and spotted blood on the hilt of his sheathed sword.

"Expecting someone else?" the rider said. "My goodness, the hospital has been very busy with ex-generals this morning." This copper-haired man with a Mountains accent seemed to be enjoying a joke with himself.

An old man was hobbling towards them, having escaped from the dozens of black-clad folk being jostled and corralled on the grass. "Stop this madness!" He waved his stick at the horseman. Seemo wondered if it were Squire Tallier—All-Ears! Oh, this must be trouble indeed if he was out of his lair!

"Don't dare to challenge me!" the man on the horse snapped. "Ye've failed Kimalloa! I didn't risk my butt in the Northern Regions for a fucking talking tent of soft-headed old squires to take my ancestral rights away. Is our Doctrine about anarchy, or is it about order? With order, we will have progress, and order is what only I can deliver. It's about time you and this slippery turncoat Raa decided whose side you are on. I've done you a great favor this morning, and you know it. You owe me!"

Seemo could see the man's spittle flying. The veterans at the front started a furious murmur of disbelief, and the ones behind them pulled and pushed to see and hear better.

"Examine your conscience, Lord Ulfan. Is this your petty revenge for one tenth of your wastelands? Quench your bitterness or ye'll quench the Eternal Spirit within you!" It was the Arch-Elder. He had a powerful voice indeed. No one would mishear his words.

"It is no use waving your staff at me, turncoat. I'm not a Sudarite who fears a magic wand."

Seemo had to make up his mind what move to make. The crowd of veterans was restless and confused. How could he guide them? He was not sure who to trust. Then, someone he *did* trust made his move. The "old" general, still in his nurse's robe, emerged from the carriage. Seemo looked around. The faces on the army men ranged from curious to terrified. Well, thought Seemo, let them stare and wonder if this was an avenging ghost. Spirit willing, that might hold off any bloodshed for a while. He felt pity for the Arbiter. His head was wrapped in a bloody bandage; he looked ill, tired, puzzled, despairing. He admired him, too. Despite his injury, he was doing his duty.

The Arbiter looked up at the man on the horse and urged, "Lord Ulfan, please don't jeopardize the peace of Kimalloa. We don't need soldiers to run a vote for a new leader."

"Ha—the once-great general, disguised as a woman. D'ye know how pathetic you look?" The man they were calling Ulfan grinned his disdain. "Ye've resisted arrest and raised a mob to march on the Seat of Government—traitor!"

Seemo yelled, "No! Not him! General Yonnis is no traitor!"

The veterans surged forward to surround Yonnis, and the soldiers were pushed back. A low, growling chant of "Whoa, General Yonnis!" started somewhere at the back of the crowd.

The man on the horse snarled, "You ignorant wretches! What are you cheering him for? His head's gone to mush because of a woman—a *Sudarite* woman. Your precious Yonnis has been harboring her and a Raia while they plotted the downfall of the Republic. You should hand him over."

Seemo was jolted by an urge to make what difference he could. With help from the coachman and a crutch, Seemo stood as best he could on the platform of the carriage. "Our Army Elders taught us the Doctrine of Truth, Lord 'Ooever-You-Are," he cried. "You're lying. You know that you're lying, and we know that you're lying. You're just trying to crush someone who'd try to stop you pushing us back into the gutter."

From his perch on the carriage, Seemo spotted soldiers, led by Norro, appearing from behind the Seat of Government Building, dragging a dozen of the small cannons that had been used to such deadly effect by the Army of Truth against King Navvan's forces. Others were carrying ammunition.

The Arbiter must have seen it clearly too. His Yerallan accent sliced through the air. "Look, they are carrying small-shot! You know what that means! This man intends our old comrades to fire on us, sure enough!"

Seemo yelled to the soldiers dragging the cannons, "Are you men of Truth or men of skulduggery? Think back a few years. We were all together—one army, one cause. Fighting for a better life, for a better Kimalloa! And we were fighting to get rid of tyranny. Who but a tyrant would order you to fire on yer old comrades?" He noticed that a small band of musketeers had their weapons trained on him. He pointed his finger at them. "If this is the new Kimalloa, where the people may not ask questions without having guns pointed at 'em, then it's a bad Kimalloa, and I pray you, shoot me, 'cause I don't wanna see it!"

The crowd cheered Seemo.

The Arbiter appealed to Lord Ulfan again. "Your Grace! Please don't create carnage here today! Remember our scriptures. A man manufactures evil for himself if he manufactures it for others. Take me as a hostage if you want. You have no argument with the people of Kimalloa. You fought for the faith you share with them."

Ulfan ignored him and yelled at the crowd. "Chaos and anarchy stop here! Right here! You folk—who should be at work—ye're in the way. Disperse! Or face the consequences..."

Squire Tallier tried to return to conciliation. "Ulfan, perhaps we have not listened to you enough in the past. Let's go back inside now, and reflect together, and all this nonsense can be forgotten."

"Reflecting and debating is for old men. This country needs action." Lord Ulfan just turned his head towards the men by the cannons. "Gunners, get ready to fire."

As his own stomach churned at the prospect of never seeing his sweet Oona smile at him again, Seemo looked from veteran to veteran in awe, with pride, with love. They did not scatter in anticipation of annihilation. They were crammed together, defying their former comrades to kill them. Good, honest folk who had hopes and ideals, who must want to go home in one piece to their families, and yet they stood together, facing a ghastly death. From their vigil at the gate, some of the women who had come to the park this morning to play with their children now picked up their skirts and started running towards the gunners, yelling, "No, brothers, no!" More and more followed them. The gun crews were stone-faced. They looked. They waited. As the fastest woman came within a breath of them and hugged her belly to a cannon, Seemo felt a flicker of recognition—was the master of that gun the man who had spat at the Arbiter at Mersin? Whoever it was, he snuffed his light with his gloved hand, and turned his back to his weapon.

Norro shot his pistol into the air. "Are you frightened of a woman, coward?! Re-light!"

Other gunners started to snuff their lights. The crowd roared its approval, and ran across to hug them. It was an overwhelming scene of joy that Seemo longed to be part of, but he was trapped on top of the carriage. Around it, the potential for tragedy still simmered.

Lord Ulfan was shouting, "Mutiny! Mutiny! Where are reinforcements? Commanders, round up those men and hang them!"

No one was taking any notice. Strangers were hugging strangers, so relieved to be human again.

Realizing that he was going to be on the losing side, Lord Ulfan looked for some consolation, and aimed a pistol at the Arbiter, who had lunged for the bridle of his horse and was urging him to dismount. "I've had enough of you, Yerallan."

Crack! Seemo thought that he had seen the last breath of Yonnis Krusa, but he was still standing, covered in blood splatter. The smoking gun was in the hands of an army commander.

"Bravo, Magg!" Squire Tallier held up his hand to acknowledge the shooter.

Lord Ulfan slumped over his horse, blood pumping from a gaping wound in his back.

The Arbiter prayed. "Eternal Spirit, please show mercy to Ulfan, son of Ardal."

"So be it!" The Arch-Elder was the only other person in prayer.

Squire Tallier was barking orders. "Squire Coppermills, get the senators and Assembly members back inside. Seemo the shepherd, bring a deputation of thirty from the veterans—others can watch from the viewing galleries or wait outside. Get Mistress Pia out of the carriage to gather some of the women! Commander Colmo, bring thirty army regulars. Gunner Kellin, the one who first turned his back—he deserves a place. And where's Duke Daggra? Your Excellency! Take Mistress Krusa to your ship—straightaway, please!"

Before he dealt with the multitude of men shouting, "Me, Seemo! I want to go!", Seemo waited to say his farewells. The Arbiter handed Ulfan's horse's reins to Pollo, clambered onto the carriage, and shook Seemo's hand.

"Thank you, Seemo. You have done great things today—you are a beacon of the Truth! I will pray for the Spirit to bless you every day!"

They hugged.

Meanwhile, Pollo was pulling at the Arch-Elder's robe. "Please, sir, someone's got to go and find Merri."

The Arbiter got down from the carriage and mounted Lord Ulfan's horse. "I'll go to the hospital. If Arlo is there, Mistress Clayhills must be as well. She will know where Merri is. Please let me through, comrades."

At this point, Esta dared to lower the carriage shutter. The Arbiter grabbed her hand to kiss it.

"I can't be sure that I will see you again. I wish you a wonderful life, dear Esta!"

Clayhills Place, New Temple Street, Nasrin. Early afternoon. The twenty-third day of the Third Moon, Year Fifty-Two.

"Is Mistress Clayhills at home?" Yonnis asked.

Mistress Clayhills' footman regarded him with undisguised suspicion.

Yonnis didn't need a looking glass to know that he was a frightening sight. "I am Yonnis Krusa, the Arbiter."

"Yes, sir."

Yonnis dismounted. He could feel that he was getting closer to Merri, and strode with growing urgency towards the door. It was opened before Yonnis knocked—by Tansi, Merri's wet nurse. He beamed at her. He wanted to cry out to the world in relief, but should he? Might there be some new twist of fate to be endured? He clasped his hands together.

"Spirit bless you, Mistress Tansi. Is she here?!"

Tansi looked terrified.

"Tansi, it is me, the Arbiter. Please tell me that all is well with Merri."

"I followed Suki here. We were told you were dead! And Mistress Esta was in prison. And Merri has to stay here with her secondary parents. It's the law."

"Let me speak with Mistress Clayhills."

"Wait... no... well, I don't know."

"Tansi, I will push past you, if you prefer? Apart from anything else, I have some grave news for her." Yonnis was not in the mood for waiting.

She led him through the brown entrance hall to a brown sitting room. Before she knocked, he heard young girls laughing and—his heart leapt—Merri gurgling with laughter too! As the door opened, Yonnis's eyes fixed immediately on a small head with a shock of black curls. Merri was sitting between Mistress

Clayhills' two daughters, playing some kind of game with them. Nothing else mattered. She was safe. Merri seemed to instantly know that the strange figure that had just entered the room was her pappa. She stretched her arms out towards him. Yonnis crouched to pick her up. Merri gurgled and squirmed. He gently stopped her trying to pull at his bandage. His headache was back. After a few moments totally immersed in the joy and relief of holding Merri, he noticed the young Clayhills girls looking fearfully at him from between their fingers.

He heard Mistress Clayhills' voice from the window seat saying, "It's Merri's pappa, girls. Don't be afraid. He's just been playing 'dressing-up' at the hospital."

The younger one piped up, laughing, "Oh, that's very good, Lord Arbiter!"

"Thank you, my dear," he replied.

"Girls, please run along to the kitchen and ask Cook to bring some beer and cheese for our guest. Yes, both of you."

The daughters scurried away. Yonnis turned his head towards Mistress Clayhills. She looked grief-stricken. He sat down opposite her. First of all, he followed her gaze out of the window to the neat garden bursting with all the joy and color of spring. Then he looked around the room and spotted Suki in a corner. She looked up from some knitting, showing no signs of apology. Reluctantly, he let her stay, knowing that she couldn't leave Mistress Clayhills alone with him.

"I'm so sorry, Mistress Clayhills, the Eternal Spirit has called Arlo to rest. I'm sorry if the messenger that Elder Yersil sent to you from the hospital did not arrive in time—"

"Oh, he did arrive. I had my reasons for not going there. You may have guessed them. You went there, I presume."

"I did. We were able to say a goodbye—of sorts…"

"I feared that, one way or another, he wouldn't last today. I wanted him to get help…" she muttered bitterly. "Perhaps it was for the best."

She started to cry. Yonnis had seen women cry, but to see a strong woman like Mistress Clayhills crying seemed especially poignant.

"I am sorry for your loss."

"History will remember him as the son of a great one, the son who lost his mind. Perhaps with some sympathy, perhaps with contempt. I'll remember a fine companion and a wonderful father to Yoshi, and to my girls. What can I tell them?"

"Tell them that he loved them. The world could see that he did. Squire Tallier writes our history. And he will be sympathetic." Yonnis looked away from Deneesa, and contemplated his dusty bare feet. He longed to know how much she knew about Arlo and Ulfan's plans to seize power, but how could he ask? "It seems that... that Squire Tallier and the Arch-Elder were expecting something to happen?"

Mistress Clayhills sighed. "There are some things that you can't be told, Lord Arbiter. I assume that's Ulfan's blood on your robe, and you're still Lord Arbiter?"

"Yes, apparently, even though I am not allowed to know what's going on."

"Ulfan, son of Ardal. He played us all. Y'know, Yersil's message said there were two blows to poor Arlo's head. What do you make of that?"

"I think that Norro was always, first and foremost, Ulfan's man."

"So, who's taking control?"

"Squire Coppermills, Squire Tallier, and Arch-Elder Yeramo. Three wise old heads. They will make a good job of it, I'm sure."

"And I see you're injured."

"I suppose that Mistress Suki has told you how that happened." Yonnis turned towards the housekeeper.

"I'm sorry for your injury, sir. All I had asked General and Mistress Clayhills about, as secondary parents, was saving the baby. The scriptures tell us to value children first. I didn't want this sweet baby to be brought up in that evil, cruel creed, and that's what would have happened if *she*—sorry, Mistress Krusa—had anything to do with it. She's an unfit parent. You indulged her, sir, which makes you unfit too. I want Merri to be brought up by Mistress Clayhills."

Yonnis stood up and snarled at her. "Mistress Suki, you are a very good housekeeper, but you do *not* get to say who brings up my daughter!"

His raised voice frightened Merri, and she howled her distress.

"Let's calm down," Mistress Clayhills ordered. "Don't forget, Lord Arbiter, that you recognized Suki's true heart when you met her at Grettin. Nothing has changed in that respect. Her duty to the child had to override her duty to you."

Yonnis let out a huge sigh of frustration. "Ladies! I am grateful to you both that Merri is safe. But, Suki, now you have learned about General Arlo's problems, can't you see that you might have placed Merri in more danger by coming here?"

Suki hung her head. "Well, sir. I didn't know."

Mistress Clayhills grumbled impatiently. "Lord Arbiter, I would very much like you to get out of my house so that I can grieve in peace, but we need to come to at least a temporary understanding about Merri. Y'know that I can get Yeribbi to support my secondary parent's rights. I can give her all the comfort she needs, and she'll be surrounded by people who love her. But what're your plans? Is Esta staying or going? The rumors change every day. And if she goes, are you staying or going?"

Yonnis slumped back down into his chair. "You may be pleased to know that Esta is at the docks, about to set sail for Osiran to marry Emperor Ikra. Is that far enough away for you? Arch-Elder Yeramo has the divorce papers if you want to see them. I would like to think that my future is sitting in soft grass by a Yerallan lake, making daisy chains with my daughter. Mistress Clayhills, Milady Deneesa, please—I know that I don't deserve your pity, but Suki will tell you how hard I fought to save Merri's life, and if ever father and daughter were bonded, it is we two."

Mistress Clayhills smiled. "She has told me. But don't imagine that it was your effort that saved her, you proud, self-pitying man! Every parent in the country was trying everything known and unknown to save their children. Some lived, and some died anyway. That's how the spotpox works. D'ye think I didn't cool my child, and poultice the spots, and stop him scratching, and keep feeding him?"

"I'm sorry." Yonnis bowed his head and stared at the brown-patterned rug.

There was a knock on the door. Tansi looked round it nervously, and bobbed a curtsy. "Sorry to disturb, mistress. There is a big, bearded man in a black fur coat with a funny accent asking to take the duke and the child to the docks."

Yonnis quaffed some beer and stood up. "Mistress, may I take Merri to say goodbye to Esta?"

Mistress Clayhills shook her head. "Sorry, Duke Yonnis. The force of your will for what you want does not move me. You go, then come back, and we'll talk some more about custody."

Yonnis handed Merri over to her. He turned to the door, then stepped back. Merri was reaching for him, and started to fret. He went to the door again. "This is cruel, Mistress Clayhills. Esta loves Merri too. She is her mother."

"Because of her vanity, she's leaving the child for a faraway throne. Be honest with yourself! Esta's love for your child has its limits. And y'know why. Because you're not a king. You're not even the consul king that you could've been if ye'd stayed in Yeralla."

Yonnis bowed, stormed out, and jumped onto a horse proffered by an Osiranian guard.

Clayhills Place, New Temple Street, Nasrin. Early afternoon. The twenty-third day of the Third Moon, Year Fifty-Two.

AS HE HEARD Yonnis leave by the front door, Squire Tallier slipped in via a door from the garden and made his own way to Deneesa's sitting room. He glared menacingly at Suki.

"You foolish girl! Get out of my sight."

"I take responsibility for her, Ellis. Suki, you may leave the room, and take the baby to Tansi. Squire Tallier's presence is a state secret, of course."

Suki hurried out with the wailing child, who left a strong aroma of her displeasure in the room. Deneesa swung her pomander and rose to open a window.

"I protected you, Deneesa. There'll be no charges against you. Now you owe me."

Deneesa turned back to Tallier, looking offended. "I thank you for giving me whatever protection you thought was necessary, brother. But I'm not sure why my integrity was in doubt. What about yours?"

Tallier admired Deneesa's dignity. He admired her intelligence, and her piety. Now she needed to step up and use them. "I like to think that you've become… one of us, a Clayhills." He paused, and wondered what kind of precedent he might be setting with his next suggestion, but he would make it anyway. "There's no law against women standing for election, and this is a country which has come to respect widows. Will you run in the Clay Hills?"

Tallier had thought hard about his offer. What could please Deneesa more than to be a woman recognized for her abilities, not just the inheritance of her first husband's money? He watched her look surprised, then baffled… and then she smiled.

"If that's what you think I owe you, I'm glad to oblige. Are

339

you sure that Arlo's… mistake… won't taint the Clayhills name?"

"Fortunately, Arlo lost. We can portray him as a victim of illness and Ulfan's double-dealing. But this is a vivid warning from the Eternal Spirit. It's not impossible for fantasists to attack the state. Even two on one day."

"What's going to happen to Yonnis Krusa? I have to make sure that Merri is safe. You know that I love her dearly—"

"That's your consideration. Mine is that I have to make sure that Kimalloa is safe. Yonnis could instantly restore morale in the army and among the veterans. He has to stay."

"He indicated to me that he wants to go home."

"Why would what he wants concern me?"

Deneesa smiled at him again. "Dear cousin! You're like a great spider, weaving webs to catch us poor flies, to be consumed at your leisure."

"What a compliment! I needed that, after my recent failures!" Tallier allowed himself a short burst of laughter. He smiled, delirious with relief for a few moments, and then his face darkened. "I must weave the new webs tighter than the old."

The docks, East Nasrin. Late afternoon. The twenty-third day of the Third Moon, Year Fifty-Two.

THERE WAS A special place on the docks for the ships whose main cargo was important people. This wharf was marked by more militiamen patrolling, and uniformed porters moving luggage around. Some ships were finely decorated with brightly painted carved wooden images at bow and stern, others were well armed. The Osiranian ship was both. As Daggra's small party arrived on the wharf, Esta appeared at the top of the gangplank, and walked carefully down it. She had already cast aside her long robes and veil, and was wearing Osiranian fashion. Her boxy headdress was short enough for her glossy curls to spill from it. Her bodice and skirt were pink silk, and she had puffy silver sleeves.

Yonnis took a few moments to take in the vision of this new Esta. "You look every bit the empress. I hope that you achieve a destiny even better than you had dreamed of."

"Thank you, dear, dear Yonnis. I'm sure that in the future, I will face decisions, and I'll ask myself, What would Yonnis do?"

Yonnis felt a warm glow. He had reached her in some way.

Daggra interrupted. "Your Majesty, this must be a short goodbye. Please get back on board. The captain is signaling that he is ready."

Esta extended her hand to Yonnis. "Goodbye, noble man of war and peace. Go and grasp a better destiny, wherever you go. And make sure that our daughter finds hers."

Yonnis shook her hand. She sashayed back up the gangplank, and waved from the top. Yonnis got back on his horse and watched the ship maneuvering away from its mooring and out onto the open river. He felt numb. The sails opened, and gusts from the southwest started to blow the ship faster. He stared for as long as he could at the little pink dot on the deck.

Eventually, Daggra decided that honor had been served. "Time to go, Duke Yonnis. Where do you live, now your home in Bankside has been violated? Do you need to come to the embassy?"

"Thank you, Your Excellency. I would appreciate that. For now, I must go back to where my daughter is staying."

"I can hear your grandmother telling me to come with you—just in case."

Yonnis smiled at Daggra. "I can hear her telling me to let you."

As they turned their horses' heads around, a posse was approaching them. Yonnis recognized Squire Coppermills, Squire Tallier, Arch-Elder Yeramo, Commander Colmo with Seemo on a pillion behind him, Elder Yeribbi, Lady Frania with Pollo, and Squire Petron, the monarchist.

Daggra growled. "Gentlemen, I hope that this is not an arrest?"

"Your Excellency, it is not," Squire Coppermills replied. "We're arranging new quarters for the Arbiter. His head needs a fresh bandage, he probably wants a change of clothes, and he must be very hungry."

"All of those things are true," Yonnis replied. "And thank you for the offer of accommodation, but I will be lodging at the Osirianian Embassy tonight, perhaps longer. Why did you all need to come? Be assured, I will write to Consul Queen Lissa and request permission to return home with my daughter. All I need from you is a direction to Mistress Clayhills to release her."

"General, no!" Pollo protested. "You have to stay with us!"

"Your daughter's too young for such a risky journey, Yonnis," said Yeribbi. "So I won't direct Mistress Clayhills to release her for it. However, I'll direct her to give you unlimited access."

Yonnis wondered where this was going. Not his way, for sure.

Lady Frania, who was sitting sidesaddle on a white horse and who had positioned herself slightly in front of the others, spoke next. "We've had a very interesting afternoon, Lord Arbiter, but we missed you."

"Your Grace, I am flattered." Yonnis congratulated himself. Had he just done that very Kimalloan thing of saying something when meaning the opposite? Had he got the tone right?

She continued. "We would like you back. Tomorrow morning, if you feel well enough."

Yonnis felt like a wet fish had been slapped across his cheek. This was a surprise indeed. "What?"

"I said that we would like you back, sir. The only way that all factions in the government see themselves working together is with an outsider at the helm—specifically, you." Lady Frania looked serious enough.

"I am sorry to disappoint the good squires. I resign. I have failed to deliver peace to Kimalloa."

Squire Tallier huffed and coughed. "I expected more resilience from you, Yonnis. You have not delivered peace to Kimalloa—*yet*. Remind us all, since you know the scriptures so well, how does Yerobis the Liberator describe a state of peace for a nation?"

"*Where all its sons and daughters can discover the Eternal Spirit of goodness within them. Where they are free and safe to apply their abilities honestly to achieve success for themselves, their families, and the common good of the country.*" Yonnis knew it well. "And Kimalloa has made some progress towards this. And maybe I did help—a bit."

"Hmm. Yes." Tallier nodded. "But have you yet made your personal journey from guilt to grace? Why not dismount, Yonnis, and let the boy Pollo explain it to you?"

Yonnis got off his horse. Pollo ran to him and hugged him. His brow furrowed as he remembered what he had heard that afternoon.

"General. Sir. Squire Tallier said that you made a solemn oath to give yourself to the peace of Kimalloa, that you were sorry for the lives lost in the war—like my pa, I s'pose—and you wanted to create a peace worthy of their sacrifice."

"He has told you most of it correctly." Yonnis was not about to trouble the boy with the complicated matter of his penitence for committing an act of vengeance against King Navvan.

"Sir. D'you think the job is finished yet?" Pollo asked.

Yonnis hesitated. Surely Seemo would not have let the boy be used to blackmail him. "Pollo, my fine boy, I cannot be the judge of that. What do you think?"

"There's more to do."

Yonnis nodded. "Pollo, there is always more to do. I could have died this morning. Other people have to take up the beacon. Young people, like you."

"Well then, you should stay to show me how." Pollo's earnest eyes were searching Yonnis's soul.

Seemo decided to put it bluntly. "Apart from all that, the way the army and veterans see it, Mr. Arbiter, is that they'd rather have the asshole that they know steering the government, rather than one that they don't. If we're going to recover quick from today's… excitement… that means you."

Squire Tallier waded in. "And the people need a new Father. My agents tell me that you're rather a good role model in that respect."

Yonnis stood up. "Sorry. I have a very bad headache. I don't know what is going on here. If you are looking for a new leader, Seemo has the qualities, and he is a true Kim."

Daggra, who had been sighing and huffing, barely able to contain his amusement at the clumsy Kimalloan way of political wooing, decided to curtail it. "The man needs some food and rest, for pity's sake. And he is coming with me, after visiting his daughter again. You may find it difficult to accept, gentlemen and lady, but perhaps Duke Yonnis finds you difficult to believe. Let's have a big breakfast tomorrow. I invite you all."

The Osiranian coast. Daybreak. The first day of the
Fourth Moon, Year Fifty-Two.

RAIN WAS LASHING and the waves were tossing the small ship up and down, again and again, as they had done three times before in the past few days. It had been going on for half a day, and Esta felt so very sick, but there was nothing left in her to throw up. Still, she dry-heaved. She had never felt so miserable. Her head ached and she felt that she was swooning. Perhaps her body was starting to shut down. She prayed in desperation to her namesake goddess and the god of the sea to deliver her safely to her new home. Everything in Esta's plush cabin that could move was moving, and she feared getting trapped. She decided to struggle up onto the deck for fresh air and the sight and hope of land.

She had been on the deck for just a few moments. How could water be so terrifying? Why did the sea rise so high—higher than a palace—and then crash down, spitting foam and making the ship toss like a toy? The sailors were hauling on ropes and the tiller. They were shouting in a way that made her feel panicked. Then a huge gust and a massive wave smashed into the ship, and as she hung on to the side, she heard a mighty wail of twisting wood.

Seawater was rushing everywhere. So near, but yet so far. She would not make her destiny after all. Then Esta felt a glow deep in her gut, like she felt when Lazzar was pointing guns at her. It was fear, but a fear mixed up with fury and overwhelming desire. Energy was pouring into her limbs to help her to survive. She wanted to survive. She had to try. She remembered Yonnis telling her that most shipwrecks happen close to shore, and if you can swim, you have a chance. Ha! This was not going to be easy, but at least she had learned how to let the water hold her up.

Quickly, Esta untied her skirt, kicked off her shoes, and ripped off her headdress. She didn't have time for the rest. She saw a person-shaped piece of wood floating in front of her. She grabbed it and splatted onto it, just as a wave cast it clear of the sinking ship. The shock of the cold, cold water hit her like a rock. The salt stung her eyes and nose and mouth. She quickly looked up. Was she going to be smashed into the harbor wall? People were on top of the wall—perhaps they would throw down ropes? Water was crashing over her and all around her, but she was not sinking, and she was able to take an occasional breath. The waves breaking against the harbor wall were buffeting her forwards, backwards, sideways. She tried to kick her feet in the water to guide the wood, to edge alongside the wall, to reach the mouth of the harbor. She felt a wave swelling behind and now under her, but looked up to see another coming at her at an angle. Would it swamp her? She closed her eyes again and prayed. She felt the board rise and twist and fall again. Then there was a rush carrying her forward. When that wave subsided, others came, but they were much less intense. She dared to open her eyes again, but everything was a blur in the rain. The smell of the salt was strong, but now she thought she could smell fish too.

She started to kick her feet again, and pull with her arms either side of the wood. She was passing fishing boats! She was in the harbor. Where could she get ashore? The rain was easing off and the wind dropped quite suddenly. Esta saw figures waving from what might be a small beach. She kicked until she was close. She felt her heart soar with joy, relief, and gratitude that she was alive, even though she still felt like death had its hand on her throat. She dared to reach down with one leg—yes, she could start to walk through the lapping foam.

She hauled herself up to her full height and waded onto the beach. Seaweed was snatching at her legs, but she would not wobble. She was Esta, Empress of Osiran, and her new people must believe that she was strong. She still had her silver sleeves and her pink bodice to give her some dignity, although her legs were probably quite evident beneath her wet shift. She shook water out of her hair, just as she had seen Nessi doing after a swim in the Binar. As she did so, the cloud broke and a ray of sunlight caught the spray above her head. She heard the people on the beach gasp in awe. Was she frightening them?

As she made her last step between the tide and the land of Osiran, people dressed like Daggra shuffled forward, looking confused, curious, but in some way happy. Esta had been learning Osiranian. She had been told that her accent was terrible, but perhaps she could make herself understood.

"I am Esta, the betrothed of Emperor Ikra. Please can you take me to him?"

There was no reply.

A lavishly carved golden sedan chair was being hurried onto the beach. Was she supposed to get into it?

A small, slight young man wearing a coronet emerged. He was clearly dismayed to be standing in the cold air, even though the rain had stopped. "Y-y-you are Esta?" he stammered.

Esta remembered Yonnis's honest description of his cousin. She sank to her knees and prostrated herself in the wet sand. "My Lord Emperor, Your Majesty. I am Esta."

"Why are you named after your goddess of the hearth, when you look like the goddess of love? P-p-please get up and let me look at you."

Esta thought that this sounded like a good start, and rose to her feet as gracefully as she could. She started to shiver uncontrollably, and was about to collapse, but footmen rushed forward with strong arms and blankets. As she searched her memory for something else to say, another sedan chair arrived, and a wizened old woman in blue was lifted from it. Esta made the best curtsy she could in her circumstances.

The old woman looked Esta up and down. "It must be her. Fetch the Empress some corn spirit and honey!" She nodded to Ikra, then she smiled at Esta. "Welcome, Esta. I am impressed at your mode of arrival. You must be a strong, resourceful woman, or perhaps you have a special form of magic or blessing upon you. This all augurs well for strong princes, which is what Osiran needs." Then she surprised Esta by suddenly switching to Pozarian. "My grandson would want me to forgive you for breaking his heart, but if, while I live, you break poor Ikra's heart as well, I will personally boil your fingers and peel off the skin."

The Seat of Government, Victory Park, Nasrin. Late evening. The thirteenth day of the Eighth Moon, Year Fifty-Two.

THE CHAMBER OF the Helm, a large meeting room in the Seat of Government, had a few high external windows. These kept it cool and secure, but Helmsman Yonnis insisted that his meetings were illuminated by the new lamps which consisted of bulbous glass chimneys over stout candles. They cast sinister shadows across the plain gray drapes that decorated the walls, but they enabled him to see clearly the expressions, and the levels of enthusiasm, of his colleagues. The new constitution was designed to fast-track decision-making, but he knew that fast decisions without the true commitment of the members of the Helm would not be well implemented.

The amended constitution, brokered by Squire Coppermills, Squire Tallier, and Arch-Elder Yeramo, had been an excellent way to divert attention from the crisis of the twenty-third of the Third, now noted in official documents as the Day of Kimalloa's Women of Truth. They had averted catastrophe. The Assembly stayed the same, the Senate stayed the same. A new Tribune of the People was formed. The Helm was a peacetime equivalent of a War Cabinet, and the Helmsman was the man previously known as the Arbiter. Yonnis was "at the helm", steering the experts in the Helm. His quest continued, and his daughter was staying in his new household. He was not dictating, but he was not averse to being strongly persuasive when something was urgent. And today's meeting was indeed urgent.

King Rolan of Pozaria had died suddenly of a seizure, and his son Fillan, in his coronation speech, had claimed Kimalloa as his, as he was the eldest great-nephew of Queen Louisa. It was not unusual for new kings to want to show their strength, and Fillan was making a reasonable calculation that if he mustered a big enough invasion, his forces would find help in several corners of Kimalloa. He would steer clear of the Mountain Regions, so fiercely for the Truth. He would steer clear of the south and east, where the Republic was popular. The west and the north were still worshipping the old gods, and despite the hard work of Elders to win the hearts and minds of young people, the diligence of the garrisons in keeping order, and the ingenuity of agents in flushing out and exiling priests, Yonnis knew that he could not be confident of holding these areas.

So here were the best minds of the country, gathered to dust off the old manuals of the logistics of war, but more importantly, to come up with something new that would defeat Fillan's forces before they even landed.

"Elder Yerbun?" Yonnis called the inventive engineer to attention. "How quickly can we chain all the harbors?"

"Within a quarter-day, and we have trap chains on all the navigable rivers as well, so we can fool them into thinking they are sailing upriver, and then haul chains at the front and back of them. Then we could use our older reserve soldiers who are good archers to shoot brands onto their ships to burn them."

Yonnis paced the room while the others sat at the table. "They will expect robust defenses in the obvious places, and the mercenaries who served in the war will have given them a lot of information about those places. We need to do more, especially if we are going to minimize casualties. We need something random that they will not expect. And we need to think of the natural resources we have which can provide a barrier to them. Things we have that they do not? That they don't understand?"

The room went quiet.

Yonnis challenged them directly. "Does anyone have any ideas?"

Still no comment.

He decided to be provocative. "Is it not the case that storms follow forest fires?"

Mistress Clayhills was quick to comment. "If you want the people on your side in the west and north, do not even think about a massacre of their trees."

"And the effect of a plume of heat on weather patterns is not fully understood," Elder Yerbun added.

"Is there any magic at all that can invoke the Kimalloan

weather, Arch-Elder Yeramo? Please, colleagues, we need some crazy ideas that just might have a grain of use in them."

"I have news for you, Lord Helmsman." Arch-Elder Yeramo dished up his sarcasm with a smile. "Magic does not work, but we do have some regularity in weather patterns which might not be known to Pozarians. The last quarter of the Ninth Moon is stormy two years in every three. If navy agents commit some sabotage in their harbors until the middle of the moon and then stop, Fillan might be tempted to sail at a bad time."

"Let's do that. But we need something else. Come on, brothers and sisters! We are a land of knowledge and ingenuity! We must have resources and technology that the Sudarites cannot counter."

"We have coal," said Squire Beechwoods.

"And?"

"I'm with you!" chimed in Elder Yerbun. "We could use cordons of coal fires to create the impression of the sea being aflame."

"Which, depending on the wind, could produce sickening smoke to deter them," Seemo observed. He was now Leader of the Tribune and a member of the Assembly, having been elected in the constituency previously held by Squire Glass, just east of Nasrin.

Arch-Elder Yeramo laughed. "And then we could hoist puppets on wires to fly through it!"

Nobody else laughed.

"Come on." The Arch-Elder followed up. "You know what the scriptures say—quantity of ideas before quality."

"I agree," said Yonnis. "More, please! No matter how mad! Where is Mistress Pia with the latest intelligence reports? That might help us to work out where the quality lies. And someone send for more food. It is going to be a long day. Once we have ideas, we must plan—rehearsals, reflections, adjustments, analysis…"

"Only if we've time for that," Squire Coppermills grumbled, ever the pessimist.

The northeast coast of Kimalloa. Late morning. The twenty-second day of the Ninth Moon, Year Fifty-Two.

THE CANVAS OF the observation tent was starting to sag. The rain was persistent, and the wind was gusting. Messages were coming in that were very encouraging. Navy signal boats had spotted the splitting of the Pozarian fleet the previous day. Forty smaller ships were heading for the wide mouth of the Binar. Yonnis could not believe that the enemy was foolish enough to head for a trap. Perhaps Fillan believed that the troops could land even if the boats were burning. They would try the north side of the estuary to head for help from Lord Aldor that was not coming, and they would find the marshes more of a barrier than any regiment of soldiers.

The bigger warships, fifty of them left after the sabotage of the previous weeks, were lining up in the strait to engage in naval warfare with the Kimalloan Navy. Perhaps the Pozarian admiral was expecting the usual close-range struggles to board and take ships. The Followers of the Truth abhorred waste, but today they had orders to aim their cannons as soon as an enemy ship was in range, aim low, and fire again and again to sink whatever they could. Another forty ships were heading for the northeast, aiming to free Lord Lazzar from the "friendly" blockade around his castle and rally local support. The coast of the northeast was unforgiving, even more so in bad weather. Wherever there was a sympathetic beach, there were sentries stoking braziers full of coal. Even if the enemy telescopes did not pick up the glow of the coals, they would see smoke and assume that there was at least a moorland fire, if not a festering fissure in the earth. Should any enemy ship be confident enough to lay anchor, the sentries were ready to set off massive firecrackers to make the illusion more frightening, then the gunners would blast their cannons.

Yonnis was wearing a breastplate and backplate and carrying a sword and pistol, which told his every instinct that he was ready for action. But he would not be in the front line if the Pozarian soldiers made land. The Army Council had been very polite about it—his muscles had wasted somewhat from the spotpox, his eyesight was not as good as it was, his reactions were slower—in short, they thought that he was getting old and weak. There were plenty of commanders of regiments and captains of ships who could do the hard work, inspired enough by the absolute necessity to defend their country and their faith.

Yonnis spoke optimistically to his commanders, but he knew that it was never over until it's over. The weather might change suddenly in Fillan's favor. Lazzar's lackeys might try an attack on the rear of the encampment. The Helm had tried to think of every reasonable possibility, and the Army of Truth, both professionals and reservists, had been well briefed. He sensed that he was not the only person in the tent that was frustrated by the slow passage of time. He asked Elder Yeribbi to lead a reflection. The Army Elder shut his eyes and bowed his head.

"Bless us today, Eternal Spirit. Our victory will be your victory, the victory of reason over superstition. Teach us to be true, honest, just, and virtuous in victory, and once again, in rebuilding a prosperous peace."

As soon as he had finished speaking, a mighty clap of thunder was heard.

The northeast coast of Kimalloa. Early evening. The twenty-second day of the Ninth Moon, Year Fifty-Two.

GLOWING BRAZIERS WERE keeping the inside of the tent tolerably warm, but the smell of damp was nauseating. The rain and wind had eased off, and seemed to be heading north. What might be left of Fillan's fleet?

Yonnis, Yeribbi, and Private Pollo were eating pottage and bread when a furious galloping was heard. An agent arrived with a collection of all the intelligence gathered from up and down the coast before the night fell.

"Fifty ships trapped in Binar. Twenty-two burnt, twenty-eight captured. Hundreds of enemy prisoners. Thirty-one enemy warships sunk in open sea off the south/southwest coast. Several dispersed westwards—alerts sent to local garrisons. Twelve ships broken up on rocks on the northeast coast. Several dispersed by the storm."

Pollo cheered, "Yes! Yes!", and punched the air.

Yeribbi offered prayers of gratitude.

Yonnis allowed himself a small smile. "Please message back to all stations—*May the Spirit bless the noble navy and army of Kimalloa. You have saved us all today. Stay vigilant!*"

Yeribbi laughed. "Well, well, Yonnis. You summoned the Kimalloan weather again!"

Yonnis shrugged. "We planned, we prepared, and we got lucky... the only card the Pozarians had to play was weight of numbers, and that is no use against a thinking opponent. So, let's go and say thank you to the sentries on the beach. I'm so glad that we have so many prisoners from the Binar expedition... no returns this time... I can't wait to see them hard at work digging the north–south canal."

"May the Spirit bless you!" Yeribbi thumped his backplate. "Allow yerself some credit. Great work, Lord Helmsman!"

The docks, East Nasrin. Late afternoon. The ninth day of the Tenth Moon, Year Fifty-Two.

A MESSENGER INTERRUPTED the meeting of the Helm as instructed. A very important ship from Yeralla had docked in Nasrin. Helmsman Yonnis left Lady Frania in charge, and boarded his carriage.

Militiamen waved people out of the way so that the carriage

could make progress through Nasrin's ever-increasing traffic. It pulled up alongside a square-rigged caravel with the distinctive brick-red sails of the Yerallan fleet. Porters were ready with luggage to be transferred to a covered river barge sporting the official flags of the Republic, which was waiting for them. The Helmsman's important guests had already disembarked. It was a cold, crisp day. His brother's widow was in a warm, dark green woolen robe and a white veil. She lowered her gray eyes and curtsied, then rose, acknowledged his bow, and shook his hand.

"My Lady Olma, it is many years since I was witness for my brother at your wedding. I am very pleased to meet you again. I am sorry that your journey had to be delayed by our problem with Pozaria. We will travel straight to my manor upstream where you can meet my daughter and household and enjoy a good supper." He hesitated, wondering how long the poor woman had been waiting after Dolfis's death for him to fulfill Kirina's wish for them to be together. Three years, perhaps four? Had she given up hope, adapted, then given up more hope, again and again, when news traveled to Yeralla of a hurried marriage to a Kimalloan queen, then a baby, then a sickness, then an attack in his home? She should have chosen someone else in that time. But she had not. Was that weakness or strength? And now that she saw him again, might she be disappointed? Lines of age on one cheek, spotpox scars on the other, a nasty scar on his head. "Of course, Grand Duchess Kirina is impatient for us to marry, but you are welcome to make your own decision in your own time. Just be assured that I would be honored to be your husband. I hope that we can have children and foster children together, and eventually retire to Yeralla."

She nodded. "Thank you, Duke Yonnis. They call you 'Mighty Yonnis' in Yeralla now."

Yonnis smiled and nodded. He had worked hard for the latest victory, but he had also ridden luck that he did not feel was his due. He looked down. Standing at Lady Olma's side was a small boy in what was probably his first suit—a smart blue-gray.

"And who is this young man?" Yonnis crouched to shake the hand of the boy, who clung shyly to his mother's robe, but looked curious.

He did not reply.

"Well, let me guess, then. Are you Karrolis, son of Dolfis?"

The boy nodded.

"I am your Uncle Yonnis. I have not been in Yeralla for a very long time, so this is our first meeting. Thank you for making such a big journey to get here. How was it?"

"It was fun!"

Karrolis had found his tongue, and Yonnis's heart lifted to hear Yerallan spoken in a child's voice. Merri was now developing from babbling to forming words, and they were Kimalloan. Still, "Pappa" was "Pappa"—the most important one to him.

"He was not sick at all, Milord Yonnis. He was bothering the sailors for stories from all the places they had been, all day long."

Yonnis noticed Lady Olma's pronounced Borielan accent, which was quite charming.

Yonnis smiled at the boy. "Well done, Karrolis. That sounds like an excellent way to spend a long journey. Well done indeed. It is good to have an inquiring mind. Do you like ships, then?"

"Yes, Uncle."

Yonnis tried to stop himself, but something about uncle meeting nephew made him ask it. "And of all the ships that you have seen in the docks here in Nasrin, which one do you like the best?" He offered a quick prayer to the Eternal Spirit that this boy was not the pugnacious little braggard that he himself had been at five years old.

"This one, Uncle. It's a Yerallan caravel. It's the best one for explorers."

"And through exploration, we gain knowledge! May the Spirit bless you, Karrolis. That's a good choice."

ACKNOWLEDGEMENTS

To all the historic figures who have inspired me, thank you. To all the teachers who have reached beyond my idiosyncrasies to encourage my writing, thank you. To all my supportive friends and family, thank you. Writing groups everywhere, I salute you, especially the two who have listened politely to extracts from the early drafts of this novel. And thank you to all the staff at Troubador for coaching me through the production of my first novel.

ABOUT THE AUTHOR

B B ELSIN is the pen name of a retired academic who switched from textbooks to creative writing to help her to cope with sudden hearing loss and late-diagnosed autism spectrum disorder. She lives near London, UK. *Heroes and Traitors* is her first novel.